Judith Lennox grew up [...] d at the University of Lanca [...] and, Iain; they have three so [...] grandchildren. She began writing in the mid-eighties, and her powerful historical novels have been widely acclaimed. Her novels, *A Step in the Dark*, *Before the Storm*, *The Heart of the Night* and *Catching the Tide* are available from Headline Review. Judith lives with her husband in Cambridge.

By Judith Lennox

JUDITH
LENNOX
The Turning Point

headline
review

First published in 2012 by HEADLINE REVIEW
An imprint of HEADLINE PUBLISHING GROUP

First published in paperback in 2013 by HEADLINE REVIEW

1

ISBN 978 0 7553 8410 5

Typeset in Joanna MT by Palimpsest Book Production Limited, Falkirk, Stirlingshire

Printed and bound by
CPI Group (UK) Ltd, Croydon, CR0 4YY

Headline's policy is to use papers that are natural, renewable and recyclable products and made from wood grown in sustainable forests. The logging and manufacturing processes are expected to conform to the environmental regulations of the country of origin.

HEADLINE PUBLISHING GROUP
An Hachette UK Company
338 Euston Road
London NW1 3BH

www.headline.co.uk
www.hachette.co.uk

To Marianne Elizabeth Smith

Acknowledgements

Thanks to my agent, Maggie Hanbury, my editor at Headline, Clare Foss, and my editor at Piper, Bettina Feldweg, for their support during the writing of this novel. Thanks, as always, are due to my family, especially my son, Dominic, for his help with the scientific parts of the book, and my husband, Iain, without whom my computer would not work and travel would be far less enjoyable.

Seil is a beautiful island off the west coast of Scotland. My thanks to the charming and welcoming owner of our B & B and to the many islanders who extended to us their warm hospitality.

Part One

Gildersleve

1952

Chapter One

It was the first cold morning of September.

A narrow lane angled sharply away from the main road, heading through a hazel wood. The chill autumn air was redolent of beginnings, of new academic years, something to get your teeth into after the torpor of late summer. A few leaves cast themselves adrift from the branches, scattering the verges with splashes of gold and crimson.

So you're going to be one of Pharoah's men. The remark, made to her by an academic acquaintance shortly after her interview six weeks ago, came back to Ellen Kingsley as she cycled up the incline. In her memory, the words were tinged with amusement and perhaps condescension. She had replied, 'I'm going to work at Gildersleve Hall, if that's what you mean,' and had felt a thrill of pleasure in saying so.

At the top of the rise she braked and looked out over

the shallow valley. The hedgerow and trees had fallen away and the fields were shaken out before her like a gold and brown quilt over the gently rolling landscape. A small grey tractor was ploughing up stubble. A flock of white birds wheeled in the blue sky before alighting on twists of earth.

Beyond the fields lay Gildersleve Hall, solid and uncompromising against this modest countryside. Half a dozen white poplars, their leafy heads shimmering silver in the breeze, stood beside the hall, and a line of cypress trees curved towards the road. A tower, wreathed in ivy, protruded from one side of the building. The heavy eaves over the two prominent bay windows gave the house the appearance of frowning, and the red-brick walls and slate roofs seemed to absorb the autumn sunshine. The house looked secretive, almost menacing, and if Ellen had believed in ghosts, she might have imagined it to be haunted.

But there was always an explanation for everything, and she knew that the heavy Victorian Gothic architecture lent itself to associations of mystery and the supernatural, and that the windows appeared blank because the scientists working in the laboratories would have put down the blinds to shut out the glare of the sun. And the flicker of apprehension she felt was caused by her excitement at this, her first day in a new job.

This was the opportunity she had worked for and longed for. This was the start of her future.

* * *

The lab in which she would grow her crystals was on the topmost floor of Gildersleve Hall.

On her arrival, a secretary had let her in, and a man of around Ellen's own age, pausing in the act of dashing upstairs, had looked back over his shoulder and said, 'You must be the new research assistant.' Introducing himself as Martin Finch, he offered to show her up to her lab. Climbing up flights of stairs, Ellen glimpsed offices and laboratories. A tall, dark-haired man hurried past them, acknowledging their presence with a nod and a word of greeting.

Martin had a plain, rather rubbery face, with a long, bulbous nose, full mouth and thick, black eyebrows. His tweed jacket was open over a jersey, shirt and tie. He wore his short brown hair parted to one side, and a spatulate fingertip jabbed at the bridge of his tortoiseshell glasses, which kept slipping down his nose.

He opened a door for her. 'These rooms are always freezing in winter,' he said. 'But you'll have your burning passion for science to keep you warm.'

That, and several jerseys, Ellen thought. A cold draught whistled through the small room. Two of the walls were lined with benches, on which stood microscopes, bunsen burners and retort stands. Two desks, the surface of one bare except for a lamp and inkwell, the other heaped with papers, pens, log books and slide rule, had been placed back to back in the centre of the room. A black metal filing cabinet squeezed into a corner, and books and box files were stacked on shelves. There was a calendar, the months written in French, pinned to a wall.

Ellen said, 'My last lab wasn't exactly luxurious, Dr Finch. Four of us in a space the size of a broom cupboard and a bomb crater outside the door.'

'You must call me Martin, Miss Kingsley. And I'm not Dr Finch, I'm a mere mister. Shall I tell you about the others?'

'Please.'

'There are two groups of scientists who work at Gildersleve Hall. Alpha and beta, I call them.'

'Who's alpha?'

'We are, of course. There's fewer of us, but we're cleverer. We're the protein group. The phage group – the betas – are in the other side of the house. There's about twenty of us scientists, as well as various other bods – technicians and secretaries, that sort of thing. You'll be sharing this lab with Mam'zelle.'

'Mam'zelle?'

'Andrée Fournier. We call her Mam'zelle. Quiet type. French. She has a cubbyhole where she brews her coffee. No men allowed in there on pain of death. She's been here about a year. She arrived a few weeks after me, does something clever with myoglobin molecules. Some of the older men have been here much longer. Who interviewed you?'

'Dr Kaminski.'

'He's been at Gildersleve for donkey's years. He joined

in the war when the hall was doing all the top-secret stuff. He's a Pole, clever bloke, was in the RAF then got shot up rather and ended up here.'

At her interview, Ellen had seen that one side of Dr Kaminski's face was a mass of scar tissue, the legacy, she assumed, of his wartime career. It had been hard to look at him without flinching and without pity.

Martin went on, 'Kaminski's Pharoah's deputy, fills in for him when he's away on one of his jaunts. Pharoah's at a conference in America just now, so Kaminski's top dog. Padfield and Farmborough are old-timers as well, ex-army types. Padfield's a first-rate batsman, captains the cricket team. We have a few matches against some of the Cambridge labs in the summer, it's jolly good fun. But I don't suppose you're interested in cricket, Ellen.'

She smiled. 'My brother's very keen, so I've learned to take an interest.'

'Padfield and Farmborough are chemists, crystallographers. You'll be making your crystals for them, as well as for Jan Kaminski. Toby Dorner works on this floor too. He's a biochemist, Jewish, came over here from Austria in the thirties, when he was just a kid.'

'And the man who passed us as we came upstairs? The tall, dark man?'

'Jock, you mean? His name's Alec Hunter, but we all call him Jock.'

'Scottish, then?'

'Very well deduced.'

She could not tell whether he was being sarcastic or not.

'I think you'll find our group's a friendly bunch,' added Martin. 'Apart from Dr Redmond, of course. He was here in the war too. Farmborough once told me he was senior to Pharoah back then. He's an odd chap.'

'Why do you say that?'

He went to the window. 'That's his cottage.'

Ellen looked out. The window looked down to the area of land behind Gildersleve Hall. There were several outhouses, including the shed in which she had put her bike. Beyond were the tall poplars she had glimpsed earlier from the road; behind them, ploughed fields and hedgerows. Following Martin's pointing finger to the skyline, Ellen caught sight of a cottage, standing beside woodland.

'It's in the middle of nowhere,' he said. 'But that's how Redmond likes it, the miserable blighter. His lab's in the tower. Gets in a huff if you go in there.'

'Perhaps he dislikes being interrupted.'

'Perhaps he doesn't care for company. I don't think he has a friend in the world.'

'Is he married?'

Finch guffawed. 'Good Lord, no. Padfield and Farmborough have wives and families. The rest of our group are footloose and fancy free.' He had taken off his glasses and was polishing them with his tie. Uncovered, Ellen noticed a sharpness in his eyes.

'Do you come from round here?' he asked.

'I'm from all over the place. My father's in the army. I went to Bristol University.'

'Hah, red-brick like me, then. Where are you lodging?'

'In Copfield. It seemed most convenient, only three miles on the bike.'

'There's a pretty decent pub in Copfield, the Green Man.' Martin put his glasses back on and blinked. 'Some of us sometimes have a drink there after work. You should join us – as I said, we're a friendly bunch.'

The door opened and Martin Finch broke off. A small, slender woman, her glossy dark hair neatly pinned up at the back of her head and her clothing hidden under a white lab coat, came into the room. She was carrying a coffee cup, covered by a saucer. Putting it down on the bench, she said, 'Hello, Martin.' And to Ellen, 'You must be Miss Kingsley. I'm Andrée Fournier.'

The two women shook hands. Then Miss Fournier said, 'Thank you, Martin. I can show Miss Kingsley where everything is,' and Martin left the lab.

Andrée Fournier was strikingly pretty. Her face was heart-shaped and her complexion was flawless and golden. She had emphasized her dark-brown eyes with a light application of liner and mascara and she wore a neat navy-blue skirt and jersey.

'Would you like a coffee, Miss Kingsley?' she asked. 'There's some in the pot.'

'Please.'

'Come with me. I'll show you where you may put your coat.'

Across the landing, Miss Fournier opened a door. This room was very small, little wider than a corridor. A small, high, narrow window framed an oblong of sky and there was an unshaded electric light bulb, a sink and a kettle. Above the sink was a mirror; to its side were coat pegs, on one of which hung a red woollen scarf and a grey coat.

Ellen hung her coat on the second hook and breathed in the aroma of coffee. 'What a gorgeous smell.'

'The coffee the others drink is vile. My mother sends me the beans from France.' There was a coffee pot beside the kettle; Andrée poured out a cup.

Ellen said, 'Martin seems very friendly.'

'Ah, yes. Though these men, and their silly names for people . . . Martin can be such a child. Help yourself to sugar.'

'I suppose nicknames can be rather tiresome.'

'You will be "Ginger", Miss Kingsley. It's inevitable.' Miss Fournier's voice was dry.

Ellen smiled. 'I was "Ginger" all the way through school and college, so I'm used to it. "Carrot-top" was worse.'

'You have beautiful hair. I used to long to have auburn hair like yours when I was a little girl.'

The coffee was delicious, rich and stimulating. Ellen asked, 'What do you do for lunch? I wasn't sure so I brought sandwiches.'

'Dr Padfield and Dr Farmborough often go home for

lunch, but most of us have sandwiches in the common room. There's a fire there, so it's warm in winter, but sometimes I prefer to come up here. The common room can be so noisy. Miriam cooks for Dr Pharoah and Dr Kaminski. When the men eat in the dining room, she cooks for them too.'

'Only the men?'

'Women aren't allowed in the dining room. It's a tradition. The others eat there when we have a visitor.'

There was a tonelessness in Miss Fournier's conversation, which Ellen put down to the difficulty of speaking in a foreign language. She said, 'Which part of France do you come from?'

A flicker of animation on Andrée Fournier's perfect features. 'Paris. Do you know it?'

'A little. I spent a week there last year. The university arranged it. It was wonderful – such a beautiful city. You must miss it.'

'Yes, I do.' Miss Fournier glanced at her watch. 'It's a quarter to nine. We should get to work.'

At one o'clock, Ellen and Andrée went downstairs to the common room. It was furnished with an electric fire, armchairs and occasional tables, as well as some hard chairs and stools. A large bay window looked out on to the gravel courtyard at the front of the house. There was an air of mild disorder: on the tabletops, apple cores and biscuit wrappings were mixed in with pens, ashtrays, newspapers and periodicals. A record player was playing a Rosemary Clooney song and the room smelled of pipe smoke and instant coffee.

Andrée sat down on a stool and began to unwrap her sandwiches. Ellen sat beside her.

'Well, well, the new recruit to our merry band!' A big, red-faced man put down his newspaper and crossed the room, offering his hand to Ellen. 'Farmborough, Bill Farmborough. Welcome to Gildersleve Hall, Miss Kingsley.'

'Thank you.' She shook his hand.

'I'll do the honours, shall I? That oaf in the corner is Denis Padfield.' There was a wave and a grunt from a balding man in a herringbone tweed jacket. 'You've met Finch, haven't you? And this is Toby Dorner. Put down that foul brew you've made, Bat, and say hello to the nice lady.'

Toby Dorner was young, short and slight, with close-cropped, curly brown hair and protruding ears, which gave him an impish look. Standing up, he took Ellen's hand. 'It's a pleasure to meet you, Miss Kingsley,' he said. 'I'm delighted that you're joining us.' His voice was gently accented.

Someone stuck his head round the common-room door. Ellen recognized him as the dark-haired man she had encountered on the stairs earlier that day, Alec Hunter.

Bill Farmborough said, 'Come and meet Miss Kingsley, Jock.'

Hunter introduced himself to Ellen, shaking her hand. He had a distracted air, as if his attention was elsewhere.

He made a quick gesture with the papers he was holding, saying, 'Kaminsky wanted these in a hurry. Any idea where he is?'

'Last time I saw him he was heading for the tower.'

'Thanks. Excuse me, Miss Kingsley.' Dr Hunter left the room.

In Alec Hunter's absence, the memory of his appearance – clear brow, almond-shaped dark blue eyes, a firm, well-shaped mouth, aquiline nose and tousled dark hair – lingered, like the after-image of a bright light.

A discussion about her lodgings followed; Ellen was fortunate in finding a room with Mrs Bryant, someone said, and horror stories were told about other digs in the area.

'Bat's frightfully energetic,' drawled Martin. 'Cycles come rain or shine. Me, I'm a lazy blighter and I drive a car.'

'It's not a *car*, Miss Kingsley,' said Denis Padfield. 'It's a rust heap. When it rains, pieces fall off it.'

Martin crumpled a sheet of newspaper into a ball and hurled it at Padfield. Andrée rose to her feet and left the room.

Padfield sighed. 'See now, Finch, you've gone and put Mam'zelle into a huff. Now she'll be ratty with us all.'

Ellen said, 'Why do they call you Bat, Dr Dorner?'

'Looks like a bat, don't you think? Skinny . . . big ears . . .'

'It's because he can find his way in the dark,' explained Martin. 'Whenever there's a blackout, Bat flits happily about while the rest of us are falling over our feet.'

13

'Are there often blackouts?'

'Now and then. This house has its own electricity generator.'

An electric kettle stood on a table near the window; the shelves above it held mugs and tea and coffee. Ellen asked whether anyone wanted a drink; Denis Padfield asked for a cup of tea. She took down two mugs from the shelf.

Bill Farmborough drawled, 'Not the striped one, it's Redmond's. Gets into a frightful bate if anyone else uses his mug.'

Ellen put back the striped mug and took down a plain one instead. They were all pleasant and friendly, she thought, though she understood why they irritated Andrée Fournier. She herself was used to schoolboyish banter: her brother, Joe, was four years younger than she was.

An older man came into the room. He was of average build but stooped, so that his gaze directed downwards. His ill-cut grey hair had thinned on top and he was wearing National Health spectacles. His clothing looked worn and not at all clean. Over an off-white shirt he wore a baggy brown corduroy jacket with leather elbow patches that were cracked and fraying.

Toby Dorner said, 'Hello, Redmond,' but the older man did not respond. He crossed the room to the table with the tea things, took down the striped mug and spooned in tea. When the kettle boiled, he poured water on to the leaves and gave the mug a vigorous stir.

'Good morning, Dr Redmond,' said Ellen, and introduced herself.

He was standing only a couple of feet away from her but he did not respond, did not even look at her. She might have been invisible. She might not have existed.

Once he had made his tea, Dr Redmond left the room, mug in hand. Dr Padfield called after him, 'And nice to talk to you too, Redmond!' and there was a murmur of laughter.

Then Bill Farmborough said, 'Pharoah, I didn't think we'd see you till the end of the week,' and immediately everyone fell silent, as if a switch had been flicked.

It was Ellen's first glimpse of the director of Gildersleve Hall, Marcus Pharoah. His tall, broad-shouldered form was flattered by a beautifully cut charcoal-grey suit. The collar of his white shirt was crisp and the silk of his tie was elegantly striped in muted shades of maroon and gold. Pharoah's features were regular and handsome, a few silver strands showing through his black hair. He held himself easily, the stance of a man used to commanding the attention of a room.

'Good morning, gentlemen. And good morning, ladies.' His dark brown eyes came to rest on Ellen. 'You must be Miss Kingsley.'

Dr Pharoah welcomed Ellen to Gildersleve, apologizing for having been too busy to greet her earlier. 'Have my troops been looking after you, Miss Kingsley?'

'Yes, thank you, very well.'

'I'm pleased to hear it. Let me tell you what I wanted to make of the hall. I wanted to create a laboratory in which I could mix all the disciplines together. Biochemists, molecular biologists, physicists, chemists, crystallographers . . . perhaps even a mathematician or two. I wanted to make an environment where new ideas might meld together and find a receptive audience. Other institutions – King's and the Cavendish, for instance – strive for the same, but I like to think we've managed it rather better. Some of our visitors tell me they find the atmosphere at Gildersleve Hall rather frantic, but I like that. I doubt if great ideas come out of monastic silences. I believe they're more likely to develop from a mixing pot, even if the bubbling and brewing makes a bit of a racket.'

There was a silence. Ellen wondered whether anyone else in the room was having to fight the desire to applaud.

Bill Farmborough spoke. 'How was America, Pharoah?'

'Useful, very useful. But we must be on our mettle, gentlemen – the race is to the swift.' Dr Pharoah smiled. 'And if no one offers me a cup of tea soon, I shall desiccate.'

'We wouldn't want that. Our lord and master reduced to a heap of powder.' Farmborough put on the kettle.

A discussion followed about the lines of research being undertaken at the hall. Opinions were batted back and forth, suppositions confronted and taken apart with surgical precision. Then Marcus Pharoah made his apologies and left the room.

Ellen ate her lunch. Bill Farmborough went back to his newspaper, a chess game started up, and Rosemary Clooney sang, her voice like honey, 'If you loved me half as much as I loved you.'

She was a Daddy's girl, she supposed. Her father, who was a Royal Engineer, had always delighted in her faculty for maths and science. He had shown her how to take apart a motorcycle engine and put it together again and they had stood together in the frosty darkness of Salisbury Plain, watching a meteorite shower. Though winning a prize at school had been important to her, winning her father's approval had mattered far more.

Her childhood had been one of new houses, new schools, different places and different people as the family had moved between army camps. She had acquired the ability to remember people's names and to fit in anywhere. At the age of twelve she had been sent to boarding school in Buckinghamshire. She had enjoyed school, which had provided her with an anchor, especially during wartime. A teacher had encouraged her talent for science; after leaving school she had taken a degree in chemistry at Bristol University, followed by a year's research. She had known by then that she was no theoretician, that her gifts were technical, for experimentation, where her methodical, careful intelligence, her powers of observation and her determination to discover the truth and to prove it as far as possible beyond doubt were assets.

Her final-year project at Bristol had been on crystallography. The growing of crystals was something she had found she had a knack for, which was why she had been offered the job of research assistant at Gildersleve Hall. This was how she would spend her days: investigating those tiny, beautiful, slivers of perfection.

A short, burly man in a camouflage jacket, a brindled bull terrier at his heels, was coming away from the outhouses when, at the end of the afternoon, Ellen went to collect her bicycle. She said good evening and he gave her a sharp look and then a curt nod.

She took her bicycle out of the shed and wheeled it to the gravelled forecourt in front of the hall. Martin was loading cardboard boxes into a small Austin parked there.

'You look rather heavily laden,' she said.

Martin looked up. He was red-faced and a line of sweat darkened the hair on his forehead. 'They weigh a ton. Have you survived your first day?'

She laughed. 'Just about.'

'I hated it at first. I felt like a new boy at school. I wanted to turn tail and run.' He glanced at the boxes. 'I'd offer you a lift but I have to take these to Mrs Pharoah. She's some charity do on.'

The lid of one of the boxes flapped open, revealing a stack of plates. Ellen said, 'It's all right, thanks, I've got the bike.'

Martin lifted a box on to the front seat of the car. 'I

thought I might call in to the jolly old Green Man tonight. Some of the others said they'd come. If you don't mind my prattle, you could always join us.'

'Thank you,' she murmured, then she said goodbye and cycled away.

Her lodgings were in a bungalow on a road that struck out from Copfield towards Cambridge. Her landlady, Mrs Bryant, was a war widow in her early thirties. Mrs Bryant had one child, a twelve-year-old daughter, Gillian. The three of them ate supper together and afterwards Ellen retired to her room, where she wrote a letter to her parents and another to her boyfriend, Daniel Risborough.

Daniel lived in London, where he shared a flat in Marble Arch with his elder brother Clarence. He was a linguist and worked for the Diplomatic Service. They had met ten months ago, on a train – or, rather, they had met just after they had left the train, because Daniel had forgotten his umbrella and Ellen had run after him with it. He had offered to buy her a drink. 'I was trying to think how to ask you out,' he said to her, 'but I couldn't work out how to do it, but now I can, to thank you for returning my umbrella.' Since then, they had met up when the opportunity arose. She went with Daniel to concerts and art galleries, and sometimes they kissed, and now and then tentative suggestions of engagement and marriage were voiced and then put aside.

In her letter, Ellen described her first day at Gildersleve Hall, emphasizing the parts that she thought might interest

Daniel: the architecture of the hall and the laboratory's connections with Cambridge (Daniel was a Trinity man). She finished by reminding him of their arrangement to meet for lunch in October (the forgetfulness with the umbrella had not been an isolated incident). Then she left the bungalow to post her letters.

The light was fading as she walked down the road and crossed the village green to a Norman church with its square central tower. The dying sun gilded the flints and stones of the ancient walls. The postbox was at the end of a winding lane overhung by hawthorns, the box itself almost lost beneath the foliage. Beyond the end of the lane was a disused RAF aerodrome, to one side of which was a new council estate, built to house the families who had come from the bombed cities to live in the Nissen huts after the end of the war.

Ellen continued her circuit of the village, eventually striking back towards its heart. The Green Man pub, which stood beside the village green, had a grey and mossy thatched roof. Remembering Martin's invitation, she went inside.

Two couples sat in the private bar, sipping their drinks in genteel silence. Noise issued from the public bar, swelling as Ellen opened the door. The room was crowded. Men turned to stare at her, their gazes running from her head to her toes. A quick scan told her that, apart from the barmaid, she was the only woman in the room.

Martin was sitting at a corner table. She waved to him.

'Ellen!' He rose to his feet. 'You don't mind sitting here, do you? The saloon bar's as dead as a mortuary. Let me get you a drink. What would you like?'

'A half of bitter, please.'

She sat down at the table. When Martin came back with the drinks she asked after the others.

'Looks like they couldn't make it. Cheers.' He chinked his glass against hers. 'I didn't think you were going to come. I saw you earlier, walking across the green.'

'I had letters to post, and,' she lowered her voice, 'my room is perfectly comfortable but there are about half a dozen different patterns in it. Curtains, eiderdown, carpet, rug . . . it's a little oppressive.' She smiled. 'My boyfriend would find it unbearable. He would have moved out by now – either that or had a nervous breakdown.'

'Boyfriend?' said Martin.

'Daniel lives in London.'

'Ah.'

'When I was leaving the hall this afternoon, I saw a man at the outhouses. Tough-looking . . . wearing an army jacket. He wasn't particularly friendly.'

'That would have been Gosse.' Martin grimaced. 'Pharoah's familiar.'

'Why do you call him that?'

'Gosse has been the janitor at Gildersleve Hall since it was first set up.' Martin cast a glance round the room. 'Just checking. He drinks here sometimes. Pharoah met him during the war. Rumour is, Roy Gosse was just out of military prison and Pharoah got him transferred here. Gosse's obnoxious to the rest of us but would do anything for Pharoah. He's useful, I'll give him that. Keeps the old place running, fixes the boiler and defrosts the pipes in the middle of winter, that sort of thing.'

'You sound as though you dislike him.'

Martin shrugged. 'I don't care about him one way or the other. I wouldn't cross him, that's for sure. He has a nasty temper. Keep-fit fanatic, used to be a boxer, apparently.' He offered Ellen a cigarette; she thanked him but declined.

He said, 'What did you think of us all, then?'

'Everyone was very kind and helpful.'

'*Everyone?* Come off it, Kingsley.' Martin flicked a lighter. 'Redmond? *Helpful?*'

'Perhaps not him. Actually, I felt sorry for him.'

'Why? He's an unfriendly devil.'

'He looked . . . uncared-for. And perhaps he's shy, rather than unfriendly.'

'Why on earth should he feel shy? He just can't be bothered, and that's the truth of it. Thinks the rest of us are beneath him.'

She did not argue the point further. Martin said, 'And Mam'zelle? Do you think you're going to like sharing a lab with her?'

'Yes, I would have thought so.'

'She's got a sharp tongue, you know. Mind you, Hunter tends to get the worst of it these days.'

'Does Andrée dislike him?'

'She used to *adore* him.' Martin rolled his eyes. 'Madly, passionately, you know, and then it all fell apart. Now, when they're in the same room together you can cut the atmosphere with a knife.'

'That's the trouble with workplace romances. If it all ends badly you still have to see each other every day.'

'I get on with Jock, on the whole, but he's lord of the manor or some such back home, and he can be a moody devil. And Mam'zelle blows hot and cold. I expect they bickered like cat and dog.'

At their meeting in the common room that morning Dr Hunter's dark blue eyes had rested on her for a moment without a flicker of a smile and had then slid aside. Ellen knew that her attraction to him was not real, that it was some transference of the hope and excitement she had invested in her new job. He was a handsome man, undeniably, but once you got to know someone, as a colleague or a friend, handsomeness was as easily forgotten as ugliness.

Martin said, 'What did you think of Pharoah's speech this morning? You know,' he put on a pompous voice, 'creating a laboratory in which all the disciplines are mixed together . . . great ideas . . .'

'I thought it was inspiring.'

'I suppose it is if you haven't heard it before.' Martin fidgeted with a beer mat. 'He adds a new bit now and then, for neophytes like you.'

'Has Dr Pharoah a family?'

'A wife, Alison, and a daughter, Rowena. They live in Barton. Alison's rather a bitch. I suppose I shouldn't say that, but it's true. Her family's very rich and she looks down on lesser folk. I think that to begin with, just after the war, the Pharoahs lived in the hall itself. Probably wasn't grand enough for Alison, so they bought the house in Barton.' Martin grinned. 'My landlady tells me there are ghosts at Gildersleve Hall.'

'Ghosts?'

'A child, a little boy, died in the house, fell downstairs or something. You're supposed to be able to hear his footsteps at night, running up and down the corridors. Creepy.' Martin made spooky movements with his hands. 'Bat has this idea that you can explain the sighting of ghosts using quantum theory.'

Ellen laughed. 'A fanciful imagination seems more likely.'

'Or a drink too many.' Martin glanced at her empty glass. 'Can I get you another?'

She shook her head. 'Thanks, Martin, but I won't. I should get back to my digs. I'm rather tired – it's been a long day.'

'I'll give you a lift.'

'There's no need. It's no distance.'

'Save you the walk.' He stood up, shrugging on his jacket.

On alternate Monday afternoons, a seminar was given by a staff member of Dr Pharoah's choosing to the entire group. 'So who's to be skewered over the hot coals today?' murmured Martin, sliding into the seat beside Ellen. She tried to imagine what it must feel like, to know that Dr Pharoah had chosen you to present your work to the group. She listened attentively to the discussions and noted her colleagues' differing contributions. Bill Farmborough deferred to Pharoah while Denis Padfield found fault with everything. Toby was pithy and incisive, but Martin's interjections, in which his words often fell over each other in his rush to make his point, were sometimes brilliant but at other times misplaced. As for Alec Hunter, Ellen noticed that for much of the time he was silent. Now and then, with an air of scowling impatience, he would lean forward and make some remark, sometimes cutting, but sometimes, she was forced to admit, shrewd. She found herself disliking him for his air of holding himself apart from other people; she wondered whether he considered his opinions too precious to be shared. And yet the attraction she had felt for him had not completely gone away but would sometimes catch her by surprise, powerful and disturbing.

Now and then, flicking through *The Times* or *Nature*, she saw Dr Pharoah's name. Funny, that, to know someone who existed in another, more celebrated world. It was almost as if a little of the magic might rub off on her. One evening, Ellen and Mrs Bryant sat in Mrs Bryant's living room, listening to Dr Pharoah give a talk on the Third Programme. Ellen was sewing on buttons and Mrs Bryant was knitting. The tip-tap of needles and the rasp of thread through the cloth, and Dr Pharoah's good-for-radio voice, murmuring of genes and proteins: like coming across a Monet in a public library, too important and cultured for the small room, with its lemon-washed anaglypta wallpaper, plump, beribboned cushions and china cats.

Marcus Pharoah was clever and amusing and commanding. But there was something else, some extra dash of an ingredient Ellen could not find the words for, some rare element or catalyst that by its presence transformed. When Dr Pharoah joined them in the common room, the air seemed charged with electricity and their discussions were whipped into life. After he had gone, they were, according to their natures, exhausted or exhilarated or fractious, each of them, Ellen suspected, rerunning the conversation in their heads, trying to judge whether they had acquitted themselves well.

'The gods have come down from Olympus,' Martin muttered to her, one Monday afternoon when Marcus Pharoah and a colleague from the Cavendish joined the regular seminar. An obvious metaphor, but Ellen could see what he meant.

She was preparing a batch of crystals for Jan Kaminski, when, from a distance, she heard raised voices. At first she disregarded them, returning her mind to the quiet, empty place that allowed her to work best. But they rose in volume, and eventually she went out to the landing. The voices were coming from the tower. One belonged to Marcus Pharoah;

she assumed that the other was Dr Redmond's. She could not make out any words, only the unpleasant angular rise and fall of the argument.

She was poised like an eavesdropper: she went back into the lab and shut the door. She heard one of the men leave the tower, his footsteps fast and clipped. Dr Pharoah, she thought – Dr Redmond shuffled as he walked, scuffing his feet. She focused her attention on making a tiny wire cage, twisting the wire so that it was exactly the right size to contain the crystal she would place inside it. A door slammed. More footsteps, then a loud clang, as if someone had stumbled against something.

After a while, checking her watch, Ellen saw that it was lunchtime and left the lab. In the corridor, her eye was caught by a scattering of sand from the fire bucket. Something was inside the bucket; she took it out. It was an Osmiroid fountain pen, tortoiseshell with a gilt cap. Her thumb grazed against a roughness on the barrel and she read the name engraved there: B. D. J. Redmond. Dr Redmond must have tripped over the fire bucket and dropped his pen.

She felt reluctant to enter the tower, knowing that she was crossing a boundary. It was quieter there than in the rest of the building, colder too, because three of the walls were exposed to the elements. On the open landing were bookshelves, bowed beneath the weight of dusty, browning periodicals.

'Dr Redmond?' she called out, but there was no reply. Even if Dr Redmond had gone back to his lab, would he answer her? During the four weeks she had been working at Gildersleve Hall, he had not spoken to her once.

She went upstairs. On the upper landing, she tapped on a door, then went inside the lab. Cluttered, you might have said, except the word in no way did justice to the accumulation of books, journals and scientific equipment there. The only light was from a tall, narrow window which looked out to the garden and copse. Through it, Ellen saw Dr Redmond standing beneath the trees, looking up with a pair of binoculars into the branches.

She returned downstairs, took her coat from the box room and went outside. The air was cool and fresh, gusts of wind shaking the bare branches of the poplars.

She called out, 'Hello, Dr Redmond!' and he turned to her.

'I brought you this.' She held out the pen. 'You dropped it in the fire bucket.'

His hand went to his jacket pocket, patting it flat. He took the pen from her.

She said, 'Have you seen anything interesting?'

'A mistle thrush.' He looked up at the sky, blinking. His eyes were large and pale blue, fringed with light-coloured lashes. 'There's always been a mistle thrush in this copse,' he said. 'Even when they cut the trees down, the mistle thrush stayed.'

'Which trees?'

'Down there.' He gestured towards the field that butted up to the perimeter of the copse. 'Before the war, these woods were twice the size. Sheer vandalism – a waste of effort as well as the pointless destruction of an ancient woodland. The ground's always been boggy. No crops have ever grown there.'

'Still, it's pretty.'

'It doesn't compare to Peddar's Wood for birds. I go there every day. I always see something.'

'How marvellous,' she said, but some movement in the upper branches had caught his attention and he had lost interest in the conversation. Turning away from her, he raised the binoculars again.

Then a brindled bull terrier rushed through the undergrowth towards them. There was a beating of wings and Dr Redmond flinched and took a step back.

'Gosse should keep that dog under control,' he muttered. Putting his head down, he walked away down the path.

The next day was a Saturday. Ellen caught the train from Cambridge to meet Daniel. Alighting at King's Cross Station, she caught sight of Dr Redmond ahead of her on the platform, among the passengers spilling out of the train. After a few moments he disappeared into the crowds heading for the Underground station.

Daniel was waiting for her by the barrier. He kissed her cheek and asked after her journey. Then they took an Underground train to Leicester Square, to visit the National Gallery. On the train, she asked him about his work and he said, 'I've been very busy. I've worked late each night this week,' and jabbed at his fringe to brush it out of his eyes.

'Poor Daniel, you must be exhausted.'

'I don't mind the extra work, but there was a concert I wanted to go to, and I had to give the tickets to Clarence.'

Inside the National Gallery, they looked at the Titians, Daniel's favourites. Daniel disliked the modern, his lack of enthusiasm extending to the nineteenth century, though he admitted a grudging admiration for Turner and Pissarro. Ellen had once said exasperatedly to him, 'Daniel, you can't just dismiss every single twentieth-century artist,' and he had turned to her, puzzlement in his great blue eyes, and said, 'But Ellen, "Diana and Actaeon" and a Jackson Pollock – how can you even *compare* them?'

He was very knowledgeable, and she had always tolerated – often enjoyed – his habit of giving lectures on each painting, but today her thoughts swung away to Gildersleve Hall, even while her gaze was fixed on the swirling draperies and contorted limbs of 'Bacchus and Ariadne'. It felt strange to pick up the strands of her previous life. She felt rusty, ill at ease, almost as if she was taking a step back.

Daniel finished speaking of brushstrokes and Titian's use of colour. Ellen said, 'It's always surprised me that "Bacchus and Ariadne" should be one of your favourites. It's so wild and forceful.'

He gave a patient smile. 'No, Ellen, you're missing the point. The painting may *appear* wild and forceful, but the composition is magnificently controlled.'

'The composition's only a means to an end, a technique for conveying whatever it is that the artist wants to say.' She studied the painted figure of Bacchus, the angle of his shoulders, the tension in his muscles and the desire in the gaze that focused on the fleeing Ariadne. 'Just look at the expressions on their faces. There's such darkness there!'

'I don't see why you should be surprised that I admire it.'

'Like it, Daniel, or love it,' she said impatiently. 'It's more than mere admiration, surely?'

He hunched his shoulders. 'I prefer not to speak of art in woolly emotional terms.'

'That's exactly what I mean. You talk in such a measured way, and yet you enjoy art that's full of desire and hunger and fear.'

They walked out of the room in silence. Their disagreement had blown up out of nowhere – they had never quarrelled before and it dismayed her. What was wrong with her? His face was set; she felt a pang of guilt and squeezed his hand.

They left the gallery shortly afterwards and lunched in a small French restaurant in the Strand. Tables were dotted round a square room whose window looked out on to a courtyard garden. One fine evening the previous summer they had dined in the garden, though Daniel had disliked the wasps.

Daniel ordered steak and potatoes and Ellen asked for an omelette and salad. When their food arrived, Daniel carefully separated the potatoes from the steak, a habit which Ellen had once found endearing but today thought childish.

He said suddenly, 'I've been offered a post in Paris.'

'Paris!' She looked up at him. 'Daniel, why didn't you say?'

'I didn't feel there was the opportunity.'

'How exciting! I'm so pleased for you.'

He looked puzzled. 'I was always convinced that when I was finally posted abroad, it would be to somewhere bleak and uncivilized. Or crashingly dull, perhaps.'

'You will go, won't you?'

'Yes, I think so.'

'I'll come and visit you.'

'Will you, Ellen?'

Something in his tone made her reach across the table and take his hand. 'Yes, of course.'

'I wondered whether to ask you to come with me. In fact, I thought I might ask you to marry me.'

'Daniel—'

But before she could go on, he added, 'But I don't think it would work.'

It was irrational, she knew, that she should feel irked that he should dismiss her so easily when she would have refused him anyway. 'Oh,' she said coldly. 'I see.'

'I think that place has changed you.'

'Changed me?' She gave him a hard look. 'I don't suppose you mean for the better.'

'I didn't say that. I just meant that you seem different. You seem,' he pursed his mouth, '*distracted*.'

'It's my first proper job. It's important to me. You don't mind, do you?'

'Mind? Why should I mind?'

'I don't know, Daniel. You've hardly asked me about Gildersleve Hall.'

'We were at the gallery. I don't believe that's a place for chit-chat. Well then, how is it going?'

'It's fine. I think it's going to work out very well.' His brisk, humouring tone annoyed her. If she had told him how she really felt about working at Gildersleve Hall – proud, exhilarated, sometimes apprehensive – he would say something deflating, she suspected.

'I don't think you'd leave Gildersleve Hall for me, would you, Ellen?'

There was a long, difficult moment when neither of them spoke. Eventually he said, 'I don't want any pudding, do you?' and she shook her head.

Daniel paid the bill and they left the restaurant. One cold kiss and mutual expressions of good will, then he walked away while she headed in the opposite direction, for the Underground and the Islington lodgings that her brother Joe shared with half a dozen other students.

She found herself, later on that afternoon and over a cup of coffee in the kitchen, telling Joe about Daniel's proposal, feeling some guilt in doing so but needing to talk about it to someone, and if not her brother, then who else? Joe, who was cheerful and athletic and had yellow hair rather than red, hooted with laughter and said, 'I bet Risborough didn't fall on his knees and beg for your hand in marriage. I bet he said "it might be a jolly good idea if we got married" or something wishy-washy like that,' and she was forced to admit that yes, that was exactly what had happened.

'You said no, didn't you?'

'I didn't have to. He more or less said it himself.'

'Just as well. You'd have made mincemeat of the poor bloke, Ellie.'

'Honestly, I wouldn't at all. You make me sound like a harpy.' Yet she had a sudden, awful vision of how marriage to Daniel might have been, tepid and restrained and ultimately stifling.

She caught the half past seven train back to Cambridge. In the carriage, her attention drifted from her book and she looked out of the window, watching the countryside rush by. She felt unsettled and was glad to be returning to Copfield. *That place has changed you*, Daniel had said. Was that true? Surely it was rather that Gildersleve Hall had informed her, allowing her to see new possibilities. She was still Ellen, and her character, principles and ambitions remained the same. She did not believe that any place had the power to alter her in a fundamental way. But she felt low nevertheless, weary of the day and its events.

She left the train at Cambridge and caught a bus to Copfield. Leaving the bus, she shivered in the sharp, cold air. As she walked past the Green Man she glanced through the window and saw Martin Finch. She had a yearning for uncomplicated friendship: she went inside.

Catching sight of her in the doorway, Martin rose to his feet. 'Evening, Kingsley. What'll you have?'

She asked for a beer, then took off her coat and sat down at the table. The room was full. The only other woman there was sitting at a high stool at the bar. She was middle-aged, a slash of red lipstick across her powdered face. She was wearing a Persian lamb jacket and a felt hat with a feather, and when she raised her glass to her mouth a chunky gold bracelet slid down her arm.

Martin came back with the drinks. He had been working that day, he told her – he liked being at Gildersleve when no one else was there. Well, only Gosse, and Redmond sometimes worked weekends, though he had not been in that day.

'I saw Dr Redmond on the London train,' Ellen told him.

Martin smiled. 'Good Lord – Redmond, going on a jaunt. Or maybe he has a secret life. How was London?'

'Not so good.' Her spirits collapsed like air out of a punctured tyre. 'I broke up with my boyfriend.' She could almost have cried, then and there, thinking of Daniel and the way they had parted.

Martin looked interested. 'That's rotten luck. You do need cheering up. I'll get you something stronger than that.'

Before Ellen could stop him, he rose and went to the bar, returning a few minutes later with a gin and tonic.

'Here, knock that back.'

'You're very sweet, Martin.'

He threw back his arms behind his head, stretching them, narrowly missing the head of the man sitting behind him. 'We aim to serve.'

'We weren't suited anyway. Daniel is very cultured.'

'You weren't in love with him, were you?'

Ellen considered that. 'No, I don't think so. He was very handsome and he was always very courteous, which I liked, and he had a knack of picking out the best, whatever it was. But I wasn't in love with him.' The gin had made her feel pleasantly fuzzy, otherwise she might not have added, 'I don't think I've ever been in love with anyone.'

She had had two boyfriends before Daniel. Giles had been in her year at Bristol, and then there had been Archie, who had been a junior doctor at the Royal Infirmary. She had lost her virginity to Archie, after a particularly wild party. Archie had been rather a mistake.

She lowered her voice, glancing at the bar. 'Sometimes I'm afraid I'll end up like *her*.'

Martin followed her gaze to the woman in the Persian lamb jacket, and sniggered. 'That old hag. I've seen her before, propping up the bar in here. Come off it.'

'How many of us are even dating anyone?'

'I think Toby has something going on with some woman in Cambridge. He's very cagey about it. And you can understand why Kaminski lives on his own, poor sod. As for Hunter, he's only got himself to blame. Women fall at his feet with sickening regularity.'

'Not Andrée.'

'Not any more, no.' His gaze settled on her. 'You're just choosing the wrong men, Kingsley.'

She laughed. 'Fall in love with another biochemist, you mean, and then perhaps we wouldn't end up quarrelling in the National Gallery.'

He laughed again, so hard he had to blow his nose and wipe his eyes. 'How middle-class you are.'

When they left the pub an hour later, a frost had begun to glisten on the road. Martin scraped a clear patch on the windscreen, then they drove out of the village. Ellen huddled in her coat, washed over by a feeling of pleasant detachment, as if much of what had occurred that day had happened to some other, quite distant person.

Martin parked the Austin outside Mrs Bryant's bungalow. 'Ellen,' he said.

'Yes, Martin?'

'I do like you a lot, you know.'

'And I'm terribly fond of you.'

'Are you cold?'

'A little.'

'Here, let me.' He reached over and put an arm round her. And then suddenly he was kissing her, his hand first squeezing her arm, then sliding beneath the folds of her coat.

She tried to say, 'Martin, don't,' but was hampered by his mouth, which was clamped wetly over her own, making it hard to breathe or speak, so in the end she gave him a shove. Then a harder shove, which startled him enough to draw back, allowing her to say, 'Martin, stop it.'

'But I thought—'

'What?'

'You're so beautiful! You must have realized how I feel about you!'

'Oh, Martin, don't be so silly!' The words snapped out of her.

His expression changed. 'Silly?'

'Yes,' she said crossly. She was annoyed with him for spoiling their evening. She opened the car door. 'You've had too much to drink. I'm going in now. I'll see you next week.'

There was an envelope on Ellen's desk when she arrived at the lab on Monday morning. She opened it and read the note inside. It was from Dr Pharoah, inviting her to Sunday lunch at his home in Barton.

She had hoped that Martin would have forgotten Saturday's embarrassing tussle in the car, but in the common room at break time, he bent over the parts of the Austin's starter motor, which he had spread out on a sheet of newspaper, and acknowledged her presence with only a grunt. She avoided him for the rest of the day, hoping that in her absence he would cool down and forgive her.

On Friday afternoon, Ellen worked late. Andrée left the lab at half past five. Time passed and the distant hum of a vacuum cleaner announced that Mary, the cleaner, had started her work. The house was quiet, and it occurred to Ellen that she and Mary might be the only ones still there.

Her work absorbed her, and by the time she had written up her notes and put away her equipment, the vacuum cleaner was long silent and the windowpanes enclosed squares of inky black sky. She turned off the light and shut the door of the lab behind her, then went to the box room to get her coat. She was doing up her buttons when the overhead light went out, plunging the box room into blackness. She fumbled for the switch and flicked it on and off: nothing. Picking up her briefcase and handbag, she felt for the doorknob, then stumbled out into the corridor.

After a few moments, her eyes accustomed themselves to the darkness, and she saw, above the condensation on a windowpane, speckles of stars. She knew that the stairs down to the first floor led off the corridor ahead, and with the flat of her hand against the wall for guidance began to move cautiously towards them. Her shin struck something hard and cold and she cried out. Stooping, her fingers padded first over sand and then touched the metal edge of the fire bucket, the same fire bucket in which she had found Dr Redmond's pen. She recalled the layout of the corridor, the fire bucket only a few feet from the topmost stair. Her right hand scooped shapes in the darkness until she found the round wooden ball of the finial at the top of the banister.

She was slowly descending the stairs when she heard

the sound. A pitter-pattering, scampering sound, like a child's footsteps. She froze. She could not tell where it was coming from. *A little boy died in the house, fell down the stairs,* Martin had told her. *You're supposed to be able to hear his footsteps at night, running up and down the corridors.*

The pitter-pattering was from above her – or no, perhaps it came from below. Or perhaps it was coming up the stairs towards her. A cry escaped her throat, and then the beating of her heart enmeshed with the sound of footsteps, louder and heavier than that dreadful pattering.

A circle of light swung up the stairs to her. 'Who is it?' someone called out. 'Who's there?'

She recognized Alec Hunter's voice. 'It's me!' she cried. 'Ellen Kingsley!'

'Are you all right?'

The torchlight swept up to her face and she put up a hand to her eyes. 'I'm fine.'

'You look as if you've had a fright.'

'I banged my leg against the fire bucket, that's all. And I thought I heard . . .'

'What?'

'There was a sound . . . Martin told me there were ghosts in the hall and I thought . . .' She broke off, feeling very foolish.

'Martin talks a lot of nonsense,' Alec said shortly. 'You shouldn't listen to him. Are you on your way home? Come, take my hand and we'll find our way out together.'

His touch reassured; slowly, they made their way

downstairs. 'I expect what I heard was Mr Gosse's dog,' she said. 'How idiotic of me to get into such a panic.'

'The mind can play tricks, especially at night.'

'So long as you don't tell the others.'

'I'm not one for tittle-tattle, Miss Kingsley. This place seethes with gossip. We work too closely together and we're too cut off from the world.'

His sudden hostility took her by surprise. She had meant it as a joke. Then she remembered Martin, in the pub, gleefully telling her of Alec Hunter's affair with Andrée Fournier, and thought she understood why he might dislike gossip.

'I'm sorry,' she said. 'I didn't mean to imply anything. How sensible of you, to have a torch.'

'I was in the basement. The lights often go out down there so I always keep a torch handy. It'll be the generator. Gosse will fix it.'

They followed the sweep of the torchlight through the house, down the stairs to the hallway. Alec said, 'I'll see you to the bike shed.'

'There's no need,' she began, but he had already opened the front door and was heading down the steps.

Her shin hurt where she had hit it on the fire bucket. She noticed that the air was growing colder. They crossed the courtyard to the path that led round by the side of the house. The gravel crunched beneath their feet and the bobbing light of the torch showed now and then the dim shapes of the outhouses and the dripping rows of winter vegetables in the kitchen gardens. Alec said, 'How are you settling into Gildersleve Hall?' and she answered, 'Very well, I'm enjoying it very much,' and all the while, as they conversed, she was aware of his presence and the compulsion to look, to touch, to prolong this moment.

As they reached the bike shed, she glimpsed out of the corner of her eye a tremulous, flickering blaze in the windows of Gildersleve Hall as the lights went back on, illuminating Alec Hunter's features. And the pang of yearning she felt was sharp and foreign to her, because she was unused to longing for what she could not have.

Dr Pharoah's house was large and imposing, late Victorian or Edwardian, and surrounded by a garden and yew hedge. By the time Ellen arrived there at midday on Sunday, several cars were already parked in the driveway.

That morning, she felt ruffled. Ruffled by the headwind which had buffeted her, cycling from Copfield, ruffled by the memories which burned in her like an intermittent fever: the touch of Alec Hunter's hand and the fragmentary glimpses of him that Friday's blackout had allowed – a profile, the flash of a dark blue, almond-shaped eye.

She propped her bicycle against the wall of Dr Pharoah's house. The door to the porch was open and the black and white tiles inside it were strewn with wellington boots and a girl's coat, lavender wool with a purple velvet collar. She rang the bell. A few moments later a middle-aged woman opened the door.

Ellen introduced herself. Her coat and beret were taken and she was shown through to the drawing room. She made a quick mental adjustment. Sunday lunch at the Pharoahs' was no intimate family get-together: there must have been twenty people in the room. The walls and curtains were papered pale primrose and cream, and French windows looked out to a terrace on which stood stone urns, garlanded with ivy. Paintings hung on the walls, some abstract and bright, others darkened by age. Arrangements of autumn leaves and berries cascaded out of vases on the mantelpiece and tables.

Alison Pharoah was in her mid-thirties, slim and of medium height. Her flaxen hair was cut short, waving round her slightly snub nose, round eyes and small, full mouth. She was wearing a white pleated skirt and a white angora sweater, set off with a row of pearls. One of her hands was playing with the pearls. Ellen noticed that her nails were very short, and that the skin around them was ragged and torn, in contrast with the rest of her immaculate appearance.

Mrs Pharoah asked, 'Have you travelled far, Miss Kingsley?'

'Only a couple of miles. I live in Copfield.'

'Did you drive?'

'No, I cycled.'

'Cycled!' Mrs Pharoah's eyebrows raised. 'In this weather?'

'I don't mind, I'm used to it. I cycle to work each day.'

Throughout their brief conversation, Mrs Pharoah's eyes had remained cold. 'Gin and tonic all right?' she said. 'Heather will get you one. Let me introduce you to the

Dorringtons. Margaret Dorrington is a keen sportswoman. I'm sure you'll have a great deal in common.'

Ellen was talking to the Dorringtons – he was a GP, she played tennis at a club in Cambridge – when Dr Pharoah joined them. He greeted her.

'Thank you for inviting me, Dr Pharoah,' she said.

'Marcus.' He smiled. 'You must call me Marcus.'

A tall, grey-haired man, catching sight of Pharoah, said, 'Marcus, where have you been hiding? We want to hear about Chinon.'

'Damned rainy,' said Pharoah. 'I've been showing Devlin my latest acquisitions in the cellar.' He turned back to the Dorringtons. 'Jimmy, Margot, so glad you could make it. Do you know Miss Kingsley?'

'We've been talking about tennis,' said Mrs Dorrington.

'Are you a tennis player, Ellen?' asked Dr Pharoah.

'Only a very amateur one.'

'You must come and play on our court in the summer. It doesn't get enough use. I haven't time and Alison isn't keen.'

If Mrs Pharoah's pale iciness chilled, Dr Pharoah's warmth melted. Ellen murmured thanks.

Margaret Dorrington said, 'I thought Rowena was shaping up to be a nice little player.'

Pharoah smiled. 'I believe she is.'

'You should get her a coach. Makes all the difference at her age.'

Another man joined them. His arched black eyebrows

and the deep channels to either side of his mouth gave him a saturnine look.

'The Côtes Hermitage with the lamb, I should say.'

'Not the claret?'

'No, too young. The Côtes.' The dark, mocking gaze took in Ellen. 'Well, hello there. Who's this, Marc?'

'This is Ellen Kingsley. She works at the hall. She's a very clever and promising young lady and we're fortunate to have her with us. Ellen, meet my brother, Devlin.'

They shook hands. 'One of Marcus's brainboxes, then,' said Devlin Pharoah.

'Not really.' Ellen could see a family similarity, though in Devlin the Pharoah handsomeness had a rakish cast. 'Dr Pharoah was being kind. Most of my colleagues at Gildersleve Hall are far more erudite than I am.'

'Not so pretty, I imagine. I visited the place once and some of the female scientists were frightful frumps.'

'Are you a scientist yourself, Mr Pharoah?'

He laughed. 'I'm not nearly noble enough for that. Too much like hard work. I'm an antique dealer. I have a few shops in London to keep me busy.'

A voice called out, 'Daddy! Daddy!' A girl of twelve or so had run into the room. She ducked through the crowd to Marcus Pharoah's side.

'Hello, darling.' Pharoah put his arm round his daughter's shoulders.

Rowena Pharoah was a strikingly beautiful child, tall and slim, with her father's strong colouring. She was wearing a turquoise wool dress with an embroidered belt, and her dark brown hair was in plaits.

'Daddy,' she said. 'I hate Rufus. He's so mean.'

'What's he done this time, Ro?' asked Devlin Pharoah.

'He's taken my wellies and won't give them back.' Rowena's voice took on a whining tone. 'He says he's going to throw them in the pond.'

'Christ, that boy,' muttered Devlin. He marched out of the room.

'Say hello to Miss Kingsley, Rowena,' said Dr Pharoah.

'Hello,' muttered Rowena. 'Daddy?'

'Yes, darling?'

'Can me and Rufus have lunch in the summer house?'

'Rufus and I,' corrected Pharoah. 'No, not this time, it's too cold.'

'*Daddy*. I'll wear my coat.'

'No, darling, I want you to eat your lunch with us. Besides, I thought you hated Rufus.'

'He's a very silly boy,' Rowena said condescendingly.

'Have you helped Heather with the table?'

'No.' A black patent sandal was scuffed along the carpet.

'Run along then, sweetheart.'

'Daddy, I don't *want* to.'

Pharoah coaxed, 'But you like choosing the glasses.'

'Do it with me, *please*, Daddy.'

Pharoah smiled at his daughter fondly. 'Would you excuse me, Ellen?'

He and Rowena left the room. The Dorringtons had

moved on to talk to someone else. Through the French windows, Ellen could see Devlin Pharoah remonstrating with a wild-looking, dark-haired boy of around Rowena's age. The wind brushed the plumes of the pampas grass and Ellen ran her conversation with Alec Hunter through her head again, testing it, tasting it, as she had done countless times since Friday evening, and felt a heady delight.

A sound from behind her made her look round. The housekeeper was gathering glasses on to a tray. Ellen made her way to the dining room.

Apart from Rowena and Rufus and a scattering of children, Ellen was the youngest person at the table. No one else from Gildersleve Hall had been invited. The talk over lunch was of plays seen and concerts attended, of holidays in Cornwall or Scotland or undiscovered parts of France.

'The Pattersons' friends, do you remember them from New Year?'

'When there's a storm, the spray hits the windows.'

'Charlie and John go fishing and we don't see them from dawn to dusk.'

'The mountains are still full of bandits. We thought our throats would be cut before we reached Turin.'

'Have you come far, Miss Kingsley? And how do you know the Pharoahs?'

Ellen explained, briefly, to the solicitor sitting beside her, about X-ray crystallography, and then, when she judged that he had had enough, listened to him talk about yachting. She saw how Mrs Pharoah ensured that the serving of the meal went off smoothly and unobtrusively, how she made sure her guests had everything they wanted, nodding to the housekeeper to let her know when to clear a course. No wine glass was left empty and every guest was drawn into the conversation.

She saw how Devlin Pharoah talked and smiled, though now and then his gaze drifted away. Was it boredom she saw in those black eyes, or contempt? The two cousins, Rowena and Rufus, sat side by side, Rowena whispering to her cousin, covering her mouth with her hand. 'Not at the table, Rowy, it's impolite,' murmured Alison Pharoah, but when she looked away the whispering started again. When fruit was served at the end of the meal, Rufus flicked orange pips with finger and thumb, pinging them off wine glasses, until his father said angrily, 'That's enough, Rufe.'

Lunch ended with a haze of cigarette smoke and a shuffling of chairs. Groups of guests dispersed through the house. Women talked in low voices of errant children and obstetric disasters, and some of the men sprawled in armchairs, making jokes, roaring with laughter. The Dorringtons were sitting in silence, not part of any group. They were makeweights, Ellen suspected, like herself.

She went to find a bathroom. Copies of Punch on a small wicker table and a bottle of Blue Grass hand lotion. She checked her face in the mirror and ran a comb through her hair; she scooped it up so that it surrounded her features like Alison Pharoah's, then let it fall to her shoulders again.

She reached down and rubbed the bruise on her leg, and felt the raised ridge left by the metal edge of the fire bucket.

On the way back to the drawing room, she looked through an open door and saw Dr Pharoah. He beckoned to her. 'Come and have a look at this, Ellen.'

She went inside the room. He pointed at a photograph. 'This was taken during the war,' he said. 'You can see the fences and barbed wire.'

In the picture, Gildersleve Hall looked muted and dingy and the wide sweep of trees that surrounded it blocked the horizon. The ivy that now grew only over the tower spread like an infection over the entire house.

Pharoah said, 'We worked twelve-hour days back then. Exhausting, but I never minded. We were young, I suppose. See this, Ellen.' He indicated another photo. 'I took this the day I knew the hall was mine. It had been empty for a year and was in a pretty rough state, but our first scientists moved in three months later. I did a lot of the work myself.' He laughed. 'I remember climbing over the roof to sort out some slates. If I'd slipped, that would have been the end of Gildersleve Hall.'

There was a footfall and Devlin Pharoah came into the room. 'Thought you might want to dig out those papers for me, Marc. Not interrupting anything, am I?'

His words had an implication that Ellen disliked. She murmured her excuses and slipped out of the door. Along the corridor, china and glasses and the stained cloth still lay on the dining table. Only Rowena and Rufus remained in the room, sitting side by side on the deep windowsill, whispering. Ellen thought Rufus looked dissolute, like his father. Silly of her – he was only a child. Rufus grabbed the girl's plaits, one in each hand, and gave them a hard tug. 'Ow, stop it, Rufe,' moaned Rowena, but Rufus did it again, jerking her towards him so that their faces were only an inch apart, and this time Rowena let out shrill laughter.

'Do you know where your mother is, Rowena?' said Ellen, and Rufus let go of the plaits.

Rowena shrugged. 'Haven't an earthly. Sorry.'

At the end of a corridor Ellen discovered a small pink and green room. Though it was no doubt charming in summer, with its white-painted chairs and bookcases of paperbacks and boardgames, the room seemed cold and unwelcoming in late October. Ellen saw a movement in the wood and glass structure that led off from the glazed side door. On the chest-height benches were orchids in pots. Their petals were pink and green and yellow, spotted and speckled, contorted and velvety, some protruding like tongues.

Alison Pharoah was in there, smoking a cigarette as she looked out of a window. Ellen was about to offer to help with the clearing up when she saw that Mrs Pharoah was crying. Her tears were silent, she hardly seemed to notice them, and while she cried she tore at her nails and the flesh around them with her teeth. A bead of blood glimmered on her finger like a ruby.

Quietly, Ellen left the room. All those people in the house, she thought, all those Jimmys and Devs and Rufes, and there was Alison Pharoah, crying alone in her conservatory. Glancing at her watch, she saw that it was past three o'clock.

Her earlier elation had vanished, replaced by staleness. The glamour of the Pharoahs' lives seemed to mask a darker undertow, and now she also saw her encounter with Alec on Friday night through more rational eyes, a conversation with a colleague, of slight significance. She longed to leave, to return to the quiet of her room at Mrs Bryant's bungalow. After thanking Marcus Pharoah for his hospitality, she fetched her coat and hat and cycled home.

Chapter Two

November: rooks jabbed their bills at the iron clods of earth and frost greyed the fields. Icy winds leaked through the gaps round the doors and windows of Gildersleve Hall. Making up salt solutions in which to float haemoglobin crystals, Ellen's hands were clumsy with cold. She noted down the size and shape of the crystals, their colouration and peculiarities and imperfections. As she adjusted the microscope, patterns shifted beneath the lens.

Alec Hunter was at the bike shed when she went there at the end of the day. Ellen said, 'Cold, isn't it?'

He looked around as if he hadn't noticed the ice and the frost and said politely, 'Yes, very.'

She wondered whether he had been waiting for her.

They walked their bicycles side by side down the path. She half-expected him to cycle off as soon as they reached the courtyard – a wave of the hand, a fast pedalling away as Alec Hunter went off to do whatever Alec Hunter did on an evening – but instead he walked on, scarcely attempting to respond to her efforts at small talk.

The cypresses beside the drive walled them off from the hall. Alec said, 'I heard Pharoah invited you to Sunday lunch.'

'Yes.' Now, there was a surprise: of all the things she might have thought – hoped, if she was honest with herself – he might be working himself up to say, that had not been one of them. She said, 'It was very pleasant.'

'Good.'

Weighted silences had never been to her taste, so she plodded on. 'Have you been to his house?'

'Me? No. Not Pharoah's sort.'

A strange remark. Mustn't they all be Pharoah's sort, those he had chosen to work at Gildersleve Hall?

They reached the end of the drive. The lamplight cast black pools of shadow on Alec's face. He said, 'I wanted to say – be careful, Ellen.'

'Careful? Of what?' Tension made her touchy. 'I didn't spill my wine down my front or eat off my knife, if that's what you mean.'

'No, of course not.' His scowl deepened. 'What do you think of Pharoah?'

'He's an extraordinary man. He's achieved so much.'

'You've had predecessors, you know. Some of them weren't quite good enough, and others . . . well, let's just say they didn't fit in.'

'I know I've a lot to prove. I work hard.'

He ran a hand through his hair. He wasn't wearing gloves or a hat: she wondered whether he did it for effect – tough, Scottish, in tune with the elements.

'Pharoah takes a liking to people sometimes,' he said. 'And that's all very nice if it's you he's taken a liking to, and while he's still keen on you, but if you disappoint for some reason, well.'

She felt a wash of disillusionment. *So that's what you think of me, Alec Hunter. You think I'm not good enough at my job.* She said coldly, 'I don't intend to disappoint.'

'Sometimes it can happen, even when you do your best. Pharoah can blow hot and cold. It might be wise to keep a wee bit of distance.'

'I hardly think Marcus Pharoah and I are likely to be close friends.' And what business was it of his anyway? 'We don't inhabit the same world.'

'Pharoah has his pets and it doesn't do to say no to him.'

Now she was angry. 'I've no intention of being anyone's pet.'

A flicker of annoyance crossed his face. 'I'm only trying to help you, Ellen.'

'I don't need anyone's help. I'll manage on my own. I always have.' Her voice was as crisp and cold as the ice that fringed the leaves of the cypresses.

They had reached the gates. She climbed on to her bicycle, bid him a curt goodbye, and cycled away.

* * *

On Sunday afternoon, Ellen went out for a long walk. The branches of the trees stood out dark and jagged against a bleached background as she tramped round the edges of the fields. The water in the gullies and ditches had frozen and was pierced by spikes of cow parsley; when she broke off a frond it gave a brittle snap, powdering the ice with fragments of stem. She thought, how dare he? How dare he tell me how to do my job, or how to behave towards my employer? It was not as if he himself was without fault. Alec Hunter, presumably, must himself be responsible for a great deal of Andrée's ill humour.

An hour of walking and she passed Gildersleve Hall, heading through the copse behind the house. The blinds were down and nothing moved in the garden. The house seemed to have retreated in on itself, as secretive as the very first time she had seen it, cycling from Copfield.

A wooden fingerpost directed her to Peddar's Wood. Circling round bare fields she reached a mass of trees surrounded by a low ridge of earth. A footpath led beneath maples, ashes and hazel. She headed into the woodland, the soles of her boots crunching on frozen leaves. Stacks of cut logs, their bark glistening with frost, lay beside the path, and the ash trees were coppiced into extraordinary shapes, great, bulbous globes that grew close to the soil. From the boles, thick branches reached up to the sky, and from the smaller, pale, hollow trunks, whiskery shoots protruded, as thin as a whip.

In the heartland of the wood, Ellen stood motionless,

her fingers aching with cold. The trees were timeless, dislocating her from the present, and she felt herself surrounded by such silence and stillness that when the crack of a branch told her she was not the only living creature in the wood, she jumped.

Catching sight of a man some distance ahead of her, at a place where the footpaths formed a crossroads, she recognized Dr Redmond. He was loading fallen twigs and branches into a wheelbarrow.

She called out to him and he looked up. She said, as she drew level with him, 'Are you collecting firewood?'

'Kindling.' The front of his duffel coat was sprinkled with leaf mould and flakes of bark. 'I leave the bigger pieces. Insects live in them and fungi grows on the rotten wood.'

'It's a beautiful place.'

'The wood was neglected when I first came here. All the trees needed coppicing. Farmers don't care about woodland any more, it doesn't make them any money. When the trees grow too tall they shut out the sunlight and then there are no spring flowers. I try to cut them back every four or five years. I've kept a record of every species I've found here since I came to live at the cottage. The first spring, there were only a dozen oxlips. Last year, there were so many I was able to do merely an approximate tally.'

Dr Redmond began to wheel the barrow along another footpath, at right angles to the one Ellen had taken from the fields. Walking beside him, she said, 'Your cottage is near here, isn't it?'

'By the farm track.'

'How long have you lived there?'

'Ten years. There was a shortage of lodgings in the war. You wouldn't have had a house like that to yourself back then. The three of us shared it, Kaminski, Pharoah and me.'

They came out of the woodland on to a broad track. The barrow rattled along the solid, rutted ground. A short distance along stood a small, brick-built house. Ellen found it hard to imagine: the three men, young then, and so unalike in character and experience. Pharoah, brilliant and ambitious, Kaminski, exiled and damaged, and Redmond – but it was impossible to picture Dr Redmond as a young man. Had they eaten together after a long day at work? Had they smoked cigarettes and drunk beer and laughed and planned their futures?

They reached the cottage. Opening the front door, Dr Redmond took out a battered coal scuttle and put it on the porch. He began to fill it with kindling.

She said curiously, 'You've known Dr Pharoah for a long time, haven't you, Dr Redmond?'

'Since before the war. After he came back from America, after his wife died. We worked together.'

She was going to make some comment – old friends, the pleasures of scientific collaboration – when his face contorted and he said savagely, 'He's changed. He was a better man, then. Marcus Pharoah is a liar and a plagiarist, but he won't get away with it. The rest of that lot might let him, but I won't!'

Then he rolled the wheelbarrow round the side of the house, leaving Ellen standing by the doorstep.

Wednesday evening: Ellen was sitting in the bar of the University Arms Hotel in Cambridge and Dr Pharoah was giving their order to the waiter. 'A lemonade, please,' Ellen said, and Dr Pharoah said, 'I think you need a gin in that, after that meeting. A gin and lemon, please, waiter, and a Johnnie Walker, water, no ice.' And, turning to her with a smile, 'Rather a marathon. These things sometimes seem to go on for ever. I hope you weren't too bored.'

'Not at all, Dr Pharoah.' Then, 'Sorry. Marcus.'

There had been three of them that afternoon at the meeting at the Cavendish: Ellen, flattered and excited to be asked along, Dr Pharoah and Dr Farmborough. As they had left the laboratory at half past six, Dr Farmborough had peeled off into the night. 'Have to see a man about a dog.'

The other tables in the bar were occupied by men in suits, flicking through newspapers or importantly checking their wristwatches. Ellen thought, I'm in a smart hotel in Cambridge, having a drink with Marcus Pharoah, the director of Gildersleve Hall. Outside, the city glittered like glass, trapped in the frost. A mist blurred the outlines of the buildings, as if they existed underwater.

'I'm afraid such meetings are part and parcel of scientific life,' Dr Pharoah was saying. 'You'll find it a useful asset, the ability to look interested when you've heard the same argument half a dozen times before.' Their drinks arrived and he touched the rim of his glass against hers. 'To your long and successful career, Ellen.'

'Thank you.'

'Tell me about yourself. Have you family?'

'Parents and a younger brother.'

His dark, hooded eyes studied her, serious, interested. Being the object of Marcus Pharoah's undivided attention made you feel significant, in a way you had not felt before. It made you feel worth listening to. But it was also a little unsettling.

'Would you like Rowena to be a scientist, Marcus?'

He smiled. 'I should love her to be one, especially if she managed to do so while being as charming and attractive as you and Mademoiselle Fournier. But she isn't the least bit interested in science, I'm afraid, and at the moment has her mind set on doing something with her art.'

'How marvellous.'

'Yes, I think so. She'll go to college when the time comes – unless, that is, some young man snaps her up before then.'

A woman in a pearl-grey evening coat came into the bar; one of the businessmen rose and kissed her cheek.

Ellen said, 'You have such a beautiful home. And Alison's so lovely and gracious. It must make such a difference, being able to rely on someone else for all the – oh, I don't know . . .'

'The background work? The running of the house, the

entertaining, the bringing up of children? Yes, it does make a difference. Although Alison hasn't been well.'

Alison Pharoah, weeping among her orchids. Oh, she thought. 'I'm sorry. I didn't realize.'

'I haven't told many people. Such things are better kept private. The hall has a reputation for gossip. I'm sure you'll keep it to yourself, Ellen.'

'I won't mention it to anyone.'

'Thank you, I knew you'd understand. Family life . . . You haven't been tempted, then?'

She was confused. 'By what?'

'By marriage.'

'No, not at all.'

He was sitting relaxed in his chair, his amused gaze focused on her. 'I'd hate to think we might lose you to domesticity,' he said.

'There's not much chance of that. Maybe one day, in the future. Most women marry eventually, don't they?'

The corners of his mouth curled. 'You sound as though you have it all worked out.'

She wondered whether he was laughing at her. Whether he thought her temporary, not a stayer. 'Women have to plan better than men because we have children,' she said. 'A man can be a little more free and easy. I can't afford that.'

'I do understand. I lost several years of my career to the war effort.' Without asking her, Pharoah signalled to the waiter for two more drinks. 'What first attracted you to science, Ellen?'

'I wanted to be part of making the future.' Enthused, she sat forward, her elbows on the arms of her chair. 'Such wonderful things are happening, aren't they? Think of the diseases we can cure now, tuberculosis, pneumonia, diphtheria – all those old killers. I want to be a part of everything, not just watching it happen from the sidelines.'

'You're very passionate, Ellen.'

Abruptly, she felt deflated. Men said that sort of thing to women: she had talked too much, had allowed her emotions to show.

Pharoah seemed to sense her discomfiture because he reached out and put a hand on her arm. 'It's all right, Ellen, passion's a quality I admire in a scientist. You could have a very promising future at Gildersleve, you know that, don't you? We're all ambitious, of course, and some will be successful and some won't. I always tell my new recruits that to succeed, you have to get everything right. Being clever isn't enough.'

Was that a warning? His hand still lay lightly on her forearm, the palm strong and square, the fingers long, well-shaped, even sensual. It was a kind, consoling gesture, she told herself, and she had no reason to feel discomforted, nor oddly disorientated, as if the fog in the streets had entered the room and the usual yardstick by which she measured events had slipped away. But voices echoed, blurred by the gin she had drunk too hastily to keep up with him. Alec Hunter's: *Pharoah has his pets.* Dr Redmond's: *Marcus Pharoah is a liar and a plagiarist.*

The waiter arrived with the drinks. Ellen thanked him and Marcus Pharoah's hand fell away. Half a dozen people came into the hotel, the women unknotting silk scarves and laughing, the men talking loudly of cars, sparking up cigarettes.

She broke the silence. 'What attracted you to science, Marcus?'

'Oh, as you say, the desire to be part of progress, to be at the forefront of new ideas.' He laughed. 'When I was young, I ran around like a wind-up toy that's been set off, expounding my latest ideas to all and sundry. Rather like Martin. But then . . .' He broke off, frowning, and his voice dropped. 'I had such ambition then, such vision,' he muttered.

The alteration in Marcus Pharoah was as if someone had drawn a curtain, shutting out the light. You would have thought, if you had glimpsed him sitting alone in a bar: another morose middle-aged man, looking for comfort in the bottom of a glass.

'When we're young, we think that if we do this and that, then we'll feel content.' He picked up his glass, swirled the contents. 'Even a little bit pleased with ourselves. We don't realize that the fear of failure never quite goes away.'

She was astonished. 'But you must feel so proud of what you've achieved at Gildersleve Hall.'

He gave a light laugh. 'Yes, naturally.'

Ellen glanced at her watch. 'I should catch my bus. Thank you for the drinks, Marcus.'

'There's no need to rush off.' He, too, looked at his watch. 'I have to stay on in town for an appointment later this evening. Why don't we go on to dinner somewhere?'

She was drawn by his voice, by its rich, coaxing quality, and by the compelling gaze of his eyes. When he looked at you like that, when he spoke to you like that, you wanted to please him. You'd do anything for him, almost anything.

And yet, in the back of her mind, the crystal of doubt hardened and glittered. 'I can't, I'm afraid,' she said with a smile. 'My landlady cooks supper for seven. I can't just not turn up, it wouldn't be fair.'

'Telephone her, Ellen.'

'She hasn't a phone, I'm afraid.'

'Then I'm sure she'll understand.' She read a challenge in his eyes.

'No, I'm sorry, I really must get back. If I hurry, there's a bus.' She rose, almost knocking over her glass in her hurry, holding out her hand.

Pharoah, too, stood up. 'It's been most interesting.'

Hurrying along St Andrew's Street, Ellen noticed that though the mist lingered, a few flakes of snow had begun to drift through the air. Her breath made vapour clouds as she ran through their conversation in her head. Had it been an act of friendship, that invitation for a drink, or had it been some sort of unofficial checking-up, a gentle hint that if she wanted to remain at Gildersleve Hall then she must improve, raise her game?

Or had it been been something more than that? It seemed

to her that they had moved too easily to the personal, the intimate. *Alison hasn't been well for some time.* There had been the implication, she thought, in Marcus Pharoah's words, that Alison was suffering from an illness of the mind. Why had he told her that? Had he simply needed to confide in someone? Was power and position so isolating that sometimes, worn down with obligations and with the added burden of a sick wife, you found yourself opening your heart to the lowest of the low? She remembered the weight of his hand on hers, the pressure of his fingertips.

Her bus was pulling away from its stop. She ran across the road and climbed on to the platform. The interior smelled of metal and rubber and cigarette smoke. You fool, Ellen, she thought as she found a seat, running away like a prim schoolgirl when you could have been dining with Marcus Pharoah. When you think of all he could offer you.

But that was the thing. What, exactly, had been on offer? Dinner at a restaurant, or something more? Somewhere along the line, the conversation had taken an uncomfortable turn. Was that what Alec had been warning her against, during their conversation the other day? But why should Alec Hunter be concerned that Dr Pharoah was showing an interest in Ellen Kingsley? Was Alec a confidant of Dr Pharoah's? She did not think so. It was Pharoah with whom Alec argued at the seminars, Pharoah's contributions he seemed to take most pleasure in picking apart.

There was so much she did not understand. Undercurrents seethed at Gildersleve Hall, factionalism, old enmities and rivalries, and it occurred to her, as she watched from the window the snowflakes whirling in the yellow light of the street lamps, that she felt more of an outsider now than she had on her very first day at the hall.

By Monday morning, a light dusting of snow had settled on the roof of the hall and the crenellations of the tower. Cycling along the path, Ellen heard the thud, thud, of Gosse's axe, as he chopped up wood.

Her eye was caught by a flash of red in the copse. She saw that Alec Hunter and Andrée Fournier were standing beneath the trees, talking. Andrée was wearing her grey coat and scarlet scarf, and her hands waved gestures as her mouth opened and closed. Ellen wondered whether she was crying. Alec's hand rested on Andrée's sleeve: Ellen felt a little stab to her heart.

Inside the hall, cold air tumbled down the chimneys, lurking like a poltergeist in the corners of the rooms. Toby was off sick; half the staff seemed to have colds or flu. Andrée, red-eyed and white-faced, came into the box room while Ellen was taking off her coat. Her head was splitting, she felt ill, she said. She was going back home to bed.

Ellen spent the morning measuring the intensities of the dots on X-ray diffraction photographs and beginning the complex mathematical calculations that would help Dr Kaminski interpret them. There were frost flowers on the insides of the window and she broke off now and then to rub the circulation back into her fingers. With both Toby and Andrée away, the top floor of the hall was quiet, only the distant percussion of Dr Redmond's sneezes from the tower punctuating the silence.

That afternoon, she heard them arguing again, Dr Pharoah and Dr Redmond, in the tower. The rise and fall of their voices was ominous and angry, like the drumbeat of Roy Gosse's axe. She went outside and stood in the corridor. The door to the tower was ajar; she pushed it open further.

'Why can't you leave me alone?' Dr Redmond's voice.

'Leave you alone?' Dr Pharoah was speaking. 'What, and have you lurking up here, like some goddamned spider, spreading poison? Not any more.'

'I'll make sure everyone knows the truth about you! I'll tell them everything!' Redmond's words had soared in pitch. 'I could destroy you, you know! I've got proof and I'll use it, don't think I won't!'

Ellen slipped back into the lab, silently closing the door behind her. The air seemed to vibrate; when she sat down at the bench, she felt her heart thump hard as she looked down the microscope, and she had to blink to focus her gaze on the geometric shape of the crystal.

More snow fell that night. The following morning, she had to push the bike much of the way to work, pitting her strength against the clogged inches of snow. A stillness had settled over the countryside, nothing moved.

In the laboratory, she found herself listening for sounds from the tower. No sneezes today, no footsteps. After weeks of careful work, her crystals had clumped together in a disordered mass, no use to anyone. She put the lot down the sink and started again. She couldn't concentrate, her mind was all over the place, skittering about, refusing to latch on to any one thing.

At midday, she went into the tower. The door to Dr Redmond's lab was shut. She tapped on it and went inside. The lab was empty, and she thought how strange it was that you could sense, lacking any solid evidence, that a room had been empty all day.

She had intended to work late that evening but she was tired, and by six o'clock the numbers had begun to swim before her eyes. She put on her outdoor things, then went to the shed and put her briefcase and handbag in her bicycle basket. Then, taking only her purse and torch, she set off over the fields.

From Gildersleve Hall, the walk to Peddar's Wood was less than a mile. The cold bit into her fingers and toes and her torchlight split the snow crystals into jewelled colours. Several times she wondered whether to turn back. Dr Redmond had probably stayed at home for the day because he had fallen out with Dr Pharoah. Or his cold had worsened and he had spent the day in bed. He wouldn't welcome her, coming to see him.

Yet the unease that had haunted her all day remained, so she kept on walking. The torch lit her way, revealing the smooth layer of snow that covered the hedgerows and fields. Inside Peddar's Wood, the trees had kept the narrow path free from snow.

She came to the crossroads where she had met Dr Redmond loading his barrow with kindling and struck off down the wider path to the left, towards the single-track road. Reaching it, she saw that light issued from the cottage windows and felt relieved. He was all right, he had taken a day off because he was unwell, that was all, silly of her to worry. She noticed that there were no footprints in the fresh snow on the farm track.

She knocked on the door of the cottage. When there was no answer, she looked through a window. She saw that the room was disordered, books pulled from the shelves and thrown to the floor. She turned the handle on the front door; it was unlocked.

She went inside the house. The door led straight into the living room she had seen through the window. 'Dr Redmond?' she called out.

No answer. Her gaze slid round the room, taking in the two armchairs, their coverings shiny with age, a threadbare sofa and a heavy, old-fashioned table and chairs. There were ashes in the grate and some of the books that had fallen on to the frayed rug had crumpled pages and broken spines. A handful of photographs scattered the floor. She picked one up. It was a snapshot of a hazel tree, pollarded like those in the wood.

A narrow kitchen, furnished with a ceramic sink, calor gas cooker and cupboard, led off from the living room. Here, too, drawers were open and the contents scattered around. A saucepan on the hob contained something brown and unidentifiable, and there was a saucer with scraps of bread and fat on the sill, for feeding birds, presumably. A mug of tea stood on the table, covered with a pale brown scum. When she touched her hand to its side, the scum swayed, heavy, frozen.

As in the lab, the house felt empty. Dr Redmond might have gone away. He might have parents, a brother, a friend to visit. A door led off from the living room, to the stairs presumably, and it occurred to her that she should check the upper storey of the house. He might be ill, his cold might have turned to flu. He might be gasping through lungs like sponges for every fluid-soaked breath, no one to help him, no other house for miles.

She tried the handle of the door. It opened an inch, no further. Something was blocking it, preventing it from opening properly. She tried again, pushing with her shoulder against the door until she was able to reach her fingers into the aperture.

Her fingertips touched cloth. The cloth felt ridged, like corduroy. She thought of the shabby corduroy jacket Dr Redmond wore at the lab every day, and her heart thudded. Like thinking you had reached the bottom of the stairs when there was one more to go, jarring, shocking.

Ellen leaned her whole weight against the door, then wedged her foot into the gap. Shoulder first, she squeezed through the opening and almost fell over Dr Redmond's body.

He was lying at the foot of the stairs. His glasses were a

short distance from his outstretched hand, their lenses fractured into stars. She touched his fingers; they felt ice-cold. She was afraid to shine the torch on his face, but when she did so, she saw that his eyes remained a little open, as if he had wanted to have one last look at the world. And then they had dulled, the light and the life extinguished.

It felt wrong to leave him there alone. The thought clawed at her as she stumbled back along the farm track to the path through the woods, but she had no alternative. There was no telephone in the cottage, and no other houses in the vicinity.

Ellen began to run, looking back over her shoulder once or twice, as if something was chasing her. The branches of the trees struck her face, and when she swung her torch in front of her along the wide path, she saw that the snow was smooth and unblemished by her footprints. She had gone too far, had missed the crossroads in the middle of the wood and had overshot the turn-off. Her breath made fast puffs of vapour in the icy air and her torch shed only a small point of light in the dense darkness.

Think.

She retraced her footsteps until she found the path that would lead her through the trees, in the direction of Gildersleve Hall. As she jogged along it, her thoughts returned to the cheerless cottage, which had been scarcely warmer inside than outside, and which had contained little of any comfort. She thought of Dr Redmond himself and the peculiar manner that had been a part of him. All gone now, all that brilliance and strangeness extinguished.

Now she was out in the open fields. The moon illuminated the roof of Gildersleve Hall and the square summit of its tower. She ran along the edge of the field, the frozen ruts of the ploughed furrows hard against the soles of her feet, tripping and stumbling on the iron-hard mud until she reached the copse, then she swung the torch ahead of her as she threaded through the trees. As she took the gravel path that led to the side door of the hall, the adrenalin that had enabled her to run from the cottage began to fade, leaving her weak with shock and exhaustion.

Inside the building, she heard the steady hum of the hoover. Mary, the cleaner, looked up as she came into the corridor.

'You've cut your face, Miss Kingsley.'

Both Dr Pharoah's office and his secretary's were empty. Ellen sat down at the secretary's desk to use the phone. Her hands were trembling, her fingers nerveless. The operator put her through to the police station in Cambridge. As she was speaking, she looked up and saw Gosse standing in the doorway.

She finished the call and put the phone down. 'There's been an accident,' she said. 'It's Dr Redmond. I'm afraid he's dead. I've just been to his cottage. It looks as if he fell downstairs. I've phoned the police but someone needs to tell Dr Pharoah.'

Gosse pushed past her, snatching the phone receiver

from her. Ellen heard him dial a number as she left the room.

Something occurred to her, and she hurried up the stairs to the top floor of the house, then entered the tower and Dr Redmond's laboratory. There, she took the lab book from the bench, tucked it beneath her coat, and then, closing the doors behind her, left the tower. From below, she heard quick, heavy footsteps – Gosse's, she assumed.

Outside, in the bike shed, she took her briefcase out of her bicycle basket and put Dr Redmond's lab book inside it. Then she went back into the hall to wait for the police.

The call came through to the station shortly after half past seven: a sudden death at a cottage in the grounds of Gildersleve Hall, the science lab to the west of Cambridge. Detective Inspector John Riley took Sergeant Claybrooke with him and arranged for two more officers to meet them at the cottage. Claybrooke drove the Wolseley with conscientious, if slightly irritating slowness, along roads that were glazed with ice. There was little traffic on this cold December night and they were soon out in open country.

As they neared the turn-off that led to the cottage, the second police car rolled up behind them and they rattled down the frozen, rutted farm track in convoy. Riley had Claybrooke park some distance from the cottage and they walked the remainder of the way, torchlights sweeping across the path. Reaching the cottage, he saw footprints in the snow, heading away from the road towards the woods.

The front door was unlocked and Riley led the way inside. The body of Dr Redmond, who looked to be in his mid-forties, lay at the foot of the stairs. There was in all sudden deaths a pathos, a collision of mischance with an exposure of vulnerability, emphasized on this occasion by the cold, disorderly cottage. Riley automatically checked for a pulse but it was obvious to him that the man had been dead for some time.

He said over his shoulder, 'Is Dr Bell on his way?'

'Should be here any minute, sir,' Claybrooke replied.

Riley and Claybrooke remained at the cottage until the doctor arrived. Shortly afterwards they left for Gildersleve Hall. Driving along icy roads ranked by trees, Riley's mind drifted to his wife, Pearl. A week ago, they had moved house to London, after Pearl had tired of Cambridgeshire. Riley was working out his notice before returning in two weeks' time to the Metropolitan Police. How were they managing, Pearl and Annie, in the new house? Did the new home still amuse and enchant, or had disappointment already set in? Though Pearl always longed for change, it invariably disturbed her.

Sergeant Claybrooke swung the car through gates and along a gravel drive, and Riley saw Gildersleve Hall for the first time. As they parked, the front door opened and a short, burly man in a camouflage jacket came down the steps towards them. Riley greeted him and showed his warrant card.

The man in the camouflage jacket said, 'Dr Pharoah isn't here yet.'

Riley nodded. 'No matter. We'll speak to him when he arrives. Who are you?'

'Roy Gosse.' Gosse didn't offer his hand or any explanation of his role at Gildersleve. 'He was at some do,' he said. 'He's on his way.'

'Let me know when he gets here. I'd like to speak to Miss Kingsley now.'

They followed Gosse into the house. A wide, curving staircase led up from a hallway tiled in black and white marble. On the first floor, Gosse flung open a door to a small room, muttered something, then stalked off.

A young woman was sitting at a chair by a desk. She was huddled in her coat, her hands tucked beneath her arms as if she was trying to warm them. She looked up as they came into the room.

Riley estimated her to be in her early twenties. Her dark red hair was caught back with a clip and her eyes were grey. Her face was oval, her mouth full, her skin pale. Even with the long, thin cut across her cheek, which she dabbed at now and then with a folded handkerchief, she was strikingly attractive. Riley noted her apparent composure and the cup of tea in front of her, which she didn't look to have touched.

He said, 'Miss Kingsley?'

She rose, gave a shadow of a smile. 'Yes, I'm Ellen Kingsley.'

'I'm Inspector Riley and this is Sergeant Claybrooke.' They shook hands. 'Do sit down, Miss Kingsley. Would you like me to find someone to see to that cut?'

'No, thank you. It's nothing, just a scratch.'

'This must have been very unpleasant for you so I'll try not to keep you too long. Do you work at Gildersleve Hall?'

'Yes, I'm a research assistant.'

'Dr Redmond worked at the hall as well, didn't he?'

'Yes.' She put a hand towards the cup of tea, seemed to think better of it, and withdrew it. 'He was very senior to me.'

'Was he a friend of yours?'

'Not a friend.' Though Miss Kingsley looked shocked, her voice was firm. 'Dr Redmond didn't really have friends. I should say we were acquaintances.'

'And it was you who found the body?'

'Yes. I went to his cottage after work. I was worried about him.'

'Why was that?'

'He hadn't been into work and I thought he might be ill. He'd had a bad cold, you see. Colds and flu are going round the lab just now.'

'So you decided to go to his cottage. How did you get there?'

'I walked. There's a footpath through the woods.'

'How did you get inside?'

'The front door was unlocked.'

'Do you know if that was usual?'

'I'd only been there once before and it wasn't locked then. The cottage is miles from anywhere, so I don't expect he usually locks . . .'

Her words trailed off. Riley had noticed this many times before, that sense of shock people felt at the realization that they were speaking of someone in the wrong tense.

He prompted, 'So you went indoors.'

'Yes.' She recovered her composure. 'I had a look round and then I thought I'd better check upstairs, in case he was ill in bed. But I couldn't open the door to the stairs. He'd fallen in front of it, you see. When I saw him I knew he was dead.'

From outside, Riley heard the sound of a car engine, followed by a door opening and closing.

Miss Kingsley said, 'I think the cottage had been searched.'

'Searched?' The same thought had occurred to him.

'The place was a mess.' Her grey eyes held his, wide and troubled. 'There were things all over the living room floor. Dr Redmond wouldn't have left it like that.'

Voices from below: Mildmay, damned unfortunate business, this.

Superintendent Mildmay: Pharoah, good to see you. I'm only sorry it should be in such tragic circumstances. Then footsteps on the stairs.

Sergeant Claybrooke opened the door. Superintendent Mildmay – fiftyish, small, pale eyes, pink scalp dusted with thinning sandy hair – was standing on the landing. Beside him was a tall, dark man: Dr Marcus Pharoah, the head of Gildersleve Hall.

Superintendent Mildmay said, 'I'll take over now, thank you, Riley. You can get back to the cottage. Miss Kingsley, nasty shock for you. You may go home now.' The pale eyes drifted back to Riley. 'Inspector, do get a move on. Dr Pharoah hasn't got all day.'

Riley left the room.

Ellen heard the door to Dr Pharoah's office close. Through the adjoining wall, there was the murmur of voices. She looked down at the cup of tea she couldn't face drinking, which reminded her of the frozen mug of tea in Dr Redmond's house. She felt sick and dazed, and when she stood up, her legs shook.

She left the room and went downstairs. A voice said, 'Ellen.' Turning, she saw Alec Hunter.

'Someone told me what's happened,' he said. 'I was working downstairs. Poor Redmond. It's bloody awful. Hard to take in.'

She closed her eyes, shaking her head. She heard him say, 'You poor girl. Here, have some of this. It'll do you good.'

Alec took a flask out of his jacket pocket and handed it to her. Ellen swallowed a couple of mouthfuls of Scotch. It was smooth and fiery and tasted of the sea.

'Thank you,' she murmured.

'Where are you heading?'

'Back to my lodgings.'

'You live in Copfield, don't you? I'll see you home. Let me get my coat. Wait there.'

It was a relief to be told what to do; she sank into a chair and waited for him. A couple of minutes later he returned, buttoning his coat.

He opened the door for her and they went outside to collect her bike. Alec pushed her bicycle along the drive. Her briefcase was in the bicycle basket. She thought of Dr Redmond's lab book inside it.

If she looked behind her, she would see the twin paths of their footprints. She said, 'I think it happened yesterday. I think he must have been lying there all day.'

A quick glance. 'You can't be sure, Ellen. Best not to think about it.'

She shuddered, seeing him in her mind's eye, and put her hands to her face. Alec propped the bicycle against a lamp post and put his arms round her. She thought how shallow of her, how *wrong*, that a part of her was enjoying the warmth of his body, the murmur of his voice.

She stepped back. 'Sorry. Have you any more of that whisky, Alec?'

'Here.' They both drank from the flask. He said, 'Do you want to talk about it?'

'Not really.'

Not yet. There was something she needed to make up her mind about. Because she – and most likely only she – had overheard the quarrel between Dr Redmond and Dr Pharoah. *I could destroy you, you know. I've got proof and I'll use it, don't think that I won't.* And perhaps only hours later, Dr Redmond had died.

They reached the road. She managed to smile, looking at him. 'It must be – what, about twenty-five, twenty-six Fahrenheit? And you're not wearing any gloves.'

'I know. My mother would scold me. I forget them, you see.'

'Perhaps this doesn't seem cold to you.'

'Och, it's balmy. You're right, though, we can have some rough winters where I come from.'

'Where's that?'

'I live on an island called Seil. It's just off the west coast of Scotland, in Argyll, a wee bit south of Oban.'

'A big island or a small island?'

'A small island. And there's another even smaller island off it, called Easdale, where only a few dozen people live now.'

The feeling of being off-balance ebbed a little. She needed this interlude, cocooned in the frozen night, with its mingling of shock and desire and foreboding.

Alec said, 'My island's made of slate. My family used to quarry slate but the quarries are all disused now. In its heyday, slates from the islands were shipped all over the world.'

'How long have you lived there?'

'Och, I've always lived there. The Hunters have always lived there.'

'Martin called you the lord of the manor.'

'You don't want to believe everything Martin says. Our glory days are behind us. My great-great-grandfather built the house back in the middle of the last century. It's a nice old place. My forebears liked to add on another few rooms whenever they felt the need, and when I was a wee boy, I found out that you can get from one end of the building to the other through the attics and eaves. You can imagine that kept me amused for days.'

'Do you have any brothers and sisters?'

'No. My father died when I was thirteen, and afterwards there was only my mother and me. When my mother went out, I'd have the whole house to myself. Sometimes, it felt as if I had the whole island.'

'You must love it there.'

'Yes, I do.'

She thought he sounded sad. Odd, that, when you'd think such belonging would be a source of pride.

They reached the main road. She heard him sigh and say, 'And sometimes I hate it too, just a little. If you belong to a place like I do, you always have to keep going back. And then, how do you make yourself a future?'

She wondered whether the future he planned for himself had once included Andrée Fournier. And whether he had finished with Andrée or she had finished with him. She suspected the former. Perhaps Andrée was still in love with Alec Hunter. Perhaps she had been in love with him all along, and that was why she was so unhappy.

'Dr Redmond loved Peddar's Wood,' she said. 'He felt he belonged there. I wonder what will happen to it now.'

'Pharoah will sell it, I should think.'

She stared at him. His profile was a black silhouette against the dim, torch-lit night. 'The wood belongs to Dr Pharoah?'

'All that land does. It's Gildersleve land. And Pharoah's

short of money. You must have noticed the hall's held together by tin tacks and paste. Pharoah's overspent and even Alison's purse isn't bottomless. Or perhaps she doesn't choose to hand out the cash any more.'

'What do you mean?'

Alec shook his head. 'Nothing. Have you heard Martin's latest theory?'

He deflected the conversation neatly to work as they walked the rest of the way to Copfield. She knew that in walking her home, he was only being kind. Next day he would be distant again; next day she would be annoyed with herself again for hoping for more.

Riley and Superintendent Mildmay returned to Gildersleve Hall the following morning. In the soupy greyness of mid-December, the hall looked less impressive than it had the previous night. Riley noticed the chips in the stone steps that led up to the front door and the peeling paint on the window frames.

They spoke first to Dr Pharoah. Pharoah claimed grief at Redmond's death but Riley sensed beneath it anger and impatience. Then Riley interviewed the other employees of Gildersleve Hall while Mildmay remained with Pharoah.

Later, he tapped on the door of Ellen Kingsley's lab and went inside. Today she looked exhausted, barely holding it together. Riley wondered whether she had slept at all the previous night. She had a redhead's milk-coloured skin, but there were patches beneath her eyes that were bluish and translucent, and the long, thin scratch across her cheek was as clear as a dark pen stroke on paper. Yet none of that altered the strong, unsettling attraction he felt towards her – unsettling because it was unexpected and unwished-for, and because it seemed to shine a glaring light on the threadbare nature of his feelings for Pearl.

There was another young woman in the room with Miss Kingsley – dark-haired, neatly pretty – who gave him a disapproving glare. Riley said, 'I apologize for disturbing you, Miss Fournier, Miss Kingsley. It was you I wanted to talk to, Miss Kingsley. Perhaps we could find somewhere.'

'Yes,' she said, and was out of the lab in two ticks, as if she couldn't wait to be free of the place.

On the landing, he said, 'Would you mind if we went to Dr Redmond's lab?'

'No, if you like.' Understandably, she didn't look keen. 'I'll get my coat, then. It's always freezing in there.'

She put on her coat and they went into the tower. 'I'm sorry about this,' he said to her when they were in the lab. He drew out a stool from beneath the bench. 'Sit down, please. I can see you'd rather not be here. But I find it hard to make sense of this place.'

'What do you mean?'

'How did he find anything?'

'I think he knew exactly where everything was. If you look carefully, you'll see that it isn't untidy, it's just cluttered. I think he was one of those men who collects things.'

'Stamps and tea cards?'

'And books and journals, and it doesn't look as if he ever threw away a piece of scientific equipment.'

'You see, when you said last night that you thought Dr Redmond's cottage had been searched, my superintendent's response was to ask how could you tell, because it was so untidy.'

'It had been searched, I'm sure of it.' She jutted out her chin. 'Dr Redmond hated things to be in a different place from where he'd put them.'

'Who might have searched it?'

'I don't know.'

He knew that she was holding something back. What was it? With long, tapering fingers she swept back a lock of hair that had fallen over her face, and said, 'When I went to the cottage last night, I noticed that there were no footprints in the snow. There was a snowfall on Monday night, so that means whoever searched it must have been and gone before then. Which means, I think, that Dr Redmond must have fallen down the stairs on Monday evening. And that means he'd lain there a whole day before I found him.' She looked upset.

'Because, you're saying, had he been able to, Dr Redmond would have tidied up?'

'Yes.'

'That does rather tie in with what we think about the time of death, I'm afraid.'

'It's funny,' she said, frowning. 'I don't have any convictions about life after death, none at all, so I don't think it can have made any difference to him, but it's still horrible to think of him all that time, lying there on his own.'

Tears glistened in her eyes; he sensed the effort she made to stop them falling. 'It's the last thing we can do for the people we've lost,' he said gently. 'Give them respect, keep a vigil. You were fond of Dr Redmond, weren't you, Miss Kingsley?'

'Yes, I was. He seemed so defenceless and so alone. But I don't know that he felt like that. And I shouldn't think he felt any fondness for me. I'm sure he never thought of me at all.' She stood up. 'If that's everything. I should get back to my work.'

'Yes, that's about it.' Riley watched her face as he said, 'Was it you who put Dr Redmond's lab book back?'

'Lab book?' He saw her go weak with shock and put out a hand to the bench.

'It wasn't there when I looked in here last night. I'm guessing it was either you or Mr Gosse who took it and put it back this morning. Or Alec Hunter, possibly. If it wasn't you, I'll go and talk to Gosse and Hunter about it.'

'It was me.'

'Why did you take it?'

She flopped on to the stool, resting her elbows on the bench, propping her head in her hands. 'I needed to check something.'

'You and your colleagues use these books to write up your work, don't you?'

'Yes, they're where we note down what we do on a day-to-day basis – experimental work, largely.'

'So you were trying to find out something about Dr Redmond's work?'

'In a way.' She paused, then said, 'A fortnight ago, Dr Redmond accused Dr Pharoah of plagiarism.'

'To his face?'

'No, he said it to me. That was why I took the book. I thought there might be something in it that would tell me what he'd meant.'

'And was there?'

'I don't think so. No, I really don't think so. And then . . .'

'Miss Kingsley?'

'They had an argument. Dr Redmond and Dr Pharoah. I overheard them.'

'When was that?'

'Monday afternoon. The day before yesterday.'

'Do you know what they were arguing about?'

'Not much. Some.'

He waited. She seemed to steel herself, as if about to take a big jump. 'Dr Redmond asked Dr Pharoah to leave him alone and Dr Pharoah said he wouldn't. Then Dr Redmond said that he could destroy Dr Pharoah, and that he had proof, and that he'd use it.'

'Those words exactly?'

'Pretty much.'

'What did he mean, proof? Proof of what?'

'I don't know. I've no idea. That was all I heard.' She

frowned. 'Dr Redmond sounded terribly upset. Furious, actually. And he was one of those people who are almost always on the same level.'

Pearl sometimes accused him of being like that. Since Annie's birth, Pearl's level had been all over the place.

A voice – Superintendent Mildmay's – called up the stairs, sharp-pitched and impatient. 'Inspector Riley? Are you up there?'

'He was upset,' said Miss Kingsley, giving him a direct look. 'People say things when they're upset, don't they?'

'They certainly do.' Riley gave her a smile, then went downstairs.

Inspector Riley was tall and broad-shouldered, with light brown hair parted to one side and patrician features: long nose, high forehead, firm jaw. Ellen had noticed the crackle of intelligence in his light hazel eyes when he had asked her about the book.

In telling him about the quarrel, she had made a conscious decision not to be one of Pharoah's men. The thought didn't make her feel proud of herself, or even frightened, just hazy with tiredness. And though she tried to tell herself that everything would be all right, she couldn't quite see how it could be. Inspector Riley would presumably ask Dr Pharoah about Dr Redmond's threat, because really, you could hardly ignore it, Dr Redmond saying he'd destroy Pharoah. And then, perhaps only hours later, dying.

The day seemed unnaturally long, too much waiting for

something to happen. She couldn't concentrate on her work and Andrée was still in a mood, so after a while she went downstairs to Alec Hunter's lab. She just slid in the door and sat on a stool and drank the coffee he made for her. She was glad he didn't talk much and she took a sharp pleasure watching him, the delicacy of his strong hands as they drew up liquid through a pipette, the small frown that settled on his forehead, the speed and clarity with which he worked. The moments passed, marked by the ticking of the clock and by the lightly falling snow outside, intimate, unvoiced.

Thursday morning: Dr Pharoah came to talk to them in the common room at break. The police were satisfied that Dr Redmond's death had been a tragic accident, Dr Pharoah told them. The coroner would make his report shortly and then the body would be released for burial. Dr Pharoah himself was making the arrangements as Dr Redmond had no close family. Unfortunately, Dr Pharoah would be absent in America at the time of the funeral – a long-standing engagement – but Dr Kaminski would represent him. He knew that there would be a strong turnout from Gildersleve Hall and his secretary would arrange the sending of flowers. Dr Redmond had been a brilliant scientist and a stalwart of Gildersleve Hall, part of the laboratory since its earliest days, and he would be greatly missed.

Pharoah left and people shuffled about. Toby and Jan

started up a chess game and Martin put the kettle on. So that's that, Ellen thought. Done and dusted. Someone, no doubt, would notice the striped mug still on the shelf and put it into a collection for a jumble sale. A new recruit would move into the lab in the tower.

Who searched your cottage? she thought. What were you and Pharoah quarrelling about? What proof had you meant to produce? Proof of what?

Martin said, 'Cheer up, Kingsley. Two weeks to go and then back home for jolly Christmas revelries.'

No one else saw anything troubling in Dr Redmond's death. No one else moved around the pieces in their heads, trying to fit them together.

They washed up their cups and left the common room. Martin walked upstairs with her. He'd had this cracker of an idea, he said, about the arrangement of inorganic ions in three dimensions. It had come to him at a party last night – yes, he knew, pretty bad form to go to a party when poor old Redmond was barely cold in his grave – well, not yet his grave, but she knew what he meant – but he'd had to get away from all the gloom, it was giving him the heebie-jeebies.

They went into the lab. Andrée wasn't there. It was a little warmer today; Ellen wiped the condensation from a windowpane and became still, looking down to the bike shed. A flash of red scarf, a dark mop of curls, and Alec's hand on the back of Andrée's neck, bending her head towards him. They kissed, she thought with a flood of pain, as if they were the only people in the world. As if it was the only thing to do in the world.

Ellen had not noticed Martin coming to stand beside her. He whistled. 'Crikey. Well, well, well. I *wondered* whether that was starting up again.' He glanced at her. 'I take it you had no idea?'

'No,' she whispered.

'I saw them together in Cambridge a few days ago. I'd have filled you in but we'd had our little tiff.'

You thought you understood but then you discovered that you were completely wrong. You had hopes, however unfounded or irrational, and then something forced you to put them aside.

After Martin had left the room, Ellen sat down at the bench, opened her lab book and unscrewed her pen. She wrote the date, underlined it, then put down the pen, put her hands over her face, and wept.

On Friday evening, as Riley was about to leave work, Ellen Kingsley phoned him at Cambridge police station.

After saying hello and apologizing for interrupting him, she dived in. 'Dr Pharoah told us that the police think Dr Redmond's death was an accident,' she said. 'Is that what you believe, Inspector Riley?'

Sergeant Claybrooke put a sheaf of papers on his desk. Riley nodded thanks. He said, 'Cause of death was a broken neck, Miss Kingsley. There was a rip in the carpet at the top of the stairs and strands of carpet had stuck to one of

Redmond's shoes, which was damp. So yes, it seems likely that his death was an unfortunate accident. The coroner will make the final verdict, of course.'

'Did anyone try to find out who'd searched the cottage?'

'I interviewed both Dr Pharoah and Roy Gosse. They claimed to know nothing about it.'

'So you're just ignoring it, not bothering.' She sounded furious.

He said, 'Where are you, Miss Kingsley?'

'I'm in a phone box in Copfield.'

Copfield was south-west of Cambridge, on his way home, more or less. Riley slid the papers into his briefcase. 'I was about to set off for London. I could stop in at the Green Man if you like. Would you mind waiting fifteen minutes or so for me?'

'No, of course not.' Some of the anger melted from her voice. 'Thank you.'

As he drove out of Cambridge he wondered what impulse had led him to suggest meeting Ellen Kingsley. It occurred to him that he was putting off going home because he wanted to extend his last few days' respite from the stormy unpredictability of his marriage.

In the private bar of the Green Man an elderly couple were sitting in a corner, the man with a beer, the woman drinking something with a cherry in it. Apart from them, Ellen Kingsley was the only other person in the room. She was wearing a green jersey over a white shirt, and her hair, which she wore tied back at work, tumbled loose to her shoulders.

Catching sight of him, she said, 'Thank you for coming, Inspector. I appreciate it.'

'John,' he said. 'Or Riley, if you prefer.' He gave a wry smile. 'There are always a great many Johns, so I've tended to stick with Riley. May I get you another drink, Miss Kingsley?'

'Ellen,' she said. 'A whisky and ginger, please.' His concern must have showed because she added, rather irritably, 'I'm not getting plastered, if that's what you're thinking. My father taught me how to appreciate a good Scotch. And I seem to feel cold all the time and it warms me up.'

'That's shock,' he told her. 'It can take a few days to set in.'

He bought the drinks. Sitting down opposite her, he said, 'Isn't it most likely that it was Redmond himself who'd searched the cottage? Perhaps you're right, perhaps he had fallen out with Pharoah. And perhaps he thought he had something to use against Pharoah but couldn't find it in all the clutter. Perhaps he was looking for whatever it was, went upstairs, searched the bedroom, tripped on the torn carpet and fell.'

'The photographs,' she said obstinately. 'There were photographs of Peddar's Wood all over on the floor. I don't think Dr Redmond loved many human beings, but he did love that wood. He wouldn't have just chucked the photos on the floor.'

'People don't always act rationally when they're angry. As for the accusation of plagiarism, isn't it possible that Dr Redmond was mistaken, or exaggerating?'

She threaded her hands together, her brow creased. 'I wondered about that. It's not always as easy as outsiders sometimes think, knowing who's responsible for a discovery. It's not always – not even usually – some experiment showing something amazing and someone crying eureka. Most scientific advances are collaborative. Someone finds a piece of the jigsaw and someone else finds another and so on. Most of the time, you're working long hours on your own. Maybe the strain was telling on Dr Redmond.'

While she talked, Riley found himself distracted by the planes and shadows of her face and the way that the firelight cast two flickers of golden light into her grey eyes. He asked, 'Do two scientists ever come up with the same theory at the same time?'

'Yes, even when they're working separately. It can be very competitive, scientific research. But there's a sort of unspoken agreement – a gentlemen's agreement – that if one scientist is working on a particular field of research then the others will leave him to it and concentrate on something else.'

'Is Dr Pharoah a gentleman?'

Sidestepping his question, Ellen said, 'If you'd been working away at something for years, and if you were pipped at the post, you might think you'd been cheated of all the glory. But it wouldn't necessarily be true. But when Dr Redmond used the word "proof", I thought at the time he meant something solid, something written.'

'Why?'

'I don't know. No, I really don't know. I suppose because he was that sort of man. Factual, literal. But maybe I got the wrong end of the stick. Maybe I shouldn't have said anything about the quarrel. Maybe I've been foolish – and disloyal.' She looked utterly miserable.

'You wanted us to find out the truth about what had happened to your friend. There's nothing foolish or disloyal in that. I'm sure Dr Pharoah will have understood that you had no alternative but to tell us what you'd heard.'

Yet he spoke with a confidence he did not feel. He had recognized something slippery in Gildersleve's director. Riley had not taken to Marcus Pharoah. And Superintendent Mildmay's rushed tidying up and skimping of procedure to protect Pharoah's reputation had left a sour taste in his mouth.

'There's something that struck me as curious.' As he glanced through his notebook, Riley heard a roar from the public bar. 'Bryan David Jeffrey Redmond . . . Did brilliantly at school, went to Cambridge when he was only seventeen, was awarded a double first. His father died while he was still at school, his mother passed away at the end of the war. He had no brothers, sisters or cousins and no one I spoke to could tell me of any friends. Yet I found old train tickets in his house. Tickets to London.'

'I saw him once, getting off the train at King's Cross.'

'I checked up at Cambridge station and the clerk and

guard remembered seeing him every month. He went to London regularly as clockwork, going back years. My sergeant found a stack of tickets in the cottage, both over-ground and underground. Odd dates on them.'

She pressed her thumb knuckle against her teeth. 'You have to give your return ticket in at the barrier. Presumably Dr Redmond only kept his when it was busy and the ticket inspector didn't get the chance to look at his ticket. That would explain the odd dates.'

'Why would he keep the tickets?'

'I told you, because he was a hoarder.'

'Do you have any idea what Dr Redmond might have been doing in London?'

'I'm afraid not.'

'Visiting a friend, perhaps. Or a lover.'

'A lover?' She smiled. 'No.'

'Most people have secrets, Miss Kingsley. I do. I expect you do too.'

She flushed, then looked away, and he realized that he had touched a nerve. She wore no ring on her finger, but was she attached to someone, secretly or otherwise? Someone, perhaps, at Gildersleve Hall?

She said, 'All those things you've just told me about Dr Redmond, I hardly knew any of them. I didn't even know he was called Bryan. That's rather sad, isn't it?' She gave a small shake of the head. 'Have you ever felt bored by your own thoughts, Riley?'

'Frequently.'

'Mine aren't getting me anywhere at all. I keep thinking I should have gone to him. On Monday afternoon, after the quarrel, I should have gone to him. He wouldn't have wanted me to, but still.'

'I doubt if it would have made any difference. He doesn't sound the sort of man to whom confidences came easily.' Riley glanced at his watch. 'I should head off, my wife and daughter will be expecting me. May I give you a lift to your lodgings?'

'Are you trying to make sure I don't sit here drinking all evening?' she said with a mocking lift of the eyebrows. But she rose and he helped her on with her coat.

As they left the pub, two men were hauling Roy Gosse out of the public bar. Forcibly ejected into the street, Gosse tumbled into the snow, cursing. Riley took Ellen's elbow to steer her out of the way.

On the short drive to her lodgings on the Cambridge road they spoke little. Outside the bungalow, Riley parked, wrote on a page from his notebook, tore it off and gave it to her. 'This will be my London number,' he said. 'I'll be transferring back to the Met shortly. Do please give me a ring if anything comes up. But for what it's worth, I think Dr Redmond slipped and fell downstairs. And not just because Mildmay and Pharoah prefer it that way.'

Miss Kingsley nodded, and climbed out of the car. Riley waited until she had opened the front door and gone inside the bungalow. Then he put the car into gear and drove away.

* * *

The new house, a pleasant, if shabby, four-bedroomed townhouse, was in Tufnell Park, in north London. When Riley arrived home at half past nine, Pearl was standing at the living-room window, smoking.

She said, 'Where *were* you?' and he felt his heart sink.

'Working.' He took off his coat and scarf. 'And the traffic was bad coming into London. Is Annie asleep?'

'She was tired, out like a light by seven.'

Pearl was wearing her old Chinese dressing gown, shiny red with embroidered dragons, over a pair of slacks and a purple jersey. She was tall and thin and had long black hair, a white skin and pale green eyes.

She flicked ash on to a saucer. 'I thought you'd be back ages ago.'

'The hours are going to be longer than usual until I'm back at Scotland Yard. I thought I explained that.'

A mistake, that last phrase. Her beautiful face contorted and she said, 'You could have been anywhere. You could have been with anyone.'

'But I wasn't.' The fact that he was, strictly speaking, lying, made him add quickly, 'Look, I'm here now. How was your day?'

'Awful. I don't know where anything is and the hall light's not working, and I can't get the fire to light and I'm freezing.' Pearl's long, thin fingers were working at the folds of her kimono. 'It's all right for you, you can just go off, but I'm stuck here all day. And there's a funny noise in the airing cupboard.'

'There's probably air in the pipes.'

'What if it's mice? I hate mice! Christ, John!'

He put his arms round her and held her until she stopped trembling. 'I'll have a look in the airing cupboard,' he said, as he stroked her spine. 'Have you eaten anything?'

'Toast with Annie.'

'I'll make us something. OK?'

'OK.' She took a gasping breath and got herself under control. Then she nodded. 'Sorry, John.'

He lit the fire then went to the kitchen, where he scratched together a tea from the meagre supplies in the larder. Cardboard boxes of saucepans and utensils were scattered around the room, and, as Pearl had said, nothing was in the right place. While a tin of soup was warming he went upstairs to check on their daughter.

Annie was four years old. She had wavy brown hair and green eyes like Pearl's. She was fast asleep in bed, her limbs flung out in a starfish shape. Riley tucked her in, kissed her and went back downstairs.

They ate in the living room, in front of the fire. Then Pearl made herself a hot-water bottle and went up to bed. Riley found a torch and had a good look in the airing cupboard, then stuck his head round the bedroom door to reassure her that there was no sign of mice.

'I suppose you think I'm imagining it,' she said and turned away from him, pulling the eiderdown over her head.

As he went downstairs he felt a sense of relief settle over

him. This was an emotion that he was familiar with, and which came upon him as soon as Pearl had gone to bed or had left the house, bringing an end to accusations and tears on her part, and to his own tiptoeing around her moods. But tonight his relief was fleeting. He felt short-changed, aware of a mixture of resentment and despair.

He had met Pearl at a north London bus stop in the spring of 1944. Their attraction had been instant and flammable, their affair all-consuming and passionate, enacted against a dreary, dangerous wartime background. By the time he had flown to Normandy three weeks later with the D-Day landing force, he and Pearl had become engaged. During the Allied armies' slow progress north through France in the summer and autumn of 1944, and then across a snow-swept Belgium and Germany into spring, he had treasured her letters and his memory of her.

At last, after almost six years of war, peace had come. After a stint in the military police in Berlin, Riley had been discharged at the end of 1946. He had returned to London, where Pearl had been waiting for him, and where their wedding was to take place a week after his homecoming. It had taken him only a day to discover that during their two and a half year parting, something had changed. She had been the same, but he had altered. He had found her wild happiness, which had formerly entranced him, disturbing, and her sudden swings from elation to dejection, which had once seemed characterful and exciting, had jarred.

Yet there had never been a moment during which he

considered voicing his reservations, or altering the future that lay before him. He had made his promises and must keep them. He had grown too used to solitariness, he told himself, and to army life. Love would return.

But it had not. The day-to-day realities of marriage, set against a cheerless post-war London, had ground down any fond, lingering memories of their three-week love affair. The succession of rented flats they had lived in before they were able to buy a house, the shortages and rationing and the appalling weather of the winter of 1947–48 would have tested the most close-knit couple. And they were not close-knit; he could neither soothe her anxieties nor satisfy her longings, and she in turn quickly found his long hours at work trying, his steadiness irksome.

A year after they had married Pearl had fallen pregnant with Annie. She had been well enough throughout the pregnancy, but soon after the birth had fallen into a deep depression. A doctor had prescribed pills and somehow they had managed. Pearl's mother, Vera, had helped with Annie, who, thankfully, had been an easy baby, easy to care for and so easy to love. Pearl's recovery had been slow and stuttering, a few steps forward followed by a backward slide into silence and sadness. There had been the added burden of trying to hide her illness from other people. Riley knew the sorts of words his colleagues used. *Nuts. Batty. A screw loose.*

It had been Pearl who had seized on the idea of the move to the countryside, partly for the fields and fresh air

– so good for Annie – and partly to make a new start. Fields and fresh air were only pleasurable in the summer, however, and she had quickly found the winters long and cold and lacking in diversion. Less than two years later, she had clamoured with equal fervour to return to London. Though Riley welcomed the move and his return to the Metropolitan Police, his thoughts drifted back to the frosty, pared-down landscape of Cambridgeshire.

And then to Ellen Kingsley. He considered her rational demeanour, her intelligence and composure, her humour. He remembered her calm grey eyes and the fall of her dark red hair. Admit it, Riley, you wanted to meet Ellen in the pub in Copfield because you wanted to see her one last time.

He had known he should not, and that afterwards he would regret it. He regretted it because half an hour in her company had shown him what might have been. Now, unpacking boxes in the kitchen, he paused for a moment, remembering the short drive from the pub to her lodgings, remembering the silence of the snowy landscape and the deep, bittersweet pleasure he had felt in being close to her.

They buried Dr Redmond in the churchyard in Copfield on a chill, windless day, and afterwards drank to his memory in the Green Man. The snow thawed, leaving puddles beside the bare hedgerows. At Gildersleve, the secretaries decorated the tree in the hall and put up paper chains. A grey, wet Christmas heaved itself closer.

Ellen went with Toby and Martin to a review in

Cambridge. Toby's girlfriend, Lise, whom he had met through his cycling club, joined them. Joe visited and they caught a train to the coast and walked along the shingle beach at Dunwich.

Dr Pharoah was still away in Boston. Ellen's relationship with Andrée was as it had always been, civil and distant, and Ellen avoided Alec Hunter. Perhaps the affair had started up again weeks ago. Perhaps Alec and Andrée had been lovers all the time that she, Ellen, had been foolish enough to begin to think that he liked her.

As for Bryan Redmond, it seemed to her that Inspector Riley's interpretation of events had probably been right. Pharoah's career had overtaken Dr Redmond's during the war. You could see how it might have happened: Pharoah the talker and the charmer, Dr Redmond hardly able to look you in the eye. Someone had to make their way through the committees and grant boards, someone had to say the right things to the right people, and that person would never have been Dr Redmond. Perhaps it wasn't what you had seen yourself doing, the bureaucracy and the toadying, but if you had a dream like Marcus Pharoah's, the price was worth paying.

It was possible Dr Redmond had never accepted the acceleration of Pharoah's career. Perhaps it had rankled, fuelling resentment that had built up over the years. Wanting to humble Pharoah, he had gone back to the cottage to try to find something, anything, that would hurt him, and in doing so had slipped and fallen to his death. And she, too, had stumbled, clumsy and cack-handed, blundering over desires and secrets she had not fully understood, blurting out misconceived notions when she would have done better to keep quiet.

She felt as if she moved precariously, stepping around other people's jealousies and broken dreams. She longed for Christmas, longed to go home. And then, in the New Year, she could return to Gildersleve Hall and begin again.

The evening before she was due to leave Gildersleve, Ellen packed her case for home. A layer of shoes, books and Christmas presents at the bottom of her case, then skirts, cardigans and blouses folded over them, underwear and stockings tucked round the sides. She was to take the train to London after work the next day; her father would meet her at King's Cross. A table was booked in a restaurant where Joe would join them, and they would spend the night in a hotel before taking the train to Wiltshire the following morning.

There was an end-of-term atmosphere at the hall the next day, people giving out Christmas cards, tidying up, writing up notes, or rushing from one floor to another, trying to find belongings that had been lent or lost. Dr Pharoah must have returned to England because his Jaguar was parked in the courtyard. Ellen heard his voice now and then, rich and mellifluous, from a lower floor.

At mid-afternoon, she went to the common room. Toby and Jan Kaminski were playing chess; one of the researchers from the 'beta' group was looking over Toby's shoulder, sucking his teeth in a disapproving manner whenever a move was made.

Dr Padfield was making punch in a chemical flask over a camping stove. Martin said, 'God, the stink, Padders, what the hell have you put in there?'

'Brandy and cloves. And my secret ingredient.'

'Snake venom . . .'

'Castor oil.'

'Who's coming to the pub later?'

'Some of us have families to go home to, Finch.'

The door opened and Dr Pharoah came in.

'Punch, Pharoah?' said Padfield.

'Thank you, Paddy, but no.'

'How was America?'

'An excellent trip. Some fascinating stuff. Let's have a drink one evening, Bill, and I'll fill you in. Jan, do you have those notes I asked you for?'

Jan Kaminski stood up. 'They're in my office.'

'Thank you. I have the Medical Research Council breathing down my neck.' Pharoah went to the door. 'Enjoy your holiday, gentlemen, and I look forward to seeing everyone in the New Year.' Then he turned to Ellen. 'When you have finished your tea, Miss Kingsley, please come to my office.'

Pharoah left the room. It was all just the same, the cloves-and-oranges smell of the punch, the click of cup and saucer, and the 'beta' group scientist sliding into Jan Kaminski's seat as Toby moved a piece on the chessboard.

But inside Ellen, something had solidified, leaden and knotted, and it was all she could do to swallow another mouthful of tea and take her cup and saucer to the sink.

In the cloakroom, she pulled a comb through her hair and checked her face in the mirror. Then she knocked on the door of Dr Pharoah's office.

And then he was calling her to come in and beckoning her to sit down, and he was telling her that things had not worked out as he would have hoped, that he was sorry, and he was sure she would find some other niche more suited to her abilities, but he must regretfully inform her that he did not wish her to return to Gildersleve Hall after Christmas. And all the while he looked at her with executioner's eyes, dark and ruthless, as he let the axe fall.

Ellen rested her forehead against the windowpane in the lab. Rain battered against the glass and she closed her eyes. 'You're leaving?' said Andrée.

'Yes.'

'When?'

'Now, I think.' She moved from the window and swept things from her desk into her briefcase: notebooks, a slide rule, sandwich tin.

'Oh, Ellen.'

So this was it, this was the beginning. Pity and shock and disapproval and maybe a little gloating: she would have to endure them all.

She went to the box room and put on her coat. Andrée

had followed her out of the lab. She said, 'How could he?' and, 'This is so *wrong*,' and then suddenly, unexpectedly, crushing Ellen's hand in hers, hugged her. 'Perhaps you've had a lucky escape.'

People were leaving the hall, calling out farewells. Ellen's legs felt unsteady as she went downstairs, and she kept a hand on the banister for support. Just then she could quite see how, giddy with shock, you might lose your balance and fall. Another flight of stairs, then she crossed the hall. Outside, rain fell from a dense grey sky.

Ahead of her on the path, Alec Hunter was going to the bike shed; she stood back in the lee of the outhouse, out of sight in the dim tunnel of honeysuckle tendrils and old man's beard, waiting till he had gone. She heard the percussive beat of Gosse chopping up wood and the bark of the dog as it ran round the kitchen garden. She watched Alec cross the path in front of her; she thought he might hear the beating of her heart, but he did not, and she clenched her fists, pressing her knuckles against her teeth. What would she tell her family? What would she say to her father? How would she endure the dust and ashes of the meal that night, which was meant to be a celebration?

Her sense of shame and of failure was so intense at that moment that it was hard to carry on. Her briefcase slid out of her hand and she leaned against the wall of the building for support. But the cool air revived her and drops of water fell on her face, and after a while she picked up her case and stumbled on.

Part Two

London

1954–1956

Chapter Three

Because she was a lot messier than Sebastian, India had the bedroom. Sebastian slept on the sitting-room sofa, folding and tidying away his bedding each morning. His clothes, a rather sparse collection, one of everything for best and one of everything for gardening, hung in the wardrobe, looking faded and uncertain next to India's frocks, which seemed to have a life of their own, slipping off hangers and edging out of the door, preventing it from shutting, as if they disliked being enclosed in the darkness.

The flat had belonged to Aunt Rachel, who had rescued them. This was how India always thought of it, rescued, with no inverted commas. When they had first come to the flat, Aunt Rachel had given India and Sebastian the bedroom and she herself had slept on the sofa. India had slept in Aunt Rachel's bed and Sebastian had had a camp bed, though he had often crawled in with India during the night. As they had grown older, Aunt Rachel had bought a folding screen from an antique shop and had put it up between India's and Sebastian's beds, to give them some privacy, she said. The screen was made out of something called découpage and was covered with pictures that looked as if they had been cut out from magazines, ladies in bonnets or holding parasols, and big-eyed, pink-cheeked children.

India tried on all her evening frocks and eventually settled for a white satin one she had found at Berwick Street Market. She dressed it up with a spray of cobalt-blue flowers, made of paper stiffened with wax, pinned to the neckline. Always accessorize, her mother used to say, peering short-sightedly into a mirror as she threaded earrings into her lobes. A dozen dresses lay on the bed; others had fallen to the floor, so that the room was filled with glorious splashes of powder blue and coral and buttercup yellow. The colours reminded India of the art supply shop in Piccadilly where she worked. Of all the jobs she had ever had, it was by far her most favourite. She liked the smell of the shop, a mixture of wax and linseed oil and paper. Pastels and watercolours nestled inside boxes beneath fragile tissue paper coverings, graded in rainbow colours from white to black. The names printed on the paper wrappings were as beautiful as the blocks of paint themselves: vermilion, cerise, ultramarine and turquoise.

The shop also stocked papers for bookbinding, swirled with amber and maroon and peacock blue like the frozen ripples of a river. Customers came into the shop and bought a sheet of marbled paper or a five-pint can of turpentine and a fine sable brush. India had met her boyfriend, Garrett, at the shop. Garrett wasn't an artist; he had been looking for cartridge paper to make posters to advertise a jazz band. He represented the jazz band, which sounded rather glamorous, though in time India had discovered that what Garrett actually did was to tramp around pubs and clubs, trying to persuade their owners to let the band play there.

Garrett Parker was twenty-three, a year older than India. He came from a small town in Leicestershire ('the sticks'). He was of medium height, muscular, black-haired, dark-eyed and olive-skinned, and he had a charming, mischievous grin. People sometimes thought he was Italian. India knew that Garrett, who had an eye for nice things, liked the contrast they made, she as fair as a wheatfield, he dark and foreign-looking. She didn't mind it herself, thought they looked pretty good together. That morning, in bed, she had tried to lie still so as not to wake Garrett, who had been sleeping beside her, but after a couple of minutes she had become bored and had wriggled round and kissed him. His eyelids had fluttered and his lashes had brushed against hers, like moths colliding near a candle flame. Then their bodies had locked together, finding familiar and favourite places before either of them said a word.

Garrett had a lot of different jobs. As well as the jazz band, he looked after half a dozen flats for a friend of his, repairing them and collecting the rent. He also bought and sold antiques. Aunt Rachel, who had known about antiques, would have called them junk, but Garrett loved his chipped creamware and amateurish oil paintings. ('Lovely piece. I'll hang on to it till it appreciates.' Garrett's flat was full of things waiting to appreciate.) Now and then, Garrett delivered cars to garages or private homes in far-flung parts of the country. A couple of times India had gone with him, once to a huge mansion in Chester, and another time to a garage in Southampton. On the Southampton trip, she had wondered, as they drove through Hampshire, whether they might come across the house in the woods. She had thought of mentioning it to Garrett, but hadn't, partly because she couldn't remember where exactly it had been, and partly because she found it hard to believe that it still existed – or whether, indeed, it had existed at all. In her memory, it was like a dream. Or a nightmare.

India sat down at the dressing table. Her hair, which was up in rollers, was thick and slightly curly, platinum blond. People thought she bleached it but she didn't, just rinsed it in lemon juice so that it kept its straw-stubble whiteness. Looking into the mirror, she pursed her lips and narrowed her blue eyes into a sultry expression. Her own image looked back at her, dreamy, beckoning. People – men – told her she was beautiful, but she couldn't always see it. Sometimes she looked in the mirror and thought, yes, you'll do, but at other times her face seemed to her as bland and featureless as a suet pudding, an empty space dotted with holes for eyes, mouth, nostrils.

India blobbed foundation on to a sponge and rubbed it into her skin. Then powder, forcing the puff into the crevices of her compact to get out the last crumbly bits and working it into the contours of cheek and chin and finishing off with quick little dabs. Leaning closer to the mirror (she had inherited her mother's short-sightedness) she drew a thin black line along each lid, flicking it up at the corners. Then she spat in her mascara, scrubbed it with the tiny brush and blackened her lashes. Eyebrow pencil, a dark red lipstick, and then she took the rollers out of her hair, scowling as they caught and pulled. She put the discarded rollers on to the dressing table, where they jostled, pink bristly plastic, with the bottles of make-up and perfume and the bracelets and tissues. She ran a comb through her hair: the curl had gone and it lay on her shoulders, as smooth and pale as the white satin dress.

She lit a cigarette and went to the window. The bedroom looked out to the back of the house, over the garden. Rachel's flat – she still thought of it as Rachel's flat, though Rachel herself had died six years ago – was in a street off Tottenham Court Road. One of the houses opposite had been struck by a bomb in the war and India remembered coming home in the school holidays and seeing the gap and the rubble and the dust. A garage had been built in the gap, though an area of wasteland still existed to one side of it. India watched as a big silver car glided into the forecourt of the garage. A boy came out of the kiosk and put petrol in the tank and wiped a cloth over the car's windscreen. A bus stopped at the near side of the road and half a dozen passengers, the women loaded with shopping bags and the men carrying a newspaper or a briefcase, climbed out. The queue of people moved up as those at the front squeezed on to the bus.

Each of the gardens visible from the window of the flat had its own character. There was the messy one, with a rusty pram and dun-coloured armchairs with holes in the seats, and the tidy one, mostly lawn, daffodils in the borders. In India's favourite garden a wisteria covered the back wall; in a month or so its flowers would hang like lilac grapes. The garden of India's and Sebastian's house was owned by the couple in the ground floor flat. They had two children, whose toys — a tricycle, a ball and dolls — were scattered over the grass. The line was full of washing, and India watched, unfocused, as the stockings, bras, vests, pants and girdles flicked in the breeze.

She turned away and scrabbled in the mess at the bottom of the wardrobe until she found a pale blue chiffon scarf, which she tied over her hair. Then she collected her coat and handbag and went outside.

Eight hours later, the white satin dress was on the floor of Garrett's room. India herself was lying on Garrett's fold-down bed. You either lay on the flat piece that formed the seat when the bed was a sofa, and whose springs stabbed you in the back, or you slid one way or the other on the rounded upper section. India had chosen the springs. She was naked and cold – Garrett's room ('my flat') was always cold – but she liked the way the lamplight made her look like a marble statue.

Garrett's flat was long and thin, part of a single large room that had been cut in half with a plywood partition. Each room could hear most of what went on in the other, so India and Garrett only went to bed when Ronnie was out. This was at India's insistence; Garrett, who was a show-off, couldn't have cared less what Ronnie heard. Apart from the fold-down bed there was a table and two chairs, a gas ring, a shelf with packets of coffee and food, a record player, radio and a wooden clothes horse, on which Garrett kept his shirts and trousers. His leather jacket hung on a peg on the door.

Garrett was walking around, no clothes on, making coffee. Garrett was even vainer than India was. He did indeed have a very nice body; when she had first seen him in the shop, she had fallen in love with the set of his shoulders and the swell of his forearm, flecked with black hairs.

Spooning instant into a cup, he said, 'Taking a car to Plymouth on Sunday. Do you want to come?'

'I can't.'

'Go on, Indy, it's be fun. We could go to the beach.'

'It's Sebastian's birthday. He's eighteen on Sunday.' India rolled on to her side. 'I need to buy him a present.'

'I found a lovely little painting the other day.' Garrett

picked up a small framed picture that was propped against the wall and showed it to her. 'It'd clean up nicely.'

India doubted it. It was hard to tell what the painting represented, the oils were so dark: the inside of a cave, perhaps, or the bottom of the sea. 'I don't think Sebastian's very keen on art,' she said tactfully. 'I thought I might buy him some books.'

'Good idea.'

'But I'm awfully short of cash.'

Garrett put the coffee on the table and sat down beside her on the edge of the bed. She rolled on to her back again and he ran his hand, warm from holding the mug, over her belly. 'Me, too, I'm afraid, darlin'. Oliver's promised me a cut of the takings tonight, but I expect it'll be weeks till I see any of it.'

She sighed. 'I wish I was rich.'

'I'm going to be rich one day, Indy. One day soon.'

'Maybe I'll marry a millionaire,' she said, teasing him.

'Bernie's going to be at the club tomorrow night. It's his birthday. Are you coming?'

'I don't like Bernie.'

'Bernie's a jerk, but the club's good fun and he'll be buying the drinks.' The pad of Garrett's thumb scooped out the curve of her waist. 'You've got goose pimples.'

'So have you.'

'Better warm us up, then.'

She gave a little yawn and arched her body, stretching her arms over her head. 'I suppose so.'

'You *suppose* so?' He sat up, made a sound that might have been outrage and might have been lust, then scooped her up in his arms, dumped her on his knee, and began to kiss her.

In a bookshop the next day, India chose for Sebastian a Hornblower and a John Creasey and tucked them under her raincoat. Then she thought that Sebastian might find the John Creasey too gruesome, so she put it back and went instead to browse the gardening section. Apart from the owner, who was sitting at the till, there were only two other people in the bookshop, a young woman and an old man. The young woman was on the opposite side of the shop, her back to India, and the old man had come in to escape the rain and wasn't even pretending to read.

India found a nice book about roses. The shopkeeper had dropped her glasses on the floor and was scrabbling under the table to retrieve them, so India slipped the book beneath her raincoat and went outside.

It was still raining. She heard the shop door open behind her, and her stomach squeezed. She didn't want to have to run for it, she was wearing high heels and she hated to be shouted at. In the seconds before she noticed that it wasn't the owner who had come out of the shop but the young woman, stories ran through her head: a sick grandmother who adored gardening, or amnesia, perhaps.

The young woman was wearing a fawn mackintosh and she had red hair, and she was looking at India in a determined – and reproving – way.

India peered at her. Then she said, 'Ellen. Oh, Ellen, it is you, isn't it?'

'Good Lord,' said the red-haired woman, staring at her. 'India Mayhew.'

'How wonderful to see you again.' India felt a bubble of happiness rise up inside her.

'And you,' said Ellen, which delighted India, though she sensed politeness.

There was a certain look in Ellen's eyes, which India remembered, so she said quickly, 'You won't tell, will you? They're not for me, they're for Sebastian.'

Ellen frowned. 'But India, you can't just *take* things.'

This made India think of school. But India, you can't just do whatever you want. When all she had suggested was nipping off the school premises or faking a headache to get out of games.

She said, 'It's Sebastian's birthday and I haven't enough money.'

'Then I'll lend you the money and you can pay me back.'

India chewed her lip. She felt cornered. 'I can't go back in,' she muttered.

'Just say you forgot to pay.'

'That woman looks such a dragon. She'll be cross with me.'

'Here, give me the books.' Ellen's expression was one that India was familiar with, a mixture of exasperation and resignation.

Ellen took the books and went inside. When she came out of the shop a few minutes later, they were in a brown paper bag, which she handed to India.

'And you mustn't do it again,' she said.

'I won't, I promise. Never, ever. You must come to tea. I live just round the corner.'

'There's no need.'

'It's the least I can do,' said India, becoming her most gracious. Her mother had used to say, good manners don't cost anything, which was perfectly true, and something India had always remembered and tried to emulate. 'You must come, Ellen,' she said. 'Then you can meet Sebastian.' She beamed at Ellen. 'It's so lovely to see you. I always knew we'd meet again. I had a *feeling*.'

India Mayhew lived a short walk from the bookshop. Her flat was on the second floor of a terraced house. The sitting room was small and pleasant and looked out over the back garden. It was immaculate, the cushions plumped up, a small pile of books and magazines neatly arranged. The ornaments on the mantelpiece – a Dresden shepherdess, Clarice Cliff jug and Venetian glass paperweight – were lined up equidistantly from each other.

'Sebastian,' called India.

A boy of eighteen or so came out of another room.

India said, 'Ellen, this is my brother Sebastian. Seb, this is Ellen Kingsley. She's an old friend of mine.'

Well, thought Ellen, I wouldn't have put it quite like that. But she said, 'Hello, Sebastian. I'm very pleased to meet you.'

Sebastian Mayhew was slight, not particularly tall, and his curling hair was a darker blond than India's. His eyes were blue, like his sister's, his features regular and classical, and his smile was incomparably sweet. He was the sort of boy, Ellen thought, to whom you would always give a second and third glance, because he was strikingly beautiful. India was beautiful too, and had the same sweet smile, but she had not that aura of goodness about her.

'Ellen was at Hayfields with me,' said India.

'P-pleased to meet you, Ellen,' said Sebastian. 'S-schools are frightful places, aren't they?'

'Your school wasn't frightful.' India explained to Ellen, 'They didn't have to do any maths or anything horrible at Sebastian's school, just woodwork and gardening.'

'Woodwork and gardening are very useful,' said Ellen.

'I think so,' said Sebastian. 'Would you like a scone? I've just made some.'

They ate scones and drank tea at the kitchen table. India talked constantly, about her job in a shop, her friends and a film she had seen. Ellen remembered that India had never been one for silences. Sebastian was quiet; Ellen wondered whether he couldn't get a word in or whether his slight stutter put him off talking. Though now she came to think of it, India, too, had had an occasional stutter at school, which had tended to come on in moments of stress, when she was at a loss or being told off.

India said, 'What about you, Ellen? Where do you live?'

'In a house in Islington. I share with my brother, Joe, and some of his friends. Joe's an engineering student. I work in a hospital in St Pancras Way, so it's not too far from work.'

'So both of us share flats with our brothers!' exclaimed India delightedly, as if this was something extraordinary. 'I'd love to meet your brother. And Sebastian would too.'

'Well,' said Sebastian. He had eaten a scone, very tidily. Ducking his head, he said, 'I should go and see Florence. I haven't been round for a week and she was worried about Arthur. Goodbye, Ellen, it's been super meeting you.'

'Sebastian gardens for lots of old ladies,' explained India to Ellen, after the door had closed behind her brother. 'They all feed him pieces of cake. If I ate as much cake as Sebastian does I'd be very fat, but he walks everywhere because he doesn't like the Tube, and then there's all the gardening, so he's always as thin as a rake. Me and my boyfriend are going out for a drink. Would you like to come with us?'

Startled by the abrupt change of subject, Ellen said, 'I don't think so, thank you. I shouldn't think your boyfriend would want me hanging around.'

'Oh, Garrett would adore meeting you, I know he would. You could have supper here and I could lend you a lovely dress and then we could all go out together.'

Ellen was remembering how India sucked you into her life. You didn't mean to succumb, but somehow it happened. 'I'm afraid I've something on,' she said. 'Another time, perhaps.' She glanced at her watch. 'I'd better go.'

'Must you?'

'Things to do . . . It's been lovely to see you again, India.'

India presented her with a piece of paper and a pencil. 'You must write down your address so I can pay you back for the books.' Ellen was aware of tides turning, storms brewing.

She took a bus back to Islington, sitting on the top deck with the smokers. The seats were crowded, but a woman with two small boys hauled them both on to her lap so that Ellen could sit down. The boys were each given a Spangle, which they unwrapped with careful concentration.

The bus shuddered away from the stop, passing a magnolia in flower, blooms the size of soup plates, seen from the top deck as a circle of pink and white splashes, and a man hunched and black with the sack of coal he was carrying on his back. Hazily green lime trees, about to come into leaf, cast shadows over a queue of people outside a cinema, plaiting the length of the street. Ellen thought of the tidy flat, that beautiful boy, and India Mayhew. India was two years younger than she was and had started at Hayfields halfway through the fourth year, when Ellen had been in the Sixth. She had been transparently defenceless, incautious and rash, one of those girls who stood out, who didn't know how to hammer herself into an acceptable form. She was always in trouble for one thing or another – lost gym shoes, talking in class. You'd see her talking to some sarcastic type, someone who liked making other girls' lives a misery, and she'd just offer herself up, fail to see it coming.

Ellen would hear them along a corridor, the usual suspects. What are you doing here, Africa, this wing's for seniors. Lost again? Shall I draw you a map? Your shoelaces are undone, America, and you haven't tied your tie properly. Blubbing again? Why don't you run home to Mummy? Oops, sorry, you haven't a mummy, have you?

Ellen sent them packing. After that, India had latched on to her. She hadn't meant to get caught up with India Mayhew, but sometimes you didn't choose someone, they chose you. And there had been nothing objectionable about India's behaviour, which had been, towards Ellen, impeccable. She was just there, trailing after her, sewn to her footsteps like a shadow, odd-looking back then, features too strong for her half-formed face, her uniform overlarge for her slender frame, enthusiastic when she should have been nonchalant, talking when she should have shut up. She had had a reputation for making up stories, embroidering the truth. Hayfields had been the sort of school where liars were ostracized, but Ellen could no more have slapped India down or told her to push off than she could have drowned an unwanted kitten.

And besides, behind the awkwardness and neediness there had been something in India that attracted. The world she alluded to – a brother, an aunt, a London life of fogs and concerts and coffee bars, had a certain rakish charm. And nothing was too much trouble for India. Ellen had never been sure whether you would call it loyalty or obstinacy. She wore you down: you let her post your letters or fetch your indoor shoes, even though you found it embarrassing.

India was fifteen when they first met, a difficult age to change school. I was expelled, India said, and Ellen, sensing confessions brimming, confidences approaching, hushed her. Some things were better not shared. Ungenerous of her, she now saw. She had been protecting herself, rejecting intimacy, when she might have helped India defuse a sense of failure and shame. Though Ellen had never been sure whether India was capable of feeling shame.

Shame wasn't something Ellen herself had had to tussle with, until the past sixteen months. She was used to acceptance, expected a certain amount of success. At first the shock of her dismissal from Gildersleve Hall had been mixed with disbelief and bewilderment. And humiliation, served up over and over again and with special panache whenever she happened to come across a former colleague or academic acquaintance. You're at Gildersleve Hall, aren't you? Then rebuttal, and explanations – there wasn't a painless way of telling people what had happened, for her or for them. She had become used to watching the expressions flicker through their eyes: surprise, then laboured tactfulness, pity or perhaps a touch of *Schadenfreude*. She found herself avoiding them, those work friends, those academic friends. Those Gildersleve friends, in particular. Once, catching sight of Martin Finch through the crowds at King's Cross station, she had hurried away down the platform, checking over her shoulder to make sure he hadn't seen her.

It had taken her six months to find another job. Staying with her parents in Wiltshire, the weather had never seemed more leadenly grey. She had read all the books she had always meant to read: *War and Peace* and *Anna Karenina* and *Crime and Punishment*, gloomy Russian novels which had suited her discouraged state of mind. After Dr Pharoah had sacked her, sometimes she had thought him bitterly unfair, but sometimes she had wondered whether she had been to blame. Whether she had reached her limit, whether he had seen something in her that had told him she would never be good enough. Never, ever.

Being academically successful had always been important to her. It had defined her. She would never forget the shock on her father's face when she told him that she had lost her job at Gildersleve Hall. Though shock had immediately been followed by sympathy and comfort, and though her family had loved her and reassured her and had offered her a space in which she could lick her wounds, she had minded very much. Retreat and regroup, her father advised her, but she had not at first known how. Nor had she realized how long it would take. The retreating was easy, it was the regrouping with which she had struggled: she could have papered her bedroom walls with the rejection letters. After a while, she had lowered her sights. A job growing cultures in a TB hospital, a lab assistant at a grammar school – anything would do. The glittering career she had once thought within her grasp – master's degree, research, maybe one day even a lectureship – slid away from her. She avoided risk, limited her ambitions. She had aimed too high, had not been good enough for Gildersleve Hall. She would not make that mistake twice.

She had become accustomed during her months in Cambridgeshire to being part of something exclusive, to being special. But she wasn't special any more, she was ordinary, and rather shabby with failure. When the letter had arrived from the hospital in St Pancras Way, offering her the position of junior lab assistant, she had felt, more than anything, relief, and had sent her letter of acceptance by return of post.

Ellen was nearing her stop. The woman beside her stood up too and Ellen offered to carry her shopping bags down the swaying spiral steps. The bus juddered to a halt and the conductor hauled a pushchair out on to the pavement. The younger child was slotted into the pushchair, the elder made to hold the handle, and bags were balanced.

Ellen walked up the main road then turned off down a side street. She had moved into the Islington lodging house at the end of June the previous year. It was a large, scruffy, rambling building, tenanted by her brother Joe and his friends, who were mostly students studying engineering and chemistry. There were several Daves, a couple of Steves, a Richard and a Mike. Their girlfriends were typists or nurses or they worked for a magazine or an advertising agency. None of them had heard of Gildersleve Hall, and none of them cared that Ellen Kingsley had once been sacked ignominiously.

Ellen was the only woman living there. She got on well enough with the Daves and Steves, as she tended to think of them. Sometimes she shared meals with them, sometimes they played poker into the night. Other times, when the humour was too juvenile or the shared kitchen too messy, she retreated to her room. It was small and narrow, on the north side of the house so rather dark, but she had furnished it herself, unlike the rooms in hall of her college days or Mrs Bryant's bungalow in Copfield. Her first real room of her own. Her parents had sent up a bed and chest of drawers from home but Ellen had bought everything else in London – a desk and chair from a junk shop, a rug from an inexpensive local store, curtains and bedspread that she had made herself. Her books and a few ornaments filled the shelves, and her dresses hung on a rail. For the first time she was living with her own taste rather than someone else's.

Here, she read books and wrote letters or mended clothes and listened to the radio. In this way, she heard of the great things that happened in 1953: the coronation of Elizabeth II, the conquest of Everest, the revelation of the double helix structure of DNA. Now and then she had the feeling that the world was going on without her, exciting and novel, while she lay on the bed reading Turgenev or listening to *Friday Night Is Music Night*.

Reaching the house, Ellen unlocked the front door and went inside. As she climbed the stairs, she noticed that the bathroom was empty, so she dashed to her room, gathered up her towel and sponge bag, ran back down a floor and bolted the bathroom door behind her. While she was soaking in the hot water, Joe tapped on the door to ask her whether she was having supper. Ellen said no, she might go to a concert. Then: what had she done today? Nothing much, she said, swooshing water with the flat palm of her hand so that it sloshed against the side of the bath. I met an old friend. And thought, was that what India was? Or did you just, after a while, find it easier to fall into India's way of thinking?

India met Garrett in Dean Street. She was wearing her silk dress, which was the intense, inarguable blue of morning glories. The dress had come from a shop in Bond Street. Ed, who worked in the City and was in his mid-thirties, plump, balding and unhappily married, had bought it for her. He had come round to the shop one day after work with a box, the dress wrapped in tissue paper inside it, tucked under his arm. 'You don't mind, do you?' he said, when he gave it to her. 'It's just that I saw it in the window and it's the same colour as your eyes.' He had gone pink as he had said it, so, to reassure him that she wasn't assuming that he was assuming anything, she had kissed him.

Just now, India was short of cash. She was only a very junior assistant in the art supply shop and Sebastian's gardening jobs brought in even less money. Neither of them spent much but they seemed to lurch between just about managing and slipping into debt. This month, no matter how she jiggled the bills and no matter how hard she thought we don't need this or that, there wasn't enough to pay both the electricity and the phone. India supposed that theoretically they could have done without the telephone but she would have hated that. And she had to pay back Ellen. She didn't want Ellen to think her the sort of person who didn't repay debts.

Ed would have lent her money, but she didn't like to borrow from Ed. India had her principles: she borrowed only from people she wouldn't feel bad about if she failed to repay. She had accepted the gift of the frock because it would have made Ed miserable if she had refused it, but money was different. And anyway, Ed was away, on holiday with his adulterous wife.

The French pub smelled of red wine and cigarettes. The small barroom was as dark as night, packed to the gunwales with drinkers. Absinthe and pastis were sold at the bar, as well as wine and beer. Some of the notices on the walls were in French, a legacy from the war, when Free French soldiers used to drink here. India, who had never been abroad, even so caught the drift of the alien, the exile.

India and Garrett squeezed into a corner with their friends. You had to shout to be heard over the noise. Vinnie Spencer, who was a saxophonist in Garrett's band, had brought along a girl called Justine. Justine's hair was cut in a choppy bob and she was wearing black slacks and a baggy black jumper. She told India about her job, dancing in a revue. 'It's pretty awful, really. I play a cat, with ears and whiskers, but it'll pay the rent until my poems are published.'

'When are they being published?'

'I don't know, I haven't sent them off yet. I've been trying to think of a title. I can't decide between *The Yellow Moon* and *Rain in the Afternoon*. What do you think?'

'*Rain in the Afternoon*,' said India, very definitely. 'You couldn't lend me a couple of quid, could you?'

''Fraid not.' Justine flicked ash on the floor. 'Pretending to be a cat doesn't pay *that* well.'

India and Garrett headed off to the Colony Room, which was above a trattoria along Dean Street. A wall of people seethed round the bamboo-clad bar, which was presided over by Muriel Belcher. Muriel had a long oval face, dark hair swept smoothly back from her high forehead, sharp black eyes and a nose which curved like the beak of a hawk.

Oliver, who owned the garage that did up the cars that Garrett delivered, was slumped in a corner at one end of the bar. If he was flush, he might lend her some cash, India thought hopefully. He was holding his head in his hands, but whenever his eyelids drooped shut an elbow would slip off the bar, jerking him awake. Garrett said hello and Oliver mumbled something back. 'Pissed as a lord,' said Muriel Belcher crossly. 'You can take him away if he causes trouble.' India mentally crossed Oliver off her list.

Vinnie caught up with them; someone had told him that Peachey was giving a party so they all meandered off to Tite Street. The door to Peachey's house was opened by a young man with curly red hair. He eyed India and her friends, drew on a small black cigarette, then exhaled smoke.

'Oh, you can come in, I suppose.'

'Hello, Simon,' said India. 'Is Laurence here?'

'Didn't you know? He's in hospital. Caught measles and nearly died.' Simon snorted. 'Rather undignified, I call it, catching measles at his age.'

Inside the house, the lights were low and Billie Holliday's voice permeated the rooms, which smelled of the heavy oriental perfume Peachey wore, underpinned by a stale mustiness. The dark purple walls of the hallway were decorated by a mirror with a gilt frame and a large painting of a nude, a big-nosed, black-eyed, salmon-pink woman, reclining on a purple couch. A chipped marble nymph stood at the bottom of the stairs, one of her arms upstretched, as if she was reaching up to change a lightbulb. Garrett hung his scarf on the statue's raised hand.

India went downstairs to the kitchen. Peachey's kitchen smelled even worse than the rest of the house. The sink overflowed with dirty crockery and cats were feeding from saucers scattered over the floor. A big white Persian cat, a giant ball of fluff sporting what India could only think of as moustaches, trod fastidiously over the debris on the draining board.

Mrs Peachey herself was sitting at the kitchen table, smoking, a tabby cat on her lap. Peachey was tall and broad-shouldered and her long, elegant face had the creased and crumpled sexlessness of old age. She was wearing a dark green satin dress, of a waistless style out of fashion since the 1920s. The cat stirred and she ran a gnarled and wrinkled hand along its back.

Spying India, Peachey glared at her. 'I'm out of gin. Those bastards have drunk it all. It's ridiculous, so early in the evening. You don't happen to have any on you, do you?'

'I'm afraid not. I was going to ask you if you could lend me a fiver.'

'Haven't a bean, darling. That's the trouble with getting old, you never have any money. If I was twenty, I'd model for John or Sickert and I'd be flush again.' Peachey added snidely, 'Hot little piece like you needn't be short of cash. You should ask Bernie, he's got a few bob.'

'Is he here?'

'No, I won't have him in my house after the last time. You want to be careful, India. He might fall for someone else.' Peachey gave a cackle of laughter and the tabby cat bristled. 'Where's that beautiful boy of yours?'

'Garrett? He's upstairs.'

'Tell him to come down here and say hello to me.'

India went back upstairs. In the sitting room, which was painted a deep strawberry pink, couples were dancing. There were other paintings on the walls, mostly nudes, of Peachey in her heyday. India had tried modelling once, but had found it tiresome and impossible, all that sitting still.

Someone put on another record. Justine began to dance, by herself at first, her long, black-clad limbs making sinuous movements, and then Simon joined her.

Vinnie said, 'How are you, India?'

'I'm very well, thank you. Peachey won't lend me any money.'

'You must have caught her in a mood, the sour old cow.' Vinnie gave her a sympathetic glance. 'I could let you have something at the end of the week.'

India wasn't sure whether they would still have a phone by the end of the week. 'Sweet of you,' she said, and squeezed his hand. Then Garrett pulled her into the centre of the room, and she tucked herself into his arms and closed her eyes, pressing her cheek against his as they danced.

Shortly afterwards, Peachey, still in a temper, threw them all out of the house. India was feeling hungry, so Garrett bought fish and chips, which they shared. Then they argued about whether to go to Bernie's party. Eventually India caved in and said all right, for an hour, so they caught an Underground train to Mayfair.

The nightclub was the sort of place that instantly made India feel happy. The glitter of light on chandelier and champagne glass and the rhythm of the band made her spirits fizz. Bernie and a dozen of his friends – men in sharp suits and girls in expensive frocks – were sitting round a large circular table.

Bernie was only a couple of inches taller than India herself, and had a stout, barrel-shaped torso and short little legs. His face was smooth and oval and brown, like a nut, and his voice was pitched high for a man of his rotundity. When she had first heard him speak India had wanted to laugh.

Bernie took his cigar out of his mouth and gave India a nod. 'Hello, gorgeous.'

'Hello, Bernie. Happy birthday.'

As she kissed his cheek he patted her bottom. 'Someone get the girl champagne,' he called, and a glass was handed to her.

'Sit down, India,' said Bernie, and the man sitting next to him stood up.

'No, I want to dance.'

Bernie gave her a look. 'Frank'll keep the seat warm for you, then,' and some of his friends laughed. 'Skittish, are we?'

'You know me, Bernie darling, I don't like sitting still.' She gave him a big smile and left the table.

There were a lot of other people she knew at the club and when she wasn't dancing, she went from table to table, talking to people. Now and then she glanced over to Bernie's party. She had the feeling that he was watching her. India had once seen a pike at an aquarium. It had had eyes like Bernie's: unblinking, dead-looking.

Garrett had met Bernie through his friend, Clive, who let out the flats. Bernie owned flats and houses throughout London, which he sublet to people like Clive, who had to hand on to him the rent, minus their cut, whether the properties had tenants or not. Clive wanted to keep in with Bernie and Garrett wanted to keep in with Clive. Garrett also enjoyed the spill-off from Bernie's fortune that occasionally reached their rocky little shore – and so did she, if she was honest. Who wouldn't enjoy a party in the Blue Duck nightclub where all the drinks were paid for, or a dinner in a West End restaurant? But she had learned long ago that there was always a price to pay, and there was something about the way Bernie looked at her that gave her the creeps. But then, the bills. Apart from the utter dreariness of the phone or the electricity being cut off, Sebastian would be alarmed. Sebastian liked life to tick along in a predictable way and he would start imagining awful things, like them losing the flat. So, Bernie. It frightened her. But, Vinnie, Oliver, Laurence, Peachey – she was running out of options.

One of Bernie's friends tapped her on the shoulder and told her they were cutting the cake. Bernie's cake was rather more splendid than the cake India had baked for Sebastian's birthday, with squirls of royal icing and thirty-five red candles, all matching. A waiter lit the candles with a flourish and Bernie blew them out with a sharp little puff.

He patted the seat beside him. 'You need to eat your cake, India.'

Reluctantly, she sat down. 'Where's Garrett?' she asked.

'I sent him on an errand. Girl like you shouldn't be wasting her time on someone like Garrett Parker.'

India cursed Garrett under her breath.

The cake was cut, Bernie's thigh pressed against hers. 'Do you like to play blackjack, India?' asked Bernie.

'I don't know.'

'Time to find out, then. Some of us are going on to one of my places.'

She unpeeled the icing from the cake. 'Card games are so boring.'

'Not if you're playing them for money, they're not.' Bernie popped a piece of cake into his mouth. 'The house always wins, of course. But if you own the house . . .' He winked.

She could feel her resolve weakening. She imagined going to the casino with Bernie and winning lots of money, paying all the bills, paying Ellen back, buying some new clothes, perhaps. But then, out of the corner of her eye, she caught a glimpse of Michael Colebrook in the crowd, and she stood up, saying, 'Sorry, Bernie, not tonight. Another time, perhaps,' then squeezed out from the table, crossed the dance floor and tapped Michael on the shoulder.

Michael turned and smiled at her. 'Hello, India. Would you like to dance?'

Michael Colebrook lived in Half Moon Street and worked for the Foreign Office. He had bright brown eyes like a robin's topped with short, thick black brows. India had met him more than a year ago, when she and her then boyfriend had had a big argument and she had stormed off, realizing too late that she had no money in her purse. They had quarrelled in Southwark, which had meant a long walk back to the flat. She had been wearing high heels and had taken them off to walk home. Michael had stopped his car as she was crossing Waterloo Bridge, and had offered her a lift. She had accepted, because she had blisters, and he had proved to be the nicest man, not a rapist or murderer at all, and had driven her home. Since then their friendship had flourished.

She said, 'Actually, darling, if you don't mind, I'd like to leave.'

Michael fetched her coat from the cloakroom and they left the club. In the taxi, India said, 'You couldn't lend me some money, could you, Michael?'

'Of course, how much do you need?'

'Ten pounds, I'm afraid. It might be for a while.'

'A birthday present.'

'It's not my birthday.'

'An early birthday present, then.' He took two ten-pound notes out of his wallet and handed them to her.

'You're very sweet.' She tucked the money into her purse. 'I should probably marry you.'

'No, you shouldn't. I would bore you within an

afternoon.' The taxi's windscreen wipers thwacked at the rain and she rested her head on his shoulder.

The laboratory was in an oblong, single-storey brick building at the back of the hospital. Through the windows came the rattle of trolleys of dirty linen and the conversation of the porters, who liked to smoke in the asphalt area between the lab and the laundry.

The laboratory's work was overseen by Professor Malik. Working for Professor Malik was very different from working for Dr Pharoah. There wasn't the competition, the jostling for position. Malik was Anglo-Indian, thin, sixtyish, never raised his voice and was calmly encouraging no matter how much work there was to be got through, even if the consultants were breathing down his neck, impatient for results. He was unfailingly civil to his staff and treated the female employees with exactly the same courtesy as the men. Ellen liked Professor Malik and almost trusted him. Almost. She seemed to have lost the capacity for absolute trust.

The samples of blood and tissue would come in from the wards several times a day, and then there would the rush to analyse them and prepare cultures and slides. Ellen's job was to label the samples, every test tube and dish, and to copy the labels on to a check sheet. Hundreds of samples a day, each one to be labelled clearly and accurately, no room for slip-ups or poor handwriting because lives depended on speed and precision. In any spare moments between the trolleys arriving, she cleaned glassware. Again, no room for error or cross-contamination. If there was a rush in the early evening she stayed on, working overtime as the victims of car crashes or patients with high fevers were taken on to the wards. She didn't mind staying late; there was a camaraderie about the lab, a sense of working closely with each other in the quiet evenings that reminded her of Gildersleve at its best.

One evening, it was almost eight o'clock by the time she got home to the lodging house. From the corridor, she heard voices from the kitchen. India's: *You have to wait until you can smell the gas or it won't light.* And Joe's: *Sounds lethal. I'll come round and have a look, if you like.*

Ellen felt tired; she wanted to kick off her shoes, peel off her stockings, lie in a hot bath, and instead, here was India Mayhew, her new best friend, in *her* house.

She went into the kitchen. Joe was standing at the sink and India was sitting at the table. A handful of Daves and Steves were in the kitchen as well, opening cans of beans and scraping the burnt bits from toast.

Joe said, 'Hi, Ellen,' and India did her smile, and all the toast-scrapers and can-openers stopped what they were doing and admired her.

'Hello, Joe. Hello, everyone. Hello, India.'

'How lovely to see you, Ellen. Joe's been looking after me so well.'

'Only a cup of coffee,' said Joe, who was washing up.

'But a simply gorgeous cup of coffee.' That smile again.

India opened a large white woven-leather handbag and delved through handkerchieves, lipsticks and scribbled scraps of paper. She found a purse and offered some coins to Ellen. 'Five shillings and sixpence. Thank you *so* much.'

'Did Sebastian like the books?'

'Enormously.'

Joe said to Ellen, 'There's some corned beef, if you want it.'

'I'm fine, thanks, I had a sandwich at the hospital.'

'Good day?'

'Long.' Ellen sat down and slid her feet out of her shoes.

'I brought you this,' said India, and, with the air of a magician taking a rabbit from a hat, produced a bottle of wine from her bag. 'It's to say thank you for helping me with, well, the bookshop. And to celebrate us meeting up again, of course.'

The wine was a 1938 Petrus. Ellen wondered how India could afford such a bottle – slipped beneath her coat, perhaps, in some dusty Soho wine merchants?

'It's kind of you, India, but there was no need.'

'A friend of mine gave it to Sebastian for his birthday, but he doesn't like wine. I thought you might like it.'

Ellen felt ashamed of herself. There was she, judging India, and yet how she hated others to judge her. Guilt, and the desire for a drink, made her say, 'Let's open it, then.'

Glasses were found, wine was poured. Someone began to fry eggs while India wandered around, opening cupboards and leafing through the books on the table and chatting to people and saying things like, 'What a sweet little vase,' and, 'You're all so brainy.' And time passed and one of the Daves went out to buy beer and crisps and Ellen could not afterwards put her finger on when or how it happened, that alteration in chemistry, that addition of a catalyst that so lifted the mood of the evening that she forgot her tiredness and didn't bother to worry about the queue for the bathroom and enjoyed herself more than she had for months.

In the kitchen of the house in Tufnell Park, every surface was covered with mixing bowls and saucepans, and more pans were simmering on the hob. The radio was turned up loud, something about Princess Margaret. Coming home from work, Riley started to wash up the dishes in the sink, but Pearl said, 'Don't do that. Sit down, I'm cooking you a special meal.'

'Are we celebrating something?'

'Does there need to be a reason for me to cook you a nice dinner?' She was staring at him, her eyes big, a whisk in one hand.

'Of course not.'

'I couldn't remember when I last made you a proper meal. Was it yesterday?'

It seemed longer, but he said, 'Yes, I think so. What are you cooking?'

'Prawn cocktail – no, no,' she flicked through a recipe book, 'shrimp and orange cocktail.'

'Sounds lovely.'

'And beef pie and lemon pudding. I bought some wine.'

A bottle of red was nestling on the windowsill among the pan scourers and washing-up liquid. Pearl topped up her own glass, looked round, found a tumbler on the draining board, and poured wine into it. Crimson splashes trailed down the sink.

'What was I doing?' she said. 'Oh, yes, the egg whites.' She tucked a bowl under her arm to whisk the egg whites. A minute's beating and then she put the bowl down and poked something bobbing in a saucepan. Then she peered into the oven, and, scooping back her hair from her forehead, said, puzzled, 'I was in the middle of something, wasn't I?'

'The egg whites. Can I do anything?'

'I *can* cook, you know,' she said, giving him a cold look. 'Honestly, John, sometimes I think you think I'm completely useless.' Then her expression lightened. 'Go and find some candles. We must have candles, I *adore* candles. They'll make the house less *dreary*.'

Riley went upstairs to look in on Annie, who was sleeping, and then to the bedroom, where he hung up his jacket and loosened his tie. Then he glanced through the day's post and unearthed the candles from the cupboard beneath the stairs. And all the time he did these things, something uneasy and cold uncoiled in his stomach.

He heard a crash and a scream and hurried back to the kitchen.

'Pearl? What's the matter?'

She was standing by the cooker, holding a saucepan, staring into it. 'The potatoes have boiled dry!' She slammed the saucepan on the hob. 'Look at them! Ruined! All that work! Why didn't you *tell* me? You must have *smelled* them! Why do I have to do *everything*?'

'It's OK, I'll sort it out.' He reached to take the saucepan but she snatched it from him, crashing it down on the hob once more, her teeth bared.

There was a cry from upstairs. Pearl hissed, 'Now look, she's woken up! It's all your fault!'

Riley walked out of the room. He realized as he went upstairs that his jaw was aching from tension.

Annie was sitting up in bed, her fists clenched. 'Daddy, I heard a noise,' she whispered.

'It's all right, sweetheart. Mummy dropped something, that's all.' He stroked her hair. 'Go back to sleep.'

Annie lay back on the pillow. While he waited for her to go back to sleep, Riley listened, alert for sounds from the lower floor of the house. It seemed to him that the only thing he and Pearl now had in common was their love of their daughter. He had learned to judge Pearl's mood from the way she looked at him, the tone of her voice and the fast see-saw of her temper. He had taught himself to detect melancholy, anger and jealousy at a glance. Tonight's was a mood he was familiar with: the frantic activity and enthusiasm, interspersed with bouts of anger and suspicion. Challenge her and she'd either dissolve into tears or hurl herself at him, screaming, beating her fists against his chest.

So he appeased her, for Annie's sake, because he did not want his daughter to grow up in a battleground. And yet he was finding it harder and harder to act out this travesty of affection, or to shake off, even temporarily, the suffocating sensation of being trapped. He could see no way out of the situation, either for himself or for Pearl. Marriage was binding, a promise made to be kept for life, in sickness and in health, until death parted them. Annie needed a father and a mother. Sometimes Pearl still claimed to need him, to love him. On his part, all that remained of the passion he had once felt for her were a few cold curlings of pity.

Annie had fallen asleep again; Riley went back down to the kitchen. Pearl was sitting at the table, her head in her hands. She looked up as he came in. 'Sorry,' she whispered. 'I'm sorry, John. I shouldn't have shouted at you.'

'It doesn't matter. You're trying to do too much, that's all.'

'I *can* do it.' Her voice quavered.

'Of course you can. Just, a bit at a time, perhaps.'

'I'm so tired. If only I could sleep . . .' She looked up at him, her eyes swimming with tears. 'You do still love me, don't you? I wouldn't blame you if you didn't, but you do, don't you?'

He put a hand on her shoulder. Her body quivered like a taut string and she leaned her head against his arm. But he couldn't find the words she wanted him to say; ashes seemed to sear his tongue, and his hand moved mechanically as he stroked her hair.

The Mayhews' flat became a refuge for Ellen from the studenty grubbiness of the Islington lodging house. India and Sebastian had inherited it from their Aunt Rachel, who had been their mother's elder sister. India showed Ellen a photograph of Rachel. A pleasant, serious face, framed by a serious wartime hairstyle, looked back at Ellen from the black and white portrait.

When Ellen asked India about her parents, India said, 'My father was killed in the Blitz. My mother died a year and a half later. She was a dancer, quite a famous one. She danced at Sadler's Wells.' Then she changed the subject.

Once a week or so, India invited Ellen to tea. Suppers with the Mayhews were unorthodox: oxtail soup followed by slices of orange, or chips, cooked in a frying pan and sprinkled with salt and vinegar, and then powdery meringues from a baker's. India always cooked and Sebastian always cleared up. Ellen found it impossible to imagine the other way round. India dropped floured fillets of plaice into a pan and fat sizzled. A cigarette in one hand, a wooden spoon in the other as she stirred a cheese sauce. Peeling potatoes, she wore a striped apron over a dress of blue silk.

Sebastian dabbed a cloth at the flour on the draining board and mopped the floor. Ellen always offered to wash up after supper and Sebastian always politely refused. If the phone rang, it was always India who answered it. If, as happened very occasionally, the call was for Sebastian, he approached it cautiously, holding the receiver a careful distance from his ear before saying hello. India always opened the door of the flat to let Ellen in, never Sebastian, as if he couldn't quite be sure what was waiting outside. Sebastian rarely started up a conversation, but sometimes, when the three of them were sitting at the table having supper, he would thread his hands together, pressing them outwards, bob his head and then look up, smiling that same sweet smile Ellen had noticed the first time she had met him, and proceed to tell a story about his day.

India liked to go shopping in Oxford Street. Inside Selfridges, she fingered fabric, testing its weight, shaking her head over the cut and finish of a blouse. Then she would slip her feet into a pair of high heels and walk up and down. Ellen felt a certain tension, shopping with India. She found herself keeping an eye on her as she came out of the changing rooms, measuring the fatness of her handbag and the bulk beneath her coat.

The summer dresses came in, full-skirted, tight-bodiced cottons and linens. The frock Ellen bought was coral-coloured, cap-sleeved and narrow at the waist, tied with a bow. *Yes*, said India, with an approving nod as Ellen came out of the changing room. All her savings, she thought, on one glorious frock, and all because India Mayhew had somehow slipped herself back into her life.

Sometimes India's boyfriend, Garrett Parker, came to tea. Garrett was dark and handsome, with flashing eyes and a beguiling grin. Inside the Mayhews' kitchen, he taught Ellen a new dance step. He put his palms on her shoulders and looked into her eyes, swaying his hips and moving in close, a smile playing around the corners of his mouth. Over the top of his head, Ellen saw India, sitting on the draining board, a hand pressed against her mouth, laughing.

Then India and Garrett demonstrated the dance step. Garrett was wearing paint-stained overalls and India had on a faded cotton dress. They kept catching each other's eyes and guffawing, but sometimes the laughter died and was replaced by heat. It felt intrusive, watching them.

Ellen turned her back and looked out of the kitchen window. Sap-green leaves were unfurling on a horse chestnut in a neighbour's garden and cars were queuing outside the garage over the road. The gramophone scratched out a tune and the room smelled steamy and stale, of cooking. No one had ever looked at her like that. Had she ever looked at a man with such longing in her eyes? She remembered gazing out of the window of her lab at Gildersleve Hall, to where Alec Hunter had walked through the copse: the catch in her throat, the tug of something she thirsted for, out of her reach. More than a year and a half ago, she had fallen in love with Alec Hunter. She wondered where he was now. On his island, she supposed, with Andrée, and into her mind came a picture of the two of them walking hand in hand along a shore pounded by winter storms.

She had not forgotten him, though she had tried. She only minded that she had not completely stopped minding.

Riley woke in the night. Switching on the light, he saw that Pearl's side of the bed was empty. When she couldn't sleep, she sometimes went into the spare room. He got up, put on the bedside light and pulled on a pair of trousers, then looked in the spare room, bathroom and Annie's room. No Pearl.

He glanced at his watch. It was ten past three in the morning and, as he walked downstairs, he felt the grey lifelessness of the house during this, the dead centre of the night. Pearl wasn't in the living room, dining room or kitchen. Out of the kitchen window, he caught a flicker of movement, a gleam of scarlet fabric and the orange tip of a cigarette.

He went outside. It was May, still cold. Pearl was wearing her red silk kimono and was walking up and down the garden.

He said, 'Pearl, what are you doing?'

She kept on walking. 'I was thinking,' she said, 'what if we went to live in Cornwall? We could go to the beach every day. Annie would adore it. It would be so lovely!'

'Come back into the house.'

'No, listen to me, John, I want to live in Cornwall!'

'No,' he said sharply. 'It's out of the question.' He took her elbow but she shook him off, and, staring at him, gave a furious hiss.

'I hate it here! I hate this horrible bloody house!'

He found himself examining her coolly, almost as if she was a suspect he was interviewing, scrutinizing her features, which were contorted with anger, and her hair, which fell in wild snaky locks around her face, before moving to the red kimono, which flapped loosely around her thin night-dress, and her bare, grass-stained feet.

'We're staying in this house,' he said. 'We're not going to move again, Pearl, so you'd better start trying to make the best of this place. If there's anything else you wish to say to me then please come indoors and we can talk there.'

She gave him an icy glare, then looked away. 'There's nothing I want to say to you, John. Nothing at all.'

Bernie was waiting outside the shop when India left for her lunch break. He offered to take her to Wheeler's and she said no thanks, she only had an hour for lunch. Doesn't matter, he said, they could do it there and back in an hour, easy. And she had shopping to do. Lee would do it; Bernie smacked his chauffeur on the back of his head. Lee liked shopping, didn't he? Lee said, 'Yes, boss.' Lee's hair, a light ginger, was cropped close, and his skin was pale, allowing India to see the flush which travelled up the back of his neck to the top of his scalp.

It seemed easier for India to say yes, too, so she climbed into the car and Lee drove them to Old Compton Street. Then she had to invent errands for Lee — soap and sugar, keep it simple or he might take hours. At a table by the front window, India and Bernie ate fish and potatoes and salad. Bernie talked about himself, mostly. It was easy enough to get Bernie to talk about himself, and she thought she had got away with it and was about to remind Bernie that she needed to go back to the shop, when he said, 'You think you're a smart little miss, don't you, India?'

She made herself meet his eyes. 'Not particularly.'

'Buy you dinner, take you to nice places.' Bernie dabbed his mouth with his napkin and inspected his fingernails. He was always fastidiously clean. 'And what do I get back?'

'I haven't asked you for anything. You asked me to lunch,' she reminded him.

'Oh yes, I did.' Bernie buffed a nail on his napkin.

'I have to go back to the shop now or I'll be late.'

'Like your job, do you, India?'

'Yes, very much.'

'I could find you a job in one of my casinos. All you'd have to do is to wear a nice frock and smile at people. You wouldn't have to get up early or nothing.'

'I'm happy where I am, thanks.'

'Can't pay much.' He took a note out of his wallet and put it on the table. 'How do you manage, you and your brother?'

India stiffened. She had never told Bernie about Sebastian. How did he know? 'You mustn't worry about me, Bernie,' she said lightly. 'I'm not short of cash. My aunt left me lots of money. I've loads of it stashed away in a bank.'

'Oh, I don't think so,' Bernie said. His eyes, the

brown-grey of mud at the bottom of a pond, surveyed her. 'I really don't think so.'

Lee drove her back to the shop and handed her the carrier bag with the shopping in it. As well as sugar and soap, there was a box of Black Magic and half a dozen packets of nylons, the sight of which made India growl like a dog. She was ten minutes late back from her lunch break and Miss Maloney told her off. Throughout the afternoon she kept doing things wrong – getting the change muddled and dropping all the watercolour brushes out of their wooden box and having to sort them back into their compartments. She was rattled and she couldn't concentrate and that was the truth of it. Bernie had rattled her. On her way home from work she gave the carrier bag of stuff that Lee had bought to an old woman who was sitting in an alleyway, begging for change. She felt some regret for the nylons, but she had her principles.

Coming into the flat, she noticed a bunch of bluebells in a vase on the centre of the table. Sebastian must have picked them from one of his gardens. The stems looked bruised and the flowers were drooping. India would have liked to chuck them away, too. She hated bluebells. How had Bernie found out about Sebastian? Had Garrett said something? Garrett had a big mouth. Had Bernie meant anything by mentioning Sebastian, or had it just been a passing comment? India was afraid that everything Bernie said meant something.

She ran a bath, undressed, and lay in the soapy water,

feeling the grime of the day float away. She wondered whether she should go to bed with Bernie, get it over and done with, and then perhaps he would leave her alone. But she recoiled from the thought of those fish eyes looking at her, those soft little hands touching her. And what if he didn't leave her alone afterwards, what if he expected to keep her in his collection, one of those silly, simpering women who went to clubs and parties with him?

The trouble was that she had got in too deep. *Buy you dinner, take you to nice places.* This was true. She had never before today dined with Bernie alone, Garrett and Clive had always been there as well. But she had known that Bernie was after her. She wasn't stupid, like Garrett, who didn't notice such things. Garrett thought Bernie was going to offer him 'business', as he put it, because Garrett lived in a world where things always worked out for the best. India had gone along with it partly to keep Garrett happy and partly because she enjoyed the glamour. The Mayfair clubs and the dinners in restaurants in Piccadilly and St James, brushing shoulders with the rich and the famous – if a rather tarnished rich and famous – had made her feel good. Had made her feel *safe*. This was all she wanted, to feel safe, her and Sebastian, because she could not feel safe if Sebastian was not safe. And Bernie's remark had unnerved her.

India climbed out of the bath and wrapped a towel round herself. She couldn't be bothered putting in rollers, and the steam had curled her hair so that it rippled away from her face. She made a cup of tea and some toast and then sat down on the sofa.

Her gaze was caught once more by the bluebells. There had been bluebells at the house in the woods when they had first gone to live there. That had been the year after her father had died. He had been killed in the London Blitz, in 1940, when India was eight and Sebastian four. He had been on leave from the army and a bomb had hit the bus on which he was travelling. Rachel had told India this afterwards, when she had been trying to sort it all out in her head.

The house in the woods was the first house that India could truly remember. She knew they had lived in other houses beforehand, but could only remember pieces of them – a basement courtyard, a bathroom papered with pale green fish. The house was surrounded on three sides by woodland, acres of it, a forest, really. No neighbours for miles. A narrow country road ran along the front of the house. Whenever a vehicle passed, she and Sebastian ran to the front gate to have a look.

Their water came from a well in the garden. Water was supposed to come out of taps; they had all been dismayed by the well. 'Like in a fairy story,' their mother said to them the day they moved in, trying to make the best of it. India had a clear memory of her mother, wearing a cotton summer dress printed with flowers, a cigarette in her mouth, hauling the arm of the pump up and down. Her mother had been called Cindy and she had been a dancer before she married

Daddy. She had had long flaxen hair which she rolled up in a sort of sausage all round her head. She had been very thin and her joints had hurt from too much dancing. 'My poor bones,' her mother often said.

India had taken over the getting of water. She hadn't minded: the crunch and press of the pump, the water squirting into the metal bucket were satisfying. When her mother's friends called, they took over the task. Men in army khaki or navy or air force blue nonchalantly operated the pump one-handed. It was fun that first summer. They had picnics in the garden and parties in the house when Cindy's friends came to stay. Another memory: her mother with a green satin flower in her hair, a cigarette in one hand and a glass of sherry in the other, laughing and dancing. Then the men went away and fetching the water was India's job again.

Going to the shops was also India's job. Cindy wrote her a list, frowning, pencil in hand, and India took Cindy's purse and a shopping bag. Sometimes she took Sebastian with her. India had a bicycle and Sebastian a tricycle, found for them who-knows-where in that austere wartime Britain by one of Cindy's friends, Neil, a naval officer. India's bike was too large for her and she had to stand on the pedals, and Sebastian was terribly slow on his tricycle, but it had a little basket on the back where they could put things. The shop was a long way away, on the main road, past the church and the school that India and Sebastian went to. It sold everything: pencils and handkerchieves and knitting wool, as well as food, though you could never be sure what exactly it would sell on any particular day.

Once, not long after they came to live in the house in the woods, the three of them walked to the shop on a fine summer's afternoon. Cindy put on a nice frock and let India wear her party dress (lilac net) and a straw hat. Sebastian wore his pale blue shorts and shirt. It was an uphill walk to the shop and they had to stop several times for Cindy to rest. When they reached the shop, they discovered that Mrs Day was out of writing paper. 'It's the war, dear,' she said to Cindy. 'I could let you have a couple of postcards.' Mrs Day, who was enormously fat and wore a flowered pinny over a mud-coloured dress, and whose stockings (also mud-coloured) were rolled down to her ankles, admired India's frock and said what a pretty little girl she was and gave her and Sebastian an apple. Cindy bought the postcards and they walked back down the hill. After they got back to the house, Cindy lay down on the sofa and India made tea for herself and Sebastian and put Sebastian to bed.

In the winter, her mother's friends visited less often. Mummy looked sad, so India tried to cheer her up by making her cups of tea and putting on the gramophone. They sang along to 'My Funny Valentine', and her mother taught India how to do the quickstep, just a few steps at a time, because of her bones. The house was cold, and often Sebastian climbed into India's bed at night, to keep warm. India told him stories about an imaginary land of hills and lakes and castles. When India described to Sebastian their voyage in a sailing boat, she heard the soft beat of the breeze in the sail and trailed her hand in cool crystal water.

At Christmas, the naval officer, Neil, came to stay. India listened to them arguing behind the closed door of the bedroom. 'It won't do, Lucinda,' she heard Neil say loudly. 'You have to think of those children.' The next day, Neil had gone and her mother took to her bed again.

Snow fell in January, marooning them in a fairy-tale forest. India and Sebastian put on their boots and coats and ran outside. India's boots were too small for her and pinched. The snowdrifts were taller than Sebastian and clods of snow slid with a satisfying flump from the branches to the ground. Because of the snow, India walked up the hill rather than take the bike. At the shop, Mrs Day said to her, 'And how's that mother of yours?' and India said politely, 'She's very well, thank you.'

But she wasn't. Mummy spent whole days resting in bed. Sometimes India heard her crying. When India asked her what was wrong, she said she missed Daddy. In the evenings, she liked India to rub her feet, which were as cold as ice. India filled hot-water bottles for her, boiling up a kettle on the stove. One day, after the snow thawed, Mummy wrote a number on a piece of paper and told India to go to the call box and phone the doctor. The telephone kiosk was on the main road, near the shop, so India cycled. The doctor came later that day and left a bottle of pills. The pills made her mother sleep, and after that things were better.

India was missing more and more school, what with looking after the house and Sebastian and her mother when she was unwell. It was a horrible school anyway, with hardly any books and a lot of going to church. The other boys and girls, tough country children with sensible, ordinary names like Mary and Joan or Bill and Peter, teased India and Sebastian for their odd names and the way they spoke. Sebastian hated school and cried the mornings she made him go; he had learned to read anyway, and if he was happier with their mother and playing in the garden, then why not let him stay at home instead of dragging him weeping up the hill?

India kept hoping that Neil would come back, but he didn't. Often, weeks went by without them seeing anyone other than Mrs Day at the shop. The house was starting to look dirty and Sebastian was growing out of all his clothes. Now and then, Cindy would have a go at the washing, carrying all the linen downstairs, putting it in to soak and hauling it through the mangle, but then she would wander off to read a book or sit in the porch and have a smoke. Sometimes a day later India would come across a basket of washing in the scullery or abandoned in the garden, still damp and oddly smelly. 'Oh dear, I wish I was a better housekeeper,' Cindy would say, picking up one of Sebastian's vests and sniffing it.

India knew that if her mother wasn't much of a

housekeeper then neither was she. She tried, but it was hard to think of things for lunch and tea, what with there being so little in the shops. She had a look in Cindy's recipe book, which told her how to make things called Steak Diane and Sole Meunière, but Mrs Day's shop didn't sell steak or sole. Cindy wrote on the shopping list 'luncheon meat' or 'tin of peas' but sometimes there weren't any of those in Mrs Day's shop either.

Mrs Day tried to teach India how to use their ration points wisely, but Mrs Day also said things like, 'Your mother can use that to make a nice stew with some mutton from the butcher,' or, 'Tell your mother to put the cabbage in a fish pie.' From this, India guessed that Mrs Day assumed that her mother did the bulk of her shopping in Andover, the nearest town. She didn't tell Mrs Day that her mother hadn't been to Andover since Christmas, and so hadn't visited a butcher or a fishmonger, because that seemed a failing, something that marked them out as deficient, not quite right. India had begun to be afraid that someone, some figure of authority, perhaps a teacher or a policeman, might decide to do something about them. So she just said, 'Yes, Mrs Day, I'll make sure Mummy knows.' Now and then, India caught the bus into town, but these days she worried about leaving Sebastian alone with Mummy for long, and it was a lot of trouble taking him with her round the shops. He whined, and he was too small to carry things.

It was also starting to worry India that they were running

out of money. She collected her mother's widow's pension from the post office each week. The post office was next to the village shop, so India went to them one after the other. Pick up the pension, buy some stamps and cigarettes for Cindy, milk for Sebastian and bread and potatoes. Put some money by for the rent and most of the cash was gone. Sometimes her mother would open her purse and stare at it, bemused.

India found her own solutions. First, she spent the money in her own money box. Then she raided Sebastian's – he never spent his money or even counted it so he wouldn't know the difference. Then she began to steal things from the shop. Small things at first, to cheer her mother up: a ribbon, a packet of hairpins, coloured chalks for Sebastian. And then, when the money really ran out, things to eat. She was very careful and never took anything big or obvious, and always waited until Mrs Day's back was turned to serve another customer or slice a piece of cheese.

Spring came. Their mother seemed to get better. She walked in the garden, carefully, because of her bones. You could see her veins through the translucent skin on her stick wrists. After supper, India put 'My Funny Valentine' on the record player and her mother smiled and told her she was a good girl and let India have a sip of her sherry. Outside, the leaves on the trees unfurled and the blackbirds sang, and the green shoots of the bluebells pressed up through the dark earth in the woods.

Chapter Four

Riley found Pearl in the back garden. She was heavily made-up, with bright red lipstick and black lines along her upper eyelids, and she was wearing shorts and a flowered top that tied at the back of the neck, the sort of outfit Riley associated with beaches and sunbathing. The gramophone was on and music was playing, and a bottle of something was bobbing in a bucket of water.

There was a man sitting in a deckchair. Riley didn't recognize him, but he was young enough to have a spray of scarlet pimples across his face. He was wearing a brown shop coat open over a shirt and trousers and he was holding a glass in his hand.

Pearl said, 'Where were you?'

'Working. What's going on, Pearl?'

'Gerry and me were dancing. We've been having fun, haven't we, darling?' Her voice slurred.

Riley lifted the needle off the record and the music died. Then he nodded to the man in the deckchair. 'Who's this?'

'Gerry works at the greengrocer's. He helped me carry my bags home.'

Riley said to Gerry, 'I should push off, if I were you.'

The youth put down his glass and hurried away.

'Spoilsport,' said Pearl. Her eyes narrowed into pale green slits.

'Where's Annie?' he said.

'Annie?' She looked round vaguely.

A moment's fear. Had she left Annie standing outside the school? Or on a bus, perhaps? Or in the greengrocer's shop where she had found Gerry?

'I remember,' said Pearl. 'She's having tea at Linda's.'

Riley felt a wash of relief. He glanced at his watch. 'I'll go and pick her up.'

As he headed back into the house, he heard her say sourly, 'It's easy for you, isn't it? If you were seeing someone else, how would I know? You'd just tell me you were working overtime and I wouldn't have a clue.'

Slowly, he turned back to her. 'I'm not seeing anyone else.'

'Why should I believe you?'

'That's up to you, Pearl.' His gaze locked on to hers. 'But if you like, I'll tell you what I was doing. In the morning, I checked witness statements connected with an arson attempt. In the afternoon, I interviewed a murder suspect.

He claims that he was drinking with his brother when I think he was strangling his ex-girlfriend in an alleyway – but then, I think both brothers are lying. In fact, I'm certain of it, and I intend to dig deep enough until I can prove it. You see, I don't believe either of them. They're volatile, they act on impulse and they fly off the handle. They're known for it in the pubs of Deptford. And you can't trust people like that, can you?'

Before her eyes dipped down, he saw the fear in them. 'Stop it,' she muttered. 'Stop it, John.'

He said curtly, 'I'm going to get Annie.'

As he walked back through the house and let himself out of the front door, he unclenched his fists, flexing his fingers. At that moment he felt nothing at all for her, not even pity, and if it had not been for Annie, he would simply have walked away.

A steel-grey sky clamped down the windless air and a cold snap made people dig their warm jackets back out of their wardrobes. March when it should have been June. Old men coughed at bus stops and films of coal dust veiled the leaves of the shrubs. If you ran your fingertips along railings, they came away blackish-yellow.

As Ellen was getting ready to leave the lab one evening, Professor Malik asked her to come to his office.

'You've been with us a year now, haven't you, Ellen?' he said, as she shut the door behind her.

She saw him run his fingers over a piece of paper on his

desk. He was frowning; she felt a ripple of apprehension. There were conversations that started like this, weren't there, and went on to include phrases such as, *I hope you can find some other niche more suited to your abilities*, or, *I regret that things have not worked out as I would have hoped.*

She said, 'I hope my work's satisfactory, Professor.'

'Very much so.' The frown deepened. 'Indeed, that's the problem.'

'I don't understand.'

'Sit down, please, Ellen. Your work is exemplary. You are quick and thorough and methodical. In fact, you are an asset to the hospital and I'm sure you will go on to have a long and successful career here, if you so choose. So this confuses me.' His thin brown fingers tapped the piece of paper again.

'What is it?'

'It's the letter that Marcus Pharoah wrote to me last year when I contacted him to tell him that I was considering you for the post here.'

She had been dismissed from Gildersleve without references. She said, 'I told you at the interview, Professor, that I was sacked from Gildersleve Hall.'

'I know you did. You told me that Pharoah didn't think you were suitable for the position and believed you would do better elsewhere. But I wanted to know Pharoah's side of the story.'

It still stung. Pharoah had discounted her as inferior, not worthy of Gildersleve Hall.

Professor Malik went on, 'When Dr Pharoah dismissed you, did he make any specific criticism of your work?'

'No.'

'Are you sure?'

'Completely. I remember every word of our conversation. You don't forget something like that. There was no specific criticism. Only the implication that I was second-rate.'

'I can see no sign of that.'

Ellen felt a surge of relief and pleasure. It was as if a load had been lifted from her shoulders. 'Thank you, Professor,' she said. 'That means a lot to me.'

'I wondered whether to bring up the subject with you. But I felt I had to.'

'I take it Dr Pharoah's comments were uncomplimentary?'

'I wouldn't say that.' Dr Malik turned the piece of paper round so that she could read it, adding quietly, 'I would say they were vituperative.'

Ellen began to read. The first time she read the typed paragraph, she couldn't take it in, so she tried again. Words pulsed like exploding stars, jarring and jabbing sickeningly. *Slovenly . . . incompetent . . . neligent.* And, most woundingly, *If she had spent less time flirting with the male staff her work would doubtless have benefited.*

Aware of a tightness in her throat, she said, 'This isn't true.'

'No, I came to the conclusion that it wasn't some time ago.'

Hateful to think that he had read that. She heard Malik

say, 'This doesn't correspond to my estimation of you at all. As I said, your work is exemplary. So unless you had some specific difficulty with what you were doing at Gildersleve Hall—'

'I don't believe so.'

'I'm sorry if this upsets you, Ellen, but I felt you should know that it exists.'

'It doesn't upset me.' She met his gaze. 'You read it, and yet you still gave me a chance. Why?'

'I'm a great believer in second chances.' His smile reached his tired brown eyes. 'I've had a few myself, in the past. You performed well during the interview and I've always preferred to trust my own judgement. Fortunately, I know your supervisor at Bristol personally, so I spoke to him, and he was able to give me a very different view of your abilities. I will admit that I kept an eye on you until I had confidence in your work.' He paused, then added, 'Pharoah is capable of being vindictive.'

'You know him?'

'We've met. We didn't get on.'

Standing up, she held out her hand to him. 'Thank you for telling me this,' she said. 'Thank you for believing in me.'

Leaving the hospital, Pharoah's damning phrases repeated themselves in her memory over and over again. *Miss Kingsley's approach to her work was slovenly, her technique incompetent and her methodology frequently misjudged. If she had spent less time flirting with the male staff, her work would doubtless have benefited.* Coldly, analytically, she surveyed her three months at Gildersleve Hall, and thought, no, none of that is true.

But any employer, reading those comments, would have crossed her off his shortlist immediately. Only Professor Malik's acquaintance with her supervisor at Bristol and the dislike of Marcus Pharoah that he had implied had enabled her to find work at all. Without that turn of fortune, what would she be doing now? Living at home with her parents. Taking some job, any job, and perhaps giving up on science for ever.

No wonder it had taken her six months to find another post, if Dr Pharoah had responded in such a manner to the inquiries of other prospective employers. She might have gone through her entire life believing that it was her poor performance at interviews that was preventing her from finding work, or a shortage of available posts, or a prejudice against female scientists. Time would have passed and soon she would have had a gap on her CV that could not be respectably filled, an open sore that could not be covered over with any acceptable explanation.

Why had Pharoah done it? Why bother? She hadn't mattered. If he had honestly not thought her suitable for Gildersleve Hall, then why not write some bland words that would rid him of her and yet allow her to continue her career? What he had done smacked of spite and contempt. It was never comfortable to find yourself the object of someone else's dislike and she could not remember it ever happening to her before. Such deceit, such treachery.

Marcus Pharoah had wanted to hurt her. He had meant to destroy her. Why?

She remembered her conversation with Alec Hunter, as they had walked together down the drive at Gildersleve Hall. 'Be careful, Ellen,' he had warned her. And then, 'Pharoah has his pets and it doesn't do to say no to him.' How right he had been.

Once, during that Gildersleve autumn of 1952, she had been to a meeting at one of the London colleges and had happened to mention to an acquaintance that she was working at the hall. *So you're at Marcus Pharoah's little fiefdom*, her friend had said. Looking back, she saw how appropriate that term had been. A word from Pharoah and they had all jumped. Impossible to imagine him at a loss or feeling guilty or ashamed of himself. Only once during her time at Gildersleve Hall had he seemed to falter. *I had such ambition then, such vision*, he had said to her in the hotel bar in Cambridge. But perhaps even those words, so apparently out of character, had been an act, designed to elicit attention and sympathy. It seemed to Ellen now that everything Pharoah had done had been with calculation. You fell under his spell and so you didn't notice. It was only afterwards, when you reflected on what had happened, that you saw this was true.

She remembered how the atmosphere had changed whenever he had come into the common room, and how the tension had ratcheted up when he had been nearby. Gildersleve Hall, with its aura of exclusivity and privilege, could not have existed without Pharoah. He had created it, nurtured it, financed it and controlled it. He controlled his staff, too, every bit as precisely as he controlled the hall – through his charm and humour, yes, but also through his unpredictability, and, when it suited him, his capacity to intimidate. Pharoah was used to having his own way. From the eminent war hero, Jan Kaminski, to young researchers like Andrée and Martin, they had all run errands for him and had leapt to do his bidding.

Ellen recalled the quarrels she had overheard between Pharoah and Dr Redmond. Redmond, who had cared nothing for the opinion of other people, had been the only person openly to disagree with Pharoah. Had anyone else dared to cross him, Pharoah would surely have taken them in the palm of his hand and crushed them. She knew this: he had done it to her.

She could not go home yet, she needed to think. Passing an open café she slipped inside, bought a cup of coffee at the counter and sat down at a table by the window. A spray of sugar speckled the cheap plastic tablecloth and the girl sitting opposite her – perm, short-sighted pale blue eyes a few inches from a paperback – glanced at her and then went back to her book.

Ellen ran her hand over the condensation on the window, making a fan shape. Passers-by blurred behind the glass. She cast her mind back to her own involvement with Marcus Pharoah. The lunch at his house, the drink at the hotel in Cambridge. The dinner invitation she had refused and the cooling-off she had sensed after that refusal. *You could have a promising future at Gildersleve*, he had said to her that evening in the hotel. What had made him alter his opinion of her during those few short weeks?

In telling Inspector Riley about the quarrel she had overheard between Pharoah and Redmond she had made a conscious decision not to be one of Pharoah's men. She could not have demonstrated her independence of mind more clearly. Had Pharoah been punishing her for that? Had he seen what she had done as an act of disloyalty?

But was disloyalty enough? You might dismiss someone for their perceived lack of allegiance, but would you set out to wreck their career? Sitting in the café, stirring her coffee, her doubts about the death of Dr Redmond resurfaced. Dr Redmond's threat, the searching of the cottage, the coincidence – and convenience to Pharoah – of his death. It wasn't that she didn't believe in the possibility of coincidence, but her instinct as a scientist told her to reach for it as an explanation only after every other avenue had been explored and dismissed. So far as she knew, she had been the only person at Gildersleve to have questioned the assumption that the death had been accidental. Well, maybe it had been. But something niggled at her; it always had.

She found herself remembering her cycle ride from Copfield to Gildersleve, how the wind had blown the red and gold leaves from the hazels and how she had breathed in the sharp cool air as she had biked down the slope. Her mind had never felt so clear; sometimes, since, she had stumbled through a fog. In her memory, the two events, her dismissal and the discovery that Alec Hunter was still in love with Andrée Fournier were inextricably entwined. Pharoah's condemnation or that embrace, seen from the window of her lab – which had been more painful to her? In cutting off all contact with everyone she had known at Gildersleve Hall, what had she been trying to escape? The shame of her dismissal or the shame of her unreciprocated feelings for Alec Hunter?

The girl with the perm waved to someone outside the window, closed her book and left the table. She had a choice, Ellen thought. She could forget it, put it behind her, get on with the rest of her life. She might even, if she continued to work hard, be able to revive her stalled career. The bruises were beginning to heal and Professor Malik had given her a second chance.

But the scars ran deep, and besides, she would not be allowed to forget Gildersleve Hall or, indeed, Marcus Pharoah himself. Switch on the radio and you heard his voice, opining on the relationship between science and the arts. Open up *The Times* and you saw his name on the byline of an article. And at the end of the column, a footnote: Dr Pharoah is the director of Gildersleve Hall. Dr Pharoah is on the governing board of this or that institution.

They should add another sentence, she thought: *Dr Pharoah destroys careers with the dash of a pen.*

* * *

At six o'clock one July morning, Riley co-ordinated a series of raids on half a dozen north London properties suspected of being used to store stolen goods. The operation was a success, the suspects were rounded up, and Riley's superintendent, an austere, quiet man, murmured approval.

It was almost eight o'clock in the evening by the time the last of the interviews were completed and the final charges drawn up. Driving home to Tufnell Park, Riley had to wind down the car window to stop himself yawning.

He let himself into the house, put his briefcase in the hall, took off his jacket and loosened his tie. He noticed the difference immediately: the quietness of the house – no radio, no gramophone, no clattering of pots and pans in the kitchen.

He put his head round the sitting room door. He didn't see her at first, and then he did, huddled in an armchair in a shadowy corner of the room, her knees drawn up, her head bowed. Riley crossed the room to her and Pearl raised her head slowly, as if it had become unbearably heavy. A glance in her eyes told him that the febrile vivacity of recent months had been wiped away, like a cloth drawn across a blackboard, revealing only darkness.

He said gently, 'Pearl, what is it? What's wrong?'

She was wearing an old cotton dress and no make-up. Her hair straggled round her face and in her eyes he saw confusion. 'I have to stop thinking,' she whispered. 'Make me stop thinking! Please, John!'

He touched her hand. In spite of the warmth of the

summer day, it felt cold and clammy. 'What do you mean?' he said carefully. 'What is it you don't want to think about?'

She made a slow and visible effort to form a response. 'I have these thoughts in my head. They just go on and on.' She licked dry lips. 'I have to buy more milk or I have to remember that Annie needs to take her plimsolls to school and my mind says it over and over again – plimsolls, plimsolls, plimsolls. I hate it. It wears me out.'

She was biting at a knuckle; he drew her hand away, saying, 'Don't, Pearl, please, you'll hurt yourself.'

'And there are the bad thoughts,' she muttered.

'What bad thoughts?'

'About you. About even Annie, sometimes. You'd hate me if I told you.' She closed her eyes. 'I see the way you look at me. I'm not a fool.'

There was nothing he could say. After a silence, she began to speak again, her voice a thready whisper.

'I'm running and running and I can't stop and I can't get anywhere either. And now and then I feel myself falling, and it's a very dark hole and I'm slipping into it, and if I keep on running maybe I'll stay out of it. I'm afraid, John. I'd rather keep on running than fall into that dark hole again.'

He cupped his hands round her face, so that she looked at him. 'Look, I'm going to go and check on Annie. And then I'll make you a cup of tea and we'll talk, and we'll try and decide what best to do.'

'I don't want to talk. I don't want to think any more.' She looked exhausted. 'I wish – I wish I could just stop *being*! I wish I could just – not be here any more!'

Annie was still awake. Her pyjama buttons were done up wrongly and her hair was still in plaits. Riley guessed that she had put herself to bed. He hugged her and sorted her out, then tucked her in and went downstairs to the kitchen and made tea.

Then he went back to the sitting room. He put the cup of tea in Pearl's hands and waited until she had drunk a few mouthfuls. He said, 'I think you'd better go and see the doctor. She'll be able to give you something that'll make you feel better.'

She looked alarmed. 'I hate those pills! I don't need them! I've been fine, most of the time, you know I have!'

'Just for a while,' he said firmly. 'Just to help you through this bad patch.'

'Oh John.' The tea sloshed into the saucer; he took it from her and she buried her head in his shoulder. 'I'm sorry,' she murmured. 'I'm so sorry.'

Dr Ellis wrote a prescription for Pearl 'to tide her over' and said that she would make an appointment for her to see Mr Morris, a psychiatrist. Pearl looked frightened and Dr Ellis explained that Mr Morris was the expert in this type of case. This type of case? What type of case? With Pearl sitting beside him, Riley didn't feel he could ask.

A week later, they went to see Mr Morris. Mr Morris

preferred to speak to his patients alone, so Riley sat for an hour in the waiting room, leafing through old copies of *Horse and Hound*. When Pearl came out, Mr Morris – imposing, pinstripes, fiftyish – boomed, 'Make your next appointment with my receptionist, Mrs Riley,' and beckoned to Riley. Then he lowered his voice. 'We may have to consider hospitalization if your wife's condition does not improve,' he said. 'We shall have to keep an eye on her.'

They went away on holiday for a week to Devon, where a reduced, dampened-down Pearl sat on a deckchair while Annie played on the beach. When they returned to London, Pearl's mother, Vera, stayed over to help with Annie and the house.

Gradually, Pearl improved. The spark flickered, and she started seeing her friends again. Vera went home to Weybridge and Pearl acted out to Riley some of her conversations with Mr Morris, mimicking his mannerisms. She didn't talk about leaving London any more, though sometimes he saw her standing in the garden, smoking a cigarette, gazing over the fence, a hungry expression in her eyes, as if she was searching for something.

Always afterwards, he remembered the weather. It was one of those disappointing late August days, the sky grey instead of blue and a sharp wind blowing, as if the year couldn't wait to turn to autumn. Before he left for work, Pearl told him that Basil was picking up Annie that morning. She had a dental appointment at ten and was getting her hair done in the afternoon, so it was easier for Annie to go to her grandparents for the day. Riley was to collect her after work from his in-laws. Vera and Basil were going to a party that evening at the golf club.

Driving to Weybridge, the traffic was heavy. Friday night, people heading off for their weekends in the country. It was almost seven by the time Riley arrived at his in-laws'. A nice house, detached, surrounded by lawns and flower beds. He parked on the drive and Basil, who was watering plants, came to meet him.

'Hello, John,' he said. 'This is a surprise.'

Riley was confused. 'Why? Have you changed your mind? Aren't you going out?'

'Going out?'

'To the golf club. Pearl said you had something on at the golf club.'

Basil shook his head. 'Not tonight. You've got the wrong end of the stick, old son. But come in and have a drink.'

Riley said, 'But you've got Annie?'

'No.'

'Pearl told me you were taking Annie for the day.'

He saw then in Basil's eyes something that mirrored his own unease. Basil said, 'I'll go and check with Vera. Don't say anything, John. No point upsetting her.' He strode into the house. Riley followed him.

Vera was in the kitchen, wiping immaculate surfaces. Basil said, 'John's in a bit of a muddle. He thought Pearl had arranged for us to take Annie today.'

Vera looked up. 'No, Pearl said she was taking her

shopping.' Her gaze darted between the two men. 'Why? What's happened?'

'Nothing's happened,' said Basil. 'Everything's fine. As I said, John made a mistake, that's all.'

As they returned outside, Basil said, 'Phone me,' and Riley nodded. On the way back to London, he tried to stop himself thinking, keeping functional only the part of his mind that enabled him to choose the quickest route home. But now and then a picture flashed into his mind. Pearl, lying on their bed. Pearl, wearing the red silk kimono with the dragons on it, eyes closed as if she was sleeping. The dragons, the black sweep of her hair, an empty bottle of pills. *I wish I could stop being. I wish I could just not be here any more.*

Riley parked outside the house and unlocked the front door. He called out Pearl's name as he ran up the stairs.

But she wasn't in the bedroom. And she wasn't in the other bedrooms, or the bathroom. She wasn't in the sitting room or the dining room or the kitchen.

Yet he knew it wasn't right. He saw a movement and went out into the garden, but it was only the branches of a neighbour's tree, soughing in the wind, casting a dappled light on the ground. Back in the house, an envelope on the sitting room mantelpiece caught his eye. Riley tore it open and read the letter inside it.

A Friday night in September, and they were giving a party at the lodging house. People squeezed into rooms and corridors and some of the hardier souls spilled out into the tangled back garden. There was the blue curl of cigarette smoke and Jacques Brel on the record player.

Someone squeezed himself on to the sofa beside Ellen. 'Simon Hacker,' he said, shouting to make himself heard over the chatter and Jacques Brel. He offered her a bowl of peanuts.

'Thanks. I'm Ellen, Joe's sister.'

'I know. I asked someone.'

She had a better look at him. Not bad. Broad shoulders, quite tall. Thirty or so, straight dark hair swept to one side, a round face with brown eyes topped with brows that were raised in a way that seemed to indicate both interest and pleasure. A little thicker round the middle, perhaps, than the sort of man she found herself thinking about, wondering about, on a bus or in a quiet moment in her lunch hour. But not bad.

He fetched two glasses of beer and sat down beside her. He told her he was a chemist, that he had been at the Dyson Perrins Lab in Oxford and had now a junior lecture-ship at Imperial. They had a mutual acquaintance; he named one of Ellen's Bristol friends. Then, shuffling himself round to face her, he said, 'So you were at Gildersleve Hall.'

'I left quite a while ago,' she said. Her usual response to such remarks.

'Can't blame you. Rats leaving a sinking ship.'

'What do you mean?'

'When did you leave?'

'Nearly two years ago.'

'All change since you were there, then.' He had the satisfied air of someone imparting startling news.

Ellen sensed exaggeration, but was interested. Simon Hacker took another draught of beer and wiped his mouth with the back of his hand. 'You'd have been there in Kaminski's time, I suppose?'

Which implied, she thought, that Jan Kaminski wasn't at Gildersleve Hall any more. Which *was* interesting.

'Le Fou du Roi' came to a rousing conclusion. Simon said, 'Cambridge offered him a fellowship. Everyone thought he'd stay at Gildersleve Hall for life. My goodness, Kaminski and Pharoah were almost *married*. Loads of the others have left too. Toby Dorner, but then Harvard's been after him for years. That pretty Frenchwoman. And the Scot, tall fellow, whatsisname, is at King's now.'

King's. Ellen's heart pounded. 'Alec Hunter, you mean?'

'That's the chap.' Simon Hacker drained his glass. 'Would you like to dance?'

They went into the kitchen. Rosemary Clooney was singing something bittersweet, and Ellen let herself be taken into Simon Hacker's embrace. So: Alec Hunter was in London, but that didn't matter because all that had been a long, long time ago, and Alec and Andrée Fournier must be married now, and didn't the bad-tempered pair of them deserve each other. It made no difference to her whether Alec was in Cambridgeshire or London or Timbuktu. And Simon Hacker's hand was running up and down her back, rather as if he were rubbing creases out of her dress, but never mind because she knew that at some point in the evening he'd ask her out to the cinema or for supper. And though she hadn't yet made up her mind what she would say, it would be nice to be asked.

India came into the room. Joe followed after her, with a moony expression on his face. Joe, you idiot, thought Ellen, then looked away, closed her eyes and let her head sink on to Simon Hacker's shoulder.

That autumn, India had decided to be more like Ellen. Ellen would never have got into the sort of mess she herself had, owing people money and being pursued by men she disliked. Ellen had a few mannerisms – that slight raising of the eyebrows when someone said something silly or did something unreasonable, and a quickness of movement as she went about her day-to-day life, as if every moment must be used well. India tried them on, like a new coat, walking a little faster, snapping her handbag efficiently shut like Ellen did. When she found herself getting bored or her mind wandering, she tried to mentally order herself back to attention. She knew how easily you could let things drift. You lay on your bed, leafing through a magazine and listening to 'My Funny Valentine', while around you, abysses opened.

Ellen was one of those people who did more or less the same thing at particular times of the day – eating, going to work, sleeping – but India's life had never been like that. She tried, but events seemed to fling themselves at her, making her do things she hadn't planned to do. Just now, she was trying very hard to arrive at work punctually each day, but it was difficult. She would be about to leave the flat in the morning when a friend would phone, or, because she had been out late the night before, she would pull the blankets over her head when Sebastian brought her a cup of tea and fall asleep again. Or she would wake up in some unexpected bed on the other side of London, with none of her belongings to hand and having forgotten to put a comb in her bag. Miss Maloney, the manager of the art supplies shop, had recently spoken to her about her timekeeping. India had found this lowering: she loved her job and didn't want to lose it. And yet she had detected a certain resignation in herself, a sense that such things were beyond her control. She had expressed this thought once to Ellen, but Ellen had been dismissive of it. 'It's up to you, India,' she had said. 'You can make your life into whatever you want.' Things were very cut and dried in Ellen's world.

India and Ellen were sitting in Ellen's bedroom, eating biscuits and drinking cocoa. Ellen was talking about her boyfriend, Simon Hacker, with whom she had been going out for some weeks. He had a motorbike, on which Ellen rode pillion to cafés or the cinema, where they watched French films. 'He has nice eyes,' said Ellen, 'and we talk about interesting things.'

India had introduced Ellen to some of her more respectable friends and some of them had fallen in love with her, but it had never gone any further than silent admiration.

They found Ellen daunting — too aloof, too brainy, too serious, too beautiful. India had often wondered how on earth it was that so many couples managed to marry. One so rarely met a man who did for everything. One man might be nice to go to dinner with, another might be fun in bed, and yet another might have money, and so on. But eventually the man for going to dinner with would let slip that he had a wife and children in Acton, and the man with the money would reveal a habit of counting every penny in his pocket and begrudge her even a chocolate bar. Or, like Garrett, he might be handsome and charming and funny, but feckless and unreliable too. Miss Maloney might say that she, India, was unreliable, but Garrett was worse. He had a habit of going off for weeks at a time without even sending her a postcard and she had more than once sat in a bar for hours, waiting for him, only to end up having a drink with a complete stranger instead.

India asked Ellen whether Simon Hacker was in love with her, and Ellen looked alarmed, from which India deduced that he might be, but that Ellen wasn't in love with him. India sympathized. There was something about a man telling you he was in love with you that made you notice his faults. Almost as if, by declaring himself to be the sort of man capable of falling in love with you, he showed his poor taste, so that adoration in itself made him undesirable.

Eventually, Ellen stopped talking about Simon Hacker.

India suggested they go and see *The Barefoot Contessa* the following evening but Ellen said that she couldn't because she was going to a lecture. 'I'll come with you,' said India. Ellen said no, it was a scientific lecture, someone she knew was giving it and India would only be bored. India was offended and Ellen, seeing that, sighed. 'Yes, all right then,' she said. 'If you really want to.'

But she *was* bored. The Royal Institution was in a very grand building in Albemarle Street and for a while India enjoyed just looking at it. The exterior was adorned with massive pillars and inside there was marble flooring and echoing corridors. India had never been in a lecture theatre before. The rows of seats were steeply raked; above them a balcony contained yet more seats. All this to listen to a man rattling on by himself for an hour.

It was at first like watching a play: the sense of anticipation, the ripple of interest as the lecturer appeared from the wings, then the applause followed by a sudden silence. India sat still, having promised Ellen she wouldn't fidget. The lecturer, who was tall and dark and film-star good-looking, distracted her for a few moments. He had a nice voice – a Bournville chocolate voice, Peachey would have called it.

But soon the silence and the murmur of the speaker's voice began to send her into an irritated stupor. She noticed every itch, every crease in her clothing. She wriggled, tugging down her skirt, hitching up a stocking. Ellen's eyebrows rose and India tried once more to sit still. She moved surreptitiously, so as not to disturb Ellen again, and scratched her leg.

The lecturer was talking about diseases, something to do with blood. India tried to concentrate, but couldn't make head or tail of what he was saying, and besides, the phrase 'bad blood' had lodged in her mind and stayed there. Could blood be bad? Could some dark taint run through it, staining your character, marking you apart? And if so, didn't that mean that you were stuck with how you were? There was luck, wasn't there, and there were the cards you were born with. Could you make yourself into a different person, as Ellen seemed to believe, or did the dark blood that ran through your veins mean that you had no choice but to submit to whatever events were thrown at you?

At last, from the floor of the lecture theatre, there was a bang and a puff of smoke and everyone clapped. Another man stepped forward and made a short speech, thanking the speaker, and then said, 'The floor is now open for questions.' Ellen was sitting on the edge of her seat, leaning forward, and India thought she might raise her hand to ask a question, but she didn't. The questions, which weren't at all interesting, seemed to go on for ever and India had to bite her lip to stifle a yawn.

Eventually, to her immense relief, there were more thanks, another round of applause, and the audience began to shuffle to their feet.

Ellen said, 'Wait here, India. I'll be back in a moment. Don't move,' and hurried down the central aisle.

India picked up her handbag, stood up and adjusted her frock (black moiré silk with a white angora bolero) and followed Ellen down the steps. Ellen was standing to one side as a group of people huddled round the lecturer. A very fat man with an almost completely bald head spoke to India. He said how interesting the talk had been. 'Dr Pharoah is such a marvellous speaker,' and India said politely, 'Yes, isn't he?' though it had been deadly dull.

Ellen was talking to the lecturer, Dr Pharoah. India went to join her. Ellen gave India a cross look – guiltily, India recalled being told to sit still.

The lecturer said, 'Aren't you going to introduce me to your friend?' and Ellen said, rather snappily, 'India, this is Dr Pharoah. Dr Pharoah, this is Miss Mayhew.' Then a voice called out, 'Ellen! How are you? Haven't seen you for ages, thought you'd emigrated!' and she turned away, looking flustered.

Dr Pharoah said to India, 'What field are you in, Miss Mayhew?'

'I wouldn't say I was in a field exactly.'

'Then you have an interest in the heritability of disease?'

'No, none at all.'

He laughed. 'If you're telling me you were bored, I'll be mortified.'

He was very handsome, quite old, and far too sure of himself. 'I was terribly bored,' she said. 'I almost fell asleep.'

He didn't look mortified at all. 'Then I shall have to remember to talk to you about something else next time we meet.'

'Oh, I doubt if that'll be necessary,' she said. 'I shouldn't think we move in the same circles at all. Good evening, Dr Pharoah.' And as she walked up the stairs of the lecture theatre, India knew that he was watching her.

One Friday evening, Ellen worked late at the hospital to help Professor Malik get through the rush. She had noticed that since their conversation about Dr Pharoah, he had encouraged her to take on more challenging tasks, running some of the tests on her own.

It was eight o'clock before her work was complete and she was able to go home. Taking with her a sheaf of results that the professor had asked her to drop off, she left the lab. She handed in the papers to Sister Casualty and walked out through the Outpatients' Hall. The hospital, and the steps that led up to the front doors, was busy, Friday night bringing its customary collection of victims of drink-induced accidents and fights.

She was making her way down the front steps when a man in navy-blue overalls staggered, stumbling against her. Knocked off balance, she put out a hand to save herself, dropping her briefcase and handbag. She caught a gust of beery breath as the man slurred curses.

A voice said sharply, 'Watch what you're doing!' and a hand reached out to her, steadying her as she fell.

Blue overalls' companion muttered, 'Ted, you lummox,' adding, 'Sorry, miss, he's had a few too many,' as he hauled his friend through the doors of the hospital. Ellen found herself sitting in an undignified manner on the steps, among the sweet wrappings and cigarette ends, holding a stranger's hand.

No, not a stranger. A voice said, 'Hello, Ellen. Are you all right?' and she looked up and recognized Inspector Riley.

He helped her to her feet. Ellen tugged at her skirt and dusted herself down. 'Yes, fine, thank you – oh no, my things!'

Her briefcase had fallen open and a cold, nagging breeze was gusting papers down the steps, strewing them like litter over the threadbare patches of lawn. As they ran around, chasing them, she expressed her surprise at meeting him here, and he explained that two of his colleagues had been injured in a car accident that afternoon, and that he had been visiting them.

When everything was gathered together again, Riley said, 'There's a café over the road. May I buy you a coffee?'

As they walked away from the hospital, she found herself looking at him, reminding herself of him. Tall, with features that were classic, almost severe, he had a kind of restrained handsomeness. A second glance beneath the flare of a street lamp allowed her to see that he looked fatigued, shadows round his eyes and a tightness to the jaw.

He said, as they crossed the road, 'How are you, Ellen? Are you well?'

'Very, thank you.' She explained, 'I work at St Stephen's.'

They entered the café. While Riley went to the counter, Ellen inspected the damage. There was a graze on her knee and, more annoyingly, a hole in her stocking, put on new only that morning. She stacked her papers into some sort of order, put them back in her briefcase and rubbed the grime off her handbag. The espresso machine hissed and gurgled and her gaze moved to where Riley stood at the counter. He had a knack of coming across her in situations that were hardly to her advantage – shocked and scratched after she had discovered Dr Redmond's body, or hurled to the ground by a drunk.

He carried the coffees to the table and sat down. She smiled at him. 'Nothing's missing and only my pride is damaged. Thank you for your help.'

His hand waved away her comment, and his eyes, with their light flickering of green and brown and gold, settled on her. 'So you decided to leave Gildersleve Hall?'

Her mood, which had lifted on seeing him, darkened. 'I didn't *leave*,' she said bluntly. 'I was sacked.'

'Sacked? I'm sorry to hear it. When was that?'

She wondered whether he was revising his estimate of her, remoulding her into the sort of woman who couldn't hold down a job. 'Nearly two years ago,' she said, adding, to spare him the calculations, 'A few weeks after Dr Redmond died.' And, finding that she did not want him to think badly of her, she explained, 'I think Dr Pharoah was angry with me for telling you about his quarrel with Dr Redmond. He told me that wasn't so, but I do believe it.'

She realized that at last she could think about what had happened without shame – and that, she supposed, was something. She told Riley about Dr Pharoah's lecture at the Royal Institution. 'I managed to speak to him when the lecture was finished,' she said. 'He'd written such unpleasant things about me to my professor at the hospital, you see, and I wanted to know why.'

'What did he say?'

'That it had been his true estimation of me at the time. That he was sorry I found my dismissal so hard to accept that I needed to invent fanciful explanations for it. And that I needed to reassess my opinion of my own abilities.'

Riley raised his eyebrows. 'Whew.'

'Quite,' she said grimly. 'I couldn't even think of anything crushing to say in response.'

'One never can at the time.' He smiled at her. 'One always thinks of just the right thing as one walks away.'

'It doesn't matter now. I enjoy my work at the hospital. And I'm loving being in London.'

Checking her watch and seeing with a sinking feeling that she was already late meeting Simon, Ellen apologized and explained that she must head off. They left the café together, she heading for the Underground station, Riley to where his car was parked.

She asked him where he was living now.

'Tufnell Park,' he said.

'And your wife – and you have a daughter, don't you? How are they?'

'Annie's very well.' Something crossed his face; she saw him look about. Then his gaze fell back towards her, unreadable and guarded, and he said, 'Pearl left me three months ago. I haven't seen her since and I've no idea where she is. I've enjoyed meeting you again, Ellen. Take care of yourself.'

Then he walked away from her, in the direction of King's Cross, and was soon lost among the crowds on the pavements.

Ellen and Simon had been going out for more than two months, long enough to get to know each other. They shared some interests, and he was a kind and well-meaning man, but she had found herself noticing certain habits of his: a tendency to fuss about his health and to talk about himself at length, as well as a way of telling anecdotes, his narratives so stretched out and pounded into submission that whatever event he was describing lost any capacity to amuse. She knew that she must break off the relationship, but so far her attempts to do so had come up against the solid wall of Simon's adoration. It was hard tactfully to part from a man who was telling you that you were the best thing that had happened to him for years. She must face up to the fact that tact – and kindness, too, if necessary – must go by the board: she must be firm tonight, and put an end to it.

Sitting on the Underground train, Ellen's thoughts turned to Riley. She was aware that she had talked largely about herself during their brief conversation — perhaps she was catching it from Simon — and yet something terrible and heartbreaking had recently happened to him. His wife had left him, and he had implied that she had also left their daughter. How did you survive something like that? She had found mere dismissal from a job almost too much to bear, and so her heart ached for him. He seemed to her a serious man, intelligent and perceptive and, she suspected, capable of deep feeling, so how would he cope with the absence of a much-loved wife? Had he friends, had he family? Or did he, like so many men, bottle up his emotions?

She knew that she had always been so fortunate in her family. Tightly-knit and united, they were always there for her. She couldn't recall ever having heard a word of criticism from either of her parents, and though Joe might tease her, she had no doubt that he would also have gone to the end of the world for her if she had needed it, as she would have done for him.

She could see clearly the effect that family break-up had on a person whenever she spent time with India and Sebastian. That lack of a solid rock, that absence of anything certain to grasp on to showed through in India's impetuosity — even, perhaps, in her need to take whatever she took a liking too. Ellen could not have said she knew Sebastian well — he was too shy, too wary to permit intimacy. India had hinted at an illness after Sebastian had been sent to boarding school, an illness that had ended up with him being sent home to attend a small, family-run day school. There was a fragility about Sebastian Mayhew that sometimes perturbed Ellen; she was instinctively gentle with him, sensing the private battles he fought.

Well now, Riley. Ellen recalled with some embarrassment now a conversation they had had during those short, unreal weeks between Dr Redmond's death and her dismissal from Gildersleve Hall. She had been angry, and had accused him of not caring enough to find the truth about what had happened to Dr Redmond. Instead of sending her away with a flea in her ear, as she had deserved, he had offered to meet her in the Green Man in Copfield. It had been a generous gesture. He must have been busy with his work and his family, and yet he had made time for her.

She took her address book out of her briefcase and leafed through it. Yes, it was still there, neatly noted, the telephone number that Riley had given her in the Green Man. She wondered fleetingly why she had bothered to note it down – habit, she supposed.

Riley always got up at six so that he could wash and shave before getting Annie up. Mornings, they had a tight time-table. Quarter to seven, he woke her up and gave her a cup of milk. She complained about the milk, said that it tasted of vegetables (Annie disliked vegetables), but he coaxed her to drink it because it was good for her. Then the bathroom, where she washed her face and cleaned her teeth. After she had dressed, Annie ate her Rice Krispies while Riley grabbed some toast and made a shopping list.

When Annie's hair was done, he checked she had everything she needed for school (handkerchief, scarf and gloves, plimsolls), and then Renée, who took Annie to school in the mornings and collected her in the afternoon, arrived. Riley said goodbye to Annie and left the house. Renée, a young Swiss woman studying English at the Berlitz School, was a godsend, filling in the hours when he needed to be at work as well as doing some light housework. Annie got on well with Renée, and had accepted her company without too much fuss.

Riley spent the first hour at work with his superintendent, discussing their strategy for dealing with the various gangland bosses who were trying to carve up London between them. Riley advocated waiting and watching: jump in too soon and you rounded up only the small fry, the puppets, and not the men who pulled their strings or the financial network that supported them. Take the foot soldiers off the streets and more would instantly spring up in their place, while their masters went to ground.

The meeting was finished when a call came in about a body found in a warehouse on Great Dover Street. Needing some fresh air, Riley took Sergeant Davies and drove across the river. The warehouse was the only building left standing on a large bomb site. There had been a frost during the night and ice seamed the water in the puddles. To one side of the area, the pink, geometric shapes of brick walls were rising out of the ground. Near the warehouse, men in overalls leaned on picks and smoked cigarettes.

The victim was forty or so, thickset, with greying black curls. Riley took a good look at him, checking if he had seen him before, but if so, he had forgotten, and anyway, a man looked different with a pickaxe through his skull. He ordered photographs and fingerprints to be taken and spoke to the owner of the warehouse, a Mr Rossiter. Riley registered the Rolex watch on Mr Rossiter's wrist as well as his cashmere topcoat.

He remained at the warehouse until the body was taken away to the mortuary, and then he returned to Scotland Yard. He had Sergeant Davies search through the files for any references to Mr Rossiter. Something nagged at him; he stood at the window of his office, looking out to the grey, scarred streets of London, digging at the memory.

But his thoughts drifted, as they had numerous times since he had encountered Ellen Kingsley on the hospital steps. He recalled his sharp delight in recognizing her, the touch of her hand and her smile. He thought back to the first time he had seen her, at Gildersleve Hall – the fall of her red hair against her white face, and the way she had fought to remain composed in spite of the shock she had suffered.

He, more than most, had reason to distrust the lightning bolt, the *coup de foudre*. Pearl had taught him that first appearances could be deceptive, and that allowing yourself to act on your initial emotional response was dangerous. He would leave a polite note with a porter at the hospital, he decided, to check that Ellen was all right. To do anything more would be to risk dragging himself into the sort of morass he had only recently crawled out of.

The phone rang. Riley picked it up, said his name.

'Hello, Riley,' said Ellen.

Garrett and Clive were doing up a house in Kensington. Heading there after the art shop closed on Saturday lunchtime, India found the door slightly ajar and went inside. It was very cold in the house so she kept her coat and gloves on while she explored. Wreaths of plaster leaves surrounded high ceiling roses, and pale winter sunlight flooded through tall windows. Inside a room overlooking the garden at the back of the house she found an oil painting of three little girls in long dresses. She wondered what it would be like to live in a house like this, to be married and to have three daughters. She found it hard to imagine, had always found a happy marriage hard to imagine, but she liked babies and remembered clearly the day that Sebastian had been born. Her father had woken her up in the morning and told her that he had a surprise for her. He had taken her to the bedroom he shared with her mother, and India had seen the baby in the crib. She had never forgotten the perfection of Sebastian's tiny features or the pearly minuteness of his fingers and toes.

Though marriage and children had rarely seemed more than a fantasy to India, that morning, curled up together in bed, Garrett had told her he loved her. Did she love him? She had little experience of such things so she found it hard to tell.

She went outside. Sitting on a low wall at the edge of the terrace she ate a Wagon Wheel. Garrett came out, shivering, turning up the collar of his leather jacket.

'Give us some,' he said, and India broke the biscuit in half and handed him a piece.

'What's up with you?' she said. He was mooching sullenly round the garden.

'I'm just sick of bloody London.'

'Let's go away then.'

He gave her a sideways glance. 'Yeah, why not? We could go to Paris. Or the south of France, that would be better.'

'Rome,' she said, joining in. 'Or Venice. We could go on a gondola.'

'No, I mean it. You just hop on a train.' Garrett's expression, which had been moody until then, had become animated. 'There's a night train from Victoria.'

'A night train,' India repeated.

'You go to sleep and in the morning you wake up in the south of France. You can catch a boat to Africa from Marseilles. We could go to Casablanca. *Casablanca* — think of it, Indy!'

'I'll go and pack my bathing costume.'

'Will you? Cool!'

'Oh, don't be so stupid! Of course I won't!'

'If it's the money—'

'Feeling flush, are you, Garrett?' she said sarcastically.

'I could get some cash.'

'Get on with it, then.' She stood up, stuffing the empty Wagon Wheel packet into her pocket. 'Then I can go to the shops instead of standing out here in the freezing cold.'

'So if I get the money, you'll come abroad with me?'

'No, Garrett,' she said, with exaggerated patience. 'I won't. And I'll tell you why. Because it's too far away. Because I have to go to work next week. And because neither of us speak French or African or anything else.'

'I learned French at school.'

'Oh yes. *Je suis, tu es, il est.* Very handy. Do you really think that'll get us jobs?'

'Something'll turn up.'

'You haven't even got a proper job here, so why would anything miraculously turn up anywhere else? Why would some Frenchman want to employ someone as dim as you, Garrett?' She was shouting at him now.

'Shut up, Indy.' He looked angry. 'We could work in a café or something. Washing up. You don't need to speak French to wash up.'

She cried, 'Oh, you can be so *stupid!*' and ran through the house and out of the front door on to the pavement. When she looked back over her shoulder, she saw that Garrett was coming after her, his expression one of black fury, and she darted across the road so suddenly that cars hooted and swerved.

A bus was pulling up to a stop ahead; she hopped on

to it. Sitting on the bus, her anger died and she began to weep. It hadn't even seemed to occur to Garrett that she would mind leaving Sebastian, that she would not for one single moment consider leaving him. She and Garrett had been going out in an off-and-on way for more than a year, and yet he had not understood this most fundamental thing about her. Tears spilled over her lids, and the older woman sitting beside her clucked and said, 'They're not worth crying over, ducks. Me, all my kiddies died in a fire in the Blitz. I couldn't stop crying for a week and I've never cried since.'

India got off the bus after a couple of stops and made her way to Oxford Street. She worked methodically, going through the cluster of little dress shops around Great Marlborough Street until she found a beautiful frock, cream-coloured with a slightly dropped waist and a black grosgrain silk bow on the bust, in a shop with only one old lady serving, who sounded flustered when a customer came in to complain about a fallen hem. In the changing room, India folded up the dress and tucked it beneath her coat, then waited until the customer was on her high horse again before slipping out. 'It's too big round the hips,' she called out as she made for the door of the shop.

Outside, she walked smartly away, looking back over her shoulder a couple of times before losing herself in the crowds on Oxford Street. Then she thought of her friend, Michael Colebrook, and headed for his flat in Half Moon Street. She loved Michael's flat, which was cool and dark and orderly. There, she had a bath, did her hair and put on the new dress. When she came back into the sitting room, Michael smiled at her and told her she was beautiful.

They sat on the sofa and watched the television, and afterwards Michael took her to the Trocadero for dinner. Friends joined them, Ed and his wife, a sulky brunette, and Oliver and Vinnie and Justine. India, who loved to be part of a crowd, had a wonderful time. Afterwards, they went on to a nightclub in Leicester Square.

Between dances, wandering round the room, she saw him. He was sitting at a table by the dance floor with half a dozen other people. It took her a moment to place him, then she remembered that Ellen had introduced her to him at the science lecture. He had had a funny name: Pharoah.

He was looking at her. India pretended she hadn't seen him as she walked slowly past his table to the bar. Making out she was searching for something in her bag, she waited to see whether he had taken the bait.

A voice said, 'I do like coincidences,' and India looked up. 'Do you, Dr Pharoah?'

'Especially this sort of coincidence. How are you, Miss Mayhew?'

'I'm very well. I didn't imagine you a nightclub sort of person.'

'I'm delighted to hear that you have imagined me at all. Now, I wouldn't have imagined I'd meet someone like you in a lecture theatre.'

'Someone like me?'

'Someone as lovely as you. May I buy you a drink?'

India asked for a Martini. She was enjoying herself. She would make him fall in love with her, she decided, just for the fun of it. She smoothed down the cream-coloured folds of her frock and chinked her glass against his.

He said, 'I take it that you're not a scientist?'

'I work in an art shop.' She shrugged her shoulders. 'It's just to pass the time. I don't need to do it.'

'Pass the time until what?'

'Until I get married, I expect,' she said airily.

'Are you planning to get married?'

She gave him a teasing smile. 'I haven't decided yet. Maybe I won't. Are you here with your wife, Dr Pharoah?'

He didn't even blink. 'Marcus, you must call me Marcus. And no, I'm with friends. My wife is at home.'

'Doesn't she like nightclubs?'

'Not much, no.'

'But you do.'

'I like to feel that anything can happen. And sometimes, in places like this, they do.'

'What is it you'd like to happen?'

'Something unexpected. Something restorative.' A smile touched his eyes. 'An adventure.'

'I wouldn't have thought you needed adventures, Marcus. You must live a very exciting life, being famous.'

He said modestly, 'Not famous, I wouldn't say. Very few

scientists are truly *famous*. Einstein, Oppenheimer, James Watson perhaps, now . . . only a few.'

India speared the olive at the bottom of her Martini glass. 'How do you know Ellen?'

'Miss Kingsley?' Again, he didn't react. 'She used to work for me.'

'Why doesn't she like you?'

This time, a small frown. 'I'm not sure that—'

'I could tell, at the lecture.'

'A colleague of mine, Dr Redmond, died a couple of years ago. It was very sad, a loss both to Gildersleve Hall and to me personally – he was a friend of mine. Miss Kingsley was working for me at the time. Because the death was sudden, the police were called in. Miss Kingsley told them that she had overheard me quarrelling with Dr Redmond shortly before his death.' Pharoah swirled his drink round his glass, swallowed it, and signalled to the barman for another. 'I'm afraid I have a temper. I'm not proud of it. I was angry with Miss Kingsley because I thought she should have shown greater loyalty. I thought she should have shown *me* greater loyalty. So I dismissed her.'

'Ellen's a very honest person.'

'People like that, one must admire them, I suppose, but they seem to hardly notice the damage they do. It must be nice to have the luxury of such frankness. I had to protect Gildersleve Hall. I've worked damnably hard for it.' His gaze raked round the room. 'And you, Miss Mayhew, how do you know Miss Kingsley?'

'We were at school together. Ellen's my best friend. My oldest friend.'

'Woman are so much better at keeping friendships than we men are.'

'I expect that's because we're more faithful.'

'Do you admire faithfulness?'

'I should think so.'

'I wonder whether it can be an excuse for stagnating, for staying in a rut.'

India wondered whether his wife felt the same. 'Perhaps you're just easily bored.'

'Perhaps I am. But I'm not bored now, so you must tell me more about yourself, Miss Mayhew, and prevent my boredom returning. You work in an art shop, and you're not married. What else can I find out about you? What else do you do?'

'Oh, I have such a busy life. I go to all sorts of places. I've been to dozens of different countries, because of my parents. Daddy's in the Diplomatic Service. We've lived in Paris . . . Rome . . . Venice . . .'

'A diplomat – perhaps I know him.'

This was dangerous: India changed the subject. 'Of course,' she said dreamily, 'my absolute favourite place in the whole world is our home. It's called Applegarth. If you saw it, you'd think it was the most lovely old house you've ever seen. There's a meadow and an orchard and the most beautiful garden.'

'It sounds idyllic. Where is it?'

'In Devon.' India had been to Devon recently with Garrett, delivering a car, and had liked it a lot.

'Are you a close family?'

'Very.'

India could see in her mind's eye the kitchen at Applegarth. It was her favourite room in the house. She knew the furnishings intimately and felt just then a pang of longing for its familiar embrace. There was one of those big old iron ranges, which kept the room warm all the time, and a large pine table laid with blue and white striped china. The curtains were prettily faded florals and the old dresser was crammed with family treasures. Their housekeeper, a rosy-cheeked Devon woman, was washing up, and India's mother was baking scones. Her father looked up smiling from his newspaper as India came into the room. He said, 'And what would my favourite girl like to do today?'

Marcus Pharoah said, 'Don't you agree?'

India started. 'I beg your pardon?'

'I said that one must be thankful that you forsake the pleasures of Applegarth from time to time.'

In his eyes, there was a flicker of something. Perhaps greed, perhaps hunger. Or perhaps he was teasing her, perhaps he had seen through her and was laughing at her. He had somehow got the upper hand in the conversation, and the elation she had brought about that afternoon by stealing the dress collapsed like a burst bubble and was replaced by emptiness, and she discovered that she didn't want to talk to him any more.

The band struck up 'Try a Little Tenderness'. India searched through the crowds for Michael.

'Thank you so much for the drink, Marcus,' she said, politely offering him her hand. 'And now you must excuse me because I'm going to dance.'

Chapter Five

Ellen had rung to ask Riley and Annie to tea. Riley accepted, and the following Sunday he stowed Annie and the bunch of golden chrysanthemums he had bought the previous day in the car and drove to Islington.

There were seven of them to tea in the scruffy kitchen of the four-storey house. Joe Kingsley was a blond, boisterous, masculine version of Ellen, with the same grey, discerning eyes. Then there were the brother and sister, India and Sebastian Mayhew. Sebastian was very young, startlingly angelic-looking, quiet, and though Riley tried to chat to him pleasantly and put him at his ease, nervous. His sister India also looked angelic but you knew instinctively that she wasn't. India Mayhew had a neat, curvy figure, big blue eyes and a bee-stung mouth. Trouble with a capital T, Riley thought privately. Though her boyfriend, Garrett, was sitting beside her, she flirted indiscriminately with all the men, including Riley himself. Riley wasn't attracted to her; he had come across too many India Mayhews in other, darker, situations, girls who were pretty and spirited and vulnerable, to be attracted to her, but he liked her. She kept the conversation going and was generous with her smiles and good humour and kind to Annie, didn't talk down to her, and let her go through her huge, grubby make-up bag and even stick a finger in the pots and potions.

And anyway, why would he have looked at any other woman in the room when Ellen was there? He noted the easy, bantering relationship she had with her brother, and her relaxed gentleness with Annie. Now and then, he caught her eye. Sometimes her amused expression seemed to reflect his own thoughts about Miss Mayhew, to say, yes, I know she makes a lot of noise and flies about, but she's fun, isn't she? And sometimes he saw something else, some emotion he had become familiar with, having seen it on the faces of the women neighbours who had called round after Pearl had walked out, offering cakes and stews and occasionally rather more.

Pity.

Better sort that out, he thought.

After tea, the Mayhews and the boyfriend left, and Ellen got out her microscope and showed Annie how it worked. Half of Riley's mind was on his conversation with Joe Kingsley about rugby, but the other half watched Annie and Ellen. For a long time after Pearl's disappearance,

Annie had woken during the night with bad dreams. By day she had seemed to regress, to go back to the thumb-sucking and tantrums of babyhood, and there had been a few run-ins at school, where she had been disciplined for bad behaviour. However he himself might feel at Pearl's absence, and however much easier he might find it to look after his daughter now that he did not also have to look after Pearl, Annie missed her mother dreadfully, and his heart ached for her. It cheered him to see her smile and exclaim at what she saw through the microscope, her dark head close to Ellen's auburn one.

At the end of the afternoon, Ellen walked outside with him and Annie to where his car was parked. She thanked him for the flowers and he thanked her for the tea. And then, before she could say goodbye and return to the house, he asked her to supper the following weekend.

The phone rang. Thinking it might be Garrett, India rolled off the sofa and picked up the receiver.

'Miss Mayhew? It's Marcus Pharoah. I wondered whether I might buy you a drink.'

India considered Marcus Pharoah's request. Then she said, 'It's very kind of you to ask but I'm afraid I'm terribly busy at the moment.' She put the phone down.

The next night, he phoned again and India put him off again. The third time he phoned, he said, 'Why won't you have a drink with me?'

'Because you're too old,' she said. 'And because you think

too much of yourself, I can tell, and I'm tired of men like you.'

'I'm forty-three,' he said. 'How old are you?'

'Twenty-two.'

There was a silence. She pointed out, 'So you're almost twice as old as me.'

'So I am. I'd have thought you older.'

'I've lived hard,' she said sarcastically.

'You have a presence. So many young women seem unformed, as if their personality hasn't settled yet.'

'You're an expert, are you, Marcus?'

'I was merely making an observation. Do you think age matters?'

'I don't know. When you say "unformed", I expect you mean boring.'

'I find a great many people boring, but I don't believe age has much to do with it. It's more a question of attitude to life. I could point out to you all the advantages of being older. I know the best places to go and I can afford to go to them. I wouldn't expect a great deal of your attention or time.'

'And,' she said, 'you're married.'

'I am married, it's true, but I haven't been happily married for a long time.'

'Men always say that,' said India sceptically.

'Do we?'

'I'm sure you know that you do. You've done this before, haven't you?'

'It depends what you mean by "this".'

'Asking girls out for drinks. You're not going to tell me I'm the first, are you?'

'No. But this is different.'

'Oh dear. They all say that, too.'

'Alison and I have lived separate lives for many years. She has her interests, I have mine. We stay together for the sake of our daughter. You mustn't misinterpret what I'm asking of you, India. You gave me the pleasure of your company the other evening and I'd like to return the compliment, nothing more.'

Liar, she thought.

'I have to go back to Cambridge this evening,' he said. 'I'll be in Claridges's bar between six and seven. Do you know it?'

'Yes. But I won't come.'

He said, 'The thing is, I can't stop thinking about you.'

India smiled, a little sadly. 'That's another thing they all say, Marcus.'

Riley's house in Tufnell Park was pleasant and spacious and contained a great many books, prints and records – a mixture, Ellen saw, leafing through them while he was putting Annie to bed, of classical (lots of Mozart) and jazz. Pearl's presence still pervaded the house. It was there, surely, in the Daphne du Mauriers and Monica Dickenses on the bookshelves, and in the bright, colourful cushions and curtains, with their stylized representations of poppies and seedheads and kites — not Riley's taste, Ellen guessed — and in the photograph on the sideboard of a laughing and strikingly beautiful woman.

When he returned downstairs Riley asked her whether she minded eating in the kitchen; Ellen said no, of course not. It was a large, airy room, the table at one end of it beside French windows looking out to the garden. Annie's paintings and drawings were stuck on the walls and fridge. Ellen guessed that Riley had many memories of eating with Pearl in the dining room, which he found too painful to revive.

'I'm afraid I haven't much of a repertoire as a cook,' he said, but the lamb chops and vegetables were delicious, and she complimented him. He had had to teach himself to cook when he was in the army, he explained, army rations benefiting from some augmentation whenever possible. There followed a discussion about army life, during which they discovered that Riley, an ex-paratrooper, and Ellen's father, then a colonel in the Royal Engineers, must have been in northern France in 1944 at much the same time and not so many miles apart.

He cleared away their plates, topped up their wine glasses, and took a chocolate cake out of a tin. He said, as he filled the kettle to make coffee, 'It's good of you to come, Ellen. I appreciate you making the time.'

'It's a pleasure,' she said. 'Besides, it's helping me to hide from my ex-boyfriend.'

'Ex-boyfriend?' He looked amused.

'He keeps coming round to the house and begging me to come back to him. No, not begging — more pointing out the error of my ways, telling me how much he knows I must miss him.'

'And do you?'

'Not at all. Thus my need to go to ground.'

In the short silence that followed, she examined her words. If there was a fault her family had in common, she thought, it was their reluctance to acknowledge difficult emotional situations with seriousness. The truth was that her break-up with Simon had been unpleasant. She had hurt him and she shrank from that, disguising her reaction with jokes and mockery in a way that was oh, so English.

She said, 'How are you, Riley?'

'Fine.'

'Oh, come off it,' she said, giving him a hard look. 'Your wife walked out on you three months ago. You can hardly be fine.'

He was making coffee; he turned to face her. 'What should I tell you? One day in August Pearl left Annie with a friend, packed a bag and walked out. I've no idea where she's gone and I've no idea whether she's planning to come back.'

'That's awful, Riley.'

'I suppose it is.'

'You must miss her so much.'

'No.' His voice remained level. 'No, I feel relieved. I feel free. I don't miss her at all. I never loved her. There are rather a lot of people I'm having to lie to about this — Annie, of course, and Pearl's parents — but I'd prefer not to lie to you.' His lids dipped down, masking the bitterness in his eyes. 'Have I shocked you, Ellen?'

'Yes,' she said honestly. 'I thought — I suppose I just assumed . . .'

He put the coffee pot on the table. 'You're trying to decide whether it's polite to ask me any more about my marriage. Or whether to tactfully change the subject.'

'I don't want to be intrusive. But I don't want you to think I'm shying away from it either.'

Fleetingly, he put a hand on her shoulder. 'I know. Forgive me. I didn't invite you here to put you through some tortuous social situation.'

She studied him. Ex-paratrooper, policeman: he was probably tough enough to cope with a searching question or two. She said bluntly, 'You must have loved Pearl when you married her.'

'No.' He shook his head.

'You don't seem the sort of man to marry on a whim.' She searched his face for signs of anger or offence; finding none, a thought occurred to her, and she said, 'Oh.'

'Wrong again.' Riley was pouring the coffee. 'Annie was born eighteen months after we married, if that's what you're thinking. Actually, you're pretty much wrong on two counts. I might not have married on a whim, but I asked Pearl to marry me three weeks after we first met.'

She said, 'Was it wartime?'

He gave a grim smile and said, 'Yes.'

'My father believes it's an evolutionary imperative, the rush to find a partner before a man goes off to battle.'

'Does he? He may be right.'

'I saw the photograph. She's very beautiful, Riley.'

'I keep the picture there for Annie.' He handed her a cup of coffee. 'Beauty's not enough, desire's not enough, I learned that very quickly. I went away for two and a half years and when I came home, whatever I'd once felt for her had gone.'

'But you married her.'

'I was bound to her. She had no second thoughts.'

'That was honourable of you.'

'Was it?' He made an impatient gesture. 'I'm not so sure now. Perhaps I cheated Pearl as well as myself.' He was quiet for a moment. She did not interrupt him, sensing the care with which he chose his words.

'I could never make her happy,' he said. 'Not for any length of time. She was never content. And when she was unhappy, she'd pick quarrels about anything. My tone of voice or the expression on my face, or some failing or habit of mine. At first you try to change. Or you fight back. My God, the arguments we used to have. Sometimes they seemed to clear the air, other times they'd go on bruising us both for days. And then Annie came along and after that I fell into the habit of appeasing Pearl. It was easier, you see, less disruptive. I'd be understanding, I'd sympathize with whatever it was that was bothering her because it made for a quieter life. Or if that was impossible I'd try cautiously to make her see sense. But after a while, you start despising yourself. You know you're lying, and that you're acting a part. And I could see that she despised me as well. So I disengaged, I cut myself off from her emotionally. And yet that didn't work either. I ended up letting Pearl get away with things I never thought I'd tolerate in a friend, let alone a wife.' Another clear-eyed look. 'You must forgive me for inflicting this on you, but I need to be honest. I was telling you the truth when I said I felt free. Though I admit I feel a certain amount of guilt as well.'

'You did your best, I'm sure, Riley.'

He frowned, and she wondered whether he was going to comment on the banality of her statement. But he said only, 'Did I? Pearl was unhappy because she was ill, Ellen. I knew then that she was ill some of the time, but it's only now, when I look back, that I can see that she was ill all the time.'

'When you say ill . . .'

'She alternated constantly between depression and euphoria. She could be good company during the early stages of the euphoric phase, but then it always cranked up out of control. Eventually, it would be as if she'd fallen over a cliff. She'd slide into depression, into silence and weeping. She always tried so hard with Annie. I could see the effort it took her sometimes just to speak, and I admired her for that. What I'm telling you is that it took me a long time to realize that the euphoria was part of the problem as well.' Frowning, he ran a hand over his face. 'After she left, I spoke to her psychiatrist. Perhaps if I'd realized sooner, something could have been done. Maybe not. But I couldn't give her what she wanted. And I think we wore each other out.'

'Riley.' She reached out across the table and touched his hand. 'We all muddle along, don't we? Oh dear,' she sighed and gave an apologetic smile, 'it seems to be my day for unoriginal remarks. But poor you.'

He shook his head. 'Poor Annie. And poor Pearl.'

'I think you're still in recovery, Riley.'

'Like an alcoholic, perhaps? You may be right.'

'I could say these things take time, but then I might have to go and shoot myself.'

'Then you'd better not. Ellen, I'm very fortunate – I have my beautiful daughter, I have a comfortable life, and I have my work.' His expression contained a measure of black humour. 'And my work teaches me that there are many lives far more chaotic than mine.'

'I suppose that's some consolation. Have you looked for Pearl?'

'Yes, for Annie's sake. But no trace so far. People disappear for a variety of reasons. Because they want to escape from their problems. Because they need a new start. Because they've started a new relationship.' He put up his palms, spreading out his fingers. 'It's possible. As I said, she wasn't happy.'

He picked up the wine bottle. There were a couple of

inches left and he shared it between them. Then he took the wine glasses and coffee things into the sitting room.

Ellen sat down in an armchair as Riley chose a record. 'I seemed to have talked endlessly about myself,' he said as he put the record on the turntable. 'How crashingly dull for you. How are you? How is your brother? And India – how is India?'

'I'm fine. Though I despair of myself slightly. And Joe's in love with India, the idiot.'

'Poor devil. Why do you despair of yourself?'

'Because I go to work, I come home, I see my friends.'

'It sounds perfectly pleasant to me.' Again, that half-smile. 'In fact I'd have thought it rather enviable.'

No, she thought, she fell too easily into routine, into cautiousness. She was twenty-four years old and sometimes it seemed to her that she might as well have been forty.

'Gildersleve was an adventure,' she said, 'even if it was a rather unpleasant one in the end. But what I do now is run-of-the-mill. You've obviously been through a rough time with Pearl, but at least you felt strongly about her once. I've never been in love with any of my boyfriends. I've never even . . .' She felt suddenly embarrassed, talking about such things with him, but she ploughed on. 'You talk about desire. I can't say I ever felt like that about Simon. Or Daniel, or either of his predecessors.'

'Give it time, Ellen.'

'Why do the wrong men always fall in love with me?' Unexpectedly, it came out as a heartfelt wail.

He said seriously, 'I expect that the others, the ones you might like, think you're unobtainable.'

'Me? Unobtainable?' She laughed, but then, remembering Gildersleve, didn't feel like laughing any more. 'No, it's me who falls in love with unobtainable men,' she muttered.

He was studying her. 'Is it possible,' he said, 'that you don't fall in love with anyone new because you're still thinking of him, the unobtainable one?'

Frowning, she looked away. 'I don't think so. I really don't think so. It was years ago, at Gildersleve. Actually, you must have met him. Do you remember Alec Hunter?'

'A little.' There was a short silence: piano music poured through the room, then Riley said, 'But it didn't come to anything?'

'No. Alec was in love with Andrée Fournier. Do you remember? We shared the lab.'

And as if it had been only yesterday, she found herself recalling the sharp coldness of the season and the equally piercing pain she had experienced on looking out of the window and seeing Alec and Andrée together.

'That was my only experience of unrequited love,' she said crisply, and swallowed the last of her wine. 'And the truth is, it wasn't much fun.'

Then she changed the subject.

India returned to the flat one evening to find Garrett sitting on a stool in the kitchen. He looked a sight, his lip swollen and puffy, a jagged cut on his eyebrow. Sebastian was dabbing at the cut with a flannel.

Garrett said, 'Fell off my bike.'

India peered at the cut. 'You should get that stitched.'

Garrett shuddered. 'Not likely.'

Sebastian dabbed on antiseptic and Garrett yelped. Then Sebastian stuck a piece of plaster over the cut.

'Poor old thing,' India said. 'You've an awful lot of bruises.' Tenderly, she kissed an undamaged part of his face.

Garrett snaked an arm round India's hips and pressed his head against her side. 'I need to talk to you, darlin',' he said.

'I'm very tired.'

'No, I really need to talk to you.'

He followed her into the bedroom and shut the door behind them. India unbuttoned her coat and Garrett said, 'Can I stay here the night, Indy?'

'I told you, I'm dead beat. And my head's splitting.'

'I don't want to go back to my flat.'

India dropped the coat on top of a heap of clothes on the floor. She looked at him suspiciously. 'What's going on?

He sat down on the bed. 'I didn't fall off the bike.'

'So what happened to your face?'

'It was one of Bernie's apes. Bloody Lee.'

She stared at him. 'Garrett, you're frightening me.'

'It wasn't my fault.' He clenched his fists. 'That stupid bastard, Clive.'

India's knees felt wobbly. She sat down at the dressing

table and blobbed cold cream on her face. 'What's Clive done? Where is he?'

'I don't know. I think he's scarpered.' Garrett sounded aggrieved. 'Typical bloody Clive, runs off when it was his idea in the first place.'

'His idea? What idea?' India swung round to face him. 'If you don't tell me what's going on, I'll black the other eye.'

'I told you, it wasn't my fault.' Reading India's expression, he added hastily, 'OK, OK. You know the houses Clive's been doing up for Bernie? Clive had this idea. Sometimes tenants want to move in before a place is finished. They can't find anywhere else, you see, and they see us working there and ask us. So Clive let them. Just a week or two early, while we were still putting the paint on.'

'But Clive told Bernie, didn't he?'

Garrett said miserably, 'No.' He dropped his head.

India felt cold inside. 'He didn't keep the rent? He didn't keep Bernie's rent?'

'It wasn't really Bernie's rent. They hadn't officially moved in.'

'And you knew?' Her voice rose. 'You should have told Clive not to be such an idiot! I suppose he gave you a cut?'

Garrett groaned. 'Just a few bob. Bernie found out somehow, and now Clive's done a bunk and Bernie blames me. When I went back to the flat, Lee was there. He's a brute. He'd have killed me if Ronnie hadn't turned up. I can't go back to the flat, Indy, I can't.'

'What did Lee want? Apart from the pleasure of beating your face to a pulp.'

'The money.' Garrett pulled down a window and flicked out his cigarette stub. 'He said I've got to pay Bernie back the money.'

'How much do you owe him?'

'About thirty quid.'

India stared at him, appalled. 'Thirty? Oh, Garrett!'

'I'll sell the motorbike.'

India thought that Garrett would make five pounds on the bike if he was lucky, but did not say so to spare his feelings.

'You shouldn't have come here,' she said. 'What if Lee had come after you? What about Sebastian?' She began to jab the pins back into her hair. 'I'll go and talk to Bernie.'

She stood up, smoothing down her dress, and inspected herself in the mirror. She was wearing her blue silk. She unpinned the waxed paper flowers and rummaged through her jewellery box until she found a brooch that was probably paste but might pass for diamonds. She pinned it on to the neckline of her frock, sprayed on some Yardley and reapplied face powder and lipstick.

She said to Garrett, 'You can stay here the night, if you like, but you're not to bother Sebastian. And if the doorbell rings, don't answer it.'

'Thanks, India,' he said, and planted his swollen lips on hers. 'Love you, darlin'.'

But he didn't, she thought, as she picked up her coat

and bag and let herself out of the flat, because if he had loved her, really, properly loved her, he would have stopped her going to Bernie.

India looked in on all Bernie's usual haunts and eventually found him in the Blue Duck nightclub in Piccadilly.

On a small stage to one side of the room, a girl in sequins was waving a couple of fans in a dispirited fashion. There was a drumroll and a tinkling of cymbals and the girl finished her number to a smattering of applause. Then the band struck up 'Mack the Knife' and couples took to the dance floor.

Bernie was sitting at a table with his entourage of women. He gave India a knowing stare.

'And what brings you here, India?'

'I'd like a word with you, please, Bernie.'

'Shove off,' said Bernie to the brunette sitting beside him. When she made an offended moue, he called out, 'Don, Gina wants to dance,' and a thickset, dark man came over to the table and yanked Gina out of her seat. Bernie smacked her bottom as they headed off to the dance floor.

Bernie said, 'Sit down, India.'

'Actually,' she said, 'I need to speak to you in private.'

His high-pitched voice squeaked up an octave. '"Actually",' he mimicked, '"I need to speak to you in private." Prissy little madam. Who d'you think you are? Maybe I've got better things to do.'

'Please, Bernie,' she said quietly.

He eyed her, then rose from his chair. She wondered whether he preferred to speak to people seated, a king at his court, because he was so short.

They found a corner away from the band, near the bar. Bernie said, 'I suppose you're here because of that toerag, Garrett Parker.'

'He'll pay you the money back.'

'Maybe that's not the point. Maybe I don't like to be cheated. Maybe I don't like to be made a fool of.'

'Garrett wasn't trying to make a fool of you, Bernie.'

'Ah, but it looks that way.' Bernie wrinkled up his nose. 'It's all about reputation in my line of work. I can't afford to look like I'm going soft. Bad for business. Everyone has to think about their reputation, don't they? You're just the same, India. That's why you turn up your nose at me. You think you're too good for me. You think you're better than those silly cows I go around with. You're thinking about your *reputation*.'

As he spoke, he stared down the front of her dress. Leaning forward, he pressed his lips into the hollow of her throat and murmured, 'I always get what I want in the end.'

India gripped her hands together, trying not to shudder. 'Garrett will give you the money in a couple of weeks,' she said steadily. 'Please, Bernie, as a favour to me.'

Another fish-eyed look, and then he shrugged. 'A week. Not a day longer. Tell your boyfriend he's got something I want. Tell him I'll have it like that,' Bernie clicked his fingers, 'if he tries to cheat me again.'

'Thank you, Bernie.'

'And don't you forget.' Slowly, as if he was sealing a bargain, his head inclined. 'You owe me, India.'

It was almost three in the morning when she got back to the flat. India let herself in quietly, so as not to wake Sebastian. Garrett was sprawled over two-thirds of the bed, snoring through his bloodied nose. India pulled off her clothes, pushed an arm and leg aside, and crawled in beside him. She lay for a long time in the darkness, kept awake by Garrett's snores and the thoughts that wouldn't stop churning through her head. She tried imagining the kitchen at Applegarth, the stove and the print curtains, the familiarity and warmth. She tried imagining her father saying to her, 'What's up, honey? You mustn't worry about anything. I'm here, it'll be all right.'

But she couldn't concentrate hard enough. Instead of the orchard at Applegarth, she saw the house in the woods, the overgrown lawns and the heavy tops of the trees, flopping back and forth in the wind, that second summer.

July 1942. Her mother hadn't left her bed for a week. India managed, just about. Sebastian hadn't been to school for ages and nor had she, but that was all right because everyone seemed to have forgotten about them.

When she took her mother a cup of tea in the morning, Cindy was asleep. India said, 'I've brought your tea, Mummy,' but her mother didn't say anything. She was lying on her side, the blanket pulled most of the way over her head, a fan of fair hair spilling over the pillow. India put the cup and saucer on the bedside table and went down-stairs to give Sebastian his breakfast.

It was a fine day, so in the morning they played in the garden. The house wasn't very nice inside by then, anyway. It had seemed to wriggle out of India's fragile control during the last few months, and there was a funny smell. They spent the morning making clay pots. India filled a bucket with water and Sebastian dug up clay with the little metal spade Daddy had bought for him, ages ago when they had gone to the seaside.

India made sandwiches for lunch, scraping out the last of a pot of jam. She made Sebastian wash his hands under the pump before he ate his lunch. She took a sandwich up to her mother, but she was still asleep. The cup of tea remained on the bedside table, undrunk, cold. She wondered whether she should wake her mother up, but she remembered Mummy saying she felt so much better after a good sleep, so in the end she just left the sandwich and carried the cup and saucer back downstairs.

In the afternoon, she and Sebastian went to the den that they had made in the woods. The den was in a box tree. The leaves made a dark green cloudy roof above the hollow inside, and they used the curving yellow branches for seats. Sebastian played with India's old tea set. He didn't seem to mind that there were only four saucers and one cracked cup left. India breathed in the dusty sharp scent of the box and watched the diamonds of light that filtered through the green cloud. She couldn't remember her mother sleeping so long before. She began to think she should go back to the house and wake her up.

Sebastian was filling up the cup with soil and holding it to the mouth of his toy giraffe. When India told him she was going back to the house, he whimpered. She told him he was to stay in the box tree and wait for her. 'I won't be two ticks,' she said. Neil had used to say this, before he went out to the pub to buy beer, though Neil was always more than two ticks. Sebastian started to cry. Hot with impatience, India said, 'I'll bring you back something nice,' and ran back through the woods.

It was very quiet in the house. She had been hoping that as soon as she opened the door she would hear her mother moving around, or the kettle purring, or 'My Funny Valentine' on the gramophone. She realized, as she went upstairs, that she was frightened, but she pushed that thought away.

Cindy was still asleep. She was lying in exactly the same position as she had been that morning, the blanket pulled up, her hair over the pillow. The sandwich was untouched.

India said, 'Mummy.' Then, louder, 'Shall I make you another cup of tea?'

Her mother didn't move. India felt angry with her. It wasn't fair that she was left to do everything, to keep Sebastian amused and think of things to eat when they hardly had any food. She gripped her mother's shoulder and shook it.

The blanket slipped back. Her hair had fallen over her

mother's face. Gently, India brushed it away. Cindy's skin felt cold, colder than it had in the winter when India had rubbed her feet for her. 'Mummy?' she whispered.

She took the sandwich for Sebastian instead and went back into the woodland. Sebastian wasn't in the box tree, which alarmed India. He might have got himself lost in the forest, like Hansel and Gretel. She ran around for a while, searching for him, calling out his name, and then she caught a glimpse of blue shirt behind a birch tree. He cried when she shouted at him but cheered up when she gave him the sandwich.

They spent the rest of the day in the garden. India didn't like being inside the house now. Sebastian wanted to kiss his mother goodnight before he went to bed, but India wouldn't let him because she had peeked into the bedroom at teatime and had seen that Cindy was still lying on her side, just the same. Sebastian cried again so India told him a story to cheer him up. She wondered whether Sebastian was crying a lot because he was hungry. She was hungry too. After Sebastian went to bed she searched the pantry for something to eat. There was no bread left, no butter, no jam. There were some crackers; she ate half a dozen, though she hated the way they stuck to her tongue and throat. Longing for sweetness, she tried eating a spoonful of cocoa powder but it was bitter and horrid. When it started to go dark, she crawled into bed with Sebastian. She knew that she should go and look at her mother again, but in the darkness she was afraid to. She lay curled up against Sebastian's warm little body, listening to the ghosts. There were ghosts in the house in the woods, she and Sebastian had both heard them. A tapping on a window, footsteps on the stairs when everyone was asleep. She thought she heard her mother walking round the house, a cold hand sliding along a banister, a door opening, the soft sigh of a cushion as Cindy lowered herself on to the sofa. India lay still and frozen in the darkness, waiting to hear the first few bars of 'My Funny Valentine'. Then she pulled the blanket over her head and stuffed her fingers into her ears.

She felt much better when she woke in the morning. Her mother would be all right now and would give her money so that she could buy some food at the shop. India padded along the corridor to Cindy's room.

But nothing had changed. Cindy's face now had an odd look, as if her skin was sinking back into her skull. India could hardly bear to touch her, but when she did, she still felt cold.

A voice said, 'Mummy?' and India, startling, looked up and saw Sebastian in the doorway.

'Go away!' she yelled at him. 'Don't come in!' and he ran off.

It took her ages to stop him crying this time, and he didn't seem right for the rest of the morning. After breakfast, she tried to coax him to have another tea party with his animals, but he shook his head and just sat on the grass, sucking his thumb and holding his giraffe. She wondered whether he was ill and, if so, whether her mother was ill too. The other possibility frightened her too much to think about; whenever it flickered into her head, her mind seemed to go blank.

In the end, she fetched Sebastian's story books and read to him. While she read, she tried to work out what to do. She thought of phoning the doctor and was cross with herself for not having thought of it before.

She let Sebastian make mud pies in the kitchen saucepans, something he was never normally allowed to do. Then she looked in the little notebook in the kitchen, where Cindy wrote lists of things, but the doctor's number wasn't there. She opened her mother's navy-blue handbag and searched for her address book among the clutter of handkerchieves and bottles of pills, lipstick and comb and powder compact.

India went upstairs. Cindy's bedroom was hot and fuggy, so she drew back the curtains and opened a window. She avoided looking at the bed and ran out of the room, closing the door behind her, as soon as she found the address book on the dressing table. Downstairs, she looked through the book. There was no one called 'Dr' anything. But Neil's phone number was there. She imagined Neil striding into the house in his navy uniform and saying, 'You have to think of those children, Lucinda,' and making everything right again.

For lunch, she put everything edible she could find on a tray and took it out to the garden. Sebastian pretended to make cakes out of very old glacé cherries and cream crackers. He wasn't crying so much now and he had stopped asking for Mummy, and when he wasn't eating, he sat with his thumb in his mouth. After lunch, India took him indoors and washed his face with a flannel. She couldn't find Sebastian's own hairbrush, so she teased out the tangles with the comb from Mummy's handbag. He looked better when she had finished with him, but not much. He had a bedraggled look; she saw, looking into the bathroom mirror, that she looked bedraggled too.

There were only a few pennies left in Mummy's purse. Searching round the house, India found a couple more down the back of the sofa. She had intended to cycle to the shop but Sebastian refused to ride his trike, just shook his head and wouldn't say anything when she asked him why not. She almost shouted at him again, but in the end lifted him on to the saddle of her own bike and told him to hold on to her as she pushed it up the road. It was very tiring pushing him all the way up the hill, and it was hard not to cry.

At the top of the hill, she propped the bicycle against a hedge and hauled open the heavy door of the phone box. Sebastian sat on the floor, watching an ant scuttle along the windowframe. India dialled the operator and asked to be put through to Neil's number. Eventually the operator said, 'Putting you through,' and a voice said, 'The Caird residence.' India asked for Neil. The voice said, 'He's not here, dear, he's at sea. Who's calling?'

India put the phone down. She gnawed her lip to stop herself crying. Of course Neil was on his ship – how stupid of her not to have thought of that! She took Sebastian's hand and dragged him out of the phone box. A black cat was walking along the path ahead of them, so she pointed it out to Sebastian, partly to cheer him up, and partly because she needed to distract herself.

Inside the shop, an old lady was talking to Mrs Day. The old lady was wearing a navy-blue beret, like the one India had worn at her London school, and a grey overcoat even though it was hot. When Mrs Day saw Sebastian, she said, 'How's my poppet, then?' Normally, India would have nudged him, because Mrs Day sometimes gave Sebastian a biscuit or an apple, but she knew that there was no point nudging today because Sebastian had stopped speaking even to her.

'Cat got his tongue, Mrs Matthews,' said Mrs Day to the old lady. Then, to India, 'What can I do you for?' She always said this; it was supposed to be a joke, though it wasn't funny at all.

India asked for a tin of pilchards. Mrs Day was very fat, and while she stretched, puffing heavily, to reach the pilchards from the topmost shelf, India stole a look at the old lady before stuffing an apple from the sack on the floor into the pocket of her dress. Mrs Day put the tin of pilchards on the counter and India asked how much it cost. One shilling and tuppence, Mrs Day said, and India said she only had fivepence.

'I don't do tick,' said Mrs Day.

'What have you got for fivepence?'

Mrs Day looked back at the shelves. 'I could do you a piece of cheese. Or some nice carrots.'

The old lady was looking through a cardboard box of old books that had been in the shop since the first time India had come there. As Mrs Day cut the cheese, India nudged a loaf of bread on the counter into her shopping bag.

India put the cheese in her bag and took Sebastian's hand. As she made for the door of the shop, the old lady said, 'Oh, no, you don't, miss.'

India tried to run for it, but the old lady, moving with surprising speed, got between her and the door. 'Look in her bag!' she crowed triumphantly as she grabbed India's arm. 'Go on, Irene, look in her bag!'

Mrs Day heaved her bulk out from behind the counter, and peered into India's shopping bag. 'Oh dearie me.'

'I was going to pay you next time.' India tried to shake off the old lady, but her grip was like iron.

'She's put an apple in her pocket as well. You want to call Constable Gilbert, Irene.'

A man came out of the back of the shop. He was wearing trousers held up with braces over a vest. 'What's all the noise about?'

The old lady said, 'This little madam's thieving.'

'Thieving?'

'I'll sort it out, Reg,' said Mrs Day.

Sebastian was crying. Mrs Day picked him up and made soothing noises. She said to India, 'Why did you do such a naughty thing? A big girl like you should know better. You've got yourself into a lot of trouble.'

'You want to call the constable,' said the old lady again.

'Thank you, Mrs Matthews,' said Mrs Day sharply.

'Thieving,' said Reg.

The policeman lived up the road. They would send her to prison and then who would look after Sebastian? It occurred to India that if Mrs Day felt sorry for her, she might not be so angry with her and then she might not be sent to prison. So she whispered to Mrs Day, 'My mother's dead.'

'Dead?' repeated Mrs Day. India nodded. Mrs Day looked shocked. 'I didn't know. You poor little things. When did she die, dear?'

'Yesterday, I think.'

'Yesterday?'

'She won't wake up.' India kept her voice low so that Sebastian couldn't hear. 'She's in bed and I brought her cups of tea and everything but she won't wake up. And she's gone all cold.'

With difficulty, Mrs Day stooped until she was level with India. Then she whispered, 'Dead? Surely not, dear.'

'I think so.'

'I expect she's just poorly. Reg can go and see if there's anything he can do to help.'

'She won't speak,' said India. 'She hasn't said anything since the day before yesterday. And there's nothing to eat.'

And because she knew that Mrs Day was fond of Sebastian, 'He's crying because he's hungry.'

'You're not fibbing, are you?' said Mrs Day, looking at India hard. 'You wouldn't fib about something like that?'

India pressed her lips together and shook her head.

She and Sebastian were taken into the back room, Mr Day's room, and sat down among the cardboard boxes and milk crates. The wireless was on, playing 'Music While You Work'. Mrs Day gave them glasses of milk and pieces of bread and butter while Mr Day, now wearing a shirt, went out. Sebastian gulped down the milk but India felt too sick to drink hers. When Mr Day came back, accompanied by the constable, India gave Mrs Day an agonized look, but Mrs Day ruffled her hair and murmured, 'We won't say any more about that. Don't fret, dear.'

The three adults talked for while. India tried to hear what they were saying, but couldn't. Sebastian clambered on to India's knee. She could feel him falling off to sleep, getting heavier in the way he had done when he had been a baby and had needed a nap every afternoon.

Through the side door, India could see a garden. Tall hollyhocks raised pink flowers the size of saucers to the sun. A chicken pecked in the dust. India imagined her and Sebastian living with Mrs Day. Sebastian could play in the garden and she could help in the shop. She could cut the cheese with the length of wire and measure out flour from the sack with the scoop and she could put the little brass weights on the scales, something she had always wanted to do.

Reg and the policeman left the shop. Much later, after the grown-ups came back, Mrs Day drew India aside and told her that her mother was indeed dead. She cried at last, though she had known it anyway.

The hard thing was telling Sebastian. He didn't really understand and kept on asking for his mother. India told him that Mummy was in heaven, that she was walking in meadows full of flowers beside a silver river. But he still cried and cried.

India drifted off as the birds sang their dawn chorus, slept through her alarm and slept through Sebastian bringing her a cup of tea. When, eventually, she woke, she looked at her wristwatch. It was half past ten. She screamed.

Garrett moved and said blurrily, 'What's wrong?'

She yelled at him, 'I'm late! I'm late for work and it's all your fault!'

India threw on some clothes, dragged a comb through her hair and ran to the Tube station. She put on a pair of dark glasses and told Miss Maloney she had a migraine, but Miss Maloney gave her a disbelieving sneer and sacked her anyway.

When she went back to the flat, Garrett had gone. India had a bath, washed her hair and lay on the sofa, leafing through a magazine. Another memory drifted through her mind, and she curled up on the sofa, trying not to think about it, but it was there, a shard of ice, and wouldn't be dislodged.

Back in the summer of 1942, India had assumed that she and Sebastian were to go on living at the grocer's shop. But one morning, Mrs Day had told them that they had a visitor. The visitor's name had been Miss Cassidy and she was going to take the two of them to live in a nice house in the countryside.

India, cutting to the quick, had asked Mrs Day whether they were to be Miss Cassidy's children.

Miss Cassidy had given a little laugh, and said, 'Oh, no, I'm just a children's nurse.'

Mrs Day had wheezily lowered her great bulk on to a low chair, looked India in the eye and explained that though she would have liked to have kept them, Reg wouldn't have it. Reg had never wanted kids. Miss Cassidy was going to take them to a lovely home and Mrs Day was sure they would be very happy.

India had said, 'We'll be together, won't we? We'll be able to sleep in the same room? He won't sleep if I'm not there.'

'Of course.'

'You promise?'

Miss Cassidy had promised. Then their things had been packed into their mother's old suitcase and they had left the shop with Miss Cassidy. A bus, two trains and another bus, and then a walk down a long, narrow road between stubble fields. Miss Cassidy had insisted on holding Sebastian's hand even though India had known he would have preferred to hold hers. 'It's the rules, young lady.' India knew that Miss

Cassidy had taken a dislike to her but she didn't seem to mind Sebastian, which was comforting.

It was a long day, and by the time they reached Charnwood, the sun was setting. Miss Cassidy hauled them through gates and down a gravel drive that led to a dusty courtyard on which prams were parked. Then they were taken through a side door and along corridors to a room in which a lady wearing a nurse's cap peered down their throats and inspected their hair for nits.

Eventually Miss Cassidy came back to the room. 'Where to, Matron?' she said.

'The girl to eleven, the boy to six.'

India said, 'We're sleeping in the same room.'

'Oh no, dear,' Matron said. 'Boys and girls never go in the same room.'

Miss Cassidy made to take Sebastian's hand. India grabbed him, hugging him to her tightly. Someone was called, and they prised Sebastian from her. Then they held her back, kicking and struggling, as Miss Cassidy had carried Sebastian screaming out of the room.

The clamour of the telephone seemed to mingle with the memory of Sebastian's screams.

India slid off the sofa and the magazine tumbled to the floor. Picking up the receiver, she said her name.

It was Marcus Pharoah. She was fed up with everything and sick of all of the people she went around with. She needed a change. When he asked her whether she was free for a drink, she said, 'Yes, if you like, I don't mind.' And in the small silence that followed, she wondered whether he felt triumphant or whether some part of him almost regretted the ending of the chase.

Christmas with her family in Wiltshire was for Ellen much as it always was, a pleasant mixture of delicious food, cooked by her mother, squabbles with Joe over boardgames, and long walks with her father over a snow-sprinkled Salisbury Plain.

Something had changed, though. It struck her, on the train back to London, that for the first time she felt that she was going home. Not *leaving* home, on this, her return to the capital, but *going* home.

She went to see her friends. A party put on by some of the men in the lab, with bread and cheese and bottles of beer from the pub. Supper with India and Sebastian, with crackers to pull and the cold remains of a Christmas pudding. And then the phone ringing and India darting out and shutting the sitting-room door while she took the call, and Sebastian raising his eyebrows as he and Ellen washed up, saying, 'Some new chap.'

Ellen wondered what had happened to dark, impudent Garrett, who had danced with her in the Mayhews' kitchen.

She and Riley went for a long walk over Hampstead Heath. Annie ran with the kite along a rough, grassy ridge and the kite thwacked and ducked and then leaped into the air, and Annie's coat flared bright red against the muted greys and browns of the trees.

*　　*　　*

India sold the Dresden shepherdess, the Clarice Cliff jug and the Venetian glass paperweight and gave the money to Garrett to pay Bernie. The sitting room of the flat looked bare without the ornaments. They had belonged to Rachel, and they had sat on the mantelpiece since the very first time India and Sebastian had arrived at her flat. Rachel had let India hold the shepherdess, a rosy-cheeked girl in a tight pink dress. It had seemed extraordinary to India that they should have come to live in a place that contained such things. Though she and Sebastian had been at the orphanage for only six weeks, its aridity had scratched her soul.

India put a vase on the mantelpiece and Sebastian put winter pansies in it, but it wasn't the same. She saw Garrett less often because that wasn't the same either. Bad things had a way of sliding off Garrett, but the scar over his eye hadn't healed well. She had been right, he should have got it stitched. She went to Christmas parties and sometimes Bernie was there and sometimes he was not, but she made sure never to be alone with him, always to be part of a crowd.

In January, she found a job waitressing in a café near the British Museum. It was OK, but it paid less than the art shop. In the evenings, Marcus Pharoah liked to drive her out to the countryside, where they dined in quiet restaurants beside rivers or in market towns. This, India supposed, was because he didn't want to run into any of his friends. He was married, after all. India didn't tell Ellen about Marcus Pharoah because she knew Ellen wouldn't approve. You told people only what they wanted to know: this was something she had learned a long time ago. As time passed, India sometimes felt guilty, but she could see how the conversation would go, and how hurt Ellen would feel that she, India, hadn't mentioned that she'd been seeing Marcus, whom Ellen disliked, for weeks. Why risk Ellen being cross with her for something that would never last?

Sometimes the tables in the smart restaurants were set up beside tall picture windows. Occasionally in the darkness, a rowboat would glide along the Thames, lit by a torch or lantern, a necklace of water tumbling from the oars. The restaurants were the sort where waiters moved silently to pick up your fork if you dropped it on the floor and to pull out your chair when you stood up or sat down. There was the chink of crystal glasses and the gleam of candlelight, and when you unfolded your napkin it was as thick and stiff as cardboard. It was all rather different to India's café in Bloomsbury, where the clientele, a bookish lot, turned pages while spraying cigarette ash on the floor and slopping coffee into their saucers.

She went along with it. A girl needed a good meal now and then, and times were hard. She wouldn't sleep with him because that only made complications. And she was tired of all that, needed a break from men wanting things from her, had begun to feel grubby with it all. India Mayhew, that fictitious creature, daughter of a diplomat, loving child of loving parents, as made-up and insubstantial as a unicorn in a forest, seemed to her almost threadbare, worn through. So she would sit in Marcus Pharoah's green sports car and go along to the smart restaurants in Henley and Newbury, for a while, at least. And then, a few months along the line, he would lose interest in her or she would break it off, and they would forget about each other, no harm done.

Chapter Six

A windy, rainswept Thursday evening in February. The seminar room at University College was already full when Ellen and Professor Malik arrived for a meeting of the Biochemical Society, so they sat in the back row. As an Oxford man stood up to give a talk on the chemical structure of enzymes, Ellen's gaze drifted idly over the audience, stopping as she reached a figure sitting several rows ahead of her.

The line of his shoulders and the mop of black curls seemed familiar to her, reminding her sharply and painfully of her autumn and winter at Gildersleve. Her view of him was partially blocked by his neighbour, a thickset gentleman who blew his nose repeatedly. But she thought – she could not be sure – that it was Alec Hunter.

If it was him, no matter. Hardly surprising that they should run into each other as the scientific community was small and self-selected. She had only to smile and say hello, how are you, and then walk away. It would get it over and done with, their first meeting after Gildersleve. Yet she felt the fast pulse of the blood through her veins as she scanned the room, searching for Andrée Fournier yet failing to find her.

The talk ended and the discussion began. An argument over the interpretation of data was soon under way, people adhering with great passion to different viewpoints. Alec – if it was Alec – said nothing at first, and Ellen remembered how he had liked to keep silent during the seminars at Gildersleve, letting the conversation flow before intervening to tell everyone else they were wrong. She felt a surge of annoyance, recalling his unwillingness to listen, his confidence in his own position, and then wanted to laugh at herself. She was not even sure that it was him. She might have taken an irrational dislike to some innocent stranger.

Then he turned to speak to the man beside her and she caught a glimpse of his profile. The straight nose, firm chin and those eyes, with their slight heaviness at the outer corners and the unlimited depth of their blueness: all these things had fascinated her, once.

He proceeded to demolish with ruthless efficiency the point made by the previous speaker. The discussion became hot-tempered, most of the audience joining in, talking over each other, their voices rising in pitch. Ellen noticed that Alec never interrupted and never allowed his enthusiasm for his subject to inform his tone. These were his faults, a detachment that amounted to indifference, a hauteur that he employed to cut himself off from other people and an impatience with the perceived slowness of others. *Hunter's lord of the manor or some such back home*, Martin Finch's voice echoed, and Ellen found it all too easy to imagine Alec striding in a lordly fashion round the ancestral estates. He was a cold fish and that was the truth of it. She felt sorry for Andrée, crazy for such a man.

Now he was saying, 'If you would merely look at the evidence . . .' and Ellen spoke for the first time.

'The evidence is inconclusive. I'm afraid Dr Hunter is mistaken if he believes the argument to be clear-cut.'

Looking back at her, Alec scowled.

'It's all too easy to draw the wrong conclusions from imperfect data.' It was hard, with that fierce blue glare directed at her, not to fidget, to brush back an imaginary lock of hair or tug at the hem of her skirt. 'Unless you know the whole picture, you can't form a true judgement.'

'There's no judgement to be drawn. These are matters of fact.'

'I disagree. But perhaps it depends on your viewpoint.'

'Not at all. A fact is a fact.'

'But we can be misled, Dr Hunter. We can believe we're seeing all the evidence when some of it is closed off to us. Surely you'd agree with that?'

'There can be good reasons for holding back information,' Alec said curtly. 'Sometimes you have no choice.'

Ellen fell silent, pressing her hands together, stilling their tremor, running her tongue over her lips to moisten them. Her heart tripped as if she had drunk too much coffee, and she had the dull beginnings of a headache.

Neither she nor Alec spoke again during the final quarter of an hour of the discussion. As the seminar ended and the participants shuffled to their feet, Ellen glanced along the rows of chairs. Alec was gathering up briefcase and jacket and turning towards her. Then someone clapped him on the shoulder, engaging him in conversation.

She and Professor Malik left the room. Sherry was served in a common room along the corridor. Warm and overly sweet, it slid down the throat, taking the sting out of a day that had become unpleasantly complicated. Malik left her to speak to one of the University College professors and Ellen found herself on the fringes of a group. She knew that there were layers of inclusion and that she was on the perimeter. She was out of touch, no longer in the heart of things. Worse still, tonight she struggled to concentrate. Phrases – long chain molecules . . . Bragg diffraction . . . carbohydrate polymers – drifted by her but did not latch on. The back of her neck prickled, almost as if she could feel his gaze. Would he seek her out? Would he speak to her? Perhaps not. After all, what was she to him? A former colleague, from a brief time, years ago.

A voice said, 'Ellen,' and she turned.

'Hello, Alec. How are you?'

'Very well, thank you. And you?'

'Marvellous. Did you enjoy the seminar?'

'Not especially. Did you?'

'Very much. How's King's?'

'Good. It's good. I didn't know you were in London.'

Was that a thread or two of silver in the black hair round his temples? Had he put on a little weight, perhaps, in the intervening years? She told him about the hospital, then waited for him to say something patronizing.

But he said only, 'Sounds interesting. Useful, too. Good to know you're doing something of benefit to people.'

Was there condescension in his voice? No, to be fair, she did not think so. She said, 'How's Andrée?'

'Fine, I assume.'

'She wasn't able to come tonight?'

'Hardly. She's in Paris.'

'Oh. Visiting?'

'Working.'

'That must be difficult.'

'Difficult?' A touch of perplexity. 'I don't think so. It was a good move for her. She needed a new start and she never particularly liked England.'

It was her turn to feel confused. 'Do you mean that Andrée's living in Paris?'

'Yes. Has been for a couple of years.'

So, Andrée Fournier had returned to France two years ago. Alec had given no hint that he and Andrée were seeing each other at weekends or writing to each other or making plans for a future together. Did that mean that the relationship had broken up again – that he, Alec, had given Andrée the push again? His uninterested 'Fine, I assume' seemed to imply so, and her anger with him returned.

'Poor Andrée,' she said. 'We were never close, but I can't help feeling sorry for her.'

He seemed about to respond when the man who had been sitting beside him during the seminar heaved into view, breathing asthmatically. 'I meant to tell you, Hunter.' A painful wheeze. 'I was speaking to Bernal the other day . . .'

Ellen took the opportunity to move away. She could no longer see Professor Malik, and the other participants of the seminar had gathered themselves into little groups, sharing gossip or debating problems. She stood by a window that looked out on to a square of asphalt. The rain had got up; she watched the patterns it churned up on the surface of the puddles.

A woman from Birkbeck came to talk to her. A quick glance round the room showed Ellen that the asthmatic man had pinned Alec into a corner and that Professor Malik had gone. The Birkbeck woman was leaving too; talking of crystallography, she and Ellen snapped up their umbrellas as they came out of the building and on to the street.

The rain made a wall of noise that almost muffled the sound of the traffic. As they walked along the pavement, a couple stepped out of a taxi and made a dash for a front door. A delivery boy slung his bicycle with a clang against some railings and hurried down a set of basement steps.

Ellen looked back. There was Alec Hunter, coming towards her, she could see the bob of his black head as he threaded through the crowds. She felt a surge of annoyance. Why couldn't he leave her alone? They had said all that was needed to be said, had exchanged a few pleasantries and a few more barbed comments. Nothing further need pass between them.

Ellen shook hands with her friend, who walked off to her bus stop. Alec drew level with her.

'You seem to think me at fault in some way,' he said. 'I'd like to know why.'

Rain glued his hair to his scalp and she remembered from Gildersleve his habit of forgetting hat and gloves, not seeming to notice the weather. It was a sort of conceit, she thought, the pretension of a handsome man who knew his appeal to women.

She saw no point in holding back. She might as well say what she had been thinking for so long. Perhaps it would puncture his self-regard. Though she doubted it.

'Have you any idea how unhappy you made Andrée? Have you any idea how she felt all the time I was at Gildersleve?'

'Naturally I knew—'

'Then how could you do it? So cruel, Alec!'

'So that's it. You think it was *me* who made Andrée unhappy.' He gave a short laugh.

His laughter fuelled her anger. 'You have to take some responsibility. All those months of moping after you finished with her the first time, and then you start the whole thing up again only to drop the poor woman once more! No wonder she's gone back to Paris!'

She began to walk fast along the pavement, winding between the girls in mackintoshes, who laughed as they ran arm in arm through the rain. Alec fell into step beside her. She waited, weary and disillusioned, for the inevitable justifications.

But all he said was, 'You're wrong, Ellen.'

'When I was at Gildersleve, I thought you had some kindness in you. I didn't think you were that sort of man.'

He caught her hand, halting her. 'That sort of man?'

'The sort of man who likes the chase but gets bored after the conquest.'

His grip slid away. They were standing in the shadow of a shop awning. Swollen drops of rain slid from the striped oilcloth, which cast channels of darkness on his features, blackening the narrowed lines of his eyes and chiselling sharp indentations round his mouth.

'No,' he said slowly. 'I told you, you've got it all wrong. You think you knew what was going on at Gildersleve, but you didn't, not at all.'

'Then tell me, Alec.'

'Not here.' He glanced at his watch. 'I have to get back to my lab, there's some work I need to finish tonight. Will you walk with me?'

She felt great reluctance. 'I don't think I want to.' Yet something in his expression, some unexpected vulnerability, made her explain, 'It was hard for me, leaving Gildersleve. It took me a long time to get over what happened there. I don't want to rake it all up again.'

'You spoke back there about not judging without knowing the true picture. I think you owe me the chance to explain.'

She met his eyes. 'I owe you nothing, Alec.'

'Ellen, please.'

Somehow she found herself continuing along Gower Street beside him. They were silent at first, keeping a distance between them, antagonistic, mutually repelling each other, their orbits never touching.

And then he said, 'Pharoah and Andrée were having an affair.'

Whatever she had expected him to say, it was not that. They were parted by a straggle of soldiers in khaki, who eyed her as she passed, but then, as they joined together once more, she said, 'Surely not.'

'It's true.'

She began to see, as they walked on, how such a thing might have been possible, how such a thing, Pharoah and Andrée, might have fitted into the silences and secrets of Gildersleve Hall.

'When?'

'It started before you came to the lab. You thought I was making her unhappy. I expect I did sometimes, though I never meant to, but Pharoah made her a damn sight more unhappy.'

It seemed to Ellen as if she had been threading through a labyrinth, confused, eyes half closed. 'I didn't know. I had no idea.'

'Andrée and I started dating not long after she arrived at the lab. At first, it was good, we were happy. But then, after a while, I noticed a change in her. Sometimes she seemed elated and sometimes she was touchy and moody. I began to wonder whether she wanted to break it off. When she told me she did, I was cut up, of course, but I accepted it. But then, one day, I found her crying in the lab. She wouldn't tell me what was troubling her at first, but eventually she admitted she'd been seeing Pharoah.'

'But he's married!' Her words, foolish and naive, seemed to echo.

Alec gave a sardonic smile. 'A wife and daughter. House in the country. The picture of the happy family. It's all false with Pharoah, smoke and mirrors. It took me a while to catch on. I was fooled by the façade, just like everyone else.'

She felt the suppressed rage in his voice, a vibration rather than an alteration in volume, like the first rumbles of thunder, a sound like stones rubbing together under the sea.

'Andrée wasn't the first,' he said. 'Pharoah had other girls at Gildersleve, before I started working there. I got Bill Farmborough drunk once and he spilled the beans.'

'Other girls?' she whispered.

'Yes.' That bitter half-smile. 'Perhaps he always has one

on the go. Perhaps he chooses them for their looks. They come to work at Gildersleve, Pharoah turns on the charm, tells the girl she has a great future, takes her along to meetings and conferences. Perhaps Andrée was flattered. Even after he'd finished with her she couldn't seem to see through him. She couldn't seem to see what he was really like, what a liar and hypocrite he was.'

A whirr, a scratch, as the pieces of the puzzle fell into place. Perhaps Pharoah had taken Andrée to a meeting at the Cavendish; perhaps Andrée, blinded by the bright light of his attention, had agreed to go for a drink with him afterwards. Perhaps they had gone on together to dinner somewhere. Andrée, a sophisticated Frenchwoman, would not have run away to the safety of the bus and her lodgings.

Perhaps Pharoah had invited Andrée to his house in Barton. Ellen remembered the Pharoahs' primrose-yellow drawing room, Marcus Pharoah's friends and family, his spoiled, beautiful daughter, and his wife, crying among her orchids. Had Alison Pharoah seen her, Ellen, as her next rival, the next insult? Had she wept because she dreaded the thought of enduring the same humiliation, the same hurt, over and over again?

There were memories she would have preferred to subdue, but they sprang at her now. The hotel in Cambridge on that strange, fogged winter evening, and Pharoah sitting opposite her.

Would you like Rowena to be a scientist, Marcus?

I should love her to be one, especially if she managed to do so while being as charming and attractive as you and Mademoiselle Fournier.

Alec said, 'I couldn't tell you about it when you were at Gildersleve, you must see that. For Andrée's sake.'

'Of course,' she murmured.

Cabs and buses were hurrying irritably along Oxford Street, hooting their horns, windscreen wipers thrashing. Alec saw a gap in the traffic, gave Ellen's hand a tug, and they dashed across the road.

As they reached the other side he spoke again. 'Andrée thought Pharoah would leave his wife and marry her. I don't suppose he considered it for a moment. It's Alison who has all the cash. Pharoah kept Gildersleve going with Alison's money. Alison would have destroyed him if it had come out into the open. She's not the sort to allow herself to be made a fool of publicly.'

Alison Pharoah had been both beautiful and glacial. Pharoah had implied that his wife was mentally ill, depressed perhaps, but maybe Alison Pharoah's depression had been a consquence of her husband's faithlessness.

'How long did it last?'

'Six months. Pharoah finished with her that autumn, a few weeks before Redmond died. He used her. He got her into his bed and then, when he was tired of her, he gave her the push.'

The crowds were being swallowed up into buses and Underground stations. Pharoah and Andrée Fournier, Pharoah dropping Andrée Fournier – and turning his attention elsewhere? To her? Was it possible? Was that, in fact, why Pharoah had sacked her, and was that why he had written that vituperative letter to Professor Malik – not because of what had happened to Dr Redmond, and not because she had told the police about the two men's quarrel, but because she had not responded to his advances, had not become his mistress?

Another memory intruded: herself, looking out of the lab window, Martin standing at her side, as she watched Alec and Andrée kissing in the copse. She said, 'Why did you stay at Gildersleve?'

'Because I hoped she'd change her mind.' Alec sounded tired. 'I thought that if I hung on she'd realize the truth about Pharoah and come back to me. Stupid of me. People go on believing what they want to believe, in spite of all the evidence. She still thought she was in love with him. It took me a long time to accept that.'

'But you still loved her, didn't you?'

His brows snapped together, as black as the rain clouds. 'All those months I'd waited for her, I went on thinking so. When Pharoah dropped her, I was glad for her sake as well as mine. She was in a state, and she was worried about her job, of course. She was in a mess and I was there, and yes, it felt good. I suppose that's why she went along with it, why she said she'd come back to me, because she needed someone then, Perhaps she couldn't face having no one. But there was nothing left. It didn't take either of us long to find that out. It was like breathing oxygen into a dead thing. You wonder, when you look back, whether it was love making you hang on or possessiveness.'

Who else might have known about Pharoah and Andrée Fournier? Not Martin: he, an inveterate gossip, would surely have passed it on to her. Could Dr Redmond have known? Could that have been what he had been referring to when he had threatened Pharoah after their quarrel? *I'll make sure everyone knows the truth about you.* Ellen dismissed the thought almost immediately. Dr Redmond had been uninterested in people. He wouldn't have noticed a love affair, such a thing would not have registered on his consciousness.

London shimmered, the light from the gas lamps fractured and pellucid. When the buildings parted, Ellen caught glimpses of the river ahead, dense and dark and oily. The wind tugged at her umbrella, turning it inside out. Alec took it from her, punching it back into shape, and now, as they walked, he held the umbrella, and they moved closer together, sheltering beneath it. When his sleeve brushed against her arm, it felt resonant, like electricity.

Reaching the Strand, they turned down towards King's. Inside, she noticed that though Alec's laboratory was larger than his one at Gildersleve, the equipment in it − X-ray apparatus, rotation camera, thermostat − gave it a familiarity. Compared to the streets outside, the room felt warm and comfortable.

Ellen draped her gloves and scarf over a radiator and squeezed the rainwater out of her hair, combing it with her fingers while Alec made coffee for both of them.

She said, 'Do you hear from Andrée at all?'

'She writes, now and then. She's working in a government lab in Paris. In her last letter she told me she'd become engaged. There was an old flame, someone she knew at school.'

'I hope she'll be happy.'

As she watched him work, she remembered doing the same at Gildersleve in the aftermath of Dr Redmond's death, sitting in his lab in the basement, letting herself be soothed by the familiar tasks, and by his presence.

'Someone told me Dr Kaminski had left Gildersleve,' she said.

'Jan left a few months after I did. I don't expect he much cared for what Pharoah did after Redmond died.'

'What do you mean?'

'Pharoah had the cottage and the woodland put up for sale. Some builder has bought it. Apparently there are plans to put up houses there.'

Ellen remembered walking in Peddar's Wood after the snow had fallen. The twisted shapes of the trees and the silence. You took pieces from the past and treasured them for ever.

'Poor Dr Redmond,' she said sadly. 'He would have hated that.'

'I think Kaminski resigned because he found it all too hard to swallow. Even good old Bill commented on the indecent haste. Now there's someone who'll stay at Gildersleve until they cart him off in a wooden box. Never the sharpest knife in the drawer, old Bill, but he knows which side his bread's buttered on.' Alec's voice was acid. 'Pharoah got someone in to do your work after you left, Ellen. Some yes-man, dull as ditchwater Cambridge type who went home to his mother at the weekends. It's getting the mix of people that makes a place work and Gildersleve wasn't working by the time I left.' He put down the pen with which he was noting down figures. 'You were missed, Ellen.'

She remembered the first time she had seen Alec Hunter, when he had passed her on the stairs at Gildersleve. That image of him had remained with her, striped by shadows and sunshine and suffused with the tang of the chilly autumn air and the promise of the day.

'I should go,' she said.

'Must you?'

He swung round on his chair, then rose. He took her scarf from the radiator and, standing in front of her, looped it round her neck. Then, with his forefinger, he gently tucked back a loose lock of hair behind her ear.

'I must look a mess,' she murmured.

'No. You look beautiful.'

And then, standing on tiptoe, she brushed her lips against his mouth. He pulled her to him and their kiss was deep and long-lasting. She could feel the beat of his heart through the damp fabric of his shirt and the warm roughness of his face against hers. Her own heart beat out its rhythm, staccato and overemphatic, and she seemed to feel the fast passage of blood through her veins. She needed him to touch every part of her, her skin cried out for him to do so. *Don't stop.* She was unsure whether she had spoken aloud or whether the words drummed inside her head. Their wet clothing caught and dragged, her hands against the flat musculature of his back, his fingertips connecting with the small bones at the top of her spine. She heard the ring of a telephone, the tick of a clock, and she wanted to consume him, and to be consumed.

India knew straight away that Marcus Pharoah was in a bad mood. He didn't get out of the car as he usually did, to hold open the door for her, but leaned across and opened it from the inside so that she could slide into the passenger seat beside him.

He said, 'You're over an hour late.'

'Am I? Darling, I'm so sorry, I've lost my watch.'

His fingers tapped the steering wheel. 'I thought you weren't going to turn up.'

'You could have come into the flat.'

She said this knowing that he felt awkward doing so. He had once, when she had been late before, done exactly this. He and Sebastian hadn't got on; Marcus had tried to talk to Sebastian, but Sebastian had been mutely terrified of Marcus.

He said, 'I don't mind ten, fifteen minutes late. It's a female prerogative, isn't it? But an hour and a quarter . . . we may have lost our table at the restaurant.'

'That's all right, I'm not hungry.' India picked up her bag and climbed out of the car.

He looked furious. 'I dislike impoliteness. Lack of consideration. It makes you look cheap.'

Cheap. Slowly, she turned to face him. 'I didn't forget and I wasn't busy. Maybe I didn't want to see you, Marcus. Maybe it's as simple as that.'

His eyes narrowed. 'Rather a change of heart. What's wrong? Haven't I come up with the cash quick enough?'

'I wouldn't touch your money!'

'Then why are you here?' He reached into a pocket, drew out a handful of change, and hurled it at her. Shillings and sixpences rolled over the pavement; she stepped back. He said, smiling, 'Go on, India, pick it up, you know you want to.'

'I might be cheap,' she yelled at him as she walked away, 'but you're a conceited pig!'

A bus had drawn into the road ahead of them. India ran along the pavement and jumped on to it. It was crowded and she had to stand on the platform. She was wearing a short black jacket with a fur collar over her blue silk; the conductor said, 'Where are you heading for, Cinderella?'

'Anywhere,' said India. She saw through the window Marcus Pharoah's car draw out from the kerb with a screech and a streak of green into the traffic.

After several stops she alighted and walked the rest of the way to Garrett's flat in Victoria. You knew where you were with old friends, she thought. They knew what you were.

India climbed up three flights of stairs and knocked on a door. She called out, 'It's me, Garrett!'

A key turned in the lock. She saw, beyond Garrett, the open rucksack on the bed. He let her in, closed the door, then rammed home the bolt.

'Where are you going?'

'Back home for a while. Oliver's driving north tonight. He said he'd give me a lift.'

'Garrett, you can't. You'll hate it.'

'Clive isn't coming back and I haven't much work. And I don't like the way Lee looks at me.' He stuffed a crumpled shirt into the rucksack.

'Were you going to leave without telling me?'

'I thought you were fed up with me.'

'I am.' With her fingertip, she traced the red line of the scar above his eye. 'You're one of the most annoying people I know.'

He looked down at her, frowning. 'I'll miss you, Indy.'

She gave him a kiss and then left him to his packing. Not bad going, India, she said to herself as she walked along the street. Quarrel with one man, say goodbye to another, all in the same night. She told herself that it didn't matter, and that both men, in their different ways, were equally annoying, but it made her feel miserable to think how these things always went wrong for her, as though they had slithering, evasive lives of their own, and she found herself longing for the sanctuary of the flat and Sebastian.

Two days had passed since the night Ellen and Alec had kissed. During that time, winter had returned, speckles of snow dancing in the grey, attenuated air. A blizzard was sweeping over the entire country, roads were blocked and vehicles abandoned, livestock stranded on hill pastures.

Alec did not call. She began to feel uneasy. She lay on the bed in her room, reading and writing letters, the radio on, waiting for the phone to ring, the knock on the door. She couldn't go out to see anyone, India or Riley or any of her other friends, because she needed the phone to ring. She found herself going through the events of the evening minutely, putting them in chronological order because that seemed to matter. He had touched her first – his finger, brushing back a lock of her hair, the memory of which even now, in its aftermath, made her shiver and squeeze her eyes shut – but it had been she who had initiated the kiss, she who had stood on tiptoe and touched her mouth to his.

Over and over, she ran it through her mind, slow motion. Perhaps he hadn't intended to kiss her. Perhaps that had been a friendly, brotherly gesture, that sweeping back of her hair. Perhaps she had taken him by surprise, kissing him, and his response had been automatic, what any man might do when a woman threw herself at him.

She phoned King's, left a message. At the hospital, she centrifuged blood samples and separated serum and waited. In the privacy of the ladies' cloakroom at lunchtime, she washed her hands and combed her hair and paused, looking at her reflection in the mirror. Her face was flushed and a film of sweat lay on her forehead. Had she been careless? Had she forgotten to wear her gloves, and brushed a finger against the contents of a test tube or petri dish and caught a fever? No, she knew she had not. It was only the memory of the shame of what had happened that brought the heat to her face. She had not merely kissed him, she had clawed at him. She had dug her fingers into his hair, had pressed her body against his. God knows what would have happened if she hadn't heard someone come to the door. She might have torn off their clothes, as wild as Bacchus's followers in the painting that Daniel had admired in the National Gallery, with their reaching, contorted limbs and dishevelled garments. She might have let him take her standing up against the wall, like a streetwalker. She had disgusted him. It was understandable that he hadn't called.

Snow pelted the pavements as she walked to work. She was becoming familiar with shame, with its twists and turns and its habit of tapping you on the shoulder in the middle of the night and keeping you awake with its sly, taunting grin. Alec might have a girlfriend. He might have been about to tell her about Andrée Fournier's successor when she had lunged at him. How would she bear it, if they were ever to meet again? She would have to leave the hospital. She would have to leave London, just as she had begun to feel truly at home there.

Snowdrifts were trapping passengers in trains and the RAF had given up hunting Russian submarines and had turned instead to dropping fodder for stranded sheep. Professor Malik told her of a job going at University College; listlessly, she began to pull together a letter of application. She went to see India, but India was in an odd mood, talking and smoking too much, and her company grated. Riley suited her better; they shared a pot of coffee and listened to 'Blue Haze' and talked about not very much. The notes of the piano fell like the raindrops that had struck the pavements as she and Alec had walked along the Strand. Riley had once told her that men thought her unobtainable. He had been wrong, though. Not unobtainable at all, just desperate. But when the record was finished, she hurried back to Islington to see if anyone had left a message.

One evening, one of the lodgers took an overdose of sleeping pills and had to be rushed off by ambulance to hospital. Ellen and Joe sat in the waiting room as Dave's parents battled through a flooded East Anglia to their stricken son. They spoke in muted tones, looking up whenever they heard the clack of a nurse's shoes on the polished lino. A girl, suggested Ellen. Joe shook his head. He didn't think so. He'd always wondered whether poor old Dave batted for the other team. He shrugged. He wasn't sure, they'd never spoken about it. Perhaps Dave had thought he would disapprove, chuck him out, call the police. Dave had mentioned a friend who'd recently been arrested on charges of indecency. Perhaps that had preyed on his mind. Joe didn't give a damn, had no interest in what other people did in bed. And anyway, you fell in love with whoever you fell in love with and there was nothing you could do about it. He sounded despondent; Ellen, looking at her brother, reached out and squeezed his hand, and thought of India, and what she did, almost without thinking, and was aware of resentment.

The next day, when she woke, the sky was a clear and flawless blue. Though the cold seared, a sharp frost made London glitter, as if made of crystal. How rarely did one act on impulse. How rarely did one allow oneself to be swept along by feelings, by passion. If she never saw Alec again, should she regret what had happened? No, because it had come from her true self. She had spoken with her true voice, had allowed her body to speak for her. When she was an old woman, when she was alone and her beauty gone, she would look back on that evening and smile.

Travelling home at six o'clock, she noticed that the intensity of the cold had ebbed a little. In the hallway of the Islington house, puddles had formed on the checkered tiles. She swept up the brown envelopes that lay muddying beneath the letter box. As she glanced through them, the telephone rang. She picked up the receiver.

The operator told her that she was putting through a

call from Nottingham. And then, on the other end of the line, she heard Alec's voice, greeting her.

Ellen sat down on the bottom stair. Thank God he had got through to her at last, Alec said, he'd been trying for days. He had been in Scotland: his mother had phoned late on the night he and Ellen had met. She had been taken ill and he had driven up through the night and the following day to be with her. But he had become stranded, marooned on Seil Island by the snow. The phone lines were down and even after his mother had recovered and he had made it back on to the mainland, many of the roads had been impassable.

Relief flooded through her like wine: she wanted to laugh. *Hoping to get home tonight — depends on the roads — snowdrifts as high as Colditz.* The line was breaking up, interspersed by crackles. The front door banged open and Ellen had to squeeze aside to allow one of the students to get past her. *Missed you*, he yelled, over the interference, and she yelled back into the receiver, *I missed you too*. He said, *When I get back*— and then the line went dead.

She put down the receiver, and sat for a while, prolonging the moment, and then she gathered up her gloves and scarf and bag and went upstairs.

The identity of the body in the Great Dover Street warehouse, the curly-haired man in the cheap suit, had been established after house-to-house inquiries. George Clancy had been a Dubliner who had lived at various addresses during the nine months he had spent in London prior to his death. A phone call placed by Riley to the Garda in Dublin had established that Clancy had a cousin there as well as a criminal record – nothing major, but ugly little crimes: extortion, assault and battery and demanding money with menaces. The Garda spoke to the cousin, who grudgingly agreed to arrange a funeral.

It was always possible, of course, that one of Clancy's past misdeeds had come back to haunt him, that some Irishman with a long memory had thought it worth his while to get on the ferry and cross the Irish Sea and stick a pickaxe in Clancy's head. But Riley didn't think so. Forensic tests had confirmed that the Dubliner had died in the warehouse, which had been used, Riley was certain, to store contraband. So, Clancy had either had an unlucky accident, had made a bad choice of place to sleep the night, or he had been lured to the warehouse by his killer. Riley suspected the latter.

So now Riley and his team were combing back though Clancy's months in London, trying to work out what he had been up to and why he had come to die in the warehouse. In the weeks before his death, Clancy had lived in lodgings near Borough Market. A West Indian family had since moved into the room; not knowing what else to do with his belongings, they had packed them into a cardboard box which they handed over to the sergeant who interviewed them during the house-to-house. In the box was a notebook containing addresses, one of which was for a house in Camden that Riley had been interested in for some time. The house was rented by a petty criminal called Terry Curran, who had served prison sentences in the past for handling stolen goods, and who went to the same drinking dens as Rex White, who ran a string of gambling houses and brothels in north London.

Riley had questioned Mr Rossiter, the owner of the warehouse, until Rossiter had brought in an expensive lawyer, who had accused the police of harassing his client. The expensive lawyer had, in the past, worked for Bernie Perlman, who was in much the same line of business as Rex White. Rossiter, his lawyer, and Perlman were sometimes to be seen sharing a table at the Blue Duck nightclub in Mayfair. Though White and Perlman had a great deal in common – greed, and a fondness for violence – they existed in competition. London gangsters each had their own patch of territory, their stake in an area which they enforced through protection rackets and brutality. Bernie Perlman's territory took in the Borough and a large area south of the river. Rivalries – someone's tame hoodlum trespassing on someone else's turf, for instance – could spark off a war to the death. It seemed probable to Riley that George Clancy had worked in some menial capacity for Rex White and had somehow stumbled upon the Great Dover Street warehouse and its contents. And that the warehouse itself was used by Bernie Perlman. Clancy's death, Riley suspected, had been intended as a warning.

He had Sergeant Davies and a detective constable watch

the Camden house, but Davies became over-enthusiastic one night, and, while the constable slipped off to buy chips, went to investigate a van parked outside the house. Davies appeared at the station the next day with a black eye and bruises. After Riley had reprimanded him for checking out the van on his own, he got Davies to describe the men who had attacked him. One had been small, bald-headed and stupid-looking, said Davies; the other – the bastard who had kicked him in the stomach – had short ginger hair and a pale, fleshy face. He looked . . . spectral, added Davies with a shudder. Riley, who hadn't suspected Davies of a poetic soul, sent him away to write up his report and help the police artist draw up a mugshot.

So far, there was nothing to link the various elements – the murder, the stolen goods, the gangland rivalries. Riley could see some of the spiders, but not the web. His desk was heaped with manilla files; more box files were stacked on the shelves and floor. Somewhere in the sheaves of paper might be the piece of evidence that he could use to bring Perlman and White to justice. Though Riley doubted it: the biggest spiders were always careful to place themselves – and their paper trail – out of reach. Words and figures jangled in front of his eyes; he slid the papers back into the file and closed it.

Riley rose and went to the window. Staring out at the sea of roofs and twists of smoke from chimneys, he let himself think of Ellen. It was over a fortnight since he had last seen her. Their careers, and Annie, and a certain wariness on his part, meant that they met only infrequently. And yet he had grown closer to her. He had confided in her the true nature of his feelings for Pearl. He remembered the bitter taste of his jealousy when she had spoken to him of Alec Hunter.

In the immediate aftermath of Pearl's leaving home, Riley hadn't looked for close involvement with anyone. He had concentrated on giving Annie a stable upbringing and on his work. And then he had encountered Ellen on the steps of St Stephen's hospital. At first he had wondered whether there was in his instant attraction to Ellen a warning echo of his infatuation with Pearl, back in 1944. By now, such reservations had fallen away. Ellen was not Pearl. She was neither changeable nor unpredictable. She was intelligent, kind, generous, thoughtful and beautiful, and he loved her, loved her completely and utterly, loved the reality of her and not the illusion. He loved the small scar on her forehead, a relic of a fall from a tree when she had been a child, and he loved her grace and her economy of movement and the passionate flow of her hands as she talked.

Riley glanced at his watch. It was nearly seven o'clock. His in-laws, Vera and Basil, were staying over at his house to look after Annie. Easy enough to squeeze a free hour out of the evening.

He went into the adjacent office, where he borrowed an *Evening Standard* from a colleague. Running an eye over the Entertainments columns, he caught sight of an advertisement for a concert at the Wigmore Hall that Saturday. What did she like, what were her tastes? He gathered his raincoat and briefcase, left Scotland Yard and drove to Islington.

One of the students let him into the lodging house. Riley went upstairs, skirting round the uncollected post, anoraks and muddy football boots scattered on the treads.

Ellen was in the kitchen. 'Riley,' she said, turning to him, kissing his cheek. 'How are you? Would you like some tea? How's Annie?'

While they talked, he noticed her smile and the way she darted around, making him tea, finding him a biscuit, removing a pile of books from a chair so that he could sit down. He found himself taking great pleasure in her response to him: it gave him optimism. You could run through a relationship like a balance sheet, totting up meetings and recollecting conversations. Or you could read the turn of a smile, a brightness of eye.

He explained about his in-laws staying over, then said, 'Are you free on Saturday?'

'I'm afraid not. What were you thinking of?'

He masked his disappointment. 'Nothing in particular.'

Ellen put the tea in front of him and dug a packet of sugar out of a cupboard. Then she said, 'Riley, I must tell you, the most wonderful thing has happened.'

A boy in a checked shirt came into the kitchen, yawning and opening cupboards. Ellen dropped her voice and sat down next to Riley.

'Do you remember I told you about Alec?' Her eyes were shining.

'Alec?' A slamming of doors, a crash, and another loud yawn as a cheese grater was unearthed.

'Alec Hunter. At Gildersleve.'

Yes, he remembered Alec Hunter. *Only a little*, he had said to Ellen when they had spoken of him before, but that had not been true. He remembered Hunter clearly enough. A little spoiled, Riley had thought, recalling how Hunter had hardly looked up from his work and had brushed off his questions with an obvious lack of interest. Clever, hand-some, and – Riley had gleaned this from the remark of another Gildersleve scientist – well-off. A man who was used to the world dancing to his tune.

He said, 'What about him?'

'I saw him a couple of weeks ago, at a meeting. He was there. I knew he was in London, and then I saw him. I could hardly believe it was him at first.'

As she spoke, the words spilled over each other in joyful little phrases. The pleasure Riley had felt, seeing her, began to shrink, and he steeled himself for what he knew must come next.

'We're going to the theatre on Saturday,' she said. 'That's why I can't come to the concert. We just – well, we hit it off straight away.' She flung him another smile. 'Do you remember what I said to you about the wrong men falling in love with me, and me falling for the wrong men? Well, this is different, I know it is. It's so wonderful – and we both feel the same!'

A heavy awareness of his own capacity for self-deception

mixed with an uncontrollable flash of dislike for Hunter. He said, 'I thought you told me Hunter and Miss Fournier were together.'

'That was all a mistake. They were seeing each other for a few months and then they broke up.' Her voice dropped to a murmur. 'Alec told me that Andrée was having an affair with *Pharoah* when I was at Gildersleve. Isn't that extraordinary?'

He could smell her perfume; he moved away from her. Disillusion made him speak harshly. 'Good God, it sounds like a hotbed of intrigue. I suppose that's what happens in these places that are cut off from normal society.'

'It wasn't *Alec's* fault, Riley.'

'No?' He rose, abandoning his tea, which now seemed to taste sour. 'Miss Fournier . . . and now you . . . He has a knack of adapting to circumstances pretty quickly.'

'*Riley.*' She had flushed.

'You are sure that the affair with Miss Fournier is really over?'

'Andrée's been living in Paris for the past two years.' Ellen sounded angry. 'I can't think why you're being like this.'

'Because I don't want to see you hurt.'

'I won't be.' The words were hard and crisp.

The silence that fell on them was interrupted by the grating of cheese and the sawing of bread. Riley picked up his briefcase.

'I should go.'

He said goodbye, managed to paste some sort of smile on his face. Which slipped away as he walked to the car. Two things were plain to him. One was that Ellen was infatuated with Alec Hunter. The other was that there had never been a moment when she had considered him as anything other than a friend. He saw himself through her eyes now: older, staid, the father of a child.

A *husband*. However much he might feel his marriage to be at an end – and however drastically Pearl herself had finally ripped it in two – they were still tied in the eyes of the law. At any moment Pearl might return home, bringing with her a trail of emotion and drama. He would not live with her again as man and wife, but Annie's presence meant that there would always be a tie between them. Ellen must see this, even if he had not, until this moment, fully realized its implications. He might *feel* free, but he was not. No wonder she had thought Alec Hunter a better bet.

Parking the car outside his house, he sat for a moment, hands resting on the steering wheel. Stop fooling yourself, Riley, he thought wearily. Ellen wasn't with Hunter because she thought him a *better bet* – or because he was younger or more dashing. And nor was she *infatuated*. Ellen had chosen Hunter because she had fallen in love with him. It was as simple as that.

India didn't hear from Marcus Pharoah for a month. She thought he'd had enough, wondered whether she cared. Though she missed the dinners, the attention.

One evening, the phone rang.

'I was trying to see whether I could manage without you,' he said, 'but I don't seem to be able to.'

'You sound as though you mind about that.'

'It would be simpler if I felt otherwise.'

'Is that what you want, Marcus, a simple life?'

He laughed. 'No, of course not.' A pause, then he said, 'I'm phoning to apologize to you. What I said to you that evening was unforgivable. I'd had a bad day. I told you that I have a temper. I try to keep it under control, but sometimes I fail.'

She was feeling generous. 'It's all right. I was awfully late.'

'Did you miss me, India?'

'Enormously.'

'Liar. I know a wonderful place by a watermill. Famous people go there – actors and politicians. I've booked us a table.'

'Rather presumptuous of you, Marcus.'

'If you turn me down I shall have to ask some dry-as-dust colleague. I'm hoping you'll take pity on me.'

They dined in a glass conservatory at the back of the building. Palms in brass pots were dotted on the black and white tiles. Outside, lanterns lit a lawn that ran down to a millpond.

India was ravenous, eating every scrap of food, and would have licked her plate had she not been on her best behaviour. The waiter poured her a second cup of coffee and at Marcus's request brought another plate of petits fours.

Marcus said, 'I was worried about you, all this time.'

'I don't believe you.' She smiled at him. 'I don't think you're the sort of person to worry about anything.'

'I worry about all sorts of things. Whether I can coax a grant out of this or that organization, whether I'll manage to stay awake through a particularly dull speech. And you, India. I worry about you. You need someone to look after you.'

'Mummy and Daddy do.' She put a miniature choux bun into her mouth whole. 'I told you.'

'Of course you did.' Pharoah took out his cigarette case and offered it to her. He flicked his lighter and India leaned forward, cupping her cigarette.

He said, 'What's the matter with your brother?'

'Sebastian?'

'I don't mean to pry, but there's something wrong, I can see that.'

She saw no reason not to say, 'Sebastian had a nervous breakdown. It was when we were children, when we were at boarding school.'

It had been wartime and Rachel had been working for the Ministry of Supply and had had to travel around the country. So, boarding schools. It must have seemed like a good idea at the time.

Pharoah slid the ashtray across the table to her. 'What happened?'

'Sebastian ran away but then they found him and brought him back to school. But in the end he had to go home to Aunt Rachel's.'

'Your parents—'

'They were busy,' she said quickly, covering herself.

'Did he see anyone?'

'A psychiatrist, you mean? Yes, lots of them. There was a nice one, Sebastian liked her, she seemed to help.'

'And—' He broke off, frowning, tapping the filter tip of his cigarette on the tabletop.

'What, Marcus?' She looked at him coolly. 'Sebastian isn't dangerous, anything like that, if that's what you're concerned about.'

'No, of course not. He seems a gentle soul.'

'He is. He's the nicest person in the world. I'd do anything for him.'

'Your loyalty does you credit. What I was going to ask you – and I hope you'll forgive my intrusion – is whether you've ever suffered similarly yourself.'

'Do you mean, have I ever had a breakdown?' She gave a loud peal of laughter and some of the other diners turned to stare at her. 'No, never.'

'Some doctors believe there's a genetic inheritance, that these things run in families, but I'm not convinced. I believe personal experience counts for a great deal. If your brother, for instance, found boarding-school life too difficult for him.'

Or if he had to play in the garden while his mother was

lying dead in the house, she thought, but said, 'Yes, I expect it was that.'

'And now? How is Sebastian now?'

'He's fine. Most of the time, anyway.'

'But you still worry about him.'

That he had noticed surprised and impressed her. 'I don't want him to be ill again, that's all. He gets upset about all kinds of things – beggars in the streets and whether there'll be a nuclear war. I never think about things like that. What's the point? I can't do anything about it so I may as well have fun now.'

'A very sensible philosophy.' He rested his cigarette on the edge of the ashtray, frowning, and said, 'It *puzzles* me, what I feel for you.'

'Puzzles you?'

'Yes, I think that's the word. I feel there should be a solution, an explanation. I feel I should be able to put my finger on it, to pinpoint exactly what it is that troubles me about you.'

'I hadn't thought of myself as troublesome.'

'Really, India?' His gaze seemed to dissect her. 'Is that true?'

She pouted her lips into the shape of a kiss. 'I expect you're drawn by my startling beauty.'

'Yes, it may well be that.'

'Or my cleverness, or my wonderful sense of humour.'

'I think it's because you like to put on this exterior. You make yourself look pretty and you laugh and you chatter.

And all the time you try not to give anything away. One longs to know what lies beneath.'

She had expected to see criticism in his eyes, or that expression of cynical perception that had disconcerted her before. Instead, to her surprise, she saw sadness.

When he spoke again, his voice was quiet, almost as if he was struggling to explain something to himself.

'Me, I like to know,' he said softly. 'I'm a scientist, after all. I like reasons, explanations. I like to understand. I don't like to feel *invaded*, taken over. I don't like to feel *touched*.'

Alec Hunter had seeped into every part of her life. His image was there, slotting itself into her mind as she worked in the lab, distracting her. It startled her to recall how, before, she had been so neat, so contained, so tidily complete. Now, her desire for him seemed to leak through her nerve endings, flowing into her world and colouring it. Her mouth was bruised with his kisses; as she looked down the microscope she ran the tip of her tongue over her lips, tasting them. She felt his touch, as if it, too, had left its mark, a bruise on her skin, invisible, painless. She had to sift him out of her thoughts or nothing would have got done.

Spring tumbled in, daffodils nodding in the lawns, blue skies showing between fleets of rainclouds. When the weather was fine, Alec waited for her outside the hospital at lunchtime. Sometimes they walked to a small park where dogs barked and sparrows flurried down from the trees and then rose up again like a gust of brown leaves. Once, a child blew bubbles from out of a plastic pot, mouth pursed up, coaxing iridescent globes that bounced and bobbled and clung to each other. A stream of bubbles danced through the air, their colours shivering from pink to blue, swirling like oil on water in the moment before they burst.

Every four weeks Alec drove to Scotland for a long weekend, to visit his mother. He followed a routine established over many years, driving up on a Friday, stopping only for short breaks, reaching the island late in the evening. He took his mother into Oban for shopping and lunch and ferried her to visit friends, and headed back to London early on Monday morning. Rather an endurance test, he admitted.

In his absence, Ellen's days mislaid a dimension and what had once been solid and substantial became flat and featureless. She picked up her old life as if it was a duty, and it took an effort to find much to savour in it. How had she existed before, in such a wilderness? She caught herself sometimes boring her friends, Alec this and Alec that. But what could she do when she struggled to find meaning and delight in anything that had no connection with him?

In his basement flat in Clerkenwell, a waxed jacket hung on a hook and books were stacked on the shelves: Graham Greene and Aldous Huxley and Schrödinger's *What Is Life?* As the weeks passed, her belongings migrated to the flat from the lodging house: a pair of socks, a paperback book, a lipstick and a bottle of shampoo.

Her clothing blotted the floor, white and navy-blue. A cream-coloured slip clung like a ghost to the back of a chair and nylons curled into question marks on the carpet. The mattress was lumpy and unforgiving, stuffed with horsehair which worked itself out in tufts through the striped ticking. The rises and falls of the mattress tried to push them together and pull them apart, but they clung on to each other, drowning sailors in a choppy sea. Afterwards, they lay between the sheets, peaceful, languorous, limbs too heavy to move, the flat of her palm on his chest, feeling the slowing pulse of his heart.

He would leave the bed and pull on a pair of trousers and wander into the kitchen. She would see the hollow of his spine and remember how she liked to place kisses along its length. She would see the sheen of sweat on his shoulders and would recall the scent of him, which was impressed on her own skin. She would watch him through the open door, filling the kettle, spooning out coffee, as he tossed phrases back to her like gifts: a word or two on the progress of his work, a remark about an acquaintance. Sometimes she wondered whether there wasn't something desperate about it, something diminishing in the urgency of their bodies, that dragged them into this room, tearing off their clothes as they fell on the bed.

Only sometimes. Mutely, their bodies spoke for them, an intimate language, a press of flesh on flesh or the touch of a finger as feathery as a penstroke. *I love you, I love you. My love, my darling, my red, red rose.*

She was making coffee. *Any Questions* was rattling away on the radio and Alec was buttoning up his shirt, towelling his hair.

'I have these nightmares,' he said. 'I get to the end of the experimental process at last and finally I've got some decent results. I've almost wrapped it all up and then I hear that some chap at Cambridge or Edinburgh has done everything I have and more. Or – and this is worse – some colleague, some chatterer, comes into the lab when I'm working, runs an eye over my notes, and says yes, but what about the something-or-other?'

'Something-or-other?'

'Some vital point I've completely managed to overlook. A hole in the entire theory that I should have noticed but haven't and when it's pointed out to me, I realize that it's all going to fall apart, years of work down the drain and me looking a complete fool.'

She kissed him. 'Get your results written up, then forget about it. We could go away for a weekend as soon as you've finished.'

He ran his fingers through his damp hair. 'It's always the same at the end of a big project. There's a sort of dread attached to it. You've been chewing over the same thoughts for months or even years and they've worn thin. You can hardly remember what it was that excited you in the first place and yet everyone's about to pick it over, looking for errors. I wonder if you ever get over it, the fear of failure.'

'Dr Pharoah once told me there were two different types of scientists. There's the single-minded and methodical, and the erratic but inspired. I'm single-minded and methodical, of course. That was why I minded so much when Pharoah said I was slovenly.'

They amused themselves, putting their mutual acquaintances into categories. Denis Padfield and Bill Farmborough had both been plodders, Alec said. He doubted if Farmborough had had an original idea in twenty years.

'Martin was erratic but inspired, obviously. Jan Kaminski had a good mind but Pharoah dumped all the administrative work on him so he didn't have the time to do original research. Pharoah might have liked to portray Gildersleve Hall as a breeding ground of genius, but there were only ever one or two people there of any real talent.' Alec swirled round the last half inch of coffee in his cup. 'Redmond was the one who had the reputation when Gildersleve first started up. Kaminski once told me that Redmond never forgot anything. He could refer word for word to a book he'd read ten years earlier.'

Alec put on his jacket and dropped his keys and wallet into a pocket. As they left the flat, he said, 'Perhaps Redmond was sidelined because he didn't fit in. He was a bit of a commie and I don't suppose that helped. There was an argument once, in the dining room. Some fellow from the Treasury came to dinner and Redmond had a go at him. He still believed all that communist claptrap – the death of capitalism, common ownership of the means of production, the whole lot.'

They walked to the Tube station. Buses lumbered along the road; through their mud-flecked windows, Ellen saw the blurred shapes of tired people, slumped in their seats. It occurred to her that whatever discussions had taken place in the dining room of Gildersleve, she would not have been privy to them, because women had not been allowed to dine there. She was aware of a sudden distaste, along with a feeling of relief that she had left Gildersleve. Other scientific institutions might not have the same prestige but neither did they treat their female staff with such casual contempt.

'Kaminski disapproved of Redmond's communism,' said Alec. He held her hand as they headed down the steps into the ticket hall. 'After all, his country was pretty well torn apart by the Russians. In the war, Redmond's politics would have been overlooked because we were all supposed to be on the same side. Times have changed, though.'

Alec bought tickets; on the escalator Ellen stood one step in front of him. His hand rested lightly on her shoulder and she threaded her fingers between his. Alec was right: with the coming of the Cold War times had changed, and America in particular no longer welcomed those with left-wing leanings.

Waiting on the platform they stood face to face, her hands tucked into his jacket pockets. They talked of their futures, which had, over the passing months, come to exist not in parallel but to converge.

A hot, rushing wind, and a train drew into the platform. The carriage was crowded and they had to stand by a door. His arms steadied her as the train rocked and screamed through the tunnels.

And she heard him say, 'I want you to come to Scotland with me, Ellen. I want you to meet my mother. And I wondered, would you marry me? Would you? I know we haven't been seeing each other all that long, but why wait? I knew after a week, didn't you?' She saw in his eyes a mixture of hope and anxiety. 'I don't know how we'll work it out, but it's what I want. Is it what you want too, Ellen?'

And she could only say with utter certainty, 'Yes, Alec. Oh yes.'

Chapter Seven

Michael's father had died. When he returned to London after the funeral, India went out for a drink with him, to keep him company. They went to the Colony Room, which Michael said was a good place for getting plastered.

He told her about the funeral. 'Awful. No grace or meaning. And no one could sing the hymns. We're a tuneless lot, the Colebrooks.'

'I've never been to a funeral. They didn't let Sebastian and me go to our mother's because they thought we were too young.'

His round black robin's eyes studied her. 'You haven't missed much. Dismal affairs.' He gave a cackle of laughter. 'I suppose that's the idea.' He took two cigarettes out of a case, lit them both and passed one to India. 'I sometimes think I envy the Catholics. At least there's some *passion*. But I don't, not really. Sex I approve of, but passion's dangerous. It makes people act out of character.'

A naval rating with a sweet, smooth boy's face asked Michael for a light and Michael passed him his cigarette. Then he said to India, 'A little bird told me someone had seen you with Marcus Pharoah,' and she shot him a glance.

'Do you know him?'

'I wouldn't say that I *know* him.' The sailor handed back the cigarette and Michael smiled at him. 'I've met him at the odd dinner or reception. But of course, one knows who he is. Did you know that he's divorcing his wife? Or I think it may be the other way round, she's divorcing him. He has rather a reputation.'

'Are you warning me off, Michael?'

'I'm telling you to be careful, that's all. Pharoah has a public face. If it became known that you and he were having an affair—'

'We're not.'

'People will assume that you're having an affair, India,' said Michael gently. 'There'll be gossip. Actually, there already is.'

If it was not a love affair, this thing between her and Marcus, then what was it? It was not a friendship, that was for sure. They quarrelled as often as they were nice to each other, and though Marcus might not have so much as kissed her, she knew that he wanted to.

Sometimes she thought she should have tried harder

at school. Then she could have been a nurse or a teacher or something like that. Then she would have been respectable. She had always meant to be respectable, could never quite work out how it had turned out otherwise. Marcus Pharoah was cool, watchful, elegant and powerful. Though these qualities attracted her, they disquieted her as well. India acknowledged power but at the same time saw it as a threat. Confronted by it, naked and gleaming, she found herself compelled to wriggle out of its hold.

Coming out of Glasgow, Alec and Ellen headed north towards Loch Lomond. Their pace slowed to accommodate the winding road which ran along the foot of the mountains where the steep, rocky slopes were darkly wooded or dense with russet-coloured bracken. To the other side of the car, the houses and trees parted now and then to reveal an island or a castle and the shining black surface of the water.

At Ardlui they stopped to drink tea in a hotel on the north end of the loch. When they had finished they stretched their legs in the hotel garden, walking down to where shrubs with dark green leathery leaves walled a narrow path that led to the shore. A yacht, white sails belling in the wind, tacked in the breeze. Standing by the chill water, Ellen's touch went instinctively to the ring on the third finger of her left hand. She and Alec had chosen it together, three diamonds on a gold band.

Back to the car and then on and on, through Crianlaroch and Tyndrum, beside mountains that rose in gaunt grey peaks to the sky, their slopes scarred by falls of scree or forested by birch and rowan. Rivers meandered through flat-bottomed valleys that even in the afternoon sunshine seemed barren, bleak and ominous, or rushed and cascaded from the heights of rock and boulder, catching the light and fragmenting it to crystal.

On again, through the port of Oban, past its harbour and hotels, and then along a narrow road that rose and fell with the contours of the hills. When another vehicle came towards them, Alec had to tuck the car up on to the verge to allow it to pass. The shores of a sea loch, strewn with bladderwrack, glittered in the fading sunshine, and fir trees made a dense impenetrable mass that fell away suddenly, revealing a sea dotted with distant blue-green islands. In the garden of a white cottage, a woman unpegged washing from a line as a flurry of rain smudged the windscreen of the car. The sun came out from behind the clouds and a rainbow shimmered before dissolving into the air.

They drove over the arched stone bridge that spanned the distance between the mainland and Seil Island. It was nicknamed the bridge over the Atlantic, Alec told her, because the water that ran through the narrow channel flowed from the Atlantic Ocean. On the island, more low white buildings – a pub, a shop, a church – clustered round the far end of the bridge, and then the road headed away from the small settlement, threading beside marsh-land where reeds swayed, feathery and fringed, and past derelict, roofless stone buildings, before winding up again into the hills. Sheep dotted the upper fields and the trees that grew on the windswept tops had bent and twisted, stooping low to keep their grip on the earth. And Ellen felt that sense of freedom that comes from the unearthli-ness of islands, from being cut off from solidity and the everyday.

As the car reached the summit of the hill, Alec braked and pulled into the side of the road. In the time it had taken them to drive from Oban, dusk had fallen. They looked down from the high ground to the coast, to a silken sea and the wide, inky sky beyond. Cliffs jutted, one behind the other, like wings on a stage set, enclosing a bay, and a strange landscape of fields and ponds and stone heaps scat-tered the shallow coastal plain. Ellen saw a dozen low, white houses as well as a few more substantial buildings. Some of the houses had small, square gardens, thickly walled, thrown like deckled grey playing cards over the undulating grass.

Where the land met the sea the sand appeared to have been scorched, burned to a band of black rubble which pushed itself up into jagged rocks on to which waves rushed and sprayed. In other places the shoreline had narrowed to a charcoal-coloured ribbon. Sheets of water, enclosed by black barricades, made glassy lakes, some square in shape, others circular or oblong. The last of the sunlight trembled on the horizon, leaving behind it a streak of luminescence and an armada of islands, some sizeable, others little more than pinnacles of rock, a few huddled close to the coast of Seil, others evanescent fragments, almost lost in the distance.

She turned to Alec in delight. 'It's so glorious.'

'Isn't it? Nearly home now.' His hand ran along her thigh. 'I'm afraid we're going to have to be on our best behaviour for the next week.'

'No creeping through the corridors at night?'

'My mother's very conventional about such things.' They were kissing. 'She's a regular churchgoer.'

'I wouldn't dream of trespassing on her hospitality.'

'I shall dream about it every night.'

The hoot of a car horn; Alec pulled away, gave a wave to the driver of the vehicle. 'That's Bill Maclean,' he said. 'He rents land from my mother.'

He put the car into gear, pulled back on to the road and headed downhill. Ellen breathed in the salty sharpness of the sea. They followed the road round the perimeter of the bay, slowing as they reached a gate set between two tall hedges.

'Home at last,' said Alec, and swung the car up a steep driveway.

It was impossible in the dusk to tell the extent of the gardens that surrounded Kilmory House, but as they headed up the drive Ellen saw lawns and borders unfolding to either side of the car. And then the drive swung round in a wide curve through trees, and there was the house itself, larger than the other houses Ellen had seen on the island, long, two-storeyed and white-walled, its roofs a series of slated gables.

Light shone through a front window and a lamp was lit in the gravel courtyard where a Land Rover was parked beside a pair of stone urns. Then the front door opened and a black Scottie dog shot out, yapping. A small, slim, dark-haired woman followed it.

'Hamish! *Heel*.'

Alec climbed out of the car. 'Hello, Mother.'

When they embraced, the top of his mother's head barely reached Alec's chin. Mrs Hunter reached out her fingertips to touch her son's face. 'Darling, I was so worried. Did you have a dreadful journey? I've been expecting you for hours. I was afraid there'd been an accident. Those roads . . .'

'There was some heavy traffic in Glasgow and we stopped at Ardlui for tea, that's all. Ellen needed a break.' Alec put his arm round Ellen's shoulders. 'Mother, meet Ellen.'

Mrs Hunter took Ellen's hand. 'Welcome to Kilmory House, dear. Alec's told me so much about you.'

'It's very kind of you to invite me to your home, Mrs Hunter.'

'Och, it's no trouble at all. Alec's friends are always welcome.' Mrs Hunter laughed and put a hand to her throat. 'So silly of me, sitting indoors all afternoon, waiting for the pair of you! And on such a wonderful fine day! I didn't dare go out, because I was sure that the moment I so much as slipped through the door to buy a bottle of milk you'd turn up.'

Alec looked concerned. 'We wouldn't have minded. You shouldn't have stayed indoors because of us.'

'Dear, I wanted to be here to welcome you, that's all. And Catriona very kindly offered to fetch the milk.'

'Cat's here?'

'Yes, she came home for a wee break. I knew you'd want to see her so I asked her to supper. But we mustn't stand out here chatting, Ellen will catch cold.'

Alec carried the suitcases into the house. The hallway was tiled in slate and panelled with dark wood. On a side table stood a bowl of tulips and two photographs, one of Alec, dressed for hiking, against a background of hills and sky, the other a portrait of a man in naval uniform.

In the better light inside the house, Ellen was able to see Mrs Hunter more clearly. Her features were regular and finely cut, and her eyes were Alec's, dark blue and almond-shaped. Her wavy dark hair was streaked with iron-grey and her complexion was tanned and seamed with a cobweb of lines. She was wearing a tweed skirt and a blue woollen jersey, on the collar of which was pinned an agate brooch bordered with pearls.

Mrs Hunter showed Ellen upstairs. The room in which she was to stay for the next week was at the front of the house. Ellen, who felt guilty, remembering the stop at Ardlui because she had wanted to see Loch Lomond properly instead of through a window of a car, as well as an earlier break to buy postcards, exclaimed about the freshness of the decor and the warmth of the fire in the grate.

'I'm afraid we still need a fire, even in May,' said Mrs Hunter. 'No doubt in London you'll be throwing windows open to let in the sun. Come down when you're ready, dear. Take your time. There's no need to rush for our sakes.' She left the room.

Ellen rushed. She unpacked her suitcase, shaking out clothes crumpled from their two-day journey, and hung them in the wardrobe. She would have loved to have soaked in a hot bath but instead quickly washed, cleaned her teeth, brushed her hair, and changed into a green and white striped blouse that seemed to have survived its incarceration in the case without too many creases. Then she powdered her nose and reapplied lipstick. She wondered who Catriona was. Alec had not mentioned her before. A schoolfriend, perhaps, or a neighbour's daughter.

A last quick glance in the mirror and then she left the room. On the landing, Chinese vases stood on the side tables, and oil paintings, seascapes mostly, hung on the walls. The corridor wound through the building, doors leading off it to more rooms, and there were unexpected steps as the floor changed level. The house had a settled look, as if what was contained inside it had been there for generations. The hollows in the crimson-brown wood of the stair treads reinforced the impression of permanence.

She found Alec in the drawing room, talking to a tall, thin man with whitening fair hair and a weatherbeaten face. He was introduced to Ellen as Donald Frazer, a friend of the family.

Alec poured her a sherry. 'Cat's helping my mother with the supper,' he said.

The predominant feature of the room was a floor-to-ceiling, five-sided bay window. Chairs and sofas were arranged inside the window, which looked out over the bay, where a dull bronze light now delineated the horizon. Standing at the window, Alec told her the names of the islands, which were melting into the darkening sea and sky. On a fine day, he said, you could see as far as Islay.

The door opened and a tall, slim young woman came into the room. 'Marguerite's made far too much, as usual,' she announced. 'We shall all have to stuff ourselves silly.'

'Cat,' said Alec, 'come and meet Ellen, my fiancée. Ellen Kingsley, this is Catriona Campbell.'

Catriona's long, dark, curling hair was caught back in a ponytail and tied with a navy-blue ribbon. Her eyes were well-shaped and thickly lashed, and her pale complexion was flushed pink along the cheekbones. She was wearing a simple pleated kilt and an oatmeal-coloured jersey, no jewellery, and, so far as Ellen could tell, no make-up.

'Welcome to Seil Island, Miss Kingsley,' said Catriona,

taking Ellen's hand. 'We've all been dying to meet the girl who's captured Alec's cold heart at last.'

'Unfair,' said Alec, smiling.

'It's perfectly true and you know it. What's your secret, Miss Kingsley? I shall have to find out. Alec, you never alter a jot. So unfair to those of us who are growing grey.' Catriona's hands had come to rest on Alec's shoulders. Her lips pressed against his, then she spun away.

'I'm dying for a drink,' she said. 'Not that frightful muck, Donald.' Mr Frazer had opened the sherry bottle. 'A proper drink.'

Catriona flung herself on to a sofa. Frazer handed Catriona a whisky. 'Go away and leave us in peace, Alec,' said Catriona. 'I want to talk to Miss Kingsley.' She patted the seat beside her and Ellen sat down. 'You must be exhausted. Seil Island's a long enough trek from Glasgow. It must be an awful fag from London.'

'Do you live in Glasgow, Miss Campbell?'

'I'm a nurse at the Royal Infirmary. I share a flat in Garnet Hill Street with some other girls.'

'Do you enjoy nursing?'

'Well enough.' Catriona grimaced. 'There are no jobs here. All the young people work on the mainland. Alec tells me you work in a hospital too.'

'Yes, in a clinical laboratory.'

'I'm sure that's much more glamorous than nursing. I'm a staff nurse, so I can leave all the bedpans and bed baths to the juniors, thank goodness. There's a ward sister's post going but I can't decide whether to apply. The pay would be better but all the ward sisters are old battleaxes. I can't help thinking it goes with the job, like a dark blue uniform.'

Ellen laughed. 'I can't imagine you a battleaxe, Miss Campbell.'

'Can't you?' Miss Campbell raised her eyebrows. 'I can. Sometimes, when it's been a hard day and I'm tired and I want to go home, I hear myself barking out orders to the pros in that tone of voice. You know – impatient, fed up with having to say the same thing twice. When I was a pro, I used to hate it when staff nurses spoke to me like that.' Catriona took a mouthful of her drink, closed her eyes and gave a satisfied smile. 'Mmm. I'll say this for Marguerite, she always keeps a good whisky in the house. But I promise I won't talk about work any more. It's such a relief not to have patients moaning at me for a day or two, so I'm not going to spoil my break by thinking about them for a moment.'

'Does your family still live on the island?'

Catriona nodded to the window. 'You see those lights over there on the far side of the bay? That's our house. My father was the doctor for the islands until he retired two years ago. If I look out my bedroom window when I wake up and can see Kilmory House, I know it's going to be a fine morning. If I can't see it then we're in for some lousy weather. But I don't mind the bad weather here. You can start the day in a rainstorm and by the end of it you'll be sitting in the sun. In Glasgow, it can rain all day, never stops, such rain and greyness.'

'This is such a beautiful part of the world. You must miss it.'

'Oh, I wouldn't say that I particularly miss the island.' Catriona's eyes, hazel flecked with green, met Ellen's. 'When Marguerite told me you and Alec were driving up, I thought of trying to cadge a lift from Glasgow. But it seemed a bit of a nerve, asking you to put up with an old girlfriend in the back of the car.'

Old girlfriend. Well, that was something Alec hadn't thought to mention. Ellen said, 'We wouldn't have minded at all. Perhaps on our way home.'

'How long will you be here?'

'A week.'

'A *week*. Goodness, how brave of you. I'm only staying a couple of nights. I've become rather attached to civilization – cafés and cinemas and decent shops, things like that.' Catriona touched Ellen's hand. 'How dreadful of me. I haven't congratulated you on your engagement. I hope you and Alec will both be very happy.' She gave a sideways glance towards the door then lowered her voice. 'You must ask yourself, though, whether you and *Marguerite* can ever be happy.'

Before Ellen could swallow her surprise at the remark and respond, Catriona went on, 'I'm dying for a cigarette but Marguerite doesn't approve of women smoking. Do you think we dare nip out for a fag? No, better not, I can hear a clanking of pots and pans, can't you? Supper must be nearly ready.'

Over a meal of Scotch broth followed by roast lamb and apple tart, Donald Frazer, tapping his plate for emphasis, told Ellen the history of the slate industry on the islands, from its modest beginnings in the late eighteenth century and its glory days in the mid-nineteenth, when the slate had been excavated from the deep quarries and taken by steamer all over the world, to its decline and eventual closure.

'You'll see the disused quarries on the island, Miss Kingsley,' he said. 'They've all been flooded for years. There was a tidal wave towards the end of the last century which drove the sea into them. They tried to get them working again, but it was the beginning of the end. They were buying slates more cheaply from other parts of the world by then anyway. That was the death knell for Seil and the other slate islands. When the industry died, the exodus of people began. It's when the young people leave,' he added, echoing what Catriona Campbell had said earlier that evening, 'that's when a place begins to die.'

'Nonsense, Donald,' Mrs Hunter said briskly. 'Dying, indeed. Stop your maundering and eat your dinner.'

The conversation moved on to some roof tiles that needed replacing, a storm-damaged tree that Alec must lop the branches from. Ellen took little part in the conversation and so was able to reflect on Catriona's earlier comment.

You must ask yourself, though, whether you and Marguerite can ever be happy. It seemed to her an extraordinary thing to say, especially on a first meeting. And it made little sense: it was Alec she was marrying, not Marguerite.

And yet she was troubled, because since she and Alec had arrived at Kilmory House, Mrs Hunter had not mentioned their engagement. It was of course possible that Alec and his mother had spoken of it while Ellen had been upstairs, changing, but it had been Catriona who had raised a glass of wine to them at the beginning of the meal. And although Mrs Hunter had joined in the toast, she had moved the conversation briskly on. 'Alec's friend', Mrs Hunter had called her, on their arrival, and for a strange, skewed moment Ellen had found herself questioning whether Alec had told his mother of the engagement – he had a habit, after all, of keeping his emotional cards close to his chest. But of course he had, she remembered him telling her that he had written, and the principal reason for this visit to Scotland had been to introduce his mother to his future wife. And yet it seemed odd that Mrs Hunter had not yet asked them about their wedding plans. Could it be that she disapproved of the engagement? No, far more likely that she was simply waiting for a quieter moment.

After they had dined, Mrs Hunter refused their offers of help with the clearing-up, though she permitted Mr Frazer to carry the dirty dishes into the kitchen and fetch logs for the fire. Alec suggested to Ellen they get a breath of fresh air. Crossing the garden, holding his hand, the blades of grass brushed against her ankles and every nerve end tingled with anticipation of their kiss.

Moonlight sketched out the perimeter of a pond and the statue of a girl standing amid the slender white trunks of silver birches. Their leaves whispered, making a faint percussion.

Alec patted the stone girl's head. 'Meet wee Jeanie. Cat and I once put one of Donald's old pipes in her mouth and a box of matches in her hand. I thought my mother would go through the roof when she saw it, but fortunately she saw the funny side.'

'Catriona told me that you and she used to date.'

'Did she?' His gaze flicked back to the house. 'That was years ago. We were just wee bairns.' A smile curled his mouth. 'Come here.' They kissed, then he said, 'So what do you think of my island?'

'I like it very much.'

'I wondered whether you might find it . . .'

'What?'

'Too cut off. We are rather perched on the edge of the Atlantic.'

A voice called out, 'Dear me, caught out. I won't tell if you won't, Alec,' and they pulled apart. A pinpoint of bobbing orange light close to the house told Ellen that Catriona had succeeded in escaping outdoors for a smoke. As they walked back through the garden, Catriona detached herself from the wall against which she was leaning, scuffed the cigarette stub beneath the sole of her shoe, and went back inside with them.

Her mind refused to settle, lying in bed that night. Images from the day darted through her head: the white-sailed yacht on Loch Lomond, the translucent waters of the shores of Loch Feochan. And Catriona, breezing into the sitting room of Kilmory House and kissing Alec. Had he not spoken of Miss Campbell because he had thought her unimportant? Or because they had at one time been close? In Catriona's teasing attitude to Alec Ellen thought she glimpsed something more than the ordinary fondness of friendship. Her imagination created a much younger Alec and Catriona, walking hand in hand along Seil's black beaches or embracing by a stormy sea.

And yet it was hard to picture Catriona capable of holding Alec's interest for long. Alec might come from a remote part of Scotland but his tastes were sophisticated. Catriona's simple clothing and freshly scrubbed face were in contrast to Andrée Fournier's cool elegance. And she had detected a hardness in Catriona that surely must eventually displease; it had shown itself in a fondness for mockery and the cynical manner with which she had spoken of her patients at the hospital.

A flurry of rain washed against the window. Ellen thought she heard from somewhere in the house light footsteps padding across floorboards. She listened, eyes open in the darkness. It must be the dog, Hamish. She rolled on to her side, pulled the eiderdown over her head, and drifted off to sleep.

The next morning there were puddles in the courtyard, but the skies had cleared and the sea in the bay was calm. Looking out of her bedroom window, Ellen saw the garden, washed with rain, glittering in the sunlight. She breathed in the cool air, noticing the absence of traffic noise and fumes. Her eye was drawn to a mass of blood-red flowers, vivid against dark conifers. Above were paths and terraces and flower borders, but she found her gaze dropping back to that crimson smear over the hillside.

She glanced at her watch. It was half past nine. Quickly, she washed and dressed and then went downstairs. The house was silent. In the dining room she saw that the table had been cleared: she must have slept through breakfast. A lonely piece of toast cooled on a plate, so she ate it, then left the room. She paused in the hall, her eye caught by the two photographs on the side table. The snapshot of Alec showed him glancing back over his shoulder, one hand raised in salute, a smile touching the corners of his mouth, as if the photographer had taken him by surprise. She wondered who had taken it. Mrs Hunter, perhaps. Or Catriona.

She picked up the other photograph, of the man in naval uniform, and looked at it more closely. This picture was formal in character, a studio portrait, she guessed. The naval officer appeared to be older than Alec was now. Strikingly good-looking, his piercing, direct gaze was searching, almost severe.

A voice said, 'He was a handsome man, don't you think?'

She looked up. Mrs Hunter was standing in the doorway. 'Is this Alec's father?' asked Ellen.

'That's my husband,' said Marguerite. 'That's Francis.'

'What was he like?'

'He was wonderful. Francis taught me everything. I was nothing before I met him, a silly wee creature who didn't know a thing about life. He told me what to wear and how to behave and what books to read. He was my whole life and I would have given my own life for him.' She took the photograph from Ellen, ran her handkerchief over the glass, then replaced the frame on the table.

'I'm sorry.' She wasn't sure why she was apologizing – for disrupting the arrangement of photographs or for Mrs Hunter's widowhood. 'I hope you'll forgive me for missing breakfast,' she said. 'I'm afraid I overslept. I don't know what happened, I hardly ever oversleep.'

Mrs Hunter smiled. 'No doubt you were tired after your journey. Shall I cook you some breakfast or would you like to see my garden first?'

'I'd love to see the garden. Where's Alec?'

'I've sent him to Oban for some messages. We didn't like to disturb you and I'm always so thankful when he's home with his car. It's a hard business for me, getting things from the shops. Mr Fleming comes round with his van, but he doesn't stock everything. Our little shop does its best, of course.'

'Don't you drive, Mrs Hunter?'

'Oh no.' A tinkling laugh. 'Francis did all the driving. He was a wonderful man with a car, he kept it going whatever the weather. Donald Frazer put the car away in the garage for me after Francis died and, do you know, when Alec was old enough to learn, the motor started the first time he tried it.'

Ellen expressed suitable admiration.

Marguerite said, as they went outside, 'Are you a gardener yourself, Miss Kingsley?'

'I'm afraid not. Do please call me Ellen.'

'And you must call me Marguerite.'

The stone slabs in the courtyard had been sheened to a satiny purplish-grey by the night's rain. Prisms of light danced on the lawn. In the sunshine, Ellen's fears of the previous evening seemed groundless. She and Marguerite Hunter needed time to get to know each other, that was all. The relationship between future mother-in-law and daughter-in-law was bound to be a delicate one.

A movement caught her eye and Ellen saw the Scottie dog rush out from behind a thicket. 'Here, Hamish!' Mrs Hunter called. 'He likes to chase rabbits. He's never caught one yet, but he likes to try.'

'I thought I heard him last night, running about the house.'

'Oh, I think you were mistaken, Ellen.' Mrs Hunter picked

a browned bud from a shrub as she passed. 'I always shut Hamish in the kitchen at night. I don't believe in a dog having the run of a house.'

The lawns were bordered by rockeries and flower beds. Ellen saw, looking up, that paths and terraces had been cut into the steep hill that rose up behind Kilmory House. They were heading up the slope, beyond the silver birches, past the statue of the girl beside which she and Alec had kissed the previous night.

'The garden was quite neglected when Francis inherited the house,' explained Marguerite. 'Francis was a keen gardener, like myself. He dug out all the terraces himself. When there's heavy rain, the soil can slip down the hillside, so you have to shore up the terraces. Not one of Francis's terraces has ever fallen down.'

'It must have been hard work.'

'He was never afraid of that. He was a practical man. I admire a practical man.'

They were passing the banks of shrubs, with their dark red blooms, that Ellen had seen from her bedroom window. In the shade, pearls of dew still clung to the scarlet petals.

'What are these?' she asked.

'These? They are my pride and joy. You've chosen a good time to see my garden, Ellen. It's at its best at this time of year, when the rhododendrons and azaleas are out. Kilmory House is famous for them. You can see them in blossom from the far side of the bay, as clear as rubies.'

They continued to walk up the hillside. Moss-covered

stones lay at the sides of the path and the streams that rushed between the rocks were bordered by ferns. The path climbed steeply on, higher and higher, into the trees, narrowing so that they had to go in single file. Marguerite led the way. The older woman was quick and agile on the paths she must know so well, and she had a wiry strength that belied her age and slight figure. Ellen's indoor shoes, not bought for rough walking, struggled to gain purchase on the damp stones. When she glanced back over her shoulder, she saw the slate roof of the house below.

Beneath the covering of trees, the air was colder and the shadows darker. A brown blanket of needles had spread itself out beneath the red trunks of the pines and there was a woody, resinous scent. Pale green lichens frilled the branches. A bridge straddled a rocky gorge where a stream surged and bubbled.

High on the escarpment, a hedge of evergreens parted to reveal another terrace. Clay pots stood to either side of a paved area, some planted with spring bulbs. A small wooden summerhouse, its front open to the elements, sheltered a table and two chairs.

'This is Catriona's favourite place,' said Marguerite. 'She'll sit here for hours sometimes. I call it her hidey-hole.' Marguerite went to stand at the edge of the terrace. 'Come and see the view, Ellen.'

'I'll stay here, I think.'

'You mustn't worry. You'll be quite safe.'

Yet her heart was thudding. Was it because of the steep

climb up the hillside or was it her awareness of the abyss just a few yards away? Or could it be the implacability she sensed in Marguerite, a spirit that was relentless and unalterable?

'I'm afraid I dislike heights,' she said, and sat down on one of the chairs in the summerhouse. After a few minutes, Marguerite joined her.

'It must be difficult for you, managing on your own,' said Ellen.

'It is, sometimes. It's a big place for one person. But I wouldn't live anywhere else. Donald is a good sort and helps me with the heavy work. And Alec comes home every month.'

'And I'm sure we'll try our best to continue to do so after we're married.'

A jolt seem to run through the older woman's body, as if she had put her hand to a nettle. Ellen said gently, 'I love Alex very much, Mrs Hunter. And I intend to make him very happy.'

Marguerite's gaze, which had been fixed ahead of her, moved slowly across the vista before coming to rest on Ellen.

'Aye, I'm sure you mean well.'

The shock of those words did not have time to die away before Ellen heard a sound, footsteps and then the rustle of branches. Looking round, she saw Alec coming up the path through the trees towards them.

*   *   *

'Where are we going?'

Marcus Pharoah had been waiting outside the café after India finished work. This evening, he was driving a big black car instead of the green Austin-Healey.

'My flat,' he said as he put the car into gear.

'I didn't know you had a flat.'

'I don't care for hotels.'

'I'd rather go to a restaurant.'

'No.' His gaze flicked to her, then back to the traffic. 'I'm not in the mood for that.'

'But I'm hungry.' It came out as a whine.

He suppressed a sigh and said, with the exaggerated patience one might use when speaking to a difficult child, 'My housekeeper will have left a cold meal. And it's all right, you don't have to worry about your dubious virtue. I'm not in the mood for that sort of tussle tonight either.'

Dubious virtue. She wondered whether to be outraged. 'You don't sound as if you're in the mood for company at all, Marcus.'

'Most company, no. But if I were to spend the evening on my own then I would drink too much, and I dislike the thought of that.'

Through the windscreen, she watched Hampstead Road peel by. 'Why me?'

'I tried to think who I could tolerate and yours was the only name I came up with.' He gave a sour smile. 'I wonder whether it's because in some ways you remind me of myself. You have a need to enhance the world, and you employ a certain economy with the truth.'

Something in his eyes, some knowledge or intimacy, made her look away. 'Stop it, Marcus.'

'That ridiculous cottage you've made up.' A wave of his hand. 'The meadow . . . the orchard.'

'Applegarth?'

'Yes, Applegarth. A tip for the future. If you're going to lie, don't over-elaborate. It's always more convincing if you don't stray too far from the truth.'

'Applegarth is true.'

'No, it isn't.' He sounded tired rather than angry. 'You might like Applegarth to exist, but it doesn't. Applegarth is a fantasy, as are the loving mother and the father in the diplomatic corps and the holidays abroad.'

She made a sound; he interrupted. 'I like to know what's going on. And I'm good at finding things out.'

So am I, she thought. You don't come from the sort of places I've come from without learning to watch your back.

She said, 'You didn't tell me you were getting divorced.'

'No, I didn't.'

'It's a big thing to leave out.'

'Yes, I suppose it is.'

He changed down gear to stop for a zebra crossing. A couple walked over it, the woman pushing a pram. India considered climbing out of the car and running away, as she had so often done before, but what then?

Instead she said, 'I'm a little tired, you see, Marcus, of being for amusement only.'

'I've never thought of you in that way. I don't know whether you're able to believe that, but it's the truth.'

He started up the car again, heading along Chalk Farm Road. They drove into Belsize Park. Outside a red-brick block of mansion flats, Pharoah slowed the car to a halt. It had rained earlier that day and puddles sheened the tarmac.

Inside the building, a porter greeted them and opened the lift for them. The flat was on the third floor. Pharoah unlocked the front door and they went inside.

In the sitting room, he took glasses from a sideboard and mixed drinks. The room was sparsely furnished in a masculine style: a shelf of books, a stack of records, architectural prints on the walls. Everything was polished and perfect. A plant in a shiny black bowl stood on the coffee table, its long, filigreed, lime-green petals reflecting in the polished surface.

'It's an orchid,' said Pharoah, following her gaze. 'I forget which type. Alison grows them, it's a hobby of hers. Perhaps I should send it back to her. I'll be living here from now on, you see. Alison insists.'

'Do you mind?'

'About losing the Barton house? No, not particularly.'

'I meant about the divorce. You look as if you mind.'

'Only for Rowena's sake.' He handed a glass to India. 'I mind that she should suffer because of me and I mind that some of the mud will inevitably stick to her. Most of all, I mind a great deal that I shall inevitably see less of her.'

'I'm sorry, Marcus.'

He gave a shrug of acknowledgement. 'I spent the afternoon at my lawyer's. A dispiriting experience. I didn't think Alison would take it so far. She wants me to suffer and she knows what to do to make it hurt.' His gaze, dark and brooding, flicked in her direction. 'What is it? I'm boring you, aren't I? I expect you'd prefer me to be treating you to a good dinner and telling you how beautiful you are. I'll make it up to you, I promise. Though, come to think of it, perhaps I'm tired of being for amusement only too. We seem to have gone on like this for some time, don't we?'

'"Like this"?'

'Playing our respective games.'

'What would you prefer?'

'A greater degree of honesty between us. You know, you tell me about the skeletons in your cupboard and I'll admit to some of mine.' A flash of a humourless smile. 'A pact between thieves, if you like. A useful metaphor, wouldn't you agree?'

India, feeling suddenly wary, did not respond.

'Your first boarding school,' he said. 'You were expelled for stealing, weren't you?'

Her heart tripped. She put down the glass and made for the door. But he, too, moved quickly, intercepting her, the flat of his hand against the door, preventing her from opening it.

'I told you,' he said softly. 'I like to know.'

'Let me go!'

'I'm not judging you, India. I've taken a few things I shouldn't have in my time. Not sweets from shops – bigger things than that.'

Tears of humiliation stung behind her lids; she swung away and sat back down on the sofa. 'It was a long time ago,' she muttered. 'It's nothing to do with you.'

'I'd rather hoped it was by now.'

She scrabbled in her bag for her handkerchief; Pharoah offered her his own. She rubbed at her face with it, streaking it with mascara, and said harshly, 'You think you know everything about me, but you don't. You don't know anything at all. People like you, you haven't a clue.'

'Then tell me.'

She shook her head, took her cigarettes out of her bag, lit one, and went to stand at the window, smoking. It was nearly dark and she could see the headlamps of the cars on the road. She would like to go away, she thought, far, far away. But then, Sebastian.

She heard him say, 'Let me tell you what I know already. I know that your mother was called Lucinda Taylor and that she was a dancer. Your father, Ralph Mayhew, was killed in the Blitz and your mother died of heart disease a year and half after that. After she died, you and your brother were sent to an orphanage, but then your aunt, Rachel Taylor, took you in.'

A cyclist passed on the street below, light flicking

between the trees. London always looked melancholy at dusk, India thought.

She turned back to him. 'The way you say it, Marcus, you make it sound careless. And it was, in a way. We'd rather slipped through the cracks, Sebastian and I. But Rachel cared. She found us. She looked after us.'

'You loved her.'

'Yes, I did.' Looking back, India wondered whether Rachel had felt guilty for having lost contact with her younger sister, and for having been away, working in Scotland, when the police had called at the flat to tell her of Lucinda's death. They had left a note. It had been 1942 and a lot of people were dying.

'Rachel was lovely,' she said. 'She was kind and gentle and she was never cross with us, even when I was bad and even when Sebastian was ill. She had to travel a lot for her work, so Sebastian and I were sent to boarding schools.'

'But it didn't work out.'

'Not for Sebastian, no. And for me . . .' She shrugged. 'I didn't fit in. How could I have?'

'Was that why you stole? Because you disliked the school?'

'No, not at all. I told you you wouldn't understand.' She flicked ash on the carpet; irritably, Marcus slammed an ashtray on to the sill beside her. 'Now it's my turn to guess,' she said. 'I expect you had a family who loved you and looked after you. Being looked after is just as important as being loved, I know this. I don't suppose you ever went hungry and I don't suppose you've ever known what it is to be completely alone. I'm sure you went to a good school and no doubt you were very clever. And then you probably went to Oxford or Cambridge, and I expect you were very clever there too.'

'Not a bad summary of my early career. I might add that I found my family stifling and that when I was fortunate enough to be encouraged by my chemistry teacher at school, I discovered what it was I wanted to do with my life.'

'How convenient, to have everything sorted out. Your brilliant career and your marriage to Alison. I shouldn't think you've ever had to worry about anything.'

'Not true,' he said. 'Actually.'

She sat down on the sofa beside him, tucking her feet beneath her. 'What?' she said scornfully. 'Maybe your cat was run over by a car. Maybe some girl you fell in love with was in love with someone else. It's a shame, but these things happen.'

'My first wife died a year after we were married.'

This shocked India. 'Oh. How awful. What happened?'

'An infection.' He gave a taut smile. 'No penicillin then. It was a long time ago, before the war.'

'You never said.'

'You and I, we don't exactly talk about the *substance* of life, do we, India? Rosanne and I were very young. I'd recently graduated from Cambridge and I was working in America at the time. We had that optimism that goes with extreme youth, that absolute conviction that everything would work out well for us.' His mouth twisted. 'After it happened, I discovered that there is a glance that says *actually I'd rather not know*. People don't want to hear about such tragedies, it reminds them of the fragility of their own happiness. I returned to England as soon as I could. One or two good friends listened to me when I'd had too much to drink, but otherwise I never spoke about it. And do you know, soon enough it was almost as if it had never happened. As if it had been nothing more than a nightmare.'

India crawled a hand along the sofa and folded it over his. She felt the warmth of his hand in hers, a small connection that for the first time seemed to tie them together.

'I'm sorry about tonight.' He raised her hand and kissed it. 'I should have kept away from you. I'm in a foul mood, I'm afraid. I never loved Alison, I knew that when I married her. She was very beautiful — she still is — and I was very attracted to her, but I never loved her. I married her for several reasons, some good, some less so. At the time, I didn't think I was capable of loving any more. But I still wanted the other pleasures that marriage can bring — a home, a family. I've never liked living alone, I'm not made for it, and I hated the thought of spending the rest of my life a single man. I don't judge myself for that, and I don't think it was wrong of me, to want to wipe the slate clean and start again. Do you?'

She shook her head. 'What were the bad reasons?'

'Oh, money, what else?' He gave a wry smile. 'Money

and power – the two are inextricably linked. Alison comes from a wealthy family. By that time, I'd learned what money can do. And what I'd once thought would satisfy me – a position in some reputable university and the funds to pursue my own research – was no longer enough. I wanted more. I needed Alison's money to unlock my future. The Josephs are financiers and they had the social connections my own family lacked. You can only get so far through talent and hard work, I'd realized. You could say that I married Alison so that in the end I was able to have Gildersleve Hall.'

'Why is she divorcing you?'

'Because of my adultery. Do you want to know the gruesome details? There have been several affairs, I admit it. The first was during the war. Alison and Rowena spent the war years in the Lake District, in Alison's parents' country house, and celibacy has never much appealed to me. There have been others since. There was a girl a couple of years ago. Alison found out about her.'

'Does she know about us?'

'Not that I know, but it would make no difference if she did. She won't change her mind now. Alison is capable of great intransigence, she always has been.'

'You can't blame her, Marcus.'

'No.' He ran a hand across his eyes. 'Though it suited her, being Marcus Pharoah's wife. She has a lover, some City type she met on the hunting field. I thought of making it difficult for her, citing him in the divorce, but my solicitor tells me it would be unwise. And besides, Rowena . . .'

She shuffled round to face him. 'What will you do now?'

'I shall try not to let her poison my daughter's mind against me. And I shall fight for Gildersleve.' He frowned. 'An occurrence can seem unfortunate, but if you take hold of it, take control, you can seize the advantage.'

'How confident you are, Marcus.' There was some mockery in her tone. 'Most of us lurch from one disaster to another, and here are you, like a captain of a ship.'

'Oh, I think you've learned to manipulate events very well, India. You know when to blow hot or cold. Clever women always do.' He scooped her up and sat her on his lap, studying her. 'I'm sorry, that sounded bitter. I wanted to avoid that. I suppose this will at least free us.'

'Us?'

'Yes. No need to hide away in corners any more. Perhaps I'll show you off.'

'Why?' she said coolly. 'For revenge?'

'Now, that would be cheap of me.' He brushed back her hair from her forehead.

'I thought it was me who was cheap, Marcus.'

'You? I don't think so.'

There was a heat in his voice, and as he touched his lips lightly against the curve of her neck he drew down the zip on the back of her dress. She closed her eyes, drawing in a breath, and he ran his hand down her back. He kissed her again, then eased first the sleeves of her dress over her shoulders, and then the straps of her slip. 'No, I really don't think so,' he murmured. 'On the contrary, India, I've always had a feeling you might turn out to be rather costly.'

Riley and Ellen had, with reasonable speed, smoothed over the disagreement that had taken place after Ellen had told him that she was seeing Alec Hunter. Riley had made the running, phoning to apologize, knowing himself to be in the wrong. Ellen had forgiven him, he thought, because, intoxicated with love, she found it hard not to be happy.

They saw each other less frequently now. Ellen naturally spent most of her time with Alec. Emotionally, Riley had tried to take a few steps back. The news of her engagement to Alec Hunter had been a body blow and he had realized that a part of him had hoped that the relationship would not last. Which had been wrong of him. Ellen loved Alec Hunter. Forget her, he had told himself. Put her out of your mind, think about something else.

So he had thrown himself into his work. But that, also, frustrated him. Progress was painfully slow. Mr Rossiter still went around in his sharp suits and gold watch, and the two gangsters, White and Perlman, carried on their violent trade without hindrance. Among those of Riley's colleagues still investigating the death of George Clancy in the Great Dover Street warehouse, there was the feeling, sometimes voiced, that after almost six months they had reached a dead end.

Riley persevered, seeking out nuggets of fact and teasing

out connections. Though Clancy hadn't been an important man or an admirable man, nothing he had found out about him had suggested that he had deserved to die such a brutal, bloody death. The warehouse itself no longer existed. It had been demolished, and the land cleared to build houses and offices. The land was owned by a property company, of which David Rossiter was a director, but the gangster Bernie Perlman's name was also there on the title deeds.

Riley sat one evening at the bar of the Blue Duck nightclub in Mayfair, spinning out a whisky, watching a skinny brunette in feathers and sequins bob around beneath a spotlight to the music of a three-piece band. The habitués of the nightclub, a mixture of businessmen and fading actors and the odd member of parliament, came and went. Two more evenings passed, and Bernie Perlman did not come to the club; two more evenings during which Riley acquired a headache from cheap whisky as well as a dislike of the song 'Blue Velvet', the skinny brunette's star number. Perhaps Perlman had gone on holiday and was sunning himself on some foreign beach. Perhaps his crimes had caught up with him and he was floating in the river, his feet encased in concrete, his short, fat corpse nibbled by whatever fish could cope with the Thames's poisonous brown water.

On Saturday night the Blue Duck was busy. Riley sat at a shady corner of the bar with a good view of the room. He chatted to a tough, vivacious woman in a shiny red dress, who told him about her hair salons and her bad marriage. Then the woman in the red dress moved away and Riley's thoughts drifted, circling until they came to rest where they so often did, with Ellen.

Since her visit to Scotland, Riley had noticed an alteration in her mood. He had sensed for the first time reservations, doubts. 'I'm sure Marguerite would rather I wasn't a career woman, and I'm sure she'd prefer it if I were Scots,' she said to him one evening, when she called round. Her tone had been light, almost joking.

Give it time, he said to her. Mothers-in-law and daughters-in-law . . . Two women in love with the same man. She had smiled and changed the subject.

The skinny brunette had left the stage and the band was whipping up the first bars of 'That's Amore'. Half a dozen couples shuffled on to the dance floor. Riley's eye was caught by a flurry of people coming into the room. One of the larger tables had been kept clear by the nightclub staff and it was to here that the newcomers – half a dozen men and five young, dolled-up women – headed. Waiters hurried to pull out chairs, girls rushed off with drinks orders.

A short, plump man sat down in the chair with the best view of the dance floor. Riley recognized Bernie Perlman. One of Perlman's men hauled a blonde in a pink dress up to dance. Waitresses brought bottles of champagne to the table, and there was a popping of corks. The dark-haired girl sitting next to Perlman lolled her head on his shoulder, closing her eyes. She looked, Riley thought, very young and very drunk.

Another man appeared in the doorway to the nightclub, then crossed the room to Bernie Perlman's table. As the spotlight circled and the newcomer was caught in its light, Riley saw his pale, pasty face, small, pink-lidded eyes and crew-cut ginger hair. *Like a spectre*: Sergeant Davies's words came back to him.

The man made his way to the table, then bent to murmur something in Bernie Perlman's ear. Perlman made an angry movement, dislodging the girl sleeping on his shoulder. With a shriek, she slid off the chair on to the floor, landing hard on her rear. The other guests roared with laughter.

Riley crossed the room to Perlman's table. He offered his hand to the girl sprawled on the floor and gave her a friendly smile as he helped her to her feet. Tears streaked sooty lines of mascara down her face. As she brushed herself down, Riley looked up and met the gaze of the ginger-haired man. Riley gave another smile, different in nature to the one he had given the girl, and then walked away.

India was dining at Le Caprice with Marcus Pharoah and his brother, Devlin.

Marcus said, 'Where's Louise?'

'She can't make it, I'm afraid.' Devlin Pharoah was reading the menu. 'She's not very well.'

'Liar,' said Marcus softly.

Devlin shrugged. 'You're asking a lot, Marc.'

The two men looked at each other. India wondered whether they were about to fight, and said, 'I'd like the fishcakes and a Bellini, please,' and Devlin Pharoah laughed and the moment passed.

'You have such immature tastes,' said Marcus. 'Nursery food and fizzy drinks.'

'Don't be grumpy. Anyway, if my tastes are immature, what does that say about you?'

'That I need to educate you.'

She made a derisive noise. 'Lots of people have tried to do that.'

'Have they? I had the impression you'd spent most of your life running wild.'

Devlin Pharoah said, 'I'm with Miss Mayhew. Nothing wrong with fishcakes and a Bellini. You hardly play by the rules yourself, Marcus,' he added pointedly.

'Unlike India, I like to give the impression of doing so.'

'I don't think so,' said Devlin. 'Not this time, anyway.'

Pharoah gave a smile. 'My little brother disapproves of you, India.'

'Not at all.' Devlin lounged in his chair, his dark eyes brimming with curiosity. 'I approve of Miss Mayhew completely. How could I not? She's utterly charming.'

'Thank you, Mr Pharoah.'

'Devlin, please.'

'Don't flirt, Dev. Disapproval I'll tolerate, but not that.'

The waiter came to take their order and the two brothers conferred over the wine list. Devlin Pharoah was slighter and shorter than his elder brother and his arched brows and hooded eyes gave him the look of a genial demon, India thought.

A claret was ordered. When the waiter had gone, Marcus Pharoah said to Devlin, 'I'm surprised Louise has allowed you out with me.'

'I'm under strict instructions.'

'To do what?'

'To make you see sense, of course.' Devlin gave a wave of his hand. 'Don't worry, I've no intention of trying.'

'Has Alison been speaking to you?'

'To Louise. Thick as thieves those two, you know that.'

'She wouldn't have me back if I went down on bended knee and pleaded with her. Which I've no intention of doing. So why does she care what company I keep?'

Devlin said quietly, 'Because it humiliates her.'

Pharoah made an angry outbreath and looked away. Devlin turned to India and gave her an apologetic smile. 'I'm sorry, Miss Mayhew, to have this conversation in front of you. Marcus can be a difficult man to get hold of.'

'I don't mean,' explained India, 'to annoy anyone. Or to humiliate anyone.'

'I'm sure you don't.'

'We're just having fun, you know.'

Devlin's eyes glittered with amusement. 'Perhaps that's what gets people's backs up. It's a characteristic of the English, isn't it, resenting those who have fun. Our Puritan side.'

Marcus said, 'Rather ironic, you, Devlin, lecturing me on my morality.'

'As I said, I'm merely the messenger. Mercury, firing a warning shot across the bows.'

'Oh, I think I've already got the message. There must be half a dozen people here whom I would have said I knew reasonably well, and yet they've hardly acknowledged me.'

'You must do as you choose. But you'll pay a price for it.'

'One worth paying.' Reaching across the table, Pharoah took India's hand.

'So long as you're sure.'

'I am. Without reservation. How's that boy of yours?'

Devlin seemed to accept the change of subject. His expression soured. 'The school won't have him back next term.'

'What happened?'

'Some silly business with a girl. I've found a place in Scotland that'll take him. Miles from anywhere so no temptation in sight.'

'What does Rufus think of that?'

'He's refusing to go. I've told him it's either that or he comes to work for me.'

'And?'

Devlin shook his head. 'I don't know. We don't speak. He's out every night, God knows where he goes. He's a moody little bugger. I've stopped his allowance, that'll make him see sense. What about Rowena?'

'She's very well. Won a prize for her painting.'

'Clever girl.'

'I haven't seen her. Just letters and phone calls.' Pharoah's brooding gaze locked on to his brother's. 'Alison's making things difficult.'

'I told you, old boy, price to pay,' said Devlin softly.

'A couple of years' time and Rowena will be able to do as she likes. Anyway, she and Alison quarrel like cat and dog, they always have done.'

On the way back to the flat, in the taxi, they sat in silence, India's head against Marcus Pharoah's shoulder, his arm round her.

'Perhaps we should stop seeing each other,' she said.

'No.' His hand, which had been stroking her hair, paused.

'Just for a while.'

'Because some silly fools gossip?'

'Because,' she said, sitting up and twitching her frock into place, 'your wife won't let you see your daughter.'

'Even if you and I never saw each other again it would make no difference. Alison would still keep Rowena from me. She wants to punish me. No – she wants to destroy me.'

He fell silent, looking out of the taxi window, as the London streets slid by. India knew that he was deeply angry, that the conversation with his brother had angered him, and all this troubled her. She said, 'I should go home,' and he said more forcefully this time, 'No.'

'I haven't seen Sebastian for days.'

'I'm sure Sebastian will survive your absence for a few more hours. I need to talk to you, India, and I need some company for an hour or two. You can do what the hell you like afterwards.'

'Shall we have a drink somewhere?'

He shook his head.

'Or a dance?' she suggested.

'Now you're tormenting me.' He kissed her hand. 'I'd prefer to go back to the flat. I promise you a proper night out tomorrow to make up for it. Who knows, I might even attempt to steer you round the dance floor.'

In his flat, Pharoah made drinks. 'I may lose Gildersleve Hall,' he told her. 'I've fought against it, I've fought damned hard. But it eats money, has been doing so for years, and I simply don't have any more.'

'Because of the divorce?'

'Yes. I spent a long, dull morning with my accountant.' He loosened the knot of his tie. 'Lawyers and accountants, that's what my life has come to. I used to be able to borrow from Alison's family but, unsurprisingly, that source has dried up.'

'If you went to a bank—'

He gave a bitter laugh. 'If only it was that easy. They're like a coven of old witches, these City money men. A rumour goes round that you're short of cash and they won't give you the time of day. I've tried everything I can think of but I'm running out of ideas. I seem to have spent a great deal of the last ten years entertaining bores and bureaucrats, trying to coax money out of them for Gildersleve, and now they slam doors in my face.'

He took a cigarette from a box on the sideboard. 'Alison's name is on the title deeds of Gildersleve Hall,' he said. 'Her father insisted when he helped me to buy the place.' He frowned. 'It's funny, I thought I'd mind more than I do. These things have a natural lifespan, perhaps. There was a time when I would have sold my soul for Gildersleve.' He gave a humourless laugh. 'Perhaps I did so.'

'What will you do?'

'I'm not sure yet. I've been offered a post at a university in America. But I've not given up on Gildersleve yet, damn them.' He struck his lighter. 'The Americans still believe in themselves. Look at us – we won the bloody war, but you wouldn't think so. We can't seem to shake off this wartime habit of cheeseparing economy. We have such small pleasures and small ambitions.'

'I don't think that's so bad,' she said. 'I used to long for a pair of proper nylons when I was at school. Just one pair. We had to wear black woolly stockings, you see.'

'The thought of you in black woolly stockings cheers me enormously, India.'

'Small pleasures . . . the restaurants, the sports car, the vintage wines . . . oh, and India.'

'You're mistaken, you know, in seeing yourself as a small pleasure.' As he spoke, he drew her to him, his hands on her bottom, pressing her against him. He said softly, 'It would mean giving up certain things, if I went away.'

'Your daughter.'

'Yes, Rowena.' His eyes were lit by dark flames. 'Perhaps it might not be such a bad idea to leave England for a few years. Let the fuss die down. But they haven't offered me enough money yet.' A smile played round the corners of his mouth. 'Not enough to tempt me away from certain small pleasures, anyway.'

Chapter Eight

In the middle of June, Ellen left the hospital to start a new job as a research assistant to a friend of Professor Malik's, Jerry Collins, a professor at London University. Jerry was American, a large man with wild, curly hair and an expansive good humour, whose big hands looked deceptively incapable of the delicate work that crystallography demanded. An expert in his field, his good humour and friendliness made him easy to get along with, and he and Ellen had hit it off from the interview.

Her task was to grow, mount and photograph crystals. She also supervised the young women who came into the lab to compute the immense and tedious calculations required for Professor Collins's work. Picking up her old occupations in the laboratory, making her solutions, examining her crystals under the microscope and noting down their flaws and measurements, she felt a deep sense of peace, as if she had come back on course after being blown about by a storm.

At the end of June, Alec drove up to Seil Island. He went on his own; it had occurred to Ellen that if she held back and made sure that mother and son had time together, then Marguerite would have the chance to get used to their engagement. She had not told Alec of Marguerite's remark in Kilmory House's garden. *Aye, I'm sure you mean well.* It seemed better to keep it to herself. Indeed, returning to London, she had questioned whether she had misheard Mrs Hunter; whether, up there on the high terrace, the whine of the wind and the rustling of the trees had transformed an innocuous response into something more ominous.

They decided that theirs would be a long engagement, lasting at least two years. She had just started a new job and Alec was soon to embark on a new research project. During that time, she and Marguerite would get to know each other. She hoped that they would grow to love each other. Marguerite must be given the chance to get used to a changed situation, and she, Ellen, must look for common ground between them, some interest that they could share. Marguerite must surely want grandchildren. If their relationship could not at first be close, then the arrival of a baby must eventually bring them together. As for Catriona, the jealousy she had felt on Seil she now brushed aside. If Catriona still had feelings for Alec then she was to be pitied rather than feared.

But it was not only Margeurite who seemed less than wholeheartedly keen on the engagement. Earlier that summer, Ellen and Alec had driven down to Wiltshire to meet her parents. Her father had grilled Alec over the dinner table. What were his prospects? How old was he? Did he intend to remain in academia? What of his family, his background, his education, his politics? Afterwards, when her father had retired to his study, Ellen had murmured to Alec that her father expected everyone to plan their future like a military campaign. He mustn't mind.

What had disappointed her more was the conversation that had taken place one evening when she and her father had gone out for a walk on the chalk hills that rose up behind the village. 'He's a pleasant chap,' her father had said, 'but are you sure he's *solid* enough for you, Ellen?' By 'solid', he had meant reliable, straightforward, lasting. 'Of course he is,' she had answered, hurt, and her father, seeing that, had tucked her hand round his arm.

'So long as you're happy, darling. He's rather decorative, that's all, and I've a tendency to doubt decorative men. Your mother thinks he's the cat's whiskers.' But the conversation had left for the first time in her life a small distance between them that had not quite been repaired.

After her first month in her job, Ellen decided to give a dinner party to thank Professor Malik for helping her find the new position. As well as the professor, his wife and Alec, she also wanted to invite Riley. She looked forward to her friend meeting her fiancé properly. Not having seen much of India for some time and needing another female guest, Ellen invited her too.

The only evening convenient for all the guests was a Friday. There was a heatwave, and there were meetings at the college that Ellen had to attend that day, so she had to rush out to the shops in her lunch hour and haul the groceries home on the Underground. There was a surprising amount of work involved in cooking for six people, and the shortcomings of the shared kitchen were soon brought home to her − the battered saucepans with their loose handles, the lack of matching cutlery or a fridge.

Riley was the first to arrive. Pulling off her apron, Ellen ran downstairs and let him in. He offered her a bunch of roses, tied up in brown paper.

'They're from my garden,' he said, following her upstairs. 'There may be the odd greenfly.'

'They smell gorgeous. And such a lovely pink. Thank you, Riley.'

'How's it going?'

'Awful. I'm worried that the fish is off. It's been sitting in my bag in the heat all afternoon. I don't want to poison everyone. And the jelly won't set.'

In the kitchen, Ellen unwrapped the package of sole and Riley sniffed it and judged it acceptable.

'And the jelly . . .' She fetched it from the windowsill.

Raspberries bobbed in a scarlet sea. Riley peered at it. 'It may be unsalvageable, I'm afraid. What are you making?'

'Trifle.'

'Have you any cream?'

Ellen nodded.

'I'll rescue the raspberries, if you like, and then we could have raspberries and cream for pudding.'

'Riley, thank goodness you're here. A cool head in a crisis. Do you mind if I leave you to it and go and get changed? I must look a fright.'

'Rubbish. You look lovely, as always.'

'Flatterer.' She dashed off to the bathroom.

When she returned upstairs, make-up applied and peppermint-green cotton frock on, she heard Riley's and Alec's voices from the kitchen.

Riley was saying, 'We met some years ago, very briefly, at Gildersleve Hall.'

Alec said, 'I'm afraid I don't remember. What on earth are you doing?'

'Fishing out raspberries.'

'How extraordinary. I'll take over, if you like.'

'There's no need, I've just about finished.'

'Riley, thank you.' Entering the room, Ellen kissed both men. 'Riley's just sorting out my rather disastrous pudding,' she explained to Alec.

'How admirably domestic,' said Alec.

'Darling, would you . . .?' She swept up her hair.

He tugged up her zip the last few inches, then drew her into his arms and brushed his mouth against hers. Ellen was aware of Riley moving away to inspect the view out of the window.

Then the doorbell rang, and she hurried downstairs again to find the Maliks and India introducing themselves to each other on the front step. Back in the kitchen, there was a flurry of introductions and wine pouring, then the tomato soup was warmed and the guests were seated. Ellen made sure everyone had bread and butter, wine and water, and was relieved that the soup was pronounced delicious.

At first the conversation was of crystallography.

Riley asked, 'When you say that the X-rays can reveal the structure of the crystal . . .'

Alec looked up from his soup. 'It's rather difficult to explain to the layman. Did you have any sort of a scientific education?'

'I struggled through the odd exam,' murmured Riley.

'I meant, a university education.'

'I'm afraid not. Wartime, you see.'

Professor Malik spoke. 'Were you in the services, Mr Riley?'

'The army.'

'I volunteered for a tank regiment,' said Malik wistfully. 'But I was turned down and told I must work in a government lab. I've always regretted that.'

'You wouldn't have liked it, dear.' Gita Malik patted her husband's arm. 'Too dark and enclosed. You know you hate even the Underground.'

'I suppose a policeman has little use for a university degree,' said Alec.

'Oh, come now, Hunter.' Malik tore a piece of bread in half. 'Detective work and scientific research must have certain elements in common. The search for the truth . . . the close scrutiny of evidence.'

Riley said, 'And a couple of years in a parachute regiment has had its uses.'

'I daresay one has to be physically fit in your line of work,' said Alec. 'All that chasing criminals and clobbering them with truncheons.'

'I try not to clobber people if I can help it.'

'But a certain amount of force must be required.'

'True, though as I said, I try to keep it to a minimum.'

'You hear stories . . .'

'You shouldn't believe everything you read in the papers, Hunter.'

What was wrong with them? thought Ellen, irritated, as she cleared away the soup bowls. Why on earth were they behaving like this? Two grown men, scrapping like schoolboys, when all she had wanted was for them to be friends. Hot and tired, she found the pair of them equally tiresome.

Then India said, 'I'm afraid I was *completely hopeless* at school. I didn't even pass the needlework exam. Our headmistress, Miss MacBeith – do you remember her, Ellen, she was absolutely terrifying – told me that if I didn't pull my socks up, I'd end up as a charlady or an adventuress.'

There was a ripple of laughter. Riley said, 'And what was your answer to that?'

India gave a demure little smile and lowered her lids. 'That I thought adventuress was a better career option. Nicer clothes, you see.'

India, too, found the dinner party rather an ordeal. Her affair with Marcus Pharoah weighed heavily on her mind throughout the evening. Though, rationally, it didn't seem likely that Ellen would find out about her and Marcus because Ellen didn't go to the sorts of places that Marcus liked, irrationally, she found herself imagining scenarios where some scientific colleague might have mentioned to Ellen that Marcus Pharoah was getting divorced from his wife and was having an affair with India Mayhew. She was afraid that if Ellen found out, she would be disapproving or furious or hurt, or all three. As both Devlin Pharoah and Michael had pointed out, there was already gossip. It would be impossible, after so many months, to pass the affair off to Ellen as temporary or unimportant, and equally unlikely that she could convince Ellen that she had not deliberately refrained from mentioning Marcus. The situation made her feel uneasy, and though she did not exactly avoid Ellen, she did not go out of her way to call on her either. Though she knew without doubt that Ellen was a nicer and better person than Marcus, there was something tiring about having to make a continual effort to make out that she herself was better than she really was. Marcus knew what she was. He didn't accept her – quite the opposite; she knew that he tried to change her, to mould her – but perhaps that was preferable to trying to live up to Ellen's exacting standards.

Dining with Marcus one evening, he talked about America once more.

'Do you remember me telling you that Midhurst College, in Vermont, has offered me a post? They've been courting me for years. It's a small place and they want to build up a biochemistry department, create it from scratch. They've come up with a decent offer at last.'

He seemed to expect a response so she said obligingly, 'That's marvellous, Marcus.'

'Marvellous?' His lip curled. 'Not, *oh Marcus, please don't leave me*? Or, *oh Marcus, I'll miss you so much*? Who else will buy you expensive frocks, India?'

He had bought her the frock she was wearing that day, which was made of a greeny-gold jacquard silk. When, earlier, they had walked into the restaurant, she had seen the men turn to look at her.

She disliked it when he was sarcastic, and he had that mean look in his eye which she had learned to be wary of, which told her his mood could so easily tip over into censure of her. To distract him, she said, 'That place . . . your laboratory—'

'Gildersleve,' he said irritably. 'It's called Gildersleve Hall.' He shook his head. 'I've decided to close it down. I'd rather make something better elsewhere than go on fighting against fools. Have you ever been to America?'

'Never.'

'You'd love it. The air seems fresher. Everywhere feels new. It gives you hope.'

Yet he looked angry rather than hopeful. Stirring his coffee, the direction of his glance drifted over the tables in the restaurant. Disliking a silence, India said, 'I will miss you, Marcus, honestly.'

His gaze snapped back to her. 'But I'm not your only – oh, what would be the word? Admirer? No, too coy. Escort? Certain unfortunate connotations, don't you think? Lover, then, I suppose we shall have to settle for that. I'm not the only one, am I?'

'No,' she said calmly. 'Does that bother you?'

'It doesn't *surprise* me.'

She made to rise but he reached out a hand and gripped her wrist. 'Stop it,' he murmured. 'Stop running away from me.'

India sank back in her seat. 'I'm not sure what you want me to say.'

'Nothing you would want to say,' he said bitterly. 'I may as well tell you – I was wondering whether you'd like to come with me.'

She said, startled, 'To America?'

'Rather than Iceland or Siam? Yes, of course.'

'Marcus—'

'I realize that you would be concerned about your brother, about Sebastian. I would make provision for him.'

'*Provision*,' she repeated. 'What sort of provision?'

'Whatever is suitable, whatever you think best. Take that

expression off your face, India. You can be so quick to take offence – it's childish of you. I only meant that I understand you feel you have a responsibility towards him and that that might inhibit what choices you make.'

She softened. 'Sebastian needs me,' she said.

'Sebastian isn't a child any more. He's a grown man. He needs to learn how to stand up for himself.'

'He can't. He's not that sort of person.'

'India, you're not doing him any favours. Sebastian won't have any sort of life if he constantly shelters behind you. To be fulfilled, to be happy, he must learn to live apart from you. You need to let him grow up.'

A part of her knew this, but she said obstinately, 'I won't leave him, Marcus. *America*. Why should I want to go to America?'

'If we were to marry.'

She laughed. 'I can't possibly marry you, Marcus.'

'Why not?'

'Because you're married already, for one thing.'

'Not for much longer. My divorce will come through in a matter of months.'

'I don't want to marry anyone. I've never wanted to marry anyone.'

He lit cigarettes and handed one to her. 'So that you have something to fidget with,' he said.

'Marcus, *honestly*, it's quite impossible. And I think that if you thought about it properly, you'd see that it was a very bad idea.'

'I have thought about it. I told you, I don't care to live alone.'

'Then marry someone else.'

'I can't seem to think of anyone else I'd like to marry. And besides, I've fallen in love with you.'

She sidestepped this, saying, 'I don't think I'd be any good at being married. I don't think I'm the right sort of person.'

'Is there a right sort of person?'

'You know what I mean. There are women who become wives and women who become mistresses. I'm the second sort, aren't I?'

'And is that how you see your life going on? Is that what you want for yourself when you are thirty, forty . . . fifty?'

For some reason, India found herself thinking of Peachey, in her mouldering flapper dresses, surrounded by the portraits that had been painted in her pomp. Perhaps she would end up like that, she thought, living on her own with half a dozen smelly moggies, surrounded by past glories.

'I don't know,' she muttered.

'Do you have no ambitions at all?'

'I've never thought, oh, perhaps I should become a film star, or perhaps I should write a book, if that's what you mean.' She twisted a pleat of her frock round a finger. 'I don't know that I've ever known anyone who was *happily* married.'

'Some people manage it. A few people. My parents were happy enough.'

'I'm not sure that mine ever were. And anyway . . .'

'What is it?'

'Do you remember the lecture I went to with Ellen? Where we first met?'

'At the Royal Institution?'

'Yes. You talked about bad blood.'

'Did I? How unscientific of me. I expect I was trying to employ some term the layman might understand.'

'Do you believe in it?'

'I was speaking about hereditary diseases. *Belief* doesn't come into it.'

'I meant, do you think that bad blood can run in a family?'

'It can do, in a sense. Where there is evidence of disease, then you could say that bad blood runs in a family.'

'Do you think those sort of people should marry? Do you think they should have children?'

'I believe that it's irresponsible to knowingly breed defectives. They can't live useful lives and there's always the risk that they'll pass on their sickness to the next generation.'

India thought of the house in the woods, the shimmer and shadow of bluebells, and her mother dancing with Neil to 'My Funny Valentine'.

She said, 'I'm not sure my mother was the sort of person who should have had children.'

'Your mother died of heart disease brought on by a bout of rheumatic fever in her childhood.'

She raised her eyebrows. 'You checked?'

'Yes, I checked. It's on the death certificate. There's no reason to believe that her poor health should be passed on to you. India, you're worrying about nothing. You are the picture of health. I've always noticed this about you, your physical perfection. You have such symmetry and form. It's quite striking.'

'You're talking about me as if I were a dog in a show. You'll be admiring my glossy coat next.'

He smiled. 'I'm sorry, forgive me. But physical health is a powerful source of attraction. Inevitably, the beautiful tend to marry the beautiful. Genetically, it makes sense. The less fortunate are left to take what they can.'

'Do you think yourself beautiful, Marcus?'

'I wouldn't put it quite like that. But I've never had a day's illness in my life. I pity those who always seem to be ailing from one thing or another. India, what do you want in life? You must think about it. You won't believe me now but time rushes on. You can end up finding it is too late to take a step in a different direction.'

They parted not long afterwards. Back at the flat, Sebastian was asleep on the sitting-room sofa. India tiptoed into the kitchen and poured herself a glass of milk. She sat down on an armchair. Sebastian lay motionless under the blankets, one arm flung out, the light from the kitchen touching his tangled fair curls. Watching him sleeping, she felt an immense tenderness for him. Marcus Pharoah might tell her that she needed to let Sebastian stand up for himself, but Pharoah did not have the memories she had, of Sebastian weeping for his mother, or Sebastian withdrawn and frightened at the orphanage or silent and uncommunicative in the aftermath of his breakdown, refusing to leave his bed, refusing to speak even to her. He did not know Sebastian's generosity and simplicity nor the fears that haunted him. Nor did he understand that she needed Sebastian as much as he needed her, because he was the one person who knew and understood her and who never, ever criticized her.

India went into her bedroom. There, she cold-creamed off her make-up, brushed out her hair and changed into her pyjamas. It was a warm night and she lay on the bed, thinking about Pharoah's offer. She had had proposals of marriage before, some serious, some less so, and had always turned them down. She didn't take Pharoah's proposal seriously. It had been made on a whim, she suspected, because he was angry about his divorce and losing his precious Gildersleve Hall. He was angry, in fact, that he had not been able to have everything his own way. Later on, he would regret the proposal. She doubted that he would ever repeat it.

But Pharoah had touched on a nerve when he had asked her what she pictured herself doing with her life. She remembered Aunt Rachel asking her the same thing, sitting at the kitchen table with her and discussing possible careers – teaching, secretarial college, nursing. None of these futures had materialized; indeed, they had all seemed improbable at the time, though India had not said this to Rachel. Since she had left school she had had a series of jobs, none of which had lasted more than six months. She knew that she often struggled to concentrate, that her timekeeping was appalling and that when she was rattled, she made mistakes. It was, if you thought about it, dismaying that at the age of twenty-three and after an expensive education, she was still waiting on tables in a cheap café. And not even doing that very well.

She wanted to be safe. And to be safe, you had to have money. Though Marcus Pharoah might claim to be hard up, it was plain to India that he didn't know what he was talking about. Poor men didn't dine at Le Caprice or run sports cars. Marrying Marcus Pharoah would take her into a different world, a better world. A girl like her, a girl who was pretty rather than clever, fun rather than studious, could better herself by marrying well. Marriage could give her the security she longed for. It would give her a home; it would give her children.

Marcus Pharoah claimed to have fallen in love with her. Often people said they were in love when it seemed to India that what they were really talking of was desire or even fondness. Love, in her opinion, should be selfless. Love meant putting another person before yourself. Rachel had loved them and had given up a lot for them. Their mother had told her and Sebastian that she loved them, and yet she had not noticed when they had gone hungry. She had talked of love while her daughter had taught herself to steal from shops and inside her son something had broken, perhaps for ever.

Love implied a certain carelessness with the emotions. Pharoah was capable of carelessness, certainly, or his wife would not be divorcing him. India herself avoided and distrusted love, was fearful of its messiness and its intemperate demands. People who loved, people who were in love, lost the capacity to see things clearly. They weren't wary, they didn't see the traps.

I've fallen in love with you. He had said it reluctantly, as if love was a disease that he had unwittingly contracted. He, Marcus Pharoah, who was never ill.

In late August, Alec and Ellen went back to Seil Island. They spent their first morning exploring the coast, following tracks that crossed fields of livestock and skirted beside beaches. Buttercups flecked the grass and rock plants in delicate miniature grew in crevices between the stones. On the beaches, waves spilled and sucked against a shoreline flecked with a mosaic of sea-smoothed slates and frilled green seaweed. Above the cliffs, a buzzard soared high in the sky, the black fingers of its wingtips outstretched to catch the air currents. Further out, crested white breakers smashed against angular rocks. The sea surrounded them, its colour constantly changing and its turbulent surface reflecting diamonds of light. The Lords of the Isles had sailed through these seas; Campbells and MacDonalds had had ownership of the lands.

In the afternoon, Alec helped his mother with the estate paperwork. Ellen offered to help in the house or the garden but was told by Marguerite that she was not needed. Feeling at a loose end, she walked to the village of Ellenabeich, at the far end of the bay. Here, tall granite cliffs smeared with tumbling sheets of scree loomed high over rows of small, white single-storey cottages. A strip of grass divided the cottages from the rubble of stones on the beach. The houses seemed caught between the rocks and the sea. The scene was pretty enough now, but Ellen found that she almost shrank from imagining what it would be like in the dark of winter, on this precipice on the edge of the Atlantic.

She posted her cards and walked to the harbour. Boats clustered against a jetty made of tightly packed slate, bobbing up and down in a livening sea. The tiny island of Easdale lay across a short stretch of water. Ellen could see, over the dividing waves, its rumpled outline and small harbour.

Someone waved to her from an incoming boat. Ellen recognized Catriona Campbell and waved back, watching as Catriona skilfully steered the yacht into the harbour and tied it up to an iron stanchion on the jetty.

Catriona ran up the slipway. Drops of water streamed from her yellow oilskins and her face was flushed. A lock of dark curling hair had come loose from her ponytail; she swept it back with her hand.

'Hello, there! I heard you and Alec were back on the island. How are you?'

'I'm very well,' said Ellen. 'I didn't know you sailed, Miss Campbell.'

'Call me Catriona, please. "Miss Campbell" might do for stuffy suppers at Kilmory House but I was hoping we might be friends. You don't mind if I call you Ellen, do you?'

'Not at all, please do.'

'Do you sail, Ellen?'

'I'm afraid not. It looks so exhilarating.'

Catriona glanced back at the boat and smiled. 'It's one of the things I miss most when I'm away from home. If I'm feeling miserable or in a bad mood I take the yacht out and it always puts me right. I'll take you out sometime, if you like. We could go to Luing, or one of the uninhabited islands. Alec too, of course, though I find he likes to take over. Men do, don't they? Where is he, by the way? I shall scold him for leaving you on your own.'

'I don't mind at all. He's looking over some legal documents for his mother.'

'Marguerite's keeping his nose to the grindstone, then. She never gives up.'

This time, she had to ask. 'What do you mean?'

'Oh, nothing really. Mothers and sons, you know. Woe betide any of us who come between them.' Catriona glanced at her watch. 'I must dash, I'm afraid. I'd offer to keep you company for the afternoon but my father wants me to come to Oban with him and I'm late already.'

Catriona had begun to walk away when she turned back to Ellen. 'How silly of me, I almost forgot. I wondered whether you and Alec would like to come to supper on Friday evening. Marguerite, too, of course.'

'That's very kind, but I don't know our plans yet, I'm afraid.'

'Oh, I'm sure it'll fit in. Eightish. Just an informal supper, no need to dress up.' With a wave of the hand, Catriona left the harbour.

On Friday, dressing for dinner at the Campbells' house, Ellen chose a cream wool skirt and a lilac jersey. When she was ready, she went downstairs. Alec and Marguerite were sitting in the drawing room. Alec was wearing a dark suit, Marguerite a full-length blue frock.

Seeing her, Ellen felt doubtful. 'Should I have dressed up more? Should I change?'

'Certainly not.' Alec kissed her. 'You look beautiful. Drink, darling?'

'You look sweetly pretty in that lilac,' said Marguerite. 'I've just the one going-out frock and I reach for it every time. So dreary of me.'

They had a gin and tonic, then put on their coats and left the house. The fine weather that had lasted since their arrival on the island had begun to break up and a wind whipped the trees in the garden. As Alec drove them along the road beside the bay, Ellen saw the white horses that crested the waves crashing on to the black rocks, sending spray high into the air.

Outside the Campbells' house, half a dozen cars were parked along the narrow track. The building, though substantial, was smaller than Kilmory House. The lower windows were lit up and as they walked up the path to the front door they heard, beneath the wild roar of the wind and the sea, the sound of voices and laughter.

A tall, smiling man with a head of thick silver hair and heavy black eyebrows opened the door and greeted them, introducing himself to Ellen as Dr Campbell. A girl took their coats and they were shown into a drawing room. Crimson velvet curtains hung at the window and Persian rugs were scattered on the dark floorboards. Couples sat on sofas or stood in groups at the window and fireplace. A glance round the room told Ellen that all the women were wearing evening frocks. Some of the women's dresses were pre-war in style, cut on the bias, straining a little across the bust; others wore long tartan skirts and white blouses. Pearls gleamed at throats, gold bracelets jangled on wrists. Ellen felt a rush of dismay. She was the only woman present wearing a knee-length skirt, the only one wearing a jersey. Should she ask Alec to drive her back to Kilmory House so that she could quickly change? No – how foolish and vain that would look.

It took a moment to register that the young woman coming towards them was Catriona Campbell. The Catriona of previous encounters, unremarkable in kilt and jersey or windswept in oilskins, had gone, replaced by a tall, slender young woman whose black velvet evening dress moulded to the curves of her body and whose upswept hair flattered the pale oval of her face. Emerald earrings and a skilful application of make-up brought out the green in her eyes.

Just an informal supper, no need to dress up. Had she misunderstood what Catriona had said to her? No, she did not think so. Or had Catriona changed her mind and had the party grown, as parties sometimes will, starting as one thing and ending up as another? This was possible, she supposed. After all, it had been she who had assumed that the five of them would be the only guests. Catriona had said nothing about numbers. Yet she counted fourteen in the room, including their own party, and it crossed her mind that occasions such as this took planning, especially on an island like Seil. Surely it would be hard to organize at the last moment food, drink, flowers and the hire of a girl from the village to pass around glasses of wine?

She felt awkward as Alec introduced her to the other guests. It seemed to her that in their gazes she saw perplexity and disappointment. She wondered whether they thought she let Alec down or whether they considered her too inept or too snobbishly English to dress up for a dinner in a remote part of Scotland. The tables had been turned: she, Ellen, was now the frumpy girl-next-door in the everyday skirt and jumper, while Catriona, vivid in black velvet and emeralds, flared like a candle. Had Catriona deliberately manipulated the situation? And if so, why?

She gave herself a mental shake. She mustn't start imagining things. What did it matter if she was not wearing her party frock? She was here, with Alec, as his fiancée. Yet she was relieved when Catriona clapped her hands and announced that dinner was served.

'Sounds like a storm's getting up.'

The man sitting at the dining table to one side of Ellen – Gillis Maclean, red hair and blue eyes – had spoken.

'Damn,' said Catriona. 'I was planning to take the boat out tomorrow.'

They had almost finished the main course. 'Might be a touch rough, Cat,' said Gillis. 'Where were you thinking of heading for?'

'Only to Luing.' Catriona, seated at one end of the table, smiled at Ellen. 'I promised you and Alec a trip, didn't I?'

'Sounds fun,' said Alec.

Marguerite frowned. 'Not if the weather's bad, Catriona dear.'

'No, of course not.'

Ellen had noticed how the other guests deferred to Mrs Hunter. Though in Catriona's demure amiability, she thought she detected only a pretence of acquiescence.

'I hope you're a good sailor, Miss Kingsley,' said Gillis.

'I haven't had much opportunity to find out. Only a steamer to France and a few ferry trips to the Isle of Wight.

There isn't a great deal of opportunity for sailing in London. Just pleasure trips down the Thames. My hours at work can be long, so I don't have much time for hobbies.'

'What do you do?'

'I'm a scientist, a biochemist.'

'Like you, Hunter.' One of the Campbells' neighbours, a gaunt, freckled man, nodded at Alec.

'These career women,' said Marguerite, with a thin smile.

'Where did you meet?'

'At Gildersleve Hall, in Cambridgeshire. We were both working there.'

'Romance among the test tubes,' said the freckled man, and there was a ripple of laughter.

'Alec's such a clever lad.' This from an older woman, a Mrs Douglas, who was wearing a white blouse with a yellowing lace jabot. 'You must be so proud of him, Marguerite.'

'How's it going, Hunter?' asked Gillis Maclean. 'Split the atom yet?'

Alec smiled. 'I think you'll find someone got there before me. And atomic science isn't really my field.'

'I suppose you'll find it hard to give all that up.'

It was Donald Frazer who had spoken. 'Give it up?' said Ellen. 'Why should Alec want to give up his work?'

'When he comes back to the island.'

'Alec has told you, Ellen, hasn't he?'

Both Donald and Marguerite spoke at the same time. It was on the tip of Ellen's tongue to say, *told me what?* but she managed not to. Across the table, she met Alec's eyes. A beat passed, she waited for him to speak, but instead he gave a quick frown and looked away.

'Alec's making a name for himself,' Ellen said, her voice level. 'It would be a terrible waste if he were to abandon his work.'

'Alec has a duty.' Marguerite's voice was clear and quiet. 'He's always known that.'

Mrs Douglas broke the uncomfortable silence that followed. 'I expect you were trying not to put Miss Kingsley off, weren't you, Alec? I daresay you were afraid that if she knew she was to live on such an outpost, she might have second thoughts.'

The remark was kindly meant but it fell flat. And shortly afterwards another discussion started up, this time about the price of land.

Because Marguerite felt tired and asked Alec to drive her back to Kilmory House straight after dinner, Ellen had no opportunity to talk to him in the bustle of movement as the party left the dinner table.

She, too, would have liked to have gone home. The evening had become stale and wearisome and the shock of the conversation that had taken place over the dinner table had not dissipated; she felt shaken, as if she had been struck by an ice-cold wave. As Catriona served coffee in the drawing room and Dr Campbell dispensed brandies, Ellen sat on a sofa, talking to Mrs Douglas. She was glad of the older woman's garrulousness, and the rambling anecdotes about grandchildren provided a cloak for her own confusion. Was it true? What had Marguerite and Donald Frazer being referring to – a promise, or some ill-defined understanding, of more significance to mother, perhaps, than son? And if Alec had given any sort of undertaking to his mother, how could he have neglected to mention something so important to her? During their many conversations about their future, they had talked of houses and children – in general terms, nothing fixed so far, not even a wedding date.

When Alec returned to the house, he sat on the arm of the sofa beside her, his hand resting on her shoulder. Though his touch should have comforted, it did not. The turmoil of her thoughts was matched by a rising wind outside that rattled the windows in their frames and made the flames of the fire gutter and flare, and Ellen was relieved when there was a general movement to the front door, where the Campbells were thanked and kisses and handshakes exchanged.

As they walked down the path to the gate, the sound of the sea, not far away, was disturbing and insistent, fighting for attention against the screaming wind.

'I'm sorry,' said Alec. 'I put you on the spot, back there at dinner.'

'It's not true, is it, what Marguerite said? That you mean to leave London and come back here?'

'Nothing's settled.'

His words – his evasion – inflicted another shock.

'So you don't rule it out.'

'I can't.'

'And you didn't think to mention this to me?'

'I was going to talk to you about it.'

'When, Alec?'

His muttered, 'I was waiting for the right moment, that's all,' was almost lost in the howling gale.

They reached the car. As he started up the engine, Alec said, 'You're making it sound as if I've kept some guilty secret from you. My mother's lived here alone since my father died. It's hard for her, she's not young any more, and she could do with someone to help with the house and the land. I can't just walk away from it without a backward glance, surely you see that?'

'To have to learn at dinner, in front of strangers . . .' In front of your mother, she wanted to say.

'I should have said something, I realize that now.'

'*Said something?*' The inadequacy of this remark left her almost speechless. 'Alec, I felt such a fool!'

The windscreen wiper had jammed; he banged at the inside of the screen with his fist, trying to free it. 'I'm sure no one thought you were a fool, darling. They all thought you were perfectly delightful.'

'Alec, you can't just brush it away like that! It was utterly humiliating. I was apparently the only person in the room not to know where we're going to set up home!'

'You're getting it out of proportion.'

She snapped, 'It was hateful! Still, I'm sure Catriona took pleasure in it.'

His gaze flashed to her. 'What are you talking about?'

'Just another little thing you failed to mention, that's all.'

Cascades of rain dashed against the windscreen so that the road ahead was absorbed into the blackness of the landscape and the night. 'I can't see a damned thing.' Alec stabbed a foot on the brake, the car came to a halt and he climbed out. As he leaned across the bonnet, wrestling with the wiper blade, Ellen saw how, above the sea, clouds like strips of grey rag parted now and then to reveal a moon that shone on the writhing waves beneath.

He got back into the car, and they moved off. 'Catriona's gone out of her way to be welcoming to you,' Alec said tightly. 'She made a special effort to come to the house when you first visited the island, just to say hello to you, she told me so. She's offered to take you out in the yacht and she's invited you to dine at her home. What more could she do?'

'She resents me, Alec.'

'Why on earth should she do that?'

'It's obvious. Because she's in love with you.' There, it was out.

'That's nonsense.' He sounded furious.

'I was the only woman there not in evening dress. When I met Catriona at the harbour, she told me that the dinner was to be informal. She said there was no need to dress up.'

But even to her, it sounded weak, a silly fuss about not having worn the right frock.

'I expect you misheard her.' She could hear the irritation in his voice. 'Or she was trying to put you at your ease, so you didn't feel you had to go to too much effort. Does it matter so much?'

'It matters that she deliberately wrong-footed me.'

'Cat isn't like that.'

'What is she like, then, Alec?' The words ripped out of her, unbidden. 'You've hardly told me anything about her!'

They had reached Kilmory House. They headed up the drive. Alec parked in the courtyard. As the car headlamps flooded the paving stones, illuminating the leaves and twigs that danced across the terrace, she turned towards him.

'How long were you together?'

'Ellen, for heaven's sake—'

'How long, Alec?'

'About a year.' An angry shake of the head. 'Something like that. What does it matter?'

'I suspect it still matters to Catriona.'

'Nonsense. You're not jealous, are you? Not of *Cat*?'

'No, of course not.'

But she was. It was an emotion she had little experience of, and she disliked the fact that she was capable of it. She disliked most of all that Catriona's scheming and her own insecurity had ended in this, a quarrel with the man she loved.

Somewhere in the distance a gate or door banged open

and shut, an irregular cannonade. A sheet of newspaper jumped and leaped like an imp, wrapping itself around pots and shrubs before bounding on down the slope. Some of her anger died away and she was able to speak more calmly.

'Alec, you've known these people all your life. But I have to walk into their homes, a complete stranger. I want you to be proud of me, and I need to understand what they mean to you. I want to know your family and friends, to like them, and one day, I hope, to love them. That's important to me because I love you.'

'And I love you, too.' Letting out a breath, he crushed her hand in his. 'You know that, don't you, Ellen? Cat's an old friend, that's all. She's the nearest thing I've ever had to a sister. We went round together for a while, it's true, but it wasn't important. We were always in and out of each other's houses, Cat and I, and I suppose one day I noticed she wasn't a little girl with skinned knees any more.' He paused, looking out of the windscreen. 'There's a side to Cat that likes to stir, to make mischief. And after a while, it began to put my back up.'

Because she had noticed those same characteristics in Catriona, she felt comforted. She said, 'So you broke it off.'

'Yes, I did. We were going our separate ways anyway. There was never a chance of anything serious coming of it. I went off to Edinburgh to study, and Cat went off to train as a nurse, and that was the end of it. And since then, she's always had someone on the go. Every time I see her there's a different boyfriend. No doubt she has this latest fellow running round after her like all the others.' He took her hand in his. 'Ellen, why are we wasting our time talking about Cat? She doesn't matter. It's you I love. Only you.'

She dropped her head on to his shoulder, closing her eyes. She heard him sigh. 'The truth is I've put off the decision for a long time and it makes me feel guilty.'

'Guilty?'

'It would have been much easier for my mother if I'd come back to the island years ago.'

'But you didn't want to?'

'No, I didn't.'

'Because of your work?'

'Among other things.' He gave a bitter laugh. 'I have become a master of prevarication. I'm not proud of it.'

Ellen had remembered something Alec had said to her on the night of Dr Redmond's death, as they had walked back to Copfield together. That sometimes he hated Seil Island, and that belonging somewhere meant that you had to keep going back. She felt a rush of sympathy for him. She, who was rootless, had no easy way of understanding what it was to be tied to a place, or how hard it might be to leave.

Now and then that night, she dozed off. Then the moan of the wind or a fusillade of rain against the windowpane jolted her awake. Lying in the darkness, she seemed to relive incidents from the evening. She had not misheard

Catriona, and no, Catriona had not been trying to put her at her ease. Quite the opposite. Of this she was certain.

It was easy to understand what, ten years ago, might have attracted Alec to Catriona. Her vividness and her athletic grace had an obvious appeal. But he, too, had noticed the dash of unkindness in her, as well as her sharpness of tongue. If Catriona had manipulated a situation in which she would make herself look good in front of Alec and Ellen would be overshadowed, the attempt had misfired.

No, she did not fear Catriona. Other memories troubled her far more: Marguerite at the dinner table, her expression touched with triumph as Donald Frazer let slip that Alec was expected to return to the island. And Marguerite in Kilmory House's sitting room, earlier that evening, dressed in the full-length evening frock that she claimed to wear for every social event. Coincidence, surely. Marguerite would not have planned to make her, Ellen, look a fool. Marguerite and Catriona would not have been in league together. No, surely not.

This, the dead heart of the night, allowed her thoughts to veer and stumble along paths she might not by daylight have ventured down. You could say that back in May, when she had first come to the island, the news of their future marriage had not been welcomed with open arms. Might you say more? That Mrs Hunter resented the engagement? Or that she would prefer Alec to marry Catriona, the island girl?

Marguerite's good opinion of her was vital. The fact of

358

Francis Hunter's early death had bound mother and son tightly together. There was the possibility that their bond might never allow admittance of another. That she might always feel an outsider, and that Marguerite might tolerate her but never like or love her.

Though they had repaired things before they went back into the house, her disagreement with Alec had left her feeling raw and despondent and she knew that out there, sitting in the car in the storm, nothing had been confronted and nothing had been decided. If Alec had promised his mother to return to the island some day, then she would have to live here with him – and with Marguerite. Could she adapt to such a different life? Could she give up all that had been so hard won?

If she and Alec were to have children, she had always known that she would have to give up work for a while. But not for any length of time, because she had seen too often how hard it was for a female scientist to have both a career and a family. Those women who took years off to bring up their children never returned to research. A little teaching, perhaps, was all that was left to them. The few exceptions employed nannies or nursemaids and came back to the laboratory as soon as their babies were weaned. To move to Seil Island would be to put an end to both their careers, Alec knew this, which was why he had put off the decision, and why, presumably, he had baulked at speaking of it to her. Her heart rebelled against it. A better way must be found.

She got out of bed and went to the bathroom to fetch a glass of water. Back in her room, she took two aspirins and opened *The Day of the Triffids*. Bill Mason's struggles, roaming through a London of blinded inhabitants, distracted her from the events of the evening. After a couple of chapters Ellen closed her book and switched off the light. Her mind had calmed and a feeling of certainty and confidence washed over her. Shared problems and shared solutions – didn't those things lie at the heart of a marriage? Dream images rose up into her unconscious like mermaids floating to the surface of the still water of the island's quarries, flickering between the memories as she felt her muscles relax and her heartbeat slow.

Something woke her. The wind had died down and she heard the sound clearly. A tap-tapping, a regular beat, a squeak of floorboard, the scuff of a shoe. She had heard the same sound on her first night on the island. Someone was walking along the corridor.

No. The footsteps came from above. This time she was sure of it, and she felt herself transfixed by a nameless and irrational fear. Something was wandering through the attics in the dark quiet of the early hours of the morning, free, untrammelled, able to roam at will. What was it?

She flicked on the light. There was a moment of sharp terror and then the items in the room resolved into reasonable, rational shapes – a wardrobe, a dressing table, her jersey hanging over the back of a chair.

The sound had stopped. It had been the dog, perhaps.

Marguerite must have thought she shut Hamish into the kitchen at night but maybe he knew a way out. Or she had been woken by the beat of her own heart, which her foolish imagination had transformed into a spectre.

Yet the wisps and shreds of fear remained and it was a long time before she was able to switch off the light and lie down and close her eyes once more.

She dreamed that she was standing on the edge of the high terrace that looked down over Kilmory House. The low wall was no longer there and her toes curled round the precipice. Far below her, scarlet petals had drifted over the garden, so that the grass and shrubs appeared to be bloodstained. She felt rather than saw the presence of someone behind her. A footstep, a light pressure on the small of her back, and she was falling . . .

Ellen woke, fighting for breath. A flare of light showed around the curtains and the clock told her that it was not quite seven in the morning. Her head ached and her eyes felt gritty with lack of sleep. Throwing on a pair of trousers and a jersey, she went downstairs and outside into the garden. Here, in the cool, fresh air, the alarms of the night slid away and the apparitions that had haunted her were dissolved into figments of the imagination by the sunshine.

She walked up the hillside. The grass was wet with dew and the scents of damp earth and new leaves were strong and fresh. Looking up, she saw ahead of her a smear of scarlet petals around the sides of the path. The petals of the roses had been torn from the branches by the force of the wind. Her dream came back to her – that vertiginous drop, that endless fall – and she realized that her unsettled consciousness had dug up her memories of the death of Dr Redmond and impressed them on to the high terraces of Kilmory House.

A movement above her made her tilt her head, shading her eyes from the sun. Alec was coming out from beneath the trees. She ran to meet him and he took her in his arms. And she closed her eyes, burying her head in his shoulder, and the sweet, fierce longing she felt for him was mixed with both fear and relief.

He said, 'Let's get out, shall we?' and she nodded.

Arm in arm, they walked down the path. Reaching the courtyard, he said, 'Wait here,' and she stood in the sunshine until he returned, carrying a small knapsack.

'Breakfast,' he said with a smile.

They went out through the gates. With every step they took away from Kilmory House towards the harbour at Ellenabeich, her heart seemed to lift. There, Alec spoke to a fisherman, and they clambered into the small boat that pitched gently up and down beside the jetty.

Crossing the short strait of water that divided Seil from its much smaller neighbour of Easdale, it seemed to Ellen that the sea had become a different element from the previous night. A few boats were moored in Easdale's narrow harbour. Alec gave Ellen his hand to help her from the boat and thanked the fisherman. The rowing boat headed back across the bay to Ellenabeich as Alec and Ellen walked from the harbour.

Their route took them over Easdale to its westernmost edge, where it faced out to the deserted island of Insh, and then beyond, across the Atlantic. This sweep of coast was a crumpled, jagged mass of sea walls. The beaches were formed of broken slates whose blue-grey sheen caught the early morning sun; the previous night's storm had cast up wreaths of glistening brown seaweed and driftwood and several beached jellyfish, which lay among the debris, their round gelatinous forms solidifying.

A narrow isthmus divided two quarries. Walking along it, Ellen saw in the still turquoise water a mass of shingled slate sloping down steeply, the stones blurring into the depths. Huge submerged rock formations, like underwater leviathans, were dimly discernible beneath the surface of the water. Old stone buildings, roofless and grown over with plants, lay in the shadow of the high land in the centre of the island, leftovers from a past that was long gone. Though the sea sparkled and a thousand flowers glittered like jewels cast into the grass, the place had a melancholy air.

They sat down on a rock overlooking the sea. Alec opened the knapsack. He took out apples, rolls, hard-boiled eggs and a thermos of coffee. He poured out the coffee and handed the cup to Ellen.

He said, 'About last night—'

'It doesn't matter.'

'I think it does. I wanted to talk to you about Cat. I wasn't fair to you, I wasn't honest. And I wouldn't want you to find out from anyone else.'

She felt a ripple of apprehension. She heard him say, 'I was nineteen, Cat was a couple of years younger. I suppose proximity had something to do with it.' He ran a hand over his jaw as he looked out to where the waves rose and fell. 'There was, back then, a kind of understanding between my mother and Dr Campbell. It was a joke, more than anything.'

'An understanding?'

'That Cat and I should marry one day. They used to tease us about it. My parents and the Campbells had always been friends, so you see it was . . .' He didn't finish his sentence. Instead, he said, 'I told you it wasn't important. It isn't now, but it was then. It lasted about a year. And then, as I said, we went our separate ways.'

It took a huge effort to hide the jolt of feeling inside her. But she had to know. 'Was Catriona your first love?'

'Yes.'

'And you were hers?'

'Yes, I suppose I was.'

Another question: *And were you lovers?* But she found she did not need to ask that – her answer was already there in Catriona's careless kiss, laden with intimacy and knowledge, as she had greeted Alec back in May, when Ellen had first come to Kilmory House. It was there, too, in the teasing way Catriona addressed him. The emotion that ran through her was, Ellen knew, unreasonable – she, too, had had lovers – and she fought to suppress it.

Alec took her hand, pressing it against his face. 'Someone had to be first,' he said.

And yet, as she took an apple and began to eat, she wished bitterly that it hadn't been Catriona. Odd that she could stomach the memory of his romance with Andrée Fournier so much more easily than the discovery of an affair with Catriona. Perhaps it was because she and Andrée were not so dissimilar in type – scientists, intellectual, self-possessed, even a little reserved. Catriona was a different kind of woman. That Alec had been attracted to her, that he had fallen in love with her, showed a side of him she did not know. That only Catriona knew.

She said, 'Would your mother still prefer you to marry Catriona?'

He laughed. 'Good God, I shouldn't think so. Why would she? She knows it's long over with.'

'Catriona's from the island. It would be understandable if your mother would prefer you to marry a girl from the island.'

He turned towards her, smiling and frowning at the same time. 'You're not worrying about that, are you? Not really?'

'I'm not sure I'm the sort of woman your mother would have chosen for you.'

'You're worrying about nothing. My mother adores you. She told me so.'

'Really?'

'Yes.'

She let out a breath. 'I'm so glad. Silly of me to worry.'

'Darling, we just need to take it slowly. You don't mind, do you? We need to give my mother time to get used to it. It's been hard for her, since my father died.'

'What happened to him, Alec?' She knew only the barest details. She had been reluctant to make him dig up painful memories.

'He died of pneumonia.' He was looking out to sea, shading his eyes from the light. 'It was in the war.'

'Was it sudden?'

'Very. He had a cold but it was nothing serious. I was away at school when it happened. I didn't even get the chance to say goodbye to him.'

She had little experience of bereavement. A grandmother, a cousin who had been killed at the D-Day landings. She had known neither well.

'You poor thing,' she said. 'And so dreadful for your mother.'

'She invited a medium to the house.'

Startled, she said, 'A medium? Ectoplasm and ouija boards?'

'Pretty much. Pernicious nonsense. Loathsome woman, utter fraud. I remember her drifting around the room, saying these things − that she could feel my father's presence in some part of the house, or that she'd seen his boat in the bay at night. Nothing that could be proved or disproved, of course. I knew she was a fraud, even then, even though I was a child, but she managed to convince my mother that my father was still there, on the island, in some sense. We've never talked about it. We talk about everything else, but not that.'

'Perhaps it gave her some comfort.'

'*False* comfort. Lazy answers and lies.'

She knew that his loathing of superstition was intractable, admitting no space for any other interpretation. She changed the subject.

'Has your mother never thought of marrying again?'

'Never, as far as I know.'

'I wondered whether Mr Frazer—'

'Donald?' Alec's expression lightened and he laughed. 'They're friends, that's all. Donald helps my mother with some of the estate work.'

'Poor Marguerite. It must be lonely.'

He picked up a slate and hurled it into the water. 'My father was the love of her life. She told me so once, not long after he died.'

There was something repellent, she thought, in the placing of such an emotional burden on a young child.

Alec climbed on to a jagged grey rock. 'All the young people know they'll probably have to leave the island. My mother won't admit it, but it's true. I had to leave and so did Cat. You go away to school and university or you go away to work. Some people return but most don't. They go to the mainland or to England or even to America. There's little work here, and anyway, island life's too hard and it's too restricting. People won't put up with it these days. I help out whenever I come home, but most of the burden falls on my mother. At some point, I'm going to have to start pulling my weight. Mother's kept the place going since my father died and now she believes it's my turn. And she's right.' He looked back at her. 'You wouldn't want me to be the sort of man who'd leave his mother to cope with everything on her own, would you, Ellen? You couldn't love that sort of man?'

'No, perhaps not. But—'

'We'll work something out, I know we will. The thing that matters most to me is to be with you.' He came to sit beside her, putting his arm round her. 'Poor girl, you look tired. I'd meant this to be a holiday for you.'

'It is. I didn't sleep well last night, that's all. The storm . . .' She had been about to tell him about the footsteps she had heard in the night, but something made her reluctant to and she said instead, 'I dreamed about Dr Redmond. I wonder why.'

'Indigestion, probably, after that enormous meal.'

She laughed. 'Too much venison and red wine? Yes, I expect you're right.'

'What did you dream?'

'That I was falling.' The bleakness returned, tumbling over her like a shadow.

He hugged her. 'We'll go for a long walk this afternoon, work it off. Not here – you'd have to do several circuits of Easdale to make even a half-decent walk.'

Tentatively, she put to him an idea that had come to her during the night.

'Alec, why don't you ask your mother to come to London next month? Buy her a train ticket, book her into a nice hotel, give her a treat. We could take her round, show her the sights. I'm sure it would be good for her.'

'She won't come.' He looked out over the sea, frowning. 'I've asked her before, many times.'

'If you tried again . . . I thought that perhaps when we're married, if we were able to find a house in London – some lovely part of London, Hampstead or Richmond, somewhere like that – we could make one of the floors into a little flat for your mother. She might take a while to get used to the change, but who knows, she might love it. If we had children, it would mean she could be close to them. She wouldn't even need to sell this house if she didn't want to. Surely some tenant or factor could be found?'

'She wouldn't consider it.' He began to pack the remains of their breakfast into the knapsack. His voice was without timbre as he said, 'Ellen, my mother will never leave Kilmory House. She would never be happy anywhere else.'

And the thought occurred to her: and if I can never be happy here?

Chapter Nine

Marcus Pharoah was away for a fortnight in America. In his absence, India sought out the company of her old friends once more. There was a certain relief in being with Vinnie and Oliver and Simon, who didn't tell her off for failing to work out what to do with her life. In fact, some of her friends were far more aimless than she was, preferring to avoid work at all costs, sleeping on other people's sofas and pretending to be artists or writers, when really they stayed in bed all day and hung around pubs at night, now and then summoning up the energy to try and persuade someone to go to bed with them.

In their undemanding company, India spent an afternoon at Peachey's house, then dashed through the rain showers on to a pub. India was wearing the greeny-gold frock Marcus had bought her, a little damp because she hadn't brought a coat. She thought how happy she was to be sitting with her friends, laughing and joking and fooling around. Ed and Justine joined them and they all wandered off to the West End. It was late, and a drizzle hung in the air, hazing the pavements, and only a few cars motored along the quiet streets.

Ed offered to pay their entrance to a nightclub. Ed was the only person who had enough money to buy drinks, and the others crowded round him at the bar, though India knew that away from him they often spoke of him as a figure of fun: Ed and his boring job in a bank and his wife who cheated on him. The room was dark and poky. India saw that the purple velvet curtains were marked with cigarette burns and the flocked wallpaper was peeling. The clientele sat at small, round tables draped with fringed cloth. India read in the faces that loomed out of the dim light expressions of boredom and envy and greed. She felt her buoyant mood of earlier in the evening start to slip away as she stood alone, smoking and listening to the three-piece band.

Then she saw him. Bernie, making his way towards her, cutting through the throng at the bar. She felt a rising panic, mixed with revulsion. Since she and Marcus Pharoah had become lovers, she had kept away from Bernie.

She dropped her cigarette on the floor and hurried out of the room. In the street, she took off her high heels and ran along the pavement until she saw a taxi. She hailed it and climbed into the back seat, where she sat, her shoes in her lap, catching her breath. Looking out of the rear windscreen, she saw Bernie standing on the pavement, his short, plump form broken into smudged, glittering fragments by the street lamps and the raindrops on the glass.

Ellen went with Riley and Annie and Annie's friend, Kathleen, to Regent's Park. There was a chill in the air and the fallen leaves were piling up on the grass.

She said, 'I may have to give up my work and go and live on the island.'

Riley threw her a glance. 'You're not serious, are you?'

'Yes, I am. I didn't understand, you see, Riley.' Briefly, she told him about the dinner party at Catriona's house, and about her mortifyingly public discovery that she and Alec were expected to live on the island after they married.

He pointed out, 'That's not the same as *Alec* expecting it.'

'But I think it will happen.' Her voice was heavy.

'Only if you agree to it. What does Alec say?'

'Not much.' She scuffed leaves on the grass.

'You weren't aware of this before?'

'No, not properly.'

She thought back to their quarrel, while the storm had whipped up the breakers on the sea. Since then, they had discussed their future on numerous occasions but had come to no conclusions.

She said, 'Alec told me that he's been putting off returning to the island for years. And that makes him feel guilty, because he knows his mother needs him. I can see that he's in an impossible situation.'

'It's difficult for him, yes.'

She sensed something held back, and said quickly, 'It's not unreasonable, Riley. It's his home.'

'But you have reservations.'

'Yes, I do.'

The girls were kicking up heaps of leaves and jumping into them.

'I love Alec,' said Ellen. 'I love him so much. So why can't I just do it, tell him that of course we'll live on Seil, without thought, without regret?'

'Because it's a big step. What is it that puts you off?'

'Oh . . . the weather.' She smiled as she looked at him. 'I know that's feeble. But I'm a southern girl. And the remoteness – I'd be so far away from my family and friends. And then, as I said, my career. I would have to give up my career.'

'Hard for you, I should have thought.'

'But not unexpected. I've always known that unless I remain single, I'd probably have to stop work for a while, especially if I had a baby. And women's careers are always thought less important than men's, aren't they?' She dug her hands into her jacket pockets and walked on. 'And it's not as if I would necessarily be the only one who has to give up work. Alec will have a better chance than me of getting a part-time lectureship in Glasgow or Edinburgh because he's published more papers. But even he couldn't be sure.'

She watched Annie and Kathleen running ahead in fits

and starts, pink-cheeked, plaits flying. She said, 'But I could cope with all those things – the cold, the remoteness, and even giving up my career. What I'm not sure I can cope with is Marguerite.'

'You don't get on?'

'We're fine on the surface. We don't argue, anything like that.' She paused, finding it hard to put into words the fears that nagged at her. 'I think I can see what she's doing. She's lost her husband and she's making sure she doesn't lose her son as well.'

'Is that how she views the marriage? As losing her son?'

'I'm afraid so.'

'What does Alec think?'

'He can think no wrong of her. He won't *allow* himself to think any wrong of her.'

Spying a large Alsatian dog, Annie ran towards it. Riley loped after her, calling out her name. Ellen heard Annie grumbling, as they walked back hand in hand, 'If I had a dog, Daddy, I wouldn't have to talk to other people's dogs.'

When she had run off to play with Kathleen again, Ellen gave Riley an amused look. 'Will you buy her a dog?'

'Probably, for Christmas. She's very keen. It will make our lives more complicated, no doubt. Renée, the au pair, goes back to Switzerland in a couple of months so I shall have to find someone else.'

They parted to skirt a woman pushing a large pram, laden with twins; when they moved together again he said,

'You're concerned that if you move to the island then you'll both be under Marguerite's thumb.'

'She's manipulative. I feel very disloyal saying that, and I'd only say it to you, Riley. For instance, she likes to make out she's frail and delicate. Now and then she's unwell and poor Alec has to go dashing all the way up to Scotland. Usually it's at some crashingly inconvenient time for us, when we've been invited for dinner somewhere nice or we're planning a weekend away. And she always miraculously recovers in a couple of days. And she keeps telling us how difficult it is for her to get to the shops or to see her friends. She has everyone running around after her – Alec and Donald and Dr Campbell, all acting as her chauffeur. But she has a perfectly good car sitting in the garage. Last time we were there, I offered to teach her to drive.'

'What did she say?'

'She just laughed, as if I'd said something ridiculous. Said that she couldn't possibly. I asked her why not and she said she was afraid not all women were as strong and practically minded as I was. But she's as tough as old boots – I've seen her in the garden, hacking away at branches and clearing out streams. Oh dear.' Ellen grimaced. 'Listen to me. I sound such a bitch.'

He smiled. 'Hardly.'

'And then there's Catriona.'

'The girl next door . . .'

'Yes. If it wasn't for Catriona's . . .' again, she searched for the word, 'her *history* with my future husband, I'd probably rather like her. When Marguerite's being particularly self-sacrificing, Catriona makes faces behind her back.' Ellen picked up a conker and passed it from hand to hand. 'Catriona's beautiful, Riley.'

'So are you.'

'Kind of you. But I'm not wild and devil-may-care. I can't sail a yacht single-handed because I'd probably be seasick, and I can't climb a mountain because I'm afraid of heights. Marguerite *adores* Catriona. But I can't pretend to be the sort of woman Marguerite would prefer me to be. I just can't, Riley, I've never been any good at pretending. And I can see Marguerite looking at me and comparing me to Cat and thinking, what on earth does he see in her? And with Cat – she thinks Catriona's such a sweet girl, and believe me, Riley, Cat may have many fine qualities, but sweetness certainly isn't one of them.'

'You're engaged to Alec, Catriona isn't. Alec has chosen you. What Mrs Hunter thinks doesn't matter.'

'But they used to be lovers.' She found it hard even to say. 'Alec and Cat.' She saw him frown.

'Some time ago, presumably.'

'Before he left the island to go to university.'

'Then—'

'Catriona's still in love with him, I'm sure of it.'

She stared moodily ahead of her, at the bronze-leaved trees and the green of the grass, already dulling with the coming autumn. 'Sometimes I think I'm imagining it,' she said quietly. 'I think about the things that are troubling me and they hardly seem anything at all. Maybe Marguerite was too busy or too tired to say something nice. Or maybe she was trying to be tactful with me and ended up putting her foot in it. You know how you do, when you're trying too hard.'

Riley didn't say anything, and after a while she went on, her voice level, 'But I don't think she likes me. Alec says she does, but I don't feel it.' No: she had felt no affection or liking from Marguerite, only a mind made up, and an obdurate will. She muttered, 'I'm not having her drive us apart.'

He gave her a sharp look. 'Is there any risk of that?'

'No, of course not. We don't have to like each other, do we? It's Alec I'm marrying, not Marguerite.'

'But you may have to live with each other.'

'Exactly, Riley. The nail hit on the head.'

'Ellen, not all things are solvable. Alec may have to make a choice, and if he does, he'll choose you.'

'How do you know that?'

'Because he's in love with you.'

They walked for some time in silence. But she said suddenly, 'I sometimes think, would I ask such a thing of Alec? If it was the other way round, would I expect him to leave his home and career and bury himself in Wiltshire with my family?'

His gaze snapped round, clear-eyed. 'Would you, Ellen?'

'No, I don't think so. It would seem too much to ask. So where does that leave me?' She broke off, pressing her fingers against her mouth. 'I can't bear to think he doesn't love me as much as I love him!'

Standing in front of her, he put his arms round her. She laid her head against his shoulder and closed her eyes, squeezing back the tears. She thought how differently she felt here in London, in Riley's company, how relieved and how free. Yes, that was it: free. Each time she went away from Kilmory House, she felt free again.

'You can't measure love,' he said gently. 'You can't weigh it up like that.'

'Can't you? Are you sure of that?'

'It's not a scientific equation, Ellen.'

She made a sound between a laugh and a sigh. 'No, I suppose not.'

'And sometimes one person has to give a little more than the other. Talk to Alec. Tell him how you feel. You'll sort it out.' He, too, laughed as they walked on, his hand lightly balanced on her shoulder. 'I don't think I'm the person to be giving you marital advice, Ellen, but there you have it, to the best of my ability.'

And yet, parting from her later that afternoon, Riley felt troubled. What Ellen was telling him was that Hunter wasn't listening. It was a measure of her loyalty and affection that she was even considering giving up her job and moving in with her future mother-in-law. Riley thought what a fool Alec Hunter was, demanding that she immure herself in the wilderness. But then, he had had Alec Hunter down as self-absorbed years ago, when he had interviewed him at Gildersleve Hall, and the dinner at Ellen's flat had done little to alter his opinion of him. Possibly unfair, he acknowledged. He couldn't help but see Hunter through a rather cracked lens.

At home, he cooked supper while Annie sat at the table and learned her spellings. They had the dog conversation again over supper, and then Annie went to bed.

In the sitting room, he put on a record of Mozart's wind quintets, poured himself a Scotch, and took a file out of his briefcase. His visit to the Blue Duck nightclub had supplied Riley with the name of another of Bernie Perlman's spiders. The ginger-haired man – Sergeant Davies's 'spectre' – was called Lee Carter. Carter worked for Perlman as a general dogsbody, chauffeur and errand boy. A teenage delinquent with an absent father during the war years, he had graduated to a career of theft and street violence before starting to work for Perlman. A few years ago, Carter had been interviewed in connection with a murder in Battersea. The victim had had his kneecaps smashed before being tied to a pier and left to drown in the muddy tidal shallows of the Thames. Riley saw in the extreme violence and the flamboyance of the violence something in common with the death of George Clancy. Carter was a nasty piece of work.

The girl that Riley had helped up from the floor of the nightclub was called Janey Kelly. He had seen her once or twice since that evening, had bought her a coffee and chatted to her, if she was in the mood. He thought she was a nice girl beneath the veneer of hardness, and he could tell that she was frightened of Carter and Perlman. Riley felt sorry for her, as out of her depth as a rabbit caught up in the blades of a combine harvester, and as likely to be crushed.

He was trying to establish the scope of Bernie Perlman's business interests. A lodging house here, a warehouse there, a nightclub, a casino or two. On a map of London, you could have seen how Perlman's empire had grown in a steady dark sprawl. Put together the pieces and something, eventually, would give up its secrets.

But tonight he couldn't concentrate. After a while, he put the file aside and sat, letting the music flow over him, remembering how it had felt to hold Ellen in his arms: the beat of her heart, the scent of her hair. *I'd only say it to you, Riley* — he found himself holding on to such fragments, as if he was searching for diamonds in the dust.

India and Sebastian were supposed to be going to tea with Sebastian's old headmaster, Mr Taylor, but India was late. She had arrived at work that morning almost an hour late and had gone on being late throughout the day — late to get the tables cleaned and set for lunch, late to clear away lunch, with some customers still eating their apple pie and custard while others arrived for scones and tea. Then she had to work late to make up the time lost and so wasn't able to leave the café until six. She couldn't afford to have her wages docked: there were bills to pay.

As she walked down the street, she unbuttoned her overall and pulled out the hair clips she used to pin back her fringe while she was working. She imagined Sebastian and Mr Taylor sitting in the chintzy back room at the school, politely waiting for her, their tea going cold. Nearing the house, she saw a big black car waiting by the kerb. Lee was in the driver's seat, Bernie was sitting beside him. India's mouth went dry and she felt a mingling of anger and dread.

She considered not bothering getting changed and turning round and walking away in the other direction, but there was a smear of gravy down her jersey, and anyway, why should bloody Bernie stop her getting into her own home?

As she approached, Bernie wound down the window of the car. 'Hello, India.'

'Hello, Bernie.'

'I haven't see you for a while.'

'I've been busy.'

'Thought the two of us could go for a drink.'

'No thanks. I'm meeting someone.'

India scrabbled in her bag for her front door key. Bernie got out of the car. He said, 'I've got the feeling you've been avoiding me, India.'

Where was the bloody key? She tried to remember what had happened that morning. Sebastian had left for work before she had got up. Had she taken her key? Had she even remembered to lock the door? Maybe she had forgotten and had just pulled it to.

'I told you,' she said to Bernie. 'I've been busy.'

'Disappointing. And after you promised me.'

'Promised you?' She looked up from her handbag. 'I've never promised you anything.'

'Oh yes, you did. All those drinks I've bought you. All those times I've treated you.'

She stared at him. She thought of his horrible parties and his stupid women and what he had done to Garrett.

She said, 'It's never a treat being with you, Bernie.'

Bernie's round, flat, walnut face altered. 'What did you say?'

India was fired up with fury and vengefulness. 'Didn't you know? People put up with you because you're rich and you think you're important, but they don't like you. Why should they? You're stupid and short and fat and ugly and you frighten people.'

Bernie grabbed hold of her ponytail and yanked her head back sharply. 'Shut up, you silly little bitch.'

He had pulled her head so far back it almost touched the roof of the car. India dropped her handbag. Tears sprang to her eyes and she gasped with pain.

Bernie gave her hair another vicious tug. 'No one talks to me like that,' he said. 'Specially not a tart like you.'

He let go of her ponytail and she staggered. Bernie's fat forefinger jabbed at her.

'You want to think about it. You want to think a bit more about what you say to me, India.'

The car roared away from the kerb in a screech of tyres. India put her hands to her head. She imagined chunks of hair coming out of her scalp, but when she cautiously explored it, only a few strands came away. Several passers-by were staring at her, but their faces were blurred by her tears. The contents of her handbag had scattered over the pavement; she scooped everything up and in doing so found her door key, tangled up with a bracelet and a rubber band. Wiping her eyes dry with her sleeve, she let herself into the building.

One of the girl computers stuck her head round the door of Ellen's lab and told her that there was a phone call for her. The phone was in an adjacent office. Ellen picked up the receiver and said her name.

'This is Catriona Campbell.'

A shock. She replied, 'Miss Campbell, hello. How are you?'

'I'm very well, thank you. I'm in London for a few days and I wondered whether we might meet up.'

'Alec has a lot on. I'd have to check with him.'

'I don't want to talk to Alec, I want to talk to you. I'm staying in Chelsea. Would you be able to meet me for lunch in Peter Jones?'

A mixture of curiosity and suspicion made Ellen say, 'Yes, at one o'clock.'

Catriona was already sitting at the table when Ellen arrived at the restaurant. Catriona was wearing a tailored peacock-blue jacket and a neat matching hat, trimmed with net. There was a stack of carrier bags beside her seat.

The two women exchanged the usual pleasantries while their orders were taken and served, but then Catriona said, 'I know you hate me, but there are things I need to say to you.'

'I don't hate you.'

'You should do, after that frightful dinner.' Catriona shrugged. 'In different circumstances I should probably have liked you. But we're both in love with the same man and that makes friendship impossible.'

'I don't want to know.' Ellen was unable to disguise her anger. 'Why are you telling me these things?'

'Because you should know what you're up against. You won't believe me, but I'm here out of kindness to you.'

And self-interest, Ellen thought. She said stiffly, 'Please say what you've come here to say.'

'I've always loved Alec.' Though Catriona spoke with composure her fingers crumbled the bread roll on her side plate. 'I can't remember a time when I didn't love him. Oh, I'm not going to pretend that I've never looked at another man – I'd have gone mad with boredom if that were true – but I've never *loved* another one.'

'But he doesn't love you.' Cruel, but it had to be said.

Catriona's reaction showed only in a small tightening of the mouth. 'Not now, I know that. But that can change in time. I can be patient, I can wait. And anyway, I would have him even under those circumstances.'

'Alec loves *me!*' Ellen rose clumsily.

'*Please.*' Catriona spoke softly, and for the first time, Ellen noticed the pain in her eyes.

She gave a small shrug: *well, if you must,* and sat down again. 'I expect you're going to tell me that Marguerite would rather Alec married you.'

'I'm sure you've worked *that* out for yourself. She makes no attempt to hide it. Dear old Marguerite, so doggedly self-absorbed. If it's any comfort to you, I don't believe that it's out of any attachment to me. She'd rather Alec married me simply because it would mean he stayed on the island.'

'There's no reason why we can't stay on the island too, after we're married.'

'Isn't there? Do you really think you could bear it? Marguerite won't change, you know. She's far too used to having her own way. That's the awful thing about people like her, you can't change them so you end up giving in to them. Marguerite sees only what she wants to see and hears only what she wants to hear.'

There was something she had to know. 'Have you and Marguerite talked about me?'

'A little, yes.'

'I suppose she tells you when Alec and I are to visit.'

'She may have mentioned it.' For the first time, a flicker of shame crossed Catriona's face. 'Ellen, I'm not at

Marguerite's beck and call, if that's what you're saying. I wouldn't sink so low. It's just that I need to see Alec sometimes. I couldn't bear not to see him at all. I've tried that and I was miserable. Of course, it's miserable too to see him with someone else, but it's better than nothing.' She gave a thin smile. 'It's dishonourable of me, I agree, to keep coming back, keep hoping he'll change his mind, but there you are. I've often thought I should marry some rich consultant and stay away from the island, but I can't seem to make myself.'

Catriona seemed then to notice her destruction of the bread roll and wiped her hand on her napkin. She said briskly, 'I expect you're waiting for Alec to put his foot down, or for Marguerite to change her mind or to realize how torn he is. I would be, in your position. Bad enough living with Marguerite, but to have to share the house with Francis Hunter's tiresome ghost as well . . .'

'I don't know what you mean.'

'Did you know that she still keeps Francis's old clothes? They still hang in his wardrobe – she has his shirts laundered each week.' Catriona's lip curled in distaste. 'I'm going to tell you the truth about him. You'll have a different version from Marguerite, no doubt, but I think you should know. I was eleven when Francis Hunter died, so I remember him a little, though not very well. I remember finding him dislikable. He was one of those men who believe it their duty to correct any mistakes a child makes, any mispronunciation or faulty manners. My mother was brought up on the island and she knew him well. She told me that Francis Hunter was a controlling bully. She said that he dominated Marguerite, and that Marguerite let him. Marguerite likes to play the defenceless little woman, you must have noticed that.'

'I don't see why this matters to me.'

'Well, why should you? These tedious old love affairs . . . Romeo and Juliet pale beside Marguerite and Francis.'

'All that's in the past. It's the present – and the future – Alec and I have to think about now.'

'But Marguerite's past will dictate your future, don't you see? Marguerite will never leave the island. Never. You must believe me, for your own sake. She clings on to Francis – to the myth of Francis – through the island. And she won't give up on Alec either. She's lost one of the men she loves and she'll do anything to hang on to the other. But the most important thing you need to realize is that Alec will, in the end, do as his mother wants. I've known him far longer than you have, Ellen, and I know his faults. Alec avoids emotional scenes. It's because of his mother, of course – he's had to endure her dramas all his life. And my God, can't Marguerite ladle it on when she wants to. Alec will never confront her and he'll never say no to her. I suppose the nearest he's come to standing up to her was when he became engaged to you. It was a shock to her, I can tell you. I expect he didn't tell her about it beforehand because he knew she would try to dissuade him.'

There was an unsettling ring of truth to that. There had been a recklessness about their engagement, and it occurred to her now that Alec had rushed into it so that he could present his mother with a fait accompli.

No. She would not believe that. She said, 'He didn't speak to his mother beforehand because there was no need to. It was between him and me. He's a grown man, he doesn't have to ask his mother's permission to get married.'

'Marguerite wants Alec home, and in the end, Alec will do what his mother wants.'

'You can't know that.'

'Oh, I do, I'm afraid. And I think you're beginning to know it too, Ellen.'

The small smile that had set around the corners of Catriona's mouth seemed at odds with the hurt and weariness in her eyes. She took a packet of John Player's out of her bag and waved them at Ellen. 'You don't, do you?'

'No thanks.'

'Coffee and cigarettes – how else would I keep going through a night shift? But what a fool I am, waiting for him! It ties me to nursing, which I loathe, and it means I'll never settle for anyone else. So there's another thing you should know. When Alec does, in the end, go back to the island, I mean to be there. I would do anything for him, you see. I would even submit to living with Marguerite. I'd marry him tomorrow, if he asked me, and I wouldn't so much as look back.'

'You had your chance.' Ellen's voice shook with anger and apprehension. 'Ten years ago, you had your chance.'

'Did I?' Catriona frowned. 'I'm not so sure. Alec wasn't ready to marry anyone ten years ago. It almost destroyed me to learn that. I'd thought he felt the same as I did. But you're capable of such self-deception, aren't you, when you're seventeen. It hurt so much to know that he could walk away from me. I'm afraid I wasn't very nice to him. In fact, I found myself wanting to make him hate me.' Catriona blew out a stream of smoke and, smiling, looked up at Ellen. 'I've sometimes regretted that. But then, they say that love and hate aren't always that far apart, don't they?'

Coming home from work a few days after her encounter with Bernie, India saw that the front door to the flat was open. She went inside. The room was in a terrible mess, as if a whirlwind had blown through it, throwing their possessions around anyhow. Books lay on the floor, splayed open, face down, and ornaments had been broken and plant pots upturned, smearing the carpet with earth.

Then she saw Sebastian. He was crouched on the floor by the sideboard, his head lowered and his arms wrapped round his knees. He had made himself into a small, tight ball. India knelt down beside him. When she put a hand on his shaking shoulder he flinched.

'Sebastian?' she said. She tried to keep the panicky rise out of her voice. 'Darling, what is it? What's happened?'

'Sorry,' he muttered. 'Sorry.'

As he straightened, wiping a hand over his face, India saw the pink marks round his neck.

'Who did this?' Though she had guessed.

'He was here.' Sebastian's eyes kept darting back to the front door. 'In the flat. When I came home. I just let him.'

India felt sick with fear. 'What did he want?'

'I don't know.' Sebastian's voice sounded hoarse. 'He didn't say. He knew my name, though. And yours, India!'

Looking at the angry marks on her brother's neck, India felt rage and an overwhelming guilt. 'Was he tall? Ginger hair? Stupid-looking?'

Sebastian nodded.

'If he's hurt you—'

'S'all right. I just fell against the wall.' He rubbed his head. Then he whispered, 'I didn't do anything! I didn't even try to stop him!'

'Well, thank God for that,' said India tartly. 'He'd have killed you if you had.' She rose to her feet. 'I'll make us a cup of tea.'

She went into the kitchen and stood for a moment, her hands on the edge of the sink, feeling sick. Lee had had fun in here as well, emptying tins and packets over the floor and pulling saucepans and crockery out of the cupboard. Aunt Rachel's bone-china tea set, pink flowers and gold leaf, lay in pieces on the floor. Consumed with fury, India knelt down and picked up the broken fragments.

Then she put on the kettle and went back into the other

room where Sebastian was trying to fit a geranium back in the pot.

India said, 'Seb, he won't come back. Honest. I'll make sure of it.'

They hugged, and then she made the tea, crushing three aspirins and lots of sugar into Sebastian's cup. They began to clear up the flat, putting the books back on the shelves, sweeping up the soil. Although India had resolved to make sure that Lee would not return, she knew that he was a headcase, so she wedged a chair beneath the front-door handle. The telephone rang several times but she did not answer it. Bernie had sent Lee to the flat to punish her for the things she had said to him, and as a reminder of a debt owed. She knew that they could change the locks, put up bolts, but someone like Lee would always find a way in.

When the worst of the mess was gone, she cooked supper. After they had eaten, they sat on the sofa side by side, listening to the radio. India smoked and chewed her nails, thinking, as some man talked about dahlias.

She had to work out what to do about Sebastian. The flat wasn't safe any more, would never be safe again. She must send Sebastian away somewhere where Bernie would never find him. Her only alternative was to go to Bernie. To offer herself up to him, to share his bed, to become one of his entourage.

She would sooner have died. She knew how Bernie liked his women, humiliated and submissive, the fight beaten out of them. By the time he tired of her, there wouldn't be much left of her.

So. They could shove a few things in a bag, she could cadge some money off friends, they could get on a train and start again somewhere else. She knew, as she considered it, that it would not do. Each time they moved — and she would always be looking over her shoulder — they would become a little poorer, a little lonelier. Sebastian would hate it, moving around all the time, never having a real home. She would find friends, she always did, but what sort of friends?

There were other futures she needed to avoid. You could be too free, she had learned that a long time ago. You would always have men friends, because you were pretty and amusing, though in your emptier moments you might find yourself lying on the sofa, leafing through a magazine and letting things slide. This was a more possible future for her than one as Bernie's tart, and because of that, equally frightening. The negligence and evasion of reality that had been a part of her mother's character was a part of her too. If she was not to repeat her mother's mistakes, then she must change. She must start again.

Sebastian had fallen asleep, huddled up on one end of the sofa. The man on the radio was still talking about dahlias. All India's choices were narrowing down to only one. She went into the hall, picked up the phone and dialled Marcus Pharoah's number.

* * *

The weather grew wilder as Alec and Ellen drove north. Darkness fell, and as they approached the Argyll coast, rain dashed against the windscreen of the car. Sometimes a twig, blown from the trees, cracked against the bonnet, and the steering momentarily lost traction as they forded deep puddles. The black landscape was relieved only by the twin beams of the headlamps, picking out the twists and turns of the road. Though she caught mere glimpses of the sea as they drove along the coastal road from Oban, Ellen was aware of its proximity, vast and formless and powerful.

It was past eight o'clock by the time they reached the island. Over supper, she heard the bow and scrape of the trees in the wind and the ricochet of dead leaves and twigs blown against the windowpanes. As Marguerite and Alec talked, Ellen's mind drifted. She found herself watching the scene as if from the outside, noticing how each participant took their allotted role, as friends and families so often do: Marguerite, queenly, directing the course of the conversation, Donald, affable and deferential, Alec, charming his mother and pacifying her moods. It came to her that this was a role he had adopted many years ago, when he had taken on the task of compensating for the absence of his father.

She had not told Alec about her lunch with Catriona. She could have predicted the conversation that would have ensued had she told him that Catriona was in love with him. He would have repudiated it. He would have said that

Cat was playing games. *Cat likes to make mischief* — she could hear his voice. Ellen had come to see that Alec shared some of his mother's reluctance to listen.

There was a pattern to their discussions about their future. She would believe they had come to a decision about where they would live after they married, only for it to disintegrate over the ensuing days or weeks. He should start to look for a junior lectureship in Glasgow, she would say, and Alec would agree. Time would pass and nothing would happen. He did not evade, but he seemed to forget — or not even that: what she saw as a resolution, he saw as merely a suggestion. She found herself filtering their relationship through the net of Catriona's words. She wondered whether, as Catriona had implied, Alec disliked the emotional fallout of confrontation so much that he hung on, hoping for circumstances to change, even after an atmosphere had become contaminated.

Ellen went to bed early. The journey had tired her and the storm unsettled her, yet she did not, as she had hoped, quickly fall asleep. Thoughts turned and roiled through her head, troubling and unresolved.

She must have been dozing shallowly when, opening her eyes, she heard it again. She sat up, listening.

A creak, a squeak, a flurry of scratches and scrapes. Someone — something — was in the attic. Against the silence of the night, the footsteps seemed resonant and unnaturally loud. The sounds settled down to a soft, rhythmic tread that moved with purpose and direction. The boundaries of her room – walls, ceiling – seemed fragile, and she found herself glancing in the direction of the door.

Ellen forced herself to rein in her fear. Alec or Marguerite must have gone up to the attic, that was the only explanation. But why?

Putting on her dressing gown, she left her room. She was about to switch on the light in the corridor when she saw beneath a door ahead a narrow band of illumination. As she watched, the light died, then shone again. She found herself hesitating, afraid of what she might find when she opened the door, and then she reached out and turned the handle.

Revealed by the intermittent light, she saw in front of her half a dozen stairs, leading upwards. Another flash of light from the interior of the attic showed the high roof beams above and opaque, bulky objects stowed on the floor. Nothing moved. Only the light oscillated once more, and now the oscillation seemed to Ellen to have some pattern to it. As she climbed the stairs she found herself stepping softly, as if not to forewarn whatever prowled there of her presence. She should have brought a torch, she thought. It was not Alec, this thing that walked at night, she was certain of that, and the thought that the light might go out and leave her in the darkness produced in her a visceral fear.

Through a skylight she saw, lit by the moon, the gusting outlines of the clouds. She heard another footstep, saw another flash of light. Its source came from some distance away; she made her way in that direction, winding between dusty suitcases and tea chests. Mentally, she matched the layout of the attic to that of the house below. Alec had told her that it was possible to walk through the attics from one end of the building to the other. She knew that she was heading for Kilmory House's westernmost end, the gable closest to the sea.

A circle of light lit up an arched window that looked out over the bay. Beside it, a figure was lit up, black against the bright light, its shadow streaking across the floorboards towards her.

A moment of cold terror: then she whispered, 'Marguerite.'

Slowly, the older woman turned towards her. She was holding a torch in her hand.

'I thought it was you.' Marguerite spoke quietly. 'Alec has always been such a sound sleeper. I can never sleep when there's a storm.'

'What are you doing?'

'I like to signal out to sea.'

Ellen suppressed a shiver. 'To whom?'

'Francis, of course. I like to think it helps him find his way home. It's just a fancy of mine. Some nights, the noise of the wind seems to come into my dreams. Come here.'

Ellen approached the window. Outside, curls of moon-light glimmered on the bay. 'Look,' murmured Marguerite. 'It's just a small boat, only a day cruiser, and it has white sails. It heads back into the bay from the open sea. The sails are torn and tattered and it seems to limp a little as it makes for the harbour. He's tired, of course, after his long battle with the storm, but he was always a fine sailor and he brings the boat safely into port.'

And for a moment Ellen found herself searching the waters of the bay, almost believing that if she tried hard enough then she might see Francis Hunter's boat coming into Ellenabeich harbour.

But the sea was empty, of course. 'There's nothing,' she murmured.

'No. He's never there, my poor darling.' Marguerite put the torch down on the windowsill.

'Marguerite, why don't we go downstairs?' Ellen spoke firmly. 'I could make us some tea.'

Marguerite shook her head. 'You go.'

'I don't like to leave you here.'

'It comforts me. Has Alec told you about that night? It was wartime, nineteen forty-one. Francis was in the Navy, guarding the Atlantic convoys. He came home on leave that autumn. He was exhausted and so thankful to return to the island. One day, he decided to go fishing. I begged him not to go to sea that day. He wasn't well, he'd had a bad cold, and the weather was on the turn. I always think I should have tried harder. I always think, if only I'd found the right thing to say.'

'You mustn't blame yourself, Marguerite.'

Again, Marguerite smiled. 'Oh, I don't. He was a man who knew his own mind. A wind got up and the storm must have swept him out to sea. The *Mairead* wasn't built for heavy weather. I often think how it must have been for him, and how he must have fought against it. I wonder whether he felt frightened. He wasn't a fearful man, but I think how lonely he must have felt and how weary. And I wonder whether he knew that he was losing the battle.' She turned towards the window again. 'I wonder if his spirit revisits that night, if he's still there in some way, struggling against the storm, if only I could push aside the veil.'

Moonlight flickered on Marguerite's face, illuminating the curve of cheekbone and jaw, the same lines and angles that made up Alec's face.

'When he didn't come home I raised the alarm, and the fishing boats went out to look for him. But there were so few of them because of the war and it took them a long time to find him. All that night and day I watched for him from the attic. You get the best view of the bay up here. I was afraid that if I let myself sleep or rest or eat, then he'd never come home. I thought that I could bring him back by the strength of my longing. But they didn't bring him home until halfway through the next afternoon. I stayed up here until I saw the boats coming in and then I ran down to the harbour. He was still alive then – just – but his cold had turned to pneumonia. Henry Campbell did his best, but it was too late. My poor Francis was dead by nightfall.'

'I'm so sorry, Marguerite.' The words sounded thin and inadequate in the face of such grief. 'How terrible for you.'

Marguerite put a hand on the glass. 'When they brought him back to the house, he didn't speak to me. He was delirious and it was hard for him to breathe. But I knew what he wanted to say to me. He died in the house he loved and with me by his side.'

'That must be some comfort to you.'

'Do you think so? What would you know?'

There was such a fierce rage in Marguerite's eyes that Ellen stepped back, saying, 'I'm sorry – forgive me – that was a foolish thing to say.'

'No, no – you're young, how could you understand?' The rage died, the gaze dropped. 'It sometimes feels as if everything that's happened since that night has been a dream. Perhaps one night I'll look out of the window and I'll see his boat coming in, and I'll run down to the harbour again. And this time it will end differently. He'll bring the *Mairead* home and I'll take him in my arms and I'll never let him go.' A small smile. 'There's that phrase, isn't there, "mad with grief". And you think, before it happens to you, that it's just something people say. But it is a sort of madness, I think, when you lose someone you love as much as I loved Francis. It's as if you've been torn to pieces. At first, you don't even want to put them together, but I had to, for Alec's sake. You can't tear your hair out and go about in sackcloth and ashes if you have a child. But it was hard. So hard. Alec was such a comfort to me. He'd let me talk for hours. He never minded, never ran off to play like other boys would have done. Such a comfort.'

'Come downstairs, Marguerite,' Ellen said gently. 'Please.'

Marguerite's eyes focused on her. 'I daresay you think I'm an old fool, coming up here at night. I don't speak to Alec about it, he doesn't approve. But I wondered whether you thought . . .'

'What?'

'I've always believed, you see, that some events have an echo of their own.'

'An echo?'

'Do you think it's possible, Ellen?' Now, Marguerite's eyes were shining. 'Do you think that a tragedy, some great event, can mark a place? Do you think that something can remain, even after they're gone, some vestige of a soul?'

And Ellen found herself remembering something that Martin Finch had once said to her in the pub in Copfield. *Bat has this idea that you can explain the sighting of ghosts using quantum theory.* And for a moment her mind flew along strange and irrational paths, producing hypotheses, conjuring up mechanisms by which happiness and tragedy might imprint itself so deeply into the stones of a house that an event might recur endlessly, bouncing off time and space, implacable, relentless.

No. Nonsense, all of it.

She said, 'Isn't it our emotions, our feelings that live on? Isn't it love that remains?'

'So rational. But after Francis died, I felt his presence in this house.'

'Alec told me you'd employed a medium.'

'Did he? He told you that?'

'He was trying to explain . . .' But she broke off, reddening, aware of a feeling of intrusion.

'It's a long time since I've felt Francis's presence.' Again, Marguerite's fingertips went to the glass, as if she was reaching out to touch her lost husband. 'It's as if time wears these things away.'

'Perhaps it's better that way. Kinder. We should concentrate on the living, shouldn't we?'

'Such a funny little thing. You try hard, don't you? I'm sorry if I frightened you. You must forgive me. But I can't disregard what I feel, I can't put it aside because it doesn't fit into whatever theory Alec and his friends think is right.' Marguerite's gaze swung back to Ellen. 'On all other matters our minds meet perfectly.'

Ellen said evenly, 'When you love someone so much it must be hard to let them go.'

'I had no intention of letting Francis go. I was convinced that he didn't want it either. Or perhaps you're speaking of Alec.'

Now the swords were drawn. Ellen said, 'He needs to be allowed to make his own way.'

'Alec's way is my way. He knows he must return to the island.'

'Only because he feels an obligation to you.' There, she had said it, though her heart was rattling like a small creature shaking the bars of its cage.

'Not only to me, Ellen, to his home. Alec loves his home. He loves the island.'

'You can love a place without being bound to it your entire life.'

'Can you? Is that what you think of as love?'

'Love should confer freedom. If you truly loved someone, you'd want to set them free.'

'Would you?' Marguerite's expression was scornful. 'Your generation has such a pallid idea of love. I would have followed Francis to the ends of the earth if he had told me to – and beyond, if I could. So tell me, what of duty, what of responsibility? Why break the ties that hold a family together? Why break the ties that hold a people to a place?'

'I've no wish to keep Alec away from his home.'

'His home will die without him, surely you see that. This island, too. The young will go and only the old will be left and that will be the end of it. Everything that Francis and the Hunters stood for, everything they worked so hard for would be meaningless if that were to happen. All those memories gone, all that history.'

'Why do you dislike me so?' The words flew from her throat. 'What have I done?'

Marguerite's eyes washed over her, measuring, dissatisfied. 'I don't dislike you. You're pleasant enough. But you are not the woman my son should marry.'

The phrase echoed like the toll of a bell.

'Would you prefer Catriona?'

'Catriona has her faults, but yes, I would. You,' Marguerite's lips pursed, 'you try too hard to oblige. You lack boldness. I've always despised timidity.'

'Civility, I'd call it.'

'Would you? No matter. It takes a certain sort of person to live here. It's so much harder, of course, if you're not born to the island. Do you remember when I showed you my garden and you were afraid to look over the edge of the terrace? I knew then you wouldn't do.'

'In your estimation, perhaps. Not in Alec's.'

'You would not be happy here, Ellen. I think you know that in your heart.'

'No, that's not true!'

Marguerite had moved closer to her. 'You know that I'm right. Think.' Her voice lowered, became soft and insinuating. 'Think what our winters are like. Think how alone you'd feel, cut off from everything you know. Wouldn't you long for home – for your home? Wouldn't you miss your work and your studies? Oh, you'd try not to be homesick, you'd try to make the best of it, to find new interests and new occupations, but wouldn't it always be there at the back of your mind, that regret, that suspicion that you'd made a mistake? A woman like you wouldn't be content to settle for the life of a rural Scottish housewife. Why should you be?'

'Because I love Alec!'

'But you don't belong here. Francis did. Alec does. But you never will.'

The torchlight illuminated Marguerite's eyes, showing them to be an implacable blue, and her words seemed to claw into Ellen's mind, voicing the questions that had tormented her for months. Because it was not only Alec who was capable of evasion, she saw that now; she was too, and it seemed to her that Marguerite was right, and that had she been a different person – a bolder person – then she might have seen the traps that lay in front of her sooner and fought harder for the man she loved.

'I only want Alec to be happy.' Marguerite's voice was gentle. 'Don't you want that too, Ellen?'

'I would make him happy!' Yet her cry sounded like a lament.

'No, you would not. You would tear him in two.' The older woman touched her hand and Ellen shuddered. 'You're cold,' said Marguerite, quite kindly. 'You must go back to bed.'

Ellen stumbled out of the attic. The torch lit her path through the old, dust-covered chattels of Kilmory House. Her footsteps, treading through the dust, weighed the building down, anchoring it to the rock of the island.

When it was light, she rose, washed and dressed and went outside. Her eyes felt gritty and her head ached. Though the wind had eased, clouds billowed across the sky, grey islands that echoed those other islands that floated weightless on the sea. The courtyard and lawn were littered with branches torn from the trees by the wind. When Ellen climbed up the paths behind the house, she saw a few scarlet maple leaves floating on the surface of the ponds. She had not dared hope that the fresh air might relieve her depression and fatigue; no, she knew that the events of the previous night permitted no such mercy. But she was thankful to be out of the house.

Reaching the topmost terrace, she went to stand by the low wall that separated it from the sheer drop below. Her fear of heights had gone, vanquished by another, much greater dread. She found herself remembering her dream in which she had fallen from this terrace, a dream which had echoed the death of Dr Redmond, and she wondered what it was in that event that had haunted her so long. They had not been close friends; indeed, she had hardly known him at all, but the memory of that evening had become a part of her, ingrained in her. Marguerite had spoken of certain events having an echo which oscillated for years, but the repulsion which Marguerite's obsession had effected in Ellen was deep-rooted and instinctive. Now, for the first time, she saw her reaction to Dr Redmond's death through Marcus Pharoah's eyes, and she knew that she had destroyed her own career through her neurotic imaginings and hysterical overreaction, just as Marguerite intended to destroy her future with Alec.

A rustle of leaves and then Hamish, the Scottie dog, pattered on to the terrace. He trotted towards her and she petted him, finding in his small, warm body some comfort. Far below, there was the sound of a door closing.

With Hamish cradled in her arms, Ellen looked down at Alec, crossing the lawn outside the house. Now and then as he headed through the garden, he would be consumed by the trees, but then he would emerge, climbing the hillside until he came through the wall of shrubs on to the terrace.

He came to stand beside her. 'You're up early. Are you all right? You look pale.'

'Did you know that your mother goes up to the attic at night to look for your father's boat?'

A frown. 'Still?'

'She was there last night.'

'She likes it up there, likes the view.'

She found herself searching his face for concealment and evasion. 'She goes to look for your father,' she said flatly.

'No, Ellen, that's not true.'

'She told me that she believes that something of your father remains. She called it an echo.'

'What are you saying? That my mother thinks she's seeing my father's ghost?'

She heard the anger in his voice, but persisted. 'Not that exactly, but that a part of her still hopes he'll come back.'

'And you judge her for that?'

'I'm not judging her. But Alec, the way your mother was talking to me, your father might have died six months ago, or maybe a year. Not fourteen years.'

'So we should set a time limit on grief? Miss someone

for twelve months but if it lasts any longer – what? It's a sign of madness?'

The dog, disliking perhaps the tenor of their voices, slipped out of Ellen's hold and pitter-patted away into the woodland.

'Last night,' she said slowly, 'although I knew that your father had been dead for so long, I still found myself looking out of the window and searching the sea for his boat. There was a moment when I almost believed that if you longed so passionately for someone you'd lost, you might bring them back to life. All my most deeply held beliefs sacrificed to irrationality and superstition. I'm not proud of that, and I don't want to be a part of it.'

Seeing him whiten, she could almost have postponed it, put off what she must say to him. It weighed so heavily on her heart that she found her gaze sliding away from him to the void below.

'You see, Alec, I don't think I can live here.'

'Not now, maybe. But we'll work something out.'

'No, not ever.' She looked up at him. 'So you must choose.'

'Ellen, that's not fair.'

'I'll visit the island two or three times a year and your mother can come and stay with us as often as she likes. But I can't live here. And I want you to make sure Marguerite knows that, Alec. I want you to speak to her today.'

'I can't do that. It would destroy her.'

'And me?'

'I'll do anything for you, Ellen, you know that.'

'Except this one thing.'

'Because it's unreasonable. No, it's worse than that, it's cruel.'

'I don't mean to be cruel. But your mother doesn't want me here.'

But as soon as she said it she regretted it, knowing it to be misjudged. His voice altered, becoming colder.

'I didn't know you could be like this. You seem to have taken against my mother from the start.'

'Is that how you see it?' The words shivered and she twisted her hands together. 'I'd have given up almost everything for you, Alec. I'd have given up my career and my home and my friends for you. But I won't give up my principles, my intellect, my beliefs. Not even for you.'

As she took hold of the ring on her finger, she heard him say, 'Ellen, please don't do this. You're upset. We need to talk about this calmly.'

Her hands were cold and the ring slid off easily. She held it out to him and he took a step back.

'Ellen, for God's sake.'

'I can't live in the same house as your mother, and your mother doesn't want me living in the same house as her. So I don't see a compromise, do you, Alec?'

'In time . . .'

But she did not wait to hear the rest of his sentence. It seemed to her that in those two words the point of no return had passed. That she had been teetering on the brink and that the long fall had now begun. She took his hand and pressed the ring into it. She whispered, 'I'm so sorry, Alec,' and walked away.

There was a saying, wasn't there, about frying pans and fire, and India knew that there would be a price to pay, because there always was.

Sitting in the back of the car, which was driven by Marcus Pharoah's employee, Mr Gosse, India reflected on the events of the last twenty-four hours. The previous evening she had gone to Marcus Pharoah's flat in Belsize Park and had told him the truth. She had told him everything, about Garrett cheating Bernie out of his rent, and about her losing her temper with Bernie and about Lee hurting Sebastian. *There is this man, and I hate him so much. Have you ever had to be nice to someone you hated? It makes you feel dirty and small, like a mouse caught in a trap. Every so often he'll reach out a paw and play with me. If it suited him, he'd crush me.*

Pharoah had asked questions, gathered facts. It had reminded India of sitting an exam at school, or an awful consultation she had had a few years ago with a Harley Street consultant, when she had thought she was pregnant. She had laid open her life in all its shabby compromise for Marcus Pharoah to inspect.

Eventually, he had gone into another room to make phone calls. When he returned, he sat down beside her. 'This is what we'll do,' he said. 'A friend of mine, Matthew Sanderson, has a farm in Devon. I've spoken to Matt and he says that Sebastian can go there. The Sandersons are good people and he'll be safe there. Sebastian can help on the farm and in return Matthew and Laura will give him board and lodging and a small wage. Gosse will drive the two of you to Devon tomorrow, India. You can settle your brother in and then you're to come back to London. You can stay here for a night or two until I find you somewhere quiet to live for the next couple of months. A seaside resort, perhaps. Yes, I know,' Marcus held up a hand, 'you're about to tell me that you'll be bored, but if you can't choose your friends more wisely then you have only yourself to blame.'

She asked about the flat and he told her that he would have it valued and put up for sale. So Aunt Rachel's flat was to be sold. Rachel who had rescued them, Rachel who had cared for them.

The journey to Devon had been long and now she was tired. India looked out of the car window, to the deep, dusky West Country lanes. The farm where she had just left Sebastian was wooded and meadowed and the Sandersons had gone out of their way to be welcoming to him. He would be fine, Sebastian had told her, when they had come to say goodbye. She had known she was leaving an important part of her life behind, and that they would never be so close again, and she had cried, her head buried in Sebastian's neck while he had hugged her.

Now, sitting in the back seat of the Jaguar, her gaze fixed on the back of Roy Gosse's neck, she thought about the conversation she had had with Marcus Pharoah the previous evening. 'I want a nice house,' she said, and he said, 'Yes, of course.'

'And a baby.'

At that, he frowned. 'I don't think I want to go through all that again.'

This she was sure of: that if she were to lose her home and Sebastian, she needed something as well as Marcus Pharoah and his vast ambition and vanity.

'I want something of my own,' she said.

'You'll have me.'

'A baby, Marcus. Just one, if you say so. But that's what I want.'

They were in the sitting room of his flat. As she waited for his answer, she heard the distant rumble of traffic, the chime of a church bell.

And at last he said, 'Very well. One child, no more.' She put her arms round him and rested her head on his chest, and thought of doors closing in a long corridor behind her, perhaps for ever.

At Central Station in Glasgow, Ellen had half an hour before the London train left. She bought herself a cup of tea in the waiting room. Already regrets had begun to seep into her consciousness, but they came up against the barrier of her conversation with Alec on the terrace, washing like the waves against the slate jetties of Seil Island. In time, he had said to her; but time had worked against her, showing her not that he loved his mother more, but that he had not loved her, Ellen, enough. The realization cut like a knife, and tears stung her eyes as she stirred her tea.

She had left Kilmory House before breakfast. She had not been able to face seeing Marguerite again and had quickly packed and asked Alec to drive her to Oban station. When he tried to stop her leaving she told him that she would walk to Oban, if necessary. In the car, he went over it all again. The hastiness of her decision, the irrationality of it. She was tired, she hadn't slept well, she had said so herself. They should go for a drive somewhere on the mainland, have a quiet chat, sort it out. The island could seem claustrophobic, he knew that. There was no need for her to rush back to London, and certainly no need to break off their engagement.

The landmarks of her journeys to Seil Island had unpeeled outside the windows of the car: the flooded quarries, the hills and marshes and the sea loch, as if her life was rushing backwards to a time before she had known him, a sparse time, as bleak as the black beaches on the island. She need say only a word, that was all, and yet her heart seemed to turn to stone a beat at a time, the cold drip-drip of her silence forming layers of disbelief and grief.

His mood, too, had changed by the time they reached Oban. As he carried her case on to the platform, he said angrily, why must she be so dramatic? And what would his mother think, her rushing off without a word?

She'll think she's won, she had thought dully.

She had gone because she had known that nothing would change. That morning would have gone on like all other mornings at Kilmory House, the routines unaltered by the conversations that had taken place in the preceding twelve hours. Had she asked too much of him? No, she did not believe so, but she felt the moment when her conviction would falter approaching, like the darkness inside a tunnel.

She left her cup of tea undrunk and went to catch her train. The red sandstone building had the melancholy of all railway stations when you are alone and unhappy, and she could almost have believed then that Marguerite had been right, and that she was sensing all the farewells that must have taken place here over the years. Waiting on the platform, her gaze went to the barrier, searching for him.

He did not come. The engine pulled in in a scream of smoke and soot and she opened a door and climbed inside. She walked along the corridor until she found an empty compartment. There was a cheap gossip magazine lying on a seat; she leafed through it as the pistons cranked and the train began to move. She longed to be back in London. She longed to be in her laboratory, working through some experiment, her mind engaged and her hands occupied with the delicate tasks she knew she did well. She needed the reassurance of measurable things.

Turning a page, she saw it. The photograph was of Marcus Pharoah and a young woman. The caption said, *Dr Pharoah, star of TV panel game 'Animal, Vegetable, Mineral', and his friend, Miss India Mayhew*. She was at first unable to take it in. This must be some other India Mayhew, surely – but no, the name was uncommon, and besides, there was India, with her pale hair and that way she had of jutting out one hip as she looked up, laughing. And she remembered that she herself had introduced them, Marcus Pharoah and India Mayhew, a year ago, at the Royal Institution. *This is my friend, Miss Mayhew*, she had said, and, guessing the chain of action and reaction that must have followed that moment, a feeling of utter betrayal washed over her.

She closed the magazine and turned to the window. And she thought of Alec, and how she had left him, and pressed her forehead against the cold glass as she stared out at the passing city.

Chapter Ten

There was no answer when, the following day, Ellen rang the doorbell of the Mayhews' flat. No answer when she telephoned the next day, or the day after. No India, an apron over her frock, a cigarette in one hand and a wooden spoon in the other, stirring pots and pans on the stove.

The sense of betrayal she had felt, seeing that photograph of India with Pharoah, faltered. She knew that she had lost touch with India during her affair with Alec. Her need to be with him had been all-consuming and India had slipped down a list. She was not proud of that.

Where was India, where had she gone? Was she with Pharoah? In the shocked, bruised aftermath of her parting from Alec, when little else touched her, that thought nevertheless troubled her. India would be attracted by Pharoah's wealth and glamour. Pharoah would use her, as he had used Andrée Fournier, and then, when he was tired of her, he would discard her.

Tuesday: Alec phoned. Hearing his voice, pleading with her to come back to him, she melted. She agreed to meet him the following evening for a meal. It was only when she saw him that she realized the depth of the emptiness she had endured over recent days. It was as if she had been hollowed out, her heart removed and put aside, raw and exhausted. He, too, looked tired and strained. As they ate an indifferent meal in a small café in the Strand, he promised to tell his mother that they would live in London after they had married. He would do whatever she wanted, if only she would come back to him.

They were together for three weeks. During that time, what began as a joyous reunion chilled. Where once, after making love, they had lain in bed together, lazily content, he now rose and dressed, saying little as he made coffee or made ready to go back to the lab. They bickered over small things – which film they would see, a difference of opinion over something they read in the newspaper. They argued about Suez: in Egypt, Nasser was buying fighter planes and reminding the British that their soldiers must leave the Suez Canal the following year.

When Ellen pointed out that Britain needed access to the canal, Alec said, 'You colonialists are all the same, you like to keep a country under your thumb.'

'*Colonialists*,' she echoed.

He shrugged. 'Military types, then. Always ready to send in the troops.'

One evening, there was a party to which an acquaintance had invited them.

'I can't see the point in hauling ourselves halfway across London,' said Alec.

'It would be a night out.'

'If you call warm beer and shop talk a night out.'

And so on, a low-grade, ill-tempered quarrel until he shrugged on his jacket, saying, 'OK, OK. I'd better not argue with you, had I?' and the shock of his words seemed to resonate inside her.

'What do you mean?'

His answer was cold-eyed and clear-voiced. 'You call the tune now, don't you, Ellen?'

A long silence, during which she tried to absorb the shock. She said, 'I don't think this is working, do you?'

He didn't reply. Fumbling around the room, gathering up coat and bag and gloves, her brain seemed to have lost the knack of telling her body what to do. Her buttons did not appear to fit into the holes made for them and her finger and thumb slipped on the clasp of her bag. Emerging from the flat, she stood for a moment on the pavement, unable to remember where to go.

The evenings were bad, the nights worse. She dreaded going to bed, anticipating the plummeting of her spirits that seemed to begin as soon as she put off the light, as if in the dark she was falling downstairs. She learned to blur the empty hours with a drink or two. Sometimes she went to the pub with Joe, and sometimes, when there were bottles of beer in the kitchen, she took a couple into her room, always scrupulous about putting cash in the kitty to pay for them. It was easier to fall asleep after a drink. And a cigarette. Some nights, she padded downstairs, reinforced by alcohol, and dialled Alec's number. When he didn't pick up, she wondered where he was, who he was with. When he did answer, she put the phone down.

Just before Christmas, she found herself sitting on Riley's sofa, listening to John Coltrane and drinking whisky. Between his dashes upstairs now and then to check on Annie, who had mumps, Ellen talked about Alec. The entire affair, hardly pausing for breath, from the first moment she had seen him on the stairs at Gildersleve Hall to that final, devastating, *You call the tune now, don't you, Ellen?* She knew that she was being boring, and she knew when she started crying that she was being even more boring and that the next day she would feel mortified and humiliated. But she couldn't stop herself. Riley patted her back, gave her his handkerchief, said soothing things. While he went to have another look at Annie, she staggered to the bathroom. Her face was red and swollen, as if she, too, had mumps; she splashed cold water on it, missing and soaking her jersey because she was drunk. Returning downstairs, she curled up on one end of the sofa, her head on one of Pearl Riley's poppy-coloured cushions.

Riley woke her up and put a black coffee in her hand.

'I've called you a taxi,' he said. 'Will you be all right?' Then he made her check she had her keys and purse, helped her on with her coat and scarf and saw her into the taxi.

The next day, her pounding head and nausea was nothing compared to her sense of shame. When she remembered Riley virtually stuffing her arms into her coat, she wanted to hide in some dark corner and never come out again. How awful for him, how tedious and embarrassing. A sick child upstairs, a weeping woman downstairs. Another wave of mortification when she remembered suggesting to him that she sleep on his sofa. Perhaps he hadn't wanted her to because he had thought she might go on weeping and jabbering about Alec all night. Or perhaps he had even been afraid that she might make a drunken pass at him. *Oh God*, she thought, *never again*.

She went to Fortnums and arranged for the delivery of a bottle of malt whisky (for Riley) and a box of jelly babies (for Annie), along with a brief, apologetic note, to the Tufnell Park address. She had wanted his forgiveness; she had come to realize what a good friend he was. Then she went home for Christmas.

This was a turning point. Her mother was quietly comforting and at frequent moments produced cups of tea, boxes of chocolates and a shoulder to cry on. Her father managed to suppress his fury towards Alec some of the time, and to distract her with discussions about science and politics. The familiar routines of Christmas – carols, Christmas dinner, social occasions with friends, and long, wintry walks – provided reassurance and a structure. Still, waking in the night, she wept, thinking of what might have been, but she was also able to acknowledge at last that passion alone had not been enough for her, and that though they could have gone on being lovers for a lifetime, she and Alec, they had lacked the day-to-day affection and mutual permission of freedom that were essential to a successful marriage.

By the time she returned to London in the New Year, Ellen had made several resolutions. No more drinking, obviously. And no more cigarettes either – she had never really liked them. And no more behaving like a madwoman, sitting on the bottom stair in the middle of the night, phoning her ex-fiancé.

And she would find her own flat. Her father had offered to help her with the money. She was twenty-six, far too old to be living like a student, and Joe would be moving out next year as soon as he finished his degree. Though it occurred to her that in doing so, she was acknowledging to herself that a chance in life had passed her by, and that she might never have the husband, children and family home that she had hoped would one day be hers, she began to look in estate agents' windows in her lunch hour.

Lastly, she resolved to try once more to find out what had happened to India. She discovered that the Mayhews' flat had been sold. None of the neighbours seemed to know where India and Sebastian had gone. When she had last seen India, she had been waitressing in a café, but

Ellen did not know which café. Sebastian had been a jobbing gardener but she had no idea where he had worked. She remembered India's boyfriend, dark-eyed Garrett, remembered dancing with him in the Mayhews' kitchen, and with a stab to the heart recalled how seeing India with Garrett had made her think with such longing of Alec.

But she hadn't a clue where Garrett lived or what his surname was or where to find him. India had had other friends, but though she recalled a name or two, Ellen recognized the impossibility of finding them among London's millions. It seemed to her, looking back, that she had hardly known India at all. India had latched on to her, and because of that, wary perhaps of a burden of unsought responsibilities, she had kept her distance.

But she did have a responsibility. It had been she who had introduced India to Marcus Pharoah. *This is what I want*, Pharoah's attitude to life had seemed to say, *and this is how I shall get it*. She wondered whether he had applied the same axiom to his courtship of India. Or whether India had made the running. Whatever, they would make a combustible pair.

She decided to try to trace India through Marcus Pharoah. She spoke to Jerry Collins, her professor. 'You know he's closed down Gildersleve Hall, don't you?' Jerry said. He hadn't mentioned it before because, well, it had seemed a sore subject. Ellen asked if Jerry knew where Pharoah had gone. 'America, apparently,' he said. 'Not sure exactly where. Not a friend of mine, you know.'

From further questioning of colleagues and acquaintances she discovered that Marcus Pharoah had taken up a position in a small New England college, and that he had married India. India had left England as Pharoah's wife. This Ellen at first found incredible. It was hard to imagine India marrying anyone, impossible to imagine her married to Pharoah, fulfilling the role Alison had once taken, running a household, handing round canapés before Sunday lunch. And what of Sebastian? Ellen may not have understood India much at all but she had never doubted her loyalty and love for her brother. Where was he? Had India taken him to New England with her? Did he live with the happy couple among the leafy hills and lakes of Vermont?

One day, at a conference in Manchester, she ran into Martin Finch. That evening, they ate Chinese food in the Ping Hong restaurant. Martin told her about his wife, who was expecting a child, and then Ellen nudged the conversation to the subject of Marcus Pharoah. Passing on gossip, Martin was in his element. Pharoah was a laughing stock, he told her. He'd married a girl half his age. You can get away with so much, but – Martin swept a finger across his neck – Pharoah had pretty much cut his own throat.

But on the train back to London, Ellen reflected that she had learned nothing of what had motivated India to marry Pharoah, or what had led Pharoah to marry India. Whether the match had been born out of love or greed or desperation. She only knew now that nothing ended tidily. That you could not tell what you yourself were capable of, let alone anyone else. Little now remained of the short flare of friendship between herself and India except memories and unease. A meeting in a bookshop, debts run up and then repaid. The purchase of a coral-coloured summer dress, and a dance in a kitchen as, outside, the sap green leaves unfurled on the trees.

Part Three

1957–1959

Vermont

Chapter Eleven

The sound of Gosse's axe echoed against the trees on the far side of the pond. Looking out of the bedroom window, India saw that only the snow on the distant mountains remained, covering the rounded peaks like a dusting of icing sugar. The thaw had turned the tracks to channels of rutted mud which glistened in the weak spring sunshine. On the trails beside the house and around the pond, the mud was pitted with boot prints.

Out of a corner of the window, India made out Gosse at the shed to one side of the pond. The axe swung down in an arc, light glinting on the blade, and bit heavily into the wood. Gosse bent to pick up the cut logs and throw them into the barrow. Then he straightened, wiping the back of his hand across his forehead, and looked round.

India took a clumsy step back, away from the window. She sank on to the bed, one hand on the dome of her belly. The baby squirmed, like an eel wriggling out of a crevice in a rock. India waited until the chopping of wood started up again. Then, hauling herself to her feet, she opened a drawer and took out gloves and a headscarf.

She was going to go out. The snow, and Dr Fisher's edict that she rest, had kept her indoors for weeks. The house, and the cold, dripping woodland that surrounded it, walled her in. She needed to feel that watery sunshine on her face; she needed to hear other voices.

Two miles away, Midhurst was the nearest town. It wasn't much of a town, just a single straight main street surrounded by a scattering of houses, garages, workshops and yards, but India imagined pottering around the shops, buying a few things and sitting in the coffeehouse, talking to people. She wouldn't stay long, an hour maybe, and would make sure to be back in time for Marcus coming home.

She did up the top two buttons of her coat, knotted her headscarf, applied lipstick and powder, then flicked a glance out of the window to check that Gosse was still at the woodshed. Then she went downstairs, holding the banister for support. The baby was due in three weeks' time and the weight she was carrying tired her.

Viola Williams only worked mornings so India was alone in the house. She plodded from room to room, collecting her things – bag, purse, car keys – then fetched her boots from the mud room and sat down on the stairs to put them on. But the zip wouldn't do up over her swollen ankles and the fur-lined leather flapped ridiculously open.

She put the boots back and heaved herself upstairs again. The problem, she thought, as she stood in the doorway, panting because of the stairs, was that she didn't own sensible shoes, such as a very pregnant woman should wear. The rows of high-heeled courts and strappy sandals looked back at her, forlorn leftovers from another life. She found a pair of lace-ups that Marcus had bought her for walking, when they had briefly imagined themselves striding out along trails together, forced her feet into them, and succeeded in tying the laces.

Chop, chop, chop. The sound of the axe reassured her. Returning downstairs, she couldn't find her bag, must have put it down somewhere, so she padded around the house, searching for it. This, she had learned, was a disadvantage of living in a big house. There were far too many places to lose things.

She found her bag in the front parlour and stood motionless, catching her breath and planning her route out of the house as the sun washed warmly through the windowpanes. If she left the house by the front door and walked to the courtyard where the cars were parked, there would be a short stretch where she would be visible to Gosse from the woodshed. It would be safer to reach the courtyard by the road, where the trees planted along the perimeter fence would hide her.

She made her way to the small lobby at the far end of the building where they kept storm lanterns and candles, then slipped out of a side door. It was still cold but there was a softness in the air which hinted of spring. Treading with great care over the muddy paving stones, India took the short path that led to the road. On the far side of the road were meadows dotted with bare, drably brown trees. Few vehicles came along this route, which led only to farms and small, insignificant townships, and India felt confident that she would be able to drive the few miles to Midhurst without difficulty. Marcus had taught her to drive last summer, before Rowena had visited. Their honeymoon period, she thought of it, cynically.

The meltwater had formed great puddles to the side of the road and the verges were awash with mud. India walked along a rut, one foot placed in front of the other, concentrating hard, afraid that if she slipped, something awful might happen to the baby.

Then she froze, one hand gripping the smooth, narrow trunk of a tree. She could no longer hear Gosse's axe. Perhaps the house blocked out the sound. Birds rustled in the branches; above her, crows flapped and dipped like black kites. The mud slodged round her feet, grey and viscous, and there was a green, woody smell.

She began to walk again. It was hard going, and she had to reach out now and then to the whippy branches of the saplings for support. But she was nearly there.

Peering round the edge of the thicket, she saw Gosse standing on the gravel, beside the Austin-Healey. He was leaning against the bonnet, smoking a cigarette. Silently, and with great care, India stepped back into the trees and began to retrace her path.

They had married in the January of 1956, after Marcus's decree nisi had come through. It had been a register office wedding, with only Sebastian and a colleague of Marcus's in attendance as witnesses. India had worn a short black jacket with a white fox-fur collar over a knee-length dress of ivory satin. Marcus had looked on edge, relieved when the ceremony was over, relieved when the moment came after their lunch in a private room in the Savoy when he could shake hands with his colleague and Sebastian and see them both off in taxis.

Making love to her, he had pressed kisses all over her body, from the soles of her feet to the folds of her ears. She had sensed his utter concentration in the cocooning luxuriance of their room at the Savoy, had heard his voice whisper over and over again of his love for her. He had run a hand along the contours of her breast and hip, pausing to press a pinch of her skin between finger and thumb, and he had drawn in breath in the darkness when she had touched him.

The following morning they had flown to America via Shannon airport in Ireland and Gander in Newfoundland. Stopping for refuelling, India had watched the snowflakes dance through the foggy air. After a few days in a bitterly cold, windswept Boston they had headed north to Cape Cod. Walking along the beach, the soles of India's shoes had crackled the frozen sand and the waves that lapped the shore had made lacy ribbons of ice. Then, north-west, through the dense, dark forests of Maine. They had kept to the routes through the valleys because of the snow, but the white bulk of the mountains had been a backdrop throughout most of their journey, disembodied above low, wispy clouds or luminous in the sunlight.

A snowstorm had forced them to spend two nights in an inn and then they had taken to the road again. Frozen opalescent lakes revealed themselves as the trees parted. Beside the road India had seen wooden shacks with logs stacked outside, a barking dog pulling on a chain and a rusty truck parked in the shadows. Covered bridges forded shallow, rushing rivers. At neat little towns they had stopped for coffee or a night's sleep.

As they drove, India had sensed Marcus's impatience. He spoke to her of his longing to start working again. He would make something new, he said, something wonderful. The Gildersleve Hall that he would create in New England would make discoveries whose significance would resound throughout the world. His voice, weighted with excitement and desire, threaded through their journey.

Now and then, India looked out of the car window. She thought of the snow in Newfoundland and the bumpy rattle of the plane through the clouds, and of the frozen sea at Cape Cod and the flare of orange light on the mountains at dusk. All these things had seemed to her to be wonders: anything was possible.

During their early months in Vermont, Marcus had still seemed to believe that he could get what he wanted. The small town of Midhurst lay in the lee of the Green Mountains; the college itself had been built three miles out of town, as if it had been feared that the main street, with its handful of old-fashioned shops, might prove a distraction to study. The college buildings, of grey granite and white clapboard, were set in a small, attractive, leafy campus.

Marcus had bought a house; they had moved in at the end of March. Fairlight House was a large, oblong building, faced with red-brown clapboard. It had formerly been a farm, and though the arable land and pasture had been sold off, there were still several acres of grounds. India had believed that was what had attracted Marcus, the thought of having *grounds*, of having your own pond and woods and meadows. Marcus, she had realized, liked to own things.

Their sea freight from England had arrived. There was the Healey, packaged up like an oversized Christmas present, and there were the boxes containing Marcus's notes and files and letters and certificates. India's possessions – embroidered linen pillowcases that had once belonged to Rachel, the pieces of the tea set that Lee had broken, a calendar Sebastian had made for her when she had been at boarding school, some books and gramophone records – had fitted in a single tea chest.

To begin with, Marcus had shown her off, much as he liked to show off the Austin-Healey. *This is my fast little European car and this is my fast little European wife.* They had been invited to dinner in the houses of lecturers and deans, white wooden houses set in smooth green lawns, where kindly women had patted India's hand and asked her if she missed her home and her family. Missing Sebastian was like a nagging toothache; she noticed it most at night when there was nothing else to crowd out the thoughts – was he happy, was he lonely, would he manage without her?

When their turn came, they gave cocktail parties and lunches. After the evenings were over, Marcus listed India's mistakes. She was supposed to pay attention to the important guests instead of perching on the table, chatting to the handful of students that had been invited. You didn't dance at a cocktail party, and you didn't sit on the sofa with your legs tucked under you, screaming with laughter when someone told you jokes.

His lectures bored her; she told him that she couldn't see the point of giving a party that no one enjoyed. He grabbed hold of her hand, pulling her round to him. The point of the evening was not to give her pleasure but to reinforce his position at the college. Did she understand?

A few of the students and one or two of the faculty wives called round now and then with offerings of cake and conversation, but much of the time, while Marcus was at work, India had for company only Viola and Gosse. India liked Viola, who told her racy stories about working in a canning factory in Chicago in the war, but she loathed Gosse. He said 'Yes, Mrs Pharoah' and 'No, Mrs Pharoah' when she asked him to take out the rubbish or fetch in logs, but India could tell that he didn't think she was the real Mrs Pharoah.

Time passed, and Marcus's satisfaction with the college waned. There was some problem with funding. The completion of the new biochemistry building had been delayed and he was having to make do with a few cramped labs in the chemistry department. He found Midhurst's smallness and isolation frustrating after London, and he disliked the Dean of Studies, a tall, thin, hollow-faced man called Lowell Crome. Mr Crome was, India conceded, very boring. He liked to steeple his hands, lean forward over his plate of pie or coffee cake, and talk for hours. When Marcus tried to interrupt, Mr Crome held up a hand and gave a little smile. 'If you would just allow me to finish, Marcus.' Mrs Crome wore her pinky-blond hair in ridges of curls, sprayed so tightly that not a single hair moved. India longed to tap them with a fingernail. When Marcus had first introduced her to Mrs Crome, the older woman's gaze had flicked between the two of them. 'My, my, you're just a little thing, aren't you?' she murmured, as her eyebrows leaped above the upswept rims of her spectacles.

In the spring, pink, white and yellow flowers had nodded in the grass. On summer's longest days, when the air was hot and humid, India liked to take out the rowing boat to the centre of the pond, from where she could see the reflections of the trees, which fractured the still surface of the water like cracks in glass. Where the narrow wooded creeks cut into the banks, the pond was alive with the flicker of fish and darting flies. Running a hand through the water, she saw the ripples flash with light.

In August, Marcus's daughter Rowena had come to stay. Rowena Pharoah was seventeen, darkly beautiful and moody. To begin with, she had ignored India, responding to her questions with an exaggerated weariness and boredom. On the second day of her stay, Marcus had had to go into college for a couple of hours. As soon as the door closed behind her father, Rowena said to India, 'Don't expect me to talk to you. I'm here to see Daddy, not you,' and then left the house to sit by the pond and smoke cigarettes. India hadn't minded: she suspected that in Rowena's shoes she might have felt much the same, and anyway, she found Rowena as tiresome as Rowena found her. All that hanging on to Marcus's arm, all that leaning her head on his shoulder and whining, *I've missed you, Daddy*. Rowena disliked the food Viola cooked; she had nothing to wear and Marcus must take her shopping, and the house and Midhurst were boring. My, my, as Mrs Crome might have said. Rowena Pharoah might be a spoiled little madam, but at least it was nice to have the weight of Marcus's attention shifted to someone else for a week.

Outings with Rowena had been equally effortful. Rowena complained of car sickness and so sat in the front of the station wagon beside her father while India sat in the back. After the first couple of days, India left them to it and remained at home. This annoyed Marcus, who felt they should get on, but there was a limit to how long anyone could put up with Rowena, and anyway, sitting in the back of the car made her feel sick. It occurred to India, when she was alone in the house, that everything was making her feel sick. Sitting on the edge of the bath, chewing her nails, trying to decide whether she was actually going to be sick, she had wondered about this.

The following morning at breakfast she had taken one look at the fried eggs on her plate and had run off to the bathroom. When she returned to the table, Marcus said perhaps she should stay in bed that day. He disliked illness, was wary of poorly people.

India said, 'I'm not unwell, I think I'm pregnant.'

And then, well. The geyser in Rachel's flat had once exploded. Watching Rowena lose her temper reminded India of that.

'Pregnant?' said Rowena.

'Yes. I'm having a baby.'

'You can't be.'

'Oh, I can, you know.' Very quiet.

'That's disgusting!'

'Do you think so?' India poured herself a cup of tea. 'But, you see, it's what happens when people get married.'

Rowena ran out of the room, sobbing. India gave a little shrug. Marcus said she could have been more tactful. India said that Rowena was behaving like a six-year-old. And so on, until he, too, lost his temper and stormed out of the room. Sitting alone at the breakfast table, running a thumbnail along the seam of her napkin, India reflected on the fact that he hadn't said *congratulations*, or, *that's wonderful news, darling*.

Rowena insisted her father drive her back to Boston that day. She hadn't visited since. She wrote letters that Marcus read, scowling, at the breakfast table and then put in his pocket. India read them later, taking them from a shelf in his study, little masterpieces of resentment and self-pity as, outside, leaves spun from the trees and the colours of the maples on the slopes of the hills turned to fire.

The pond darkened, becoming brackish, and there was a smell of decay. Light filtered grudgingly from a bruised sky. As she walked in the woods, the dead leaves, frilled with frost, scratched underfoot. Ice crawled from the banks of the pond towards its centre, dulling the surface of the water.

She liked the differences. She liked the rhythm of the voices in drugstore and coffeehouse, the fizz of the soda fountain and the strange shapes of the pumpkins and gourds on the roadside stalls. She liked to see the mountains when she woke in the morning, and she liked not knowing the names of the trees or where the roads led to.

She had been sick for three months and then had felt quite well for three months, and then her ankles had puffed up and her fingers had turned into sausages and Dr Fisher had told her to rest. Marcus drove her once a week to Midhurst for her appointment with Dr Fisher; after the snow fell, that was her only outing.

In the coldest months, she sat with her feet up on the sofa by the window, watching the drift and speckle of the snow and the bird pecking at the peanuts. She wrote to Sebastian and to Michael and to Justine. Justine sent her a poem, Sebastian wrote back long, earnest letters about the farm and the Sandersons, and a girl he had met from a nearby village. Michael sent her picture postcards with London buses and the Tower; when India closed her eyes she could see the rows of soot-blackened houses, the people queueing at bus stops, the umbrellas jostling on the pavement, all that was familiar to her.

Boredom made her mind wander. She wondered whether her baby would be a boy or a girl. She wondered whether it would have fair hair like her or black hair like its father. She wondered whether she regretted the bargain she had made: safety for Sebastian, comfort and security for herself, in return for marriage to Marcus Pharoah.

She wondered whether Marcus regretted his side of the bargain. She suspected that though he might never have loved Alison, he might prefer to have an Alison in his life. He needed a wife who said the right things, talked to the right people. There was love and there was desire and there was usefulness. Alison had been the useful wife, India was the desired one. The only person Marcus loved – loved properly, in India's eyes – was Rowena.

She wondered whether he would love the baby. He had changed towards her since the day she had told him she was pregnant. She had thought at first that he had been angry because the news of her pregnancy had upset Rowena; in time she had come to question whether his bad mood had been caused by the pregnancy itself. They quarrelled more: she knew how to rile him, how to give the indifferent shrug that infuriated him, how to scratch and probe at his weak spots, his hunger for status and recognition, his need to control. Marcus had wanted a wife who dedicated herself to satisfying his needs and furthering his career; what he had got was one who squirmed away from any attempt to impose authority.

Lying on the sofa, the silence seemed to enfold her like a blanket. The trees shrank back into the fog and a heavy grey pall fell over the rounded peaks of the mountains. She could lie there for hours, looking out of the window. Sounds seemed muffled, and there was an absence of echoes. She was surrounded by a wall of glass, a shell of ice; if she spoke, no one would hear her. It wouldn't have surprised her if she'd looked down at herself and discovered that she was turning invisible.

She couldn't afterwards remember exactly when it was that she had come to think that Roy Gosse was watching her. Gosse drove for Marcus, mended and cleaned the cars, cut logs and did any necessary repair work to the house. He didn't talk much and he slept and ate in the barn. He was the sort of man, India thought, who always seemed to be on the verge of losing his temper.

Go out for a walk, and when she looked back, there would be Gosse, sitting on the back porch, cleaning the shotgun he used to kill vermin, or washing the cars and pick-up truck, hands cupped as he lit a cigarette. She might have thought he liked looking at her had she not known that he despised her. Of course, a man might despise her and still want to go to bed with her, as Bernie had done, but India did not think that this was true of Gosse, in whose glance she read only the same industriousness that he applied to replacing a tyre or trapping mice, or carrying out any other order of Marcus's. She wondered whether Marcus had been drawn to Fairlight House's isolation because, after all, it was a lot easier to keep an eye on your wife if she was marooned in the middle of nowhere.

She wasn't certain. Often she thought that the falling snow and the silence were playing tricks on her, and that her fear that she had made a mistake was only a product of those other fears that came to her when she woke in the night, her fear of having the baby, of being hurt, of something unspeakable happening.

She wondered whether, once the baby was born, she would mind less that she had come to dislike her husband. As the days passed, this question nagged at her.

She went into labour a week early. Marcus drove her to the nursing home in Midhurst, a Gothic red-brick building set in velvety green lawns. Afterwards, India could remember the daffodils in the borders by the tarmac drive, bobbing their frilled yellow heads in the wind, and she could remember the smell of the polished lino in the corridors of the nursing home and the heavy dread that had settled on her inside the building. Schools, orphanages, hospitals: she just wasn't much good at them. But she could not remember Abigail's birth at all, could not remember her first cry. Dr Fisher told her that they had anaesthetized her, but still, it seemed negligent of her to have missed those first moments of her daughter's life.

Feverish during the days after the birth and weak from loss of blood, India dreamed of monsters with bug eyes and gaping jaws, and of gardens with acres and acres of luridly coloured flowers, stippled points of bright colour that stretched on for miles. When her temperature dropped, what remained was exhaustion. She had to lie down to recover after a visit to the bathroom or a walk to the nursery; stay on her feet too long and a hot and cold faintness washed over her.

There were days following the birth when she felt as if she was swimming underwater. Now and then she would bob to the surface and one of the nurses would put Abigail into her arms and she would study her, finding in her perfection, alternately overwhelmed with love for her and terrified by her. This persisted, this mixture of love and anxiety, an anxiety that she wouldn't be up to scratch, that she would drop Abigail in the bath or stick a nappy pin in her, as well as a deeper fear that she would make as ham-fisted a job of motherhood as her own mother had, that she would mess it up, just as she had messed up every other job she had ever taken.

But love itself was a revelation, immediate and undeniable, and by the time she left the nursing home when Abigail was a fortnight old, it had changed her chemistry, pulling her this way and that, hammering her into a different shape so that her heart and mind seemed as raw and bleeding as her post-partum body.

The baby was crying. India's eyelids fluttered open and she hauled herself up on the sofa cushions. The nurse that Marcus had engaged to help in the first six weeks must be in the yard, smoking a cigarette or making up to Gosse. India supposed that because Marcus was out, Miss Forrest thought she could get away with it. She was glad to have Abigail to herself, but she could have told Miss Forrest that she was wasting her time, that all the hair-patting and leg-crossing wouldn't get her anywhere.

Abigail was waving her limbs and squirming, making mewing little cries like a cat's. India went into the kitchen, put a pan of water to heat on the stove, took a bottle of baby milk out of the refrigerator and placed it in the pan to warm. Abigail's cries were gathering momentum, like a car engine igniting. As waves of heat and nausea washed over her, India leaned against the stove, closing her eyes. She was feeling much better now, almost well sometimes, and she had walked round the pond that morning, with lots of stops for rests, but there was still that gluey exhaustion, like fighting your way through a blanket of spiders' webs.

Opening her eyes, she folded a tea towel to take the bottle from the pan and shook a few drops of milk on to the back of her hand to test the temperature. Then she went back into the sitting room, lifted Abigail out of the Moses basket, and sat down on the sofa. Abigail latched on to the teat and began to suck, then wriggled, kicking out her legs and pulling away from the teat with a gasp and a short, high-pitched cry. India stroked her head, with its down of fine, fair hair, and the baby started to suck again.

Voices murmured beyond the window, Miss Forrest's and Roy Gosse's. India looked at the clock. It was almost three. It was so easy to lose track of time, to close her eyes and let the parts of the day, morning, afternoon and evening, blend into each other. Even now, the voices were leaching away, as though the colour had been washed out of them, and when she prised open her eyes the bottle was almost empty, and she put a hand to her forehead, wondering whether she had a temperature again.

She was dozing on the sofa when the doorbell rang. Dragging herself awake, she went to the front door and opened it.

The woman standing outside said, 'Mrs Pharoah?'

'Yes?'

'My name's Mrs Hester Devereux. We haven't met before.'

Hester Devereux was wearing a rust-coloured coat, mended at the elbows, and a cream woollen scarf and hat. Her straight dark hair was windswept and streaked with white and a sunray of shallow lines spun out from the corners of her steel-grey eyes.

'I hope you'll forgive me for interrupting your afternoon,' Mrs Devereux said. 'I knew your husband many years ago and I wondered whether I might speak with you.'

'Marcus is at work, I'm afraid.'

'Yes, I made sure of that. It's you I wanted to speak to, Mrs Pharoah.'

India found herself glancing over her shoulder. It was a fine, sunny day and Gosse was outside, painting the back porch.

She said, 'If you're a friend of Marcus's—'

'I'm not. I was a friend of Rosanne's.'

Blurred from sleep, it took India a couple of seconds to place the name. Then she said, 'Marcus's first wife.'

'Yes.'

India showed Mrs Devereux indoors. In the mud room, Mrs Devereux took off her boots and gave her coat to India to hang on a peg. There was a front sitting room with a piano and bookcases, well away from the porch and Gosse. India invited her visitor to sit down.

'Can I get you a coffee, Mrs Devereux?'

'No, thank you. I appreciate the kind offer but I won't take up your time.'

'If you'll excuse me a moment, I just need to go and check on my baby.'

India went upstairs to the nursery. Abigail was sleeping,

arms flexed, hands fisted. In the bathroom, India splashed cold water over her face, then returned downstairs.

She closed the door behind her. Hester Devereux said, 'How old is your baby, Mrs Pharoah?'

'Abigail's almost two months old.'

'How lovely.' Hester Devereux's voice was toneless. 'Congratulations.'

'Thank you.'

'You're English, aren't you? Have you been married long?'

'A year and a half.'

'And you're happy?' Mrs Devereux leaned forward in her chair.

India heard the doubt in her voice. 'You told me you knew Rosanne. What was she like?'

Mrs Devereux's strained face relaxed. 'She was a perfect darling. Pretty as a picture. Blonde, like you. I used to tell her she was as fair as thistledown. We met at Bourchier University, in Maine, in nineteen thirty-two. We were only eighteen years old, both freshmen.'

'You were friends?'

'Best friends. But then she married Marcus Pharoah and left school. At first we kept in touch.'

'At first?'

'I had to leave Bourchier because my father was very ill. After he died, I came back to visit and I found that they'd moved out of town. I asked Marcus for the address but he wouldn't give it to me. We didn't get on, you see.'

'You didn't like him?'

'No, I'm afraid not. He was a jealous man. When he and Rosanne were courting, I could see that he didn't like her spending time with me. I've often thought since that I should have found out where she was and visited her anyway, but I didn't like to come between husband and wife.' Hester Devereux twisted her hands together. 'I'm sorry, Mrs Pharoah, you must think me very impolite, coming here and saying such things, and I don't mean to upset you. I have a friend in Midhurst, Mrs Ingalls, her husband teaches at the university, and she mentioned in a letter that she'd met you. It's such an uncommon name, isn't it, Pharoah, so I felt I had to ask Elizabeth whether it was the same Pharoah, whether he'd come back to America. And then, when she told me he'd married again . . .' Frowning, Hester Devereux cast a glance round the room. 'I remember those days so fondly, you see. Rosanne and I were firm friends from our first day at Bourchier. It was the first time I'd been away from home. Since then, I've never been so carefree. My husband died two years ago and we have three children. The two eldest have married but my youngest is still at home. It's been very hard. I don't think I'm the same person as I was then, no, not at all.'

India said gently, 'Are you sure you won't have a cup of coffee?'

'I don't want to trouble you.'

'Actually, I'm ravenous,' she said. 'I was going to have a piece of cake when you knocked at the door. May I get some for you too?'

'Then, thank you, Mrs Pharoah.'

Her visitor offered to help but India refused. In the kitchen, making coffee and cutting cake, she thought through what Hester Devereux had told her. It was easy to picture Marcus resenting the emotional bond between the two women and putting up a barrier between them. It occurred to her that she had allowed – invited – Marcus to separate her from her brother and her friends.

She took the tray back into the front room, put the side plates on occasional tables, and poured out the coffee. She said, 'You must have been awfully sad when Rosanne died.'

'I didn't know at the time. That's always troubled me. After Daddy died there was no money for me to go to college, so I had to leave. I didn't find out about Rosanne till nearly six months later. I recall every detail of that day, even though so many years have passed. It was summer and I was working in New York, in a department store. I'd met Henry, my husband, by then, and I was expecting a child of my own, though I hadn't told my employers because I was afraid I'd lose my job. Work was hard to come by back in the thirties. I remember I felt tired and sick, and then I came home and found that letter. It was from a girl I'd known at Bourchier. When I read it, I just cried.' She cut up the cake with the fork. 'You can get so caught up with your own life you neglect old friends. I've always felt bad about that. It was such a sad thing to happen. Poor Rosanne had longed for that baby.'

'Baby?' repeated India.

Hester Devereux looked up. 'Yes. Rosanne Pharoah died in childbirth. Didn't you know?'

India remembered sitting on the sofa in Marcus's flat while he told her about Rosanne. She was sure he had said that his first wife had died of an infection. *No penicillin then*, he had told her. She remembered that she had reached out and taken his hand.

India shook her head. Mrs Devereux looked stricken. 'I'm so sorry . . . So clumsy of me, I just assumed . . . It was different back then, and they were living in such a remote area. I'm sure you have wonderful physicians in Midhurst.'

'Wonderful,' echoed India. 'And the baby?'

'Well, that's the thing. That's why I thought I'd make the journey. I never knew. It's been preying on my mind since Henry died. I don't know why it should start to bother me now, but perhaps at such times you find yourself thinking of all the loose ends.' She put down her plate and turned to face India. Her expression was wounded and puzzled. 'I never found out what had happened to Rosanne's baby. Marcus had gone back to England by the time I heard of her death, but there was no mention of a child. I tried writing to a friend I knew at Bourchier, but they didn't know anything either. I thought you might be able to tell me, Mrs Pharoah, but I can see I was mistaken.'

Hester Devereux's voice had taken on a mollifying tone, but the puzzlement in her eyes remained. Shortly afterwards, the older woman got up to leave. At the door, turning to India, she said, 'No one seemed to know what had happened to that baby. Isn't that just terrible? No one seemed to have the least idea.'

The conversation had exhausted her; India lay down on the sofa and fell asleep. When Marcus came home, he sat on the sofa arm, stroking her hair.

She said, 'Tell me what Rosanne was like.'

'Why?'

'Was she as pretty as me?'

'Yes,' he said shortly.

'Where were you living?'

'North. Far north.' He looked down at her. 'Why do you want to know?'

'I had a visitor. A Mrs Devereux. She said she was a friend of your first wife.'

The hand stilled. 'Devereux . . .'

'Hester Devereux.'

He rose and looked out of the window at the porch, where Gosse was packing up paint cans and rags. 'She was a rather sad woman, I recall. A meddler. I had to send her packing in the end. I hope you did the same, India.'

'She told me that Rosanne died in childbirth.'

'Did she now?' Slowly, he swung round to face her.

'Is it true?'

'Yes, it is.'

'You didn't tell me.'

'It was no business of yours.'

'What happened to the baby?'

'Leave it, India.'

She wriggled herself into a sitting position, turning to look at him. 'Did it die?'

The sun dipped through the sky, painting the pond with streaks of gold. In the distance, the summits of the mountains also caught the liquid gold light.

'It was stillborn,' he said. The anger in his voice was at odds with the heaviness in his eyes. 'There, India, does that satisfy you? I didn't want to upset you, that's all, talking about such things.'

In the middle of the night, feeding Abigail, memories of her conversation with Hester Devereux shifted uneasily.

Rosanne Pharoah . . . pretty as a picture . . . only eighteen.

No one seemed to know what had happened to that baby. Isn't that just terrible?

Why had he lied to her? Because he *had* lied to her, two years ago, in his flat in Belsize Park. He had told her that Rosanne had died of an infection when in fact she had died giving birth to a stillborn child. Rosanne could have died of an infection *after* the birth, India supposed. She herself had had an infection, after all, which had made her very ill. *No penicillin then.* Or perhaps an infection had *caused* the stillbirth. But then, why hide it? Because he couldn't bear to talk about it? Or for some other reason?

Hester Devereux's visit had cut like a knife through the weeks of drowsy disorientation that had followed Abigail's birth. India took the bottle of pills Dr Fisher had prescribed to help her sleep and flushed them down the lavatory. Over the next couple of days she felt as if she was rising out of the mud into a sharp new clarity.

At night, she dreamed of babies. Sometimes the baby was Abigail and sometimes it was that other baby, the child of Rosanne Pharoah. In her dreams, she discovered Rosanne's baby beneath beds, in boxes, and floating beneath the frozen surface of Fairlight Pond. Always alive, though white and waxy and silent, her fingers swaying like fronds of seaweed, her mouth opening and closing as if she was trying to speak.

Marcus was at the college and Gosse had taken the pick-up truck to the garage in Midhurst, so India was alone in the house.

She opened the door to Marcus's study. There was a desk, filing cabinets, bookshelves, prints and photographs on the walls. She flicked through the compartments above the desk, where Marcus kept Rowena's letters. Then she opened the drawers. She wasn't sure what she was looking for – a letter, a diary, a birth or death certificate. When she heard a car on the road she started and hurried to the window. But it was only a lorry, logs chained to the flatbed, rattling along the road, and she went back to her searching.

A small cardboard box contained a sheaf of photographs. India snapped them one by one on to the desktop, like dealing playing cards. There was a photo of Marcus in his academic gown, and several of Rowena, in party dress or school uniform or hard hat and hacking jacket, seated on a horse. Another snapshot was of an old house with a tower to one side of it, the jagged little teeth of crenellations notching its top. But no pretty fair-haired young wife. No baby. All those years before they had met, she thought as she put the pictures back in the box, all those years of which she knew nothing. She hardly knew him at all.

Leafing through a bundle of documents in a file, something caught her attention. The paper was the yellow-buff of milky tea, powdery and torn at the edges. The two pages both bore the same heading: Charnwood Children's Home, near Winchester, Hampshire. The date was 18 July 1942. Scanning the two sheets of paper, India saw that the information on them was divided into sections: health, educational attainment, behaviour, character, background. Typed at the top of each page was the name of a child. One of the names was Sebastian's and the other was hers.

It took her several moments to absorb the fact that Marcus had in his desk reports that the orphanage had written about her and Sebastian after they had arrived at Charnwood following the death of their mother. It took more moments before she could begin to read them.

As she read, something inside her seemed to chill and solidify. Their physical health had been satisfactory, though they had been judged ill-nourished and underweight. Her own level of education had been considered average but Sebastian had been thought backward. In the section headed 'Character', someone had written, 'India is given to violent outbursts and appears to have little understanding of right and wrong.' The same hand noted further down the page: 'The mother was neglectful but it is believed that with proper care the children should be capable of becoming useful members of society.'

India heard the rumble of a car engine so she put the papers back into the file and returned it to the drawer. Looking out of the window she saw the pick-up truck pull off the road into the drive. She left the room.

But she must have been careless because at dinner that night, Marcus said, 'Did you find anything?' and she blinked, her nerves taut.

His knife sliced through his steak. 'I was going to get rid of Mrs Williams,' he said, 'but then I realized that it must have been you, India. If you're going to be devious and underhand, you should remember in future to take more care.'

They ate for a while. Cutlery clicked, she could hear herself chew. Then he said, 'Well, did you find what you were looking for?' and she shook her head.

'I was trying to find a bottle of gum. I wanted to mend my tea set.'

His look said, liar. The next day Gosse put a lock on the door of the study.

Ellen's colleague, David Shapiro, had had a paper accepted by *Nature*. They toasted him that evening in the lab with warmish beer drunk out of chemical beakers. Jerry Collins joined them and there was some gentle ribbing by Tom MacPhee of Shapiro for the length of time it had taken him to write the paper. Then they peeled off, Shapiro and some of the others to the pub, Professor Collins to a meeting, the other female junior lecturer in the department, Freya Hawks, to meet her sister at the cinema, while Ellen stayed on to write up her notes.

She had been appointed a junior lecturer four months earlier, at the end of 1956. On hearing the news of her promotion, her parents had come up from Wiltshire and had taken her out to celebrate. She enjoyed her work, the increased contact with students and the greater responsibility, and she attended conferences in her own right now rather than as Jerry Collins's research assistant. Her colleagues were a friendly bunch; she and Freya went hiking now and then and sometimes she accompanied Tom MacPhee to concerts.

Riley had been made chief inspector at much the same time as Ellen had been promoted. They went to the Royal Opera House to see *The Firebird* and afterwards shared a bottle of champagne. When they were not working late, she and Riley talked on the phone most nights. Those conversations could flow and expand like the estuary of a river, stemmed only by the late hour and fear of the phone bill. They didn't always agree, but then neither did she ever become bored, talking to him. His opinions were neither easy nor rigid and until brought up against the solid rock of his principles, they had a fluidity. You might have thought, if you totted up the hours they had talked together, that they must have covered every subject under the sun and yet there were always new things to say. It had become part of her routine: come home, cast off coat and brief-case, run bath, think about supper, call Riley.

Tonight, she finished her work by seven and left the building. Her flat in Earl's Court was only a short distance away so she walked home. She had moved into the flat a year ago and it never failed to give her pleasure to come home, scoop up her post from the pigeonhole in the shared hallway, then walk up the stairs and unlock her front door.

There was a kitchen, sitting room, bathroom and bedroom. No more queuing for the bath, no more breathing in other people's ashy toast over breakfast. A woman came in twice a week to clean and she sent her sheets and table-cloths to a laundry. She was twenty-eight and she had got her life in order and she didn't intend to let it ever become disordered again.

She saw that in the pile of post she had collected from the hallway, among the circulars for window cleaners, the gas bill and a postcard from a friend, was a blue airmail letter. It had been forwarded from her old address in Islington. She turned it over in her hand, then read the name and address on the back.

Frowning, Ellen reached for a paper knife, slit open the letter, and sat down. Then she flattened out the flimsy blue paper and began to read.

*   *   *

'What are you doing now, Riley?' She always asked him this when she phoned him. She liked to be able to picture him as if she were there.

'Sitting on the sofa, enjoying the quiet, wondering whether another drink will make my headache better or worse. Kitchen's a wreck and I don't think Annie's asleep yet.'

'How's the new au pair?'

'Hendrika? Fine.'

'That good?'

'Hmm,' said Riley.

She had him in her mind's eye now, sitting on the living-room sofa with the poppy print cushions, nursing a Scotch, listening out for Annie, aware of the latest au pair sullenly crashing pots and pans in the kitchen. He would be wearing . . . what? A white cotton shirt, top button undone, navy-blue tie loosened. His hair would be dishevelled because he had run his hand through it. His light hazel eyes, with their multitude of shades of brown, green and gold, would be drenched with ironic humour.

'How was your day, Ellen?'

She told him about India's letter. She could almost hear him frown.

'That's rather out of the blue, isn't it?'

'Nothing for nearly two years and now this.'

'How is she?'

'Well, that's the thing, I'm not sure. She's had a baby, a girl. It's rather an odd letter.' The air letter was lying open on the coffee table. India's spidery handwriting, which contained a spelling mistake or two and covered only half a page, didn't really answer Riley's question. It was the sort of letter, Ellen thought, that you might write if you were in a hurry.

She said, 'She wrote to ask me whether I knew anything about Dr Pharoah's first child. I don't mean Rowena, Alison's daughter. Apparently there was another child before that, when Pharoah was in America in the thirties.'

'Excuse me a moment, Ellen . . .'

Doors opening and closing; Riley's voice, distant now, calling Annie to go to sleep. Muffled noises as he picked up the receiver again.

'Sorry about that. She had some friends round and she's still full of beans. Were you aware that Pharoah had another child?'

'No, not at all. I remember Dr Redmond telling me that Pharoah had been married before Alison but he didn't say anything about a child.'

'Two decades ago. It's a long time.'

'If there was a child, it hardly seems to have left a trace.'

'There's always a trace. It's just a question of finding it.'

'India doesn't say why she wants to know. And why doesn't she ask Marcus himself, or his family and friends?'

'Presumably she doesn't want to.'

'Exactly. Why?' There wasn't an answer to that which Ellen did not find disquieting. 'And why me, Riley? After all this time.'

'Because she trusts you. And because you knew Pharoah.'

Ellen sighed. 'I think about them sometimes,' she said. 'How India and Sebastian let me into their lives. I was lonely when I first came to London. Pretty miserable, actually. You know how usually with people it takes you a while to get to know them? They hold back till they're sure about you. But with India it was as if we'd parted only the day before. She never held back.'

'She struck me as a nice kid.'

'We had fun. I've always felt I should have warned her about Pharoah.'

'And told her what, exactly? She wouldn't have listened to you. People fall in love with people and often it doesn't make much sense to anyone else.'

He sounded tired. She said, 'You're all right, aren't you, Riley?'

'Yes, and all the better for talking to you.'

She let it go, though she didn't believe him. 'How's work?'

'Busy. Very busy. I've only just got home and I'll have to go out again shortly.'

'How's your gangster?'

'Continuing his business unimpeded by me or anyone else, I'm afraid.' He gave a short, dry laugh.

'It's odd, isn't it,' she said, 'how you can look back on a part of your life that seemed so difficult at the time, that you wouldn't have thought you'd remember with any fondness, and yet you feel nostalgic for it.'

'Are you thinking of Alec?' he said sharply.

Surprised, she said, 'Alec? No, not at all. I was thinking about when I first came to live in London. The lodging house with that awful shared kitchen, and my job at the hospital. And all the new people I met then, all the new friends. When I remember, it seems so clear, so bright. It's as if I felt more *alive*.' She made a self-conscious, exasperated sound. 'I suppose it's because I was young then.'

'You're hardly decrepit. *Annie*.'

Faintly, a child's voice, 'Daddy, I can't sleep.'

Riley said crisply into the phone, 'My love, I'm going to have to go, I'm afraid. I'll call you back tomorrow night.'

He put the phone down. In the silence, Ellen was aware of a continuing feeling of restlessness, almost dissatisfaction.

And confusion. *My love, I'm going to have to go.* 'My love'? He had never called her that before. Had he meant to use the endearment to Annie but accidentally said it to her? Tired and harassed, had he, as one sometimes did, muddled his words?

Rising, she picked up India's letter and went to the window. She glanced at the scrawled text but did not read it, her gaze flicking away to the squares of garden at the backs of the houses. A few forgotten items of washing hung limp on the lines; roses flopped heavy heads in the dusk. *My love* . . . She was rolling the edge of the thin blue paper between finger and thumb, testing those words in her mind. Strange how two words could produce such an onrush of feelings. Or perhaps it was not that, perhaps this sudden, sharp inclination to laugh or cry was a consequence, as she had said to Riley, of remembering, of the door to the past that India's letter had unlocked.

There's always a trace, he had told her. It's just a question of finding it. The past left traces and so did the people who made it. On reflection, those early years in London seemed so vividly coloured. She was aware of a sense of loss. Are you thinking of Alec, he had asked her, but the traces were not of him.

She had achieved so much, this flat, her career, prizes that had once seemed unobtainable. Why then this nagging, disturbing feeling of regret? Carefully, analytically, she found herself inspecting the events of her early years in London. The amusement and distraction of India's company, that had helped jolt her out of the shock and loss of confidence which had followed her dismissal from Gildersleve Hall. Her gradual discovery of satisfaction in her new job. And Riley: their meeting on the hospital steps, the friendship that had begun that day.

She would do as India asked and try to find out whether another child of Marcus Pharoah's had ever existed, because that was her nature. She knew that once a question formed in her mind, she had to go on digging until she answered it.

My love . . . Did she mind that he had called her that? No, not at all. But that, too, raised questions because his words had left their own trace of absolute delight, as if they were a magic incantation that cast an enchantment. She found that she could hardly bear to think he might have said them by mistake. She found she wanted him to have meant them with all his heart.

She was sitting at a corner table in a café in Tottenham Court Road. Catching sight of her through the window, Riley went inside.

'Hello, Janey,' he said.

As she turned her head slowly towards him, he saw the yellowing bruises down one side of her face. She was a pretty girl, very young, small and delicate-looking, her straight dark-brown hair cut in a fringe and swept up in a ponytail. Irish; beneath the cosmopolitan twang still sang an Irish lilt.

He had first met Janey Kelly in the Blue Duck nightclub two years ago. Janey was one of Bernie Perlman's girls. Riley had given her his hand to help her up after she had fallen on the floor on the night he had seen Lee Carter. Since then, he had bought her a coffee now and then, food when she looked hungry.

She said, 'What do you want, Riley?'

'Just thought I'd see how you were. Shall I get you another coffee?'

She shrugged and he went to the counter. He bought buns as well, because she looked stick thin, then carried the tray to the table and sat down opposite her.

'You look as if you've been in the wars, Janey.'

'I tripped.' She hunched her birdlike shoulders, sucked on her cigarette. 'Silly of me.'

'How's Bernie?'

'Fine.'

'And Lee?'

She tilted back her head, narrowing her eyes, letting out a thin channel of cigarette smoke. 'I hate Lee.'

'Only takes a word, Janey.'

'And I've a faceful of stitches. No thanks.' She bit at a hangnail.

'Someone like Lee doesn't know when to stop,' he said quietly. 'I think he's killed two people already. I don't want there to be a third.'

Her pretty little face creased into a scowl; she pulled down the sleeves of her yellow cardigan over her narrow blue-veined wrists and looked out of the window. 'Shove off, Riley.'

'I don't want you to get hurt.'

'Oh, how touching. Bet if I offered you a quick one round the back you wouldn't say no.' She blew smoke in his face. 'Long time since you had it, is it, copper? You're all the same. Just leave me alone.'

Driving home, Riley found himself remembering Ellen's friend, India. Another pretty girl, with her come-to-bed eyes and tousled blond hair, coupled with a jumpy, attractive, careless vivacity. Like Janey, she had that air of wildness, instability even, that some men went for. Men like Pharoah and Bernie Perlman. India Mayhew and

Marcus Pharoah, Janey Kelly and Bernie Perlman. Perhaps, to begin with, they were looking for protectors, these girls. Someone strong, who'd look after them.

Sometimes he thought he was getting somewhere with Janey and sometimes, like today, he suspected that he was wasting his time. During the past three years he had painstakingly built up a dossier on Bernie Perlman's business enterprises, each fragment of information contributing to the larger picture. Recently, Perlman's attention had begun to move away from gambling dens and protection rackets to the acquisition of property – houses, flats and offices in central London. Property was where Perlman thought the money was, where fortunes would be made in the second half of the twentieth century. Perhaps Bernie Perlman had decided to step aside from the violent activities of his youth in favour of a career that verged on respectability. This possibility frustrated Riley: two years, five, and it would be forgotten that Perlman's empire had been built on terror and extortion. People had short memories. He knew that he was running out of time.

He had spent the past two years patiently waiting for Janey to change her mind and help him put Bernie Perlman behind bars. He had spent those same years waiting for Ellen. It seemed to him that he had waited long enough. He wanted more than friendship. 'My love' – the term had slipped out but he would not have taken the words back even if he had been able to. He knew that he was reaching the point where he must make his feelings clear to her even if that meant risking losing her as a friend. It was time for a decision. One way or the other. For ever, done with, for good or ill.

The first time she met him, India was hauling the carrycot out of the coffeehouse in Midhurst – the heavy door to be kept ajar with an elbow, the wheels to be lowered carefully down the steps – when he dashed across the road, held open the door for her, then lifted the pram down the steps so gently Abigail didn't stir at all.

He was young, about her own age, she guessed, and he had thick, curly brown hair and a smile that spread over his tanned face like the sun coming out. He was about a foot taller than she was and he wore dark drill trousers and a plaid shirt. When she got to know him better, she saw that round the pupils of his blue eyes was a ring of amber-brown.

The next day, he opened the door of the coffeehouse for her as she arrived. And the next, and the next. She said, 'Don't you ever work?' and he pointed across the road to the upper storey of a red-brick building.

'That's my office, ma'am. I said to myself, Linc, you go out for a coffee every afternoon and so does that lady, so why don't you go out ten minutes earlier and help her get her baby carriage up those steps.'

'Linc?' she said.

He held out a hand. 'Lincoln Strawbridge. It's a pleasure to meet you, ma'am.'

'India Pharoah,' she said. 'And this is Abigail.'

He leaned over the pram. 'May I?'

Abigail was stirring, her fat little hand dipping to the blanket, her pursed mouth opening and closing. 'Yes, of course,' she said.

Very gently, cradling Abigail's head in the palm of his big hand, he picked her up. She looked so tiny, supported against his broad chest. 'Well, aren't you a honey?' he murmured to her. 'Aren't you just a honey? She takes after you, ma'am.'

'She does, doesn't she?' India took the baby from him and stroked a silver-fair curl. 'Do you have children of your own, Mr Strawbridge?'

'No, I'm not married, but I'm the eldest of seven. My youngest brother's just eighteen months old.'

She offered to buy him a coffee but he insisted, gravely courteous, on buying one for her. He told her he had been born in Midhurst, had gone away to college to study architecture, but had come back to the town after he had qualified. 'I missed my family,' he said. 'Do you miss yours, Mrs Pharoah?'

Abigail was grizzling. India thought of Sebastian, and nodded, then unrolled the bottle from its covering of a spare nappy.

One afternoon, he told her about the houses he built. He had brought with him a long roll of paper which he flattened out on the table so that she could see the ink sketches. The houses had porches and dormer windows and long, shady verandas.

'I like to build in the vernacular style,' he said. 'It suits the landscape. If there's anything I detest, it's a house that should be in Miami or Los Angeles thrown into a town in Vermont. Vermont houses are quiet and modest. They don't like to blow their own trumpet. Same with the people. My homes are built solid to weather the winds. The walls are thick and the doors are well-fitting to keep the house warm when there's snow outside. I make my windows out of two thicknesses of glass—' He broke off. 'Aw, listen to me. You don't want to hear the technical details, do you?'

'Yes, I do,' she said. Sun was pouring through the window of the café; she adjusted Abigail's bonnet. 'Do you live in a house like this?'

He leaned back in his seat, stretching out his long legs, which struggled to fit beneath the table. 'I live in a shack a little way north out of town, where the road forks. It's not much of a place, just a couple of rooms, but I like it there. It's in a valley, and there's a fine view of the mountains and I can sit on the stoop and watch the hummingbirds. One day, I'll build a house there. I'm just starting out, Mrs Pharoah, and so far I've had only a couple of clients reckless enough to let me build them a home. Most of the work that comes to me is making a garage or adding on a sunroom. But that will change, I know it will.'

Some afternoons India sat in the café, spinning out cups of coffee, playing with Abigail. She got to know the waitresses and some of the other customers. When Linc wasn't there, she looked out of the window to where the hot summer sun painted the shadows of the passers-by across the sidewalks. A convertible rolled along the street. The girl sitting in the passenger seat was wearing sunglasses and her head was covered by a flowered scarf. She leaned towards the driver, her arm along the back of his seat.

India imagined Linc standing on a building site, shading his eyes from the sun as he looked up to where the bare bones of his house rose out of the soil. She imagined him running a hand along a span of wood, testing the strength of a joist.

A letter arrived from Ellen. India waited until she was at the café to open it. It was a very Ellen sort of letter, its news presented in a factual and undramatic fashion, sent with love and best wishes, which was good of Ellen, all things considered. After she had read it, India folded it and put it back in her handbag.

Two years ago, she had sat in a nightclub in Mayfair in her stolen dress, talking to Marcus. She had asked him why Ellen disliked him and he had told her about the quarrel with his friend, his friend's death and the inquiries of the police. Now the friend had a name, Bryan Redmond. It seemed to India, after reading Ellen's letter, that Marcus had left a lot of things out.

It was so hard to know what to make of it. Marcus had a way of moulding the past into what he wanted. Suppose, after his first wife had died, Marcus hadn't wanted the baby. Suppose he had looked at Rosanne's baby with the same critical, assessing eye with which he looked at Abigail.

Suppose it had been Rosanne he had wanted, Rosanne he had longed for with all the intense possessive power of which he was capable. He might even have blamed the baby for Rosanne's death.

What might he have done? He might have put the baby in an orphanage. He might then have told anyone who asked him that it had been stillborn. He might have returned to England and hidden the baby's existence. He might have started again while his child was left stranded, alone for ever among strangers. Marcus was good at remaking himself; Marcus liked to shut doors on the past.

Chapter Twelve

A rush to finish a series of experiments which she hoped to use in a paper to be presented at a conference the following spring, and then a week's holiday, camping with Freya Hawks in Wales, had delayed Ellen from following up her promise to India to find out anything she could about the first Mrs Pharoah and her child. Returning to London in late August, she had only two more days before going back to work.

Friends and family, that's where to start, Riley had suggested when they had spoken earlier. Marcus Pharoah had a daughter, Rowena, a brother, Devlin, a nephew, Rufus, and an ex-wife, Alison. Recalling the sardonic glitter in Devlin Pharoah's brown eyes, Ellen had decided to telephone Alison Pharoah. Mrs Pharoah agreed to talk to her. After putting the phone down, Ellen remembered that Jan Kaminski, once Pharoah's right-hand man, was now a Fellow at Cambridge.

Ellen wrote to him, explaining that she would be in the area and asking whether they could meet. Kaminski had written back by return of post, inviting her to lunch.

Earlier that morning, she had called at Riley's house to borrow his car to drive to Cambridgeshire. Stopping and starting through the rush-hour city traffic before heading north on the A1, she was aware of his belongings: the notebook, Polos and I-Spy book stuffed into the glovebox, the scarf on the back seat. After Royston, she turned off the main road on to narrower country lanes, walled with hedgerows. Soon, the landmarks became familiar to her. A church spire, a village green and a shop recalled to her weekend cycle rides she had taken during the time she had worked at Gildersleve Hall.

Driving into the village of Barton, she parked on the road by the yew hedge and was assailed by memories. She remembered the night of the power cut, how the velvety darkness had seemed to press in on her as, blinded, she had made her way along the corridor. Her horror and her relief when she had encountered Alec. She remembered how the wind had whisked the frayed seedheads of the pampas grass in the Pharoahs' garden, and the confusion of her feelings that day. Yet those events seemed distant now; they had happened to a younger, different self.

Leaving the car, she walked up the gravel driveway. The house looked much as she remembered it, large, pleasant and gracious in the summer sunshine. A horsebox was parked on the courtyard; pansies and petunias spilled from stone urns and a white rose rambled over the front door.

Alison Pharoah, her fair head bright in the morning sun, was kneeling in front of a border, a trowel on the lawn beside her, tapping a geranium from a pot. Ellen called out a greeting and Mrs Pharoah turned, then stood up. She was wearing a tweed skirt and a short-sleeved pale pink jersey.

'Miss Kingsley?'

'Yes. Thank you for agreeing to talk to me.'

Mrs Pharoah took off her leather gardening glove before shaking Ellen's hand. 'I'll get on with this, if it doesn't bother you.' Alison Pharoah's tone made it clear that she expected Ellen's agreement.

'Please. It's such a beautiful garden, Mrs Pharoah.'

Alison Pharoah surveyed the borders and lawns. 'It's a lot of work. It's so hard to get decent help these days. Marcus wanted me to sell the house but I'll be damned if I'll do that.' Her cold, pale green eyes settled on Ellen. 'You said that you had some questions for me.'

In other words, get on with it, I'm busy. Ellen asked a few anodyne questions about Marcus Pharoah's career, then said, 'You weren't Dr Pharoah's first wife, were you, Mrs Pharoah?'

'No.' A short, contemptuous outbreath. 'Nor his last.'

'His first wife was American, wasn't she?'

'From somewhere in New England. He married her when he was very young.'

'She died, didn't she?'

'Yes.' There was a packet of cigarettes on a nearby stone urn. Alison tipped one out and lit it.

'Do you know what of?'

Mrs Pharoah gave a quick shake of the head. 'Pneumonia or something. Marcus never talked about it. He was always very odd about illnesses. I've met you before, haven't I?'

'I came here for Sunday lunch once, about five years ago.'

'Were you one of Marcus's girls?'

'I was an employee of his.'

A sceptical smile curled the corners of Mrs Pharoah's mouth. Ellen said coolly, 'Nothing else. What did you mean when you said that Dr Pharoah is odd about illnesses?'

'He can't bear sick people.' Alison Pharoah balanced the cigarette on the edge of the urn and picked up another pot. 'Marcus likes the people around him to be good-looking, healthy and conventional. I can see now what a dull man he was. Why do you want to know? What was it you said you were doing when we spoke on the phone?'

Ellen repeated the lie that she and Riley had concocted: that she was writing a few paragraphs on Dr Pharoah, an overview of his life and work, for a scientific journal. She had never been much of a liar and she could tell that Mrs Pharoah was unconvinced. A whack on the underside of the pot with the trowel and another geranium was neatly upended, then plunged into a hole in the soil.

Ellen said, 'Did Dr Pharoah and his first wife have any children?'

'No, none. We only had the one child, our daughter, Rowena. Marcus didn't want any more.' Mrs Pharoah stood up again, peeled off her gloves and picked up the cigarette. 'I would have liked more.' A mixture of discontent and sadness settled over her face. 'I always wanted a son. You'd have thought Marcus would have wanted a boy, but he didn't. And yet he always loved Rowena far more than he loved me. You'd have thought that—' She broke off, pressing the back of her hand against her mouth. 'Forgive me,' she murmured. 'I haven't been well.'

'I'm sorry, Mrs Pharoah.'

Alison Pharoah's expression altered. 'I'm well rid of him. To tell the truth, I miss Gosse more than I miss Marcus. Marcus insisted on taking Gosse with him to America. Damned annoying and of course the wretched boiler broke down the day after he left. Gosse was a nasty little man, but he was good with the horses.' The cigarette stub was crushed into the urn and Mrs Pharoah glanced at her watch. 'And now, if you'll excuse me, I'm meeting my fiancé for lunch.'

Returning to her car, Ellen felt a longing to head home to London. These long ago events, these people with their skewed morality and their egotism, produced in her feelings of distaste. It was a relief to sit in the car, with its intimacy, its reminders of Riley, as she rested her hands on the steering wheel and ate a Polo.

A Rover drove at speed out of the Pharoahs' driveway. Ellen started up the car and headed for Cambridge. It was a market day and the traffic was heavy, and she was almost ten minutes late for her lunch with Dr Kaminski.

As a senior research fellow, his rooms overlooked a garden where a fig scrambled along ancient brickwork and a handkerchief tree flailed its greenish-white pennants. Not far away, punts slid along the olivine surface of the river. Brushing off Ellen's apologies for her lateness, Dr Kaminski showed her to a small table, set for lunch, in the bay window.

'How are you, Miss Kingsley?'

'I'm very well, thank you. And thank you so much for inviting me.'

'A pleasure, a pleasure. I thought a cold lunch in this warm weather. Then we need not be interrupted.'

They discussed their work; as they spoke, Ellen thought that he had changed little since she had last seen him, only taking on, perhaps, the look of the academic, rumpled and tweedy.

They had finished the first course when he said, 'I am enjoying my life here. There is some dissension, of course – among intelligent, ambitious people that is inevitable – but only comparatively minor matters. The atmosphere at Gildersleve Hall had become poisonous by the time I left. You said that you wanted to talk to me about Pharoah, Miss Kingsley. Why is that?'

Instinctively she knew that she must tell him the truth. She said, 'A friend of mine has married him. She wrote to me, asking me to find something out for her.'

'And what was that?'

She told him about Rosanne Pharoah and the stillborn child. Jan Kaminski shook his head. 'I'm afraid I can't help you. Pharoah rarely spoke of personal matters to me. I knew Alison, of course, but . . .' He spread out his hands.

'It doesn't matter.' She smiled at him. 'It's lovely to see you anyway.'

Dr Kaminski cleared away their plates to the sideboard. His back to her, he said, 'I did, however, know poor Redmond reasonably well. I should have thought that would have been of interest to you.'

She glanced at him sharply. 'Yes, it is.'

He put a strawberry tart and a jug of cream on the table. Sitting down, he pressed his folded knuckles against his forehead and, in the squares of light that poured through the mullioned windows, she saw for the first time that he had aged after all, that he looked tired, and that the eye on the undamaged side of his face was now surrounded by deep lines. 'A headache,' he said, catching her looking at him. 'I get a lot of headaches.'

'I have some aspirins.' She made to open her bag.

'No, thank you. Let's talk. It will distract me.'

She said, 'You lived in Dr Redmond's cottage during the war, didn't you?'

'From nineteen forty-two. The three of us lived there. Pharoah and Redmond moved in first and I joined them some time later. It was Pharoah who recruited me. I had certain skills that were useful to the work of Gildersleve

Hall during the war.' He cut the tart into four, put one of the pieces on a plate, and handed it to Ellen. 'Please help yourself to cream, Miss Kingsley. I'd thought I was finished. I'd been pretty badly shot up and my nerves were wrecked. When I was well enough, I started going to scientific meetings in London. Sat at the back, so people didn't have to look at me, put my hands in my coat pockets so that no one would notice them shake. There were kind people who came to talk to me and someone must have mentioned me to Pharoah because he phoned me and we had a chat. I started work at Gildersleve Hall two days after that conversation took place. Pharoah cut through all the red tape to get me there. He was good at that sort of thing. He knew what he wanted and he got it. I was deeply grateful to him. There are few things worse than believing you'll never be of use to anyone any more, that you have no further part to play.'

Ellen found herself recalling the six months after she had left Gildersleve Hall, six months without work, during which a drab pall of isolation and futility had settled over her.

'It must have been very difficult,' she said.

'Yes, it was. For me, that was worse than the physical pain.' He nodded towards the window. 'I would have none of this now had it not been for Pharoah. I doubt if I'd have survived. I would have hoped a bomb would fall on me. So, as I said, Pharoah and Redmond were already living at the cottage by the time I went to Gildersleve Hall. After a couple of weeks, Pharoah asked me to join them. I was relieved – my lodgings were unpleasant and my landlady was suspicious of me because I was a foreigner. We three got on well. We had certain things in common, we were all young men, uprooted from the places of our birth, and we shared an interest in science. We liked to play chess and solve crosswords and to walk in the grounds of the hall and Peddar's Wood. In the evenings one of us would cycle to the pub to fetch a jug of beer and would bring it back on the handlebars of his bike. It was a matter of honour to do so without spilling a drop, in the blackout, whatever the weather. We'd drink and talk until the early hours of the morning. I remember those conversations. I've never had conversations like them since. They were exhilarating and wonderful. We talked about everything, of the future of science, the marvellous developments the post-war years would bring, of the lives we hoped for.' He smiled. 'I was happy. Six months earlier I'd thought I'd never be happy again. We believed that we could change the world. You do when you're young.'

'Did you always get on well?'

'Not always. Sometimes we argued. I remember once telling the pair of them they were fools and walking out of the house. I sat in the wood, listening to the owls calling, and then after a couple of hours I went back.'

'What did you argue about?'

'Politics. Yes, I would say that was our main area of disagreement.'

'Dr Redmond was a communist, wasn't he?'

'I couldn't shake them out of it. It infuriated me, how two intelligent people could refuse to see what was staring them in the face. They wouldn't listen, they didn't seem to have the capacity to understand what it is to live in a country that is not free.'

Ellen's heartbeat had speeded up. 'Are you saying that Dr Pharoah was a communist too?'

'For a while, yes.' Kaminski's eyes narrowed as if he was staring back into the past. 'Communism was fashionable in the thirties, you understand, among a certain section of young people. Redmond was a card-carrying communist up to his death, so far as I know.'

'And Dr Pharoah?'

'I believe that for a short time, before the war, he may have been a party member. I'm not convinced, though, looking back, that Pharoah ever had strong political convictions. Redmond was unshakeable in his faith but I don't think it was ever as important to Pharoah. I remember feeling proud of myself, wondering whether it was my influence that had made him change his mind, but I don't suppose it had anything to do with me. I'm sure that Pharoah had by then worked out what he wanted to do and was clear-sighted enough to see that extreme left-wing politics would only be a hindrance to him.'

'Do you mean what he wanted to do after the war was over?'

'Yes.' Jan Kaminski had risen from the table. Silhouetted

blackly against the window, he looked outside. The shrieks of laughter from the punts had died down; from somewhere, Ellen heard the liquid notes of a violin.

'We had a nickname,' he said, 'the three of us, during the war. The Triumvirate, that was what our colleagues at Gildersleve Hall called us. And the Triumvirate worked it out together in those long evenings at the cottage. I think it was Redmond's idea first, that we would set up our own research institution after the war was over. Pharoah, being the only presentable one of the three of us, was to head it, to be the public face. He had that knack of inspiring loyalty in people. You wanted to please him. All Redmond cared about was having somewhere to pursue his work uninterrupted. He never wanted fame or success or money. I offered to undertake the routine work, the chasing up of funds, the bringing in of projects on time. You need someone methodical and conscientious to do that and I knew I was capable. We discussed the organization of such an institution and which branches of research we would pursue – genetics, crystallography, biochemistry. We would, of course, become world-renowned.' Jan Kaminski's mouth stretched in a shallow smile and his fingers tapped the windowsill. 'After a while, what started as a pipe dream seemed to become a possibility. Though I think that Pharoah always believed in it.' He turned back to Ellen. 'Will you have some coffee, Miss Kingsley?'

'Yes, thank you.'

'Shall we take it out to the Fellows' garden?'

Dr Kaminski made the coffee, then put on a hat over his thin blond hair and carried the tray outside. They sat in the shade of the handkerchief tree.

'Then something happened,' said Kaminski. 'In nineteen forty-four I went away for a week to oversee some tests on Salisbury Plain. When I came back to the cottage, Pharoah and Redmond were no longer speaking to each other.'

'They'd fallen out?'

'Yes.'

'Do you know why?'

The patchy shade of the tree darkened the burned skin on Jan Kaminski's face to a livid purple. 'I asked, but neither would say. Pharoah brushed it off and Redmond refused to talk to me. It was a habit of his to shut himself away for days at a time and he did so then. I wondered at the time whether Redmond had felt it a betrayal that Pharoah should alter his political allegiance so absolutely. Perhaps he'd told Pharoah so. Pharoah dislikes criticism.' He added pointedly, 'But you know that, Miss Kingsley.'

She could only say, 'Yes.'

'But I came to doubt that was the reason. It was Pharoah's attitude to Redmond that had altered rather than the other way round. Redmond remained unswervingly loyal to Pharoah for a long time after they had quarrelled. He had always admired Pharoah intensely. I suppose Pharoah could do so easily the things Redmond found impossible – talking to people, charming them, persuading them to do what he wanted. Anyway, they patched it over – Gildersleve needed both of them – but it was never the same after-wards. To some extent, before that time, I had always been a little on the outside. Pharoah and Redmond had known each other for several years before I came along. When there are three of you, there'll always be two who have the deeper bond. I noticed that they began to communicate through me. I became closer to Pharoah while Redmond lived more and more apart from us. Then the war ended and all Pharoah's energy went into making his dream a reality. He was impressive. He had his plans in place – he'd got to know the right people and he and Alison were living together again, and he had persuaded her father to finance the hall. The War Office had no further use for it. It was a ramshackle old building, as you know, and they were happy enough to sell it to him.'

Jan Kaminski fell silent. Ellen said gently, 'It must have been exciting.'

'It was. So much so that I'm afraid I overlooked certain things. I've often asked myself, was that out of loyalty to Pharoah, because I owed him so much, or was it because they were good times for me, too, and I didn't want to rock the boat?'

In the silence, Ellen saw the flicker of shadows on the grass. Two men in academic gowns came out of a doorway; Dr Kaminski raised a hand in greeting as they went to sit on a bench on the far side of the garden.

He said, 'I let Pharoah pass off some of my work as his own. He had done little new research work for some time.

He claimed that the setting up of the hall had fully occupied him. Can't give a good impression without a few papers in *Nature*, he said to me, and would I mind helping him out. Gildersleve Hall would die an early death if it got round that its director was running out of ideas. When he had the chance to do some solid work, he'd pay me back.'

'And did he?' Her voice was a whisper.

'No. In fact, it happened again. And again. After a while, he didn't even ask me, he just took. We'd be at a meeting or seminar and I'd hear him come out with some theory I was working on. As if he'd thought of it himself. Perhaps by then he believed he had. So there we were, Pharoah with his growing reputation for brilliance, and me – well, I could see that my colleagues were starting to think that it was me who was burned out.'

'Did you say anything to Dr Redmond?'

'Never.'

But Redmond had known, Redmond had guessed. Ellen recalled the afternoon in Peddar's Wood, when he had called Dr Pharoah a liar and a plagiarist: the sting of snow in the air and the way that the coppiced trees had clawed at the heavy sky.

Jan Kaminski's pale blue eyes looked straight ahead. 'In nineteen thirty-nine, after the Germans and the Russians invaded Poland, I travelled to England. It was a long, arduous journey that took me almost six months, but I found my way. But once I started giving in to Pharoah's demands, I couldn't find my way back. What Pharoah did was wrong, but what I did was equally wrong.' He smiled sadly. 'It was dishonest. There, it's a relief to admit that at last.'

'You were loyal to him,' she said gently. 'That's not such a terrible thing.'

'Do you think so? But perhaps Pharoah demanded too much loyalty.'

This, she herself had learned the hard way. Pharoah had demanded absolute allegiance and he had also demanded silence. Those who had not given him what he wanted had received summary justice.

Kaminski gave a soft sigh and said, 'In the years after the war, Redmond retreated from us. He saw me as Pharoah's man, I suspect. He'd always liked his own company, and he was an odd man, and I'm afraid he became odder over time. He changed. He was never *sociable*, but when I first knew him, he had a few close friends.'

'Dr Pharoah.'

'Yes, Pharoah, for many years. And there was a woman.'

Now she said incredulously, 'A girlfriend?'

'Yes, in London. He visited her each month. Once, Redmond and I were on the same London train. When we reached town, we found that we were both heading in a similar direction so I travelled on with him.'

'And he was visiting his girlfriend? He *said* that?'

'Not in so many words. To tell the truth, I don't think he said anything at all. But I guessed. I'm afraid I teased him a little.'

Now, Ellen felt utterly confused. But she had the

presence of mind to say, 'Where was this, Dr Kaminski? In which part of London?'

'Finsbury Park,' he said. 'Woodstock Road.'

Before she headed back to London, Ellen took the road out to Copfield. She drove past Mrs Bryant's bungalow and into the village, past the Green Man pub and the church and out along the hazel-fringed rise that led to Gildersleve. The hedgerows were thickly leaved and she realized that she had never before seen Gildersleve Hall in summer, that her memories were of the frozen monotones of winter.

At the summit she braked, looked down and saw the hall. Parking the car, she got out and climbed on to the verge. Absently, she snapped off a twig as she peered through the branches of the hazels. The hall seemed for an instant just the same, almost as if it was waiting for Martin to run down the front steps at a clip or for Bill Farmborough to emerge from the building, briefcase in hand.

She had learned that day about the consequences of betrayal. Pharoah had betrayed Alison and her pain and bitterness remained visible. He had betrayed Dr Redmond and Jan Kaminski as well, had taken their admiration and friendship and used it for his own ends. Once, the three men had shared their excitement for the future but now Redmond was long dead, Pharoah had left the country, and only Kaminski remained, haunted by regret and disillusion.

At Gildersleve, she had been unable to see the truth, had

fumbled in the dark, stumbling against other people's desires and ambitions. She saw clearly now, and, glancing a second time, Gildersleve Hall seemed little more than a husk of a house, ivy creeping over the walls and tower, a relic from a dusty and dishonourable past.

That morning, when she had collected the car from Riley, he had sat with her in the vehicle, running through the various controls. She had been aware of him beside her, of the brush of his hand and the warmth of his skin. Touch had its own chemistry, a fierce, igniting power that filled the spaces left by words. Touch told you that you wanted someone. Touch told you they wanted you. Before they had parted, he had said to her, 'Are you sure about this? Are you sure you want to go back there?' She had reassured him, and now, as she returned to the car, she knew that she had been right to do so.

Her three months at Gildersleve had been a turning point in her life but now she was poised at another juncture. Both she and Riley had been bruised by former relationships. Neither of them, she thought, loved lightly. In law, Riley was still married to Pearl. For herself, there were all her old reservations about the difficulty of mixing marriage and career, the fear of jeopardising what had been so hard won.

And yet, as she started up the car and drove on, she was filled with a bright optimism. You could not say that anything had been easy for them. The circumstances of their first meeting, in the shocked aftermath of Dr Redmond's death, had not been auspicious. Pearl's illness and disappearance, her own broken engagement to Alec: these events had left a long shadow. In spite of this, they had survived. Their friendship had blossomed and deepened. They would manage, she thought, she and him. No, more than manage, because she found it unbearable to imagine life without him. He was threaded into her thoughts, into her heart. A successful partnership – and here she considered her parents – was not necessarily of two people with similar characters, backgrounds and tastes, but of a couple so deeply rooted together they became different parts of the same person, like the facets of a crystal. One might sometimes look one way, one another, but they were together a whole, precious and harmonious.

Reaching the farm track, she had intended to park at the entrance to Peddar's Wood, so as not to get mud over Riley's car, but as she neared the turn-off she noticed that the rutted track was now tarmacked. Swinging on to the new road, she drove a short distance along it. The wood had been felled and not a single tree remained. In place of their enchantment, new houses, boxy in shape, their bricks a raw red, had sprung up.

Redmond always loved that woodland, Dr Kaminski had said to her as they had parted that afternoon. *Pharoah knew that. It would have been a fitting memorial to his old friend to preserve it as he had loved it, but Pharoah chose to destroy it. That was his greatest crime. Though I suppose you could say that in the end, it set me free.*

*　　*　　*

It was one of those rare English days when the heat lingers into the evening. Ellen was sitting in Riley's garden and they were sharing a bottle of beer.

'I know what happened now,' she said. 'I know what Dr Redmond meant when he told Pharoah he could destroy him.'

She explained to Riley about Marcus Pharoah passing off Jan Kaminski's work as his own and about his youthful communist sympathies. 'Pharoah went to America several times during the months I was at Gildersleve,' she said. 'He attended conferences and gave lectures there. He was feted in America, even more so than he was here. If Dr Redmond had made public that Pharoah had dabbled in communism then Pharoah might not have been able to travel to America any more. He might have had his visa revoked, like Professor Bernal at Birkbeck. Couple that with accusations about plagiarism – even if Dr Kaminski had refused to confirm what Redmond said, rumours can do a lot of harm. Pharoah must have known that his career might never recover.'

Riley uncapped another bottle of beer and topped up their glasses. 'It makes sense. And the child?'

Ellen shook her head. 'Nothing. Jan didn't know anything about a child. Neither did Alison Pharoah.'

'A dead end, then.'

'Yes, in some ways.'

She saw him look at her quizzically. Why couldn't she just tell him what she had come here intending to say the moment he had opened the door to her? Why instead, after she had parked his car outside, had she talked to him about the drive, and Annie, even the *weather*, for heaven's sake? Why, now that they were alone, Annie in bed and the au pair out for the evening, did she sit on the garden bench, fidgeting and reddening like a schoolgirl, the confidence she had felt that afternoon at Gildersleve having deserted her?

They might go on in this way for ever, she thought despairingly, both aware of an attraction but unable to bring it into being, both reticent and reserved in character, the sort of people who delved into a problem, analysing it, tearing it apart, until it lay in meaningless fragments. Mutually incapable of putting it together again, of making something new.

Another thought occurred to her. What evidence had she that he was attracted to her? A brush of a hand, sitting in the car that morning. An endearment, quite possibly voiced in error. Almost nothing. There was, if you looked back critically at their history, little indication that he had anything more than a friendly affection for her. And *friendship* had come to have such a dull, spinsterish sound. Even back in the early days of their acquaintance, before Alec, Riley had never asked her out, never made a move. She remembered that evening in the aftermath of the break-up of her engagement when, drunk, she had suggested sleeping overnight on his sofa, and how he had bundled her out of the door and into a taxi as if she had an infectious disease. There had been numerous occasions during the past two years when all he had to do was to reach out and take her hand. He wouldn't even have needed to *say* anything. Would she have turned him away? She knew that she would not.

But then . . . She thought of their long phone conversations, sometimes late into the night until they could hardly speak for yawning, as though neither of them could bear to be the one who ended the call. She thought of the days they had spent together, the concerts they had attended, the hours they had sat in this garden or his house, listening to music or just talking. Oh, it was all too complicated! She gave a loud sigh, wishing such things could be weighed, measured, put on a balance, total totted up, conclusion written, line drawn.

'Riley—'

'Ellen.'

They had both spoken at once. 'I'm sorry,' she said. 'You go ahead.'

'No, you first.'

'No, you. What were you going to say?'

He sat down beside her. 'It's funny, you wait, thinking one day the time will be just right but it never is. There's never a moment when there isn't risk. And you've made mistakes before, so you're wary.'

'Wary of what?' She peered hard into his eyes.

'Of speaking from the heart.'

Her own heart was racing. She whispered, 'If you were to speak from the heart, Riley, what would you say?'

'That I love you. That's what I was going to say. What were you?'

She felt herself teetering on the edge of great happiness. 'I was going to say that though today was a dead end in some ways, in another it was a revelation. But Riley, what did you mean when you said that you were afraid I might be a mistake? Did you mean like Pearl?'

'Never.' His voice roughened. 'Good God, no. I've been sure from the first moment I saw you. Oh, you tell yourself that it's mere attraction – and perhaps at first it is only attraction and desire, perhaps it's being in love rather than really loving. But for me none of what I first felt for you has ever diminished, it's only gathered pace. It's become a part of my life, a part of me. I love you, Ellen, and that love is as essential to me as the bones that hold me up and the blood that flows through my veins. But you may not feel the same. In fact, I can think of a number of reasons why you'd be sensible not to feel the same.'

'I can't think of any.' Her voice was small but clear.

In his eyes, a fire flared. 'Are you sure?'

'Never more so.'

'Listen, Ellen.' He gripped her hand. 'I have a child – and yes, I know you love Annie and she loves you, but nevertheless, it's a huge commitment. I have a job that can be ridiculously demanding, that takes me away at all hours, often without warning.'

'None of that matters.'

'I'm married. *That* matters. I have a failed marriage behind me that I'm still legally tied to. I've spoken to a solicitor about a divorce but it won't be straightforward with Pearl nowhere to be found. I wonder what your family would think of that?'

'My father would dislike it.'

'Yes, I would have thought so. Quite understandably. I daresay he wouldn't be too thrilled either at the thought of you taking on another woman's child.'

'No, probably not. But he would come round.'

'Ellen—'

'And if he didn't, I'd live with it.' She was looking at him and though she knew she was smiling, she was aware also of tears aching around her eyes. Tears of joy, she thought, but also of regret for the time that they had already spent apart, those unreclaimable years.

'Joe's always liked you,' she said tremulously. 'And my mother will adore you. She loves handsome, capable men.'

A flicker of a smile. 'Even if that's so—'

'Riley, you're not going to put me off. I may as well point out to you that I'm a career woman and though I know how to bake a cake and mop a floor, I don't choose to spend much of my time doing so.'

'I've no wish to tie you to the kitchen sink.'

'Don't look so grim, darling. I love you and I'm only explaining that if we were to—'

She broke off. She had got rather ahead of herself. She felt herself go pink.

'If we were to marry? Was that what you were going to

say?' Threading his fingers through hers, he raised her hand and kissed it. 'If it was, if it's something you'd seriously consider as soon as I'm free, then you would make me indescribably happy.'

Embarrassment and uncertainty fell away, replaced by elation. She felt a deep contentment and a complete pleasure in the moment and was calm again. She was sharply aware of everything around her: of the papery rustle of a bumble bee in the trumpet of a flower, of the distant whine of traffic on the main road, and of the presence of the man sitting beside her, the pressure of his hand on the back of her neck as he drew her to him to kiss her.

'It's my life, Riley,' she said gently, breaking away for long enough to speak. 'No one else's. My decision. And anyway, what's wrong with living in sin?'

'Your father would probably shoot me.'

They kissed as the sun sank beneath the rooftops of the buildings. 'I suppose there is that,' she said. Then they kissed some more.

Once, India drove north, out of Midhurst, past Linc's place. The small wooden building was set well back from the road, halfway up the slope of the hill, among a stand of birches. India was driving the station wagon that day and Abigail was sleeping in the carrycot on the back seat. She parked and looked up at the house, and imagined Linc sitting on the raised stoop at the front, watching the hummingbirds. She pictured his strong brown hands holding a coffee mug or a glass of beer. The sleeves of his plaid shirt would be rolled up to his elbows and the sun would throw shadows that would pick out the curve of his lip and gather round his deepset eyes.

A pick-up truck, painted a dull green, was parked on the slope. She thought she saw a movement in the meadow behind the house – a shadow, the to-and-fro of a branch – and she turned the car and drove home.

She stopped going to the coffeehouse. She knew how easily such things began, and how, the deeper you waded in, the more they clung to you. She thought of her mother and Neil dancing in the garden, how the open air had swallowed up the music of the gramophone and how her mother had rested her head against Neil's navy-blue shoulder. *Lucinda, you have to think of those children.* She, now, had a child to think of.

She applied herself to being a good wife and mother. In the afternoons, instead of driving to town, she spread a blanket on the grass and laid Abigail upon it so that she could watch the shivering leaves on the trees. She carried Abigail round the pond, showing her the fish and the sparkle of water and the pale flowers that grew in the dampest, darkest part of the woods. She wanted Abigail to be the sort of woman who knew about everything, like Ellen.

Marcus decided that they should give a summer party. He told her where she should have the invitations printed and specified the thickness of card and the wording. He dictated the guest list to her: his colleagues from Midhurst, academics from other colleges and research institutions, a scattering of wealthy and important people from the area. India wondered who she would have invited, had Marcus asked her. The grocer's boy, the waitresses in the coffee-house. The old man she sometimes spoke to at the gate, when he was out walking his dog. Viola. Linc.

She made lists, placed orders for food and liquor, engaged maids to hand around drinks and canapés, had her nails and hair done. On the afternoon of the day of the party, she lay on the sofa in the sitting room, playing with Abigail. Her hands round her baby's middle, India lifted her up until her arms were straight and then whooshed her gently down. 'Abby's going up in an aeroplane . . . higher and higher into the sky . . . and zoom, down she goes.' Abigail chortled, her gummy mouth wide open.

The front doorbell rang. Marcus was working in his study and Viola had gone home for a couple of hours, so India laid Abigail on a blanket on the floor and went to answer it. It was the florist, with the arrangements for the party. India helped him take in the flowers, then looked for her purse. She heard Abigail start to cry and called out to Marcus to go to her. She found her purse in a coat pocket in the mud room; the baby was still crying as she fumbled urgently for notes to pay the bill.

The florist left; India went back into the sitting room. Abigail was lying on the floor, red-faced and screaming, and Marcus was standing a few yards away. It crossed India's mind that he was looking at his daughter with the same appraising eye with which he might have regarded one of his scientific experiments.

Pushing past him, India picked Abigail up. Then she held out the infant to him. 'Hold her,' she said. It was hard to speak for fury. 'Go on, hold her. She's your daughter, Marcus. Why won't you touch her? What's wrong with you? If you really didn't want another child, then why agree to letting me have one?' The effort of not shouting made her voice shake.

'To keep you busy,' he said softly. 'So you wouldn't make a spectacle of yourself, dawdling round town and talking to strangers.'

Then he walked out of the room. As she cradled Abigail against her shoulder, India found herself fighting for breath, as if she had been running.

She went into the kitchen. Warming Abigail's bottle in a pan, staring at the tiny bubbles which set themselves free from the metal base of the pan before rising to the surface to burst, she found herself concentrating on the task because the other part of her mind flinched from closely examining the scene that had just taken place. When the bottle was ready she took Abigail upstairs to feed her. She sat down in the low chair beside the nursery window, and tucked the baby into the crook of her arm.

They had engaged a children's nurse to look after Abigail during the party, Marcus had insisted, so after feeding her, India changed Abigail's nappy and made sure that everything was ready. Viola returned to put the finishing touches to the food. When the nurse arrived, India showed her where everything was and then went away to dress for the party. After she had bathed, she wrapped herself in a towelling robe, then searched through her wardrobe for a frock. At the end of the rail she caught sight of the white silk she had bought years ago from Berwick Street Market. She had bought it secondhand and had worn it many times. The silk ruffles round the low-cut bodice had yellowed and the edging of the slit up the front of the bell-shaped skirt had begun to fray.

She stepped into it, cranking round awkwardly to do up the zip. Then, sitting down at the dressing table, she rubbed powder into the planes and hollows of her face, painted on black wings of eyeliner, and pencilled in her eyebrows to make them dark and sooty. She chose the brightest, reddest lipstick she possessed. *Always accessorize*, she muttered to herself, and opened her jewellery box. She had lost the spray of blue waxed flowers somewhere on the long journey between the London flat and Vermont, but Marcus had bought her for her birthday a large, flashy diamond brooch in the shape of a shooting star. She pinned it on to her bosom. Satisfied, she looked in the mirror and pursed her mouth into the shape of a kiss.

She remained in the dressing room until she heard the first few cars draw up in the courtyard. There was a tap on the door; she opened it.

Viola's eyes widened, seeing her. 'Mr Pharoah says could you come downstairs, Mrs Pharoah.'

India ran her hands down her ribs, smoothing out the creases in the silk. 'Do you like it?'

Viola gave a bark of laughter. 'You're a sight for sore eyes, Mrs Pharoah. You look like Marilyn Monroe.'

India walked slowly downstairs. Half a dozen guests were in the hall, taking off summer coats and hats. She greeted them and showed them to the back veranda, where cocktails were being served. The evening sun spun a wash of apricot over the meadows and the pond.

The perfect hostess, India moved from guest to guest, enquiring after their holidays and their children, making sure everyone had a drink and a canapé. Out of the corner of her eye she saw Marcus turn to look at her.

As he drew her aside, his fingers pinched into the soft flesh of her arm. 'What do you think you're doing?' he hissed. 'You look like a tart. Go and change.'

'I like this dress, Marcus.' Where he had whispered, her voice was normal in pitch, and heads turned towards them.

The Dean of Studies was standing a few feet away. India touched his hand. 'Lowell, how delightful to see you! Let me find you a drink. It's a glorious evening, isn't it?'

After the guests had gone, after the maids and the children's nurse had been paid and sent home, he came to her in the kitchen, where she was tidying up.

'Never do that again,' he said.

Drying a glass, India held it up to the light to check for streaks. 'Do what, Marcus?'

'Try to make a fool out of me.'

'I thought it all went rather well.'

'You may be resentful of me,' he said softly, 'you may even dislike me, but you need me. You'd be nothing without me.'

'I managed perfectly well before I met you.' She put the glass away in a cupboard. 'And yes, I do dislike you. I didn't to begin with but I do now. I dislike the things you do. You've told Gosse to spy on me, haven't you? And you wrote to the children's home about me, I saw the letters in your desk. How could you do that, Marcus? How could you be so underhand?'

'I needed to find out what I was getting. Surely you can understand that.'

'I suppose if you'd found me to be inferior, you'd have got rid of me.'

'You're not inferior.' He was leaning against the door of the fridge, drinking. He pulled at the knot of his tie. 'A little shop-soiled, perhaps, but not inferior.'

'Neither is Abigail. She's a beautiful, healthy, perfect baby and you hardly even look at her.'

'I don't find small children interesting. I daresay I'll like her better as she grows older.'

India took out a cigarette, snapped her lighter. 'You mean, ignore her for the first few years of her life and then indulge her, so that she grows up as spoiled and desperate for your attention as Rowena is.'

The grip on his glass tightened. 'Stop it, India.'

'What? I can't say what I think of your darling daughter but you can ignore ours?'

Something malevolent crossed his face. 'I suppose I should have guessed that, in the end, breeding will out.'

'What do you mean?'

'Bad blood.' His voice was soft and low. 'Don't you remember asking me about it? Your mother had bad blood. Perhaps she's passed it on to you.'

'Shut up, Marcus,' she said sharply.

'She wasn't a fit person to bring up children. She was negligent. Face up to the truth, she didn't care enough about you or Sebastian to make the effort. Maybe you take after her. After tonight's little performance I'm starting to think so. I shall have to keep an eye on you. For your own sake, and for our daughter's.'

She hugged her arms round herself, as if to hold in her anger. It didn't do to lose your temper with Marcus, you didn't win. 'I'm a good mother to Abigail,' she said levelly. 'And I'll tell you something. I'll never be ashamed of my child. However she grows up, however plain or pretty she turns out to be, however clever or slow, I'll always love her and I'll always be proud of her.'

'*Ashamed?*' he repeated. 'What are you talking about?'

'You've had three children. There's the one you spoil, the one you ignore, and the one you never mention.'

In his eyes, something flickered. He said, 'I told you, the baby was stillborn.' Then he turned and walked out of the kitchen.

India's head pulsed painfully and she found that was trembling. The firestorm that had run through her that night seemed to have left her nerve endings exposed. She went outside to the veranda. As she walked slowly down the steps and along the moonlit path that led to the pond, she felt dreamy and glassy, almost beyond thought, and so light-headed she could have risen into the air like thistledown. She stood on the bank of the pond, letting the cool night air wash over her. Stars dabbed the still surface of the water and in the distance there was the cry of a bird.

Just before Marcus had left her, she had seen something that had shocked her. The expression that had passed over his face had contained an emotion she had never seen there before.

Fear.

Two days after the party, India drove to Midhurst. Parking in a vacant lot, she lifted the carrycot out of the station wagon and pushed it along the sidewalk. She bought a few odds and ends from the shops and then went to the café.

There, the waitress greeted her like an old friend and offered to warm Abigail's bottle for her. The feed was almost finished and India was wiping a dribble of milk from Abigail's chin, when she looked through the window and saw him, coming across the road.

'Hello, Linc,' she said, as he came into the café.

He smiled at her. 'I was beginning to think you'd gone back to England. It's been pretty dull, having my coffee without you.'

She settled Abigail, a round, compact little package, on her knee, and smiled at him. 'I'm sure you found someone else to talk to.'

'Not the same.'

She might have gone on with this mild flirting, as she had done on many previous afternoons, but instead she said flatly, 'I'm married, Linc.'

He sat down opposite her. 'But not happily.'

'How can you tell?'

'Happily married women talk about their husbands, but you never do. They say things like, "Do you know what John said to me last night?" or, "John took me to the most adorable restaurant."'

His voice had lifted in pitch and she knew he meant to make her laugh, but she bit her lip and stared out of the window.

'Hey,' she heard him say gently. 'I'm sorry, I've upset you.'

'You haven't.'

He stood up. 'Let's go for a walk. I'll push honeybunch and you can tell me to keep quiet when I put my foot in it.'

So they went for a walk, down the main street, past the shops and the garages, Abigail lying in the blue-grey shade, her hands reaching out to the fringes of the sun canopy.

He said, after a while, 'I missed you.'

'Linc—'

'I think you need to know. And I need to say it.'

'You shouldn't like me.'

'I do, though.'

'Not just because of Marcus. I'm not a nice person.'

He peered at her. 'Let me see . . . you shot your lover and pushed him into a creek?'

She gave a fleeting smile. 'No. But I used to steal things.'

'Ah.'

'The first time I did it I was ten years old, and the last time – oh, it was a couple of years ago.'

He whistled. 'Quite a criminal record. What are we talking about? Gold bullion, diamonds, unmarked banknotes?'

'Food, to begin with, because we were hungry, Sebastian and me.' She bit a nail. 'When I was at school, I took things that belonged to the other girls. Just little things. Nothing valuable.'

'Keepsakes.'

'Yes. I got thrown out, I had to move to another school.'

'That's tough.'

'No, not really, it was a horrible school, it was a relief. And then—'

He put his hand over hers, stopping her tearing at the piece of skin round her nail. 'You don't have to tell me. We've all done stuff, India.'

'Even you?'

'Yeah. Do you want to know? Smashed myself up on a motorbike when I was sixteen, broke my leg pretty bad. Dropped out of school the same year, travelled around for a while doing this and that, none of it very edifying, got in trouble with the police after I'd had a few drinks too many. It took me a year to realize what an idiot I was, then I stopped drinking, came home, got a job in a store, went to night school, sorted myself out. Where was your mom, while all this was going on?'

'She died when I was ten. Yes, yes, I know,' she added quickly. 'I was stealing to comfort myself for losing my mother. It's so obvious, isn't it?'

They had left the outskirts of the town and were heading along the road that led north. 'Where are we going?' she asked him.

'My place.' He grinned at her. 'I promise I make better coffee than the café.'

In the fields to either side of the road, the hay had been mown, leaving shorn, buff-coloured stalks. A veil of golden dust had settled over the grassy verges. As they walked, India told Linc about the house in the woods, about Sebastian and Neil and Mrs Day at the shop, and about the death of her mother. It struck her that it was the first time she had told anyone the whole story. Perhaps being in a different country enabled her to speak more freely. Or perhaps it was Linc that made the difference.

Reaching his home, he pushed the pram up the slope, then made coffee while India sat on the stoop, looking out for hummingbirds. He brought out two enamel mugs and sat down beside her.

'Seems to me,' he said, 'you did rather well. You kept your little brother fed, you did your best to protect him.'

A long time ago, Rachel had said much the same thing to her. She thought how much she missed Rachel and how much she could have done now with her sensible, concerned advice.

She said, 'Marcus says that I have bad blood.'

'Helpful of Marcus. I'm taking a dislike to him.'

She wrapped her hands round her knees and leaned forward, looking down to the road. 'I don't think my blood's any different from anyone else's, not really. But I do worry that I won't be a good enough mother to Abigail.'

'India, you're a terrific mother to Abigail. You love her, you feed her, you play with her. That's all babies need. She's a credit to you.'

'But you learn from your parents, don't you? When you're a child, you think that however you live is normal, however strange or wrong it seems to everyone else. And that belief is very deep, I think, it runs right through us. What if I slip back into that? What if I'm lazy or I'm careless, and she gets hurt? I don't suppose my mother meant to neglect us. I expect she did her best.'

He put his hand over hers. His big palm was warm where he had been holding the coffee cup, and she squeezed it. He said, 'People can change. Lives can change. If two people find each other, they help each other.'

She whispered, 'I'm afraid, Linc.'

'The best things often happen by chance. Like me being bored one afternoon at work and looking out the window and seeing you trying to get that baby carriage through the café door.'

Then he kissed her. His body was warm and resilient against hers. When, eventually, she opened her eyes, she saw that, in the shade beneath the branches of the birches, something darted and hovered, a flash of iridescent light.

She spoke to him that evening, after dinner. He was working in his study; the door was ajar.

'I want you to let me go, Marcus,' she said.

She saw him still, then swivel round in his chair. 'Let you go?' he repeated.

'Yes.'

'If you're bored, we'll have a holiday. We'll go to Cape Cod.'

'I'm not bored, it's not that. Lonely, sometimes.'

'You have the baby.'

'I'm not complaining. But I can't stay here with you.'

'No.' Softly.

'We don't make each other happy, do we?'

'Happy?' In his eyes there was bitterness and regret. 'Is that what you want, happiness?'

'Some of the time, at least. I don't mind if it's just flashes, like hummingbirds. But I'm never happy when I'm with you. And I don't think you're happy with me.'

'I've always thought it such a shallow aspiration, happiness, when there are so many other things one might have.'

'Well.' She wound her hands together. 'That's what I think. I suppose you'll say I'm running away again, but I don't think I am.'

'Who are you planning on leaving me for? That man you meet at the café?'

'I'm not leaving you for anyone but myself. You're trying to change me, I can see that you are. If you loved me, really, properly loved me, you wouldn't do that. I always think you're trying to make me into, oh,' she raised her shoulders, gave a shake of her head, 'some idea you have, some idea I don't really understand, and I hate it.'

'You're such a funny little thing. What do you expect me to say? "Very well, pack your bags, off you go?" No, India.'

'Marcus, please.'

'No.'

'You can't keep me here.'

'Perhaps not, but I shall keep the child.'

Was he taunting her? No, studying his face, she did not think so.

She said, 'But you don't love her.'

'I love *you*.'

'No, you don't. Whatever it is you think love is, you're mistaken. And I don't love you, I never have.'

He swung away, saying coldly, 'If you leave me, I shall keep the child. No court in the land would award you custody, surely you see that? The neglectful mother, the mentally disturbed brother. I have the reports from the children's home and, of course, Sebastian was rejected for National Service. Written documentation, evidence, that's what counts with the law, and I have plenty of it. If you leave me, I'll make sure that you're judged an unfit mother. Custody of Abigail will be awarded to me, and you'll never see her again.'

He unscrewed the cap of his pen, and with a flourish dashed off his signature at the foot of a letter.

Climbing out of bed that night, India left Marcus sleeping beside her and walked silently out to the landing. Sebastian's letters told her that he was happy in his new home and she felt grateful to Marcus for that. They had managed, she and Sebastian, they had survived. Really, considering the circumstances, that wasn't so bad at all.

But she had to go. If she looked back, she saw that every time she found herself trapped, she had always managed to escape. The house in the woods, her first boarding school, Bernie – on each of these occasions she had, however clumsily and with however much difficulty, set herself free. And with Marcus, she could not be free.

There was not the smallest chance that she would let him take her baby from her. In threatening her, he had only reinforced her conviction that she must leave. She knew that she would have to change. No more flitting from job to job; she must find whatever work she could carry out while looking after Abigail, and she must stick to it.

And she needed to stop taking things that weren't hers: a book, a dress, someone's husband, someone's lover.

India looked out of the landing window. Threadbare clouds scurried across the face of the moon. Resting her forearms on the sill, she saw how, when the clouds moved aside, the tops of the trees turned to silver.

In the morning, Marcus drove the station wagon to college. After he had gone, India packed her bags. Viola was vacuuming downstairs and Gosse was repairing the roof of the front porch. She listened out for the tap of the hammer, footsteps on the gravel.

While Gosse was having his coffee, India went to the toolshed and took out a screwdriver. Back inside the house, she unscrewed the lock on the study door. In the study, she searched through Marcus's desk. She took out Abigail's birth certificate, her own passport, and the letters from the orphanage. In the back of a drawer she discovered a fat bundle of dollars tied up in an elastic band so she took that too, along with the keys to the Austin-Healey, Marcus's favourite car.

Then, checking that Gosse was still in the kitchen, she put the bags in the boot of the Healey. Afterwards, she fed and changed Abigail and ate her own lunch. Viola stuck her head into the dining room to say goodbye, then left the house.

India put on her mackintosh and headscarf and picked up the carrycot. The hammering at the porch started up again as she put the carrycot on the passenger seat of the

Healey. Then the car roared up the gravel drive, brushing against the hedge as India screeched on to the road. She thought she heard Gosse's yell. She drove through Midhurst, past the café and the shops and out of town. As she passed the shack by the fork on the road, she slowed and looked, but did not see Linc.

Driving north, she was soon heading along unfamiliar roads. Frequently, she looked in the mirror, checking the road behind her. She did not know at first where she was going to, but as the afternoon wore on, it became clear to her.

Chapter Thirteen

In Woodstock Road in Finsbury Park bursts of rain swept across the street and the wind jigged at Ellen's umbrella. The tall, terraced houses, some of which had been split up into flats, contained families with small children, pensioners, and a young couple in denim jeans and checked shirts, who were knocking out the fireplace in their front room. Ellen started at one end of road, ringing doorbells, showing the people who answered a photograph.

The photograph had been taken at Gildersleve Hall during the war. Years later, she had found it in Dr Redmond's lab book, when she had taken it on the night of his death. In the snapshot, the group of young men appeared relaxed and happy. There was Jan Kaminski, standing a little apart from his colleagues, his head turned to one side so that the scarred aspect of his face was hidden. And there were Bryan Redmond and Marcus Pharoah. Pharoah was looking at the camera but Dr Redmond had turned towards Pharoah and was smiling.

An old friend . . . lost touch during the war . . . someone thought he might live here. Some of the neighbours gave the photo a quick glance, others fetched their reading glasses and peered at it, frowning, but all shook their heads.

There she was, Ellen thought, so happy with Riley, and there was India, married to Marcus Pharoah. She didn't understand why India had married Pharoah, but it made her feel uneasy, which was why she was out in the rain, knocking on strangers' doors.

Ellen walked up another path and rang the bell to the basement flat. Rain poured from a broken gutter, splashing on to her shoes. No answer, and blinds were pulled down over the basement windows.

Next she tried the first floor flat. The man who opened the door was slight and of medium height, with a thatch of dark brown hair. His liquid dark eyes were set in a boyishly handsome face. He was wearing grey flannel trousers and a pale blue shirt.

Ellen said good morning and introduced herself. Then she held out the photograph to him. The alteration in his expression, sleepily curious before, was immediate and unmistakable.

'What do you want?' he said.

She pointed out Dr Redmond. 'Did you know him?'

'I said, what do you want?'

'To talk to you, that's all. I was a colleague of Dr

Redmond's. I worked at Gildersleve Hall in the autumn of nineteen fifty-two.'

'Fifty-two? Were you there when he died?' His voice, which had a gentle West Country accent, was urgent and brusque.

'Yes. It was me who found his body.'

His lips parted, then he nodded. 'You'd better come in,' he said.

'I didn't know until several weeks after his death. No one told me. He used to come here regular as clockwork, every month, and then, that December, he didn't turn up. I knew something was wrong then. Bryan was always very reliable. He'd never just not turn up.'

His name was Tony Ferrers and he was pacing around the front room as he spoke.

'Had you and Dr Redmond been friends for long?' she asked.

'A while,' he said.

'I didn't know him well,' she said. 'But we talked a few times and I liked him. I respected him.'

'He was a good man. Bryan was one of the best.'

'You were fond of him?'

'Yes, very.' A touch of defiance. He sat down on the sofa. 'I never wrote to him at the cottage. Bryan was very strong about that, said I mustn't.'

This confused Ellen. 'I don't see . . .' Though, even as she spoke, she was starting to understand.

As he looked up at her, his mouth twisted into a wry smile. 'I don't suppose it matters now. Bryan's been dead for years. Let's just say that ours wasn't the sort of friendship you'd want to make public, Miss Kingsley.'

'Oh. Oh.'

'Quite.'

Her gaze flicked to the photo, which was lying on the coffee table, then she looked back at Tony. 'I'm glad,' she said. 'I'm glad he had someone.'

'I've never been much of a one for reading the newspapers, just the sport in the *People*, so I didn't know what had happened. In the end, I phoned the hall. Said I was a friend. The woman who answered told me that Bryan was dead. Just came out with it, like that. I couldn't think what to say.'

'I'm sorry,' she said gently.

'Yeah. Well, I went to the library, looked up old copies of the papers. I found some articles about Bryan. "Death of a Boffin", that sort of rubbish. I cut them out when no one was looking. I wanted to know what had happened. And I wanted to remember him. Not that I'd ever forget him. The newspaper article said he'd fallen down the stairs.'

'I'm afraid so. I went to the cottage because I was concerned about him. He hadn't been into work that day and I thought he might be ill. When I got there, he was lying at the bottom of the stairs.'

'He was dead?'

'Yes.'

'For how long?'

She had hoped he wouldn't ask her that. 'A few hours, the police thought.'

'I hate to think of him dying alone. It used to frighten me, when I was in the desert, the thought of getting cut off from my mates and something happening.' He was looking away; he ran the back of his hand over his eyes.

'Shall I make us some tea?'

'No, I'll do it. Sorry.'

He heard him blowing his nose as he left the room. A few minutes later he returned with a tray.

She said, 'You were a soldier?'

'Yes. I was wounded at El Alamein and they sent me home. That was when I met Bryan.'

'Where did you meet?'

He gave her a look that was a mixture of shame and humour, and said, 'In some rotten little pub in Chelsea, in nineteen forty-three. Not the sort of place you'd know, Miss Kingsley. I was on my uppers, rather. I was still on sick leave from the army and I didn't have anywhere to go. I couldn't go home.' He poured out the tea. 'I come from deepest, darkest Somerset. Home life was Sundays where nothing ever happened and my dad ranting on about queers and Jews. Jesus. Anyway, Bryan was there, at the bar. Funny bloke, I thought, sort of awkward, didn't look you in the eye. We got talking and he offered to buy me something to eat, and I was lonely and I had nowhere to go, so . . .' He shrugged. 'But I liked him. He didn't talk much, but he listened. And he was clever and he was funny and he was good to me.'

'Did he tell you about the place where he worked?'

'Not much. Said it was all very hush-hush.' Then, looking at her, he said, 'There was someone he was close to there. They shared a cottage.'

'Jan Kaminski and Marcus Pharoah.'

'That's the one, Pharoah. Do you know him?'

'He was my boss when I worked at Gildersleve Hall.' Ellen pointed out one of the figures in the photograph. 'That's him. That's Dr Pharoah.'

'Handsome devil. You can see why you'd fall for him.'

Her gaze returned to the photograph. Once more, she noticed how Dr Redmond had turned to Pharoah, and the light in his eyes.

'Had he?'

'Bryan? Oh yes, hook, line and sinker, the poor sod. He told me about him quite soon after we met. Wanted to get it straight with me, he said. I didn't need him to spell it out, though, I could tell by the way he talked about him, about Pharoah.'

Dr Redmond had remained loyal to Marcus Pharoah for a long time after their quarrel. Was it possible that what Redmond had felt had been not mere admiration, but love? Time and success had corrupted Pharoah, and yet in spite of their differences, Dr Redmond had stayed at Gildersleve. He had kept this photo, tucked into the lab book he used each day. Could that have been because love, on his part, had never completely died?

She chose her words carefully. 'I knew they used to be friends.'

His eyes flashed, full of ironic humour. 'Just good friends,' he said. 'Dr Pharoah was a ladies' man, Bryan told me.' His tone was mocking. 'Bryan was always very careful. It's hard, that, always watching yourself.' He leaned forward in his seat, studying the snapshot, frowning. 'I always pictured him as some bluff, rugby-playing type, but he doesn't look like that, does he? Anyway, somehow he caught on that Bryan was queer. Gave him the works – disgusting, deviant, couldn't he get treatment for it, all that.' In an odd, vengeful little gesture, Tony ground a knuckle into the image of Pharoah's face. 'The poor bugger,' he muttered. 'He didn't deserve that. It wasn't as if he wanted anything from Pharoah. Just to be near him.'

'When was this?'

'It must have been a couple of months before the end of the war. After the war ended, Bryan stayed on in the cottage and the other two moved out. He came down here once a month and we had a good time. I made sure he had a good time. But you could see it, eating away at him. He changed, and in the end he wasn't the same person. He'd always been quiet but he seemed to go in on himself. Something had knocked the life out of him, you see. I think that eventually he hated Pharoah.'

'Why do you say that?'

'Last time I saw him he was spitting nails.'

'When, Mr Ferrers?'

'Autumn fifty-two. A short time before he died. November, it must have been. It was because of the woodland. Bryan thought of it as his, the cottage as well, but they weren't, not really, they belonged to Pharoah. When Bryan heard that Pharoah was thinking of selling them, he offered to buy both the house and the land. Pharoah agreed but then he told Bryan he'd had a better offer. I'd never seen Bryan so angry. He never usually lost his rag but he did then. And there's another thing.'

'What's that?'

'He was scared.'

'Of what?' But she thought she knew. 'That Pharoah would expose him?'

'Oh no, Bryan never worried about himself. He was afraid for me. The last time I saw him, Bryan told me he was putting this flat in my name. I told him he didn't have to do it, but he said he wanted to because that way I'd be safe.' Tony pushed the photograph back across the tabletop to her. His mouth twisted. 'A couple of years ago a friend of mine was charged with indecent behaviour. They sent him to prison for six years. He only lasted a couple of weeks — he hanged himself with a bedsheet.'

She could think of nothing adequate to say so she remained silent. Tony rose and opened the door and a golden Labrador dog ambled into the room, nails tapping on the polished wooden floor.

She said, 'Did Dr Redmond ever speak to you about Dr Pharoah's first marriage?'

Tony shook his head. 'Not that I remember. He was never one for gossip.'

Ellen thanked him for the tea and for talking to her. As she stood up, Tony spoke again.

'After Bryan went back to Cambridge that last time,' he said, 'I never heard from him again. He didn't like talking on the phone and he was never much of a letter-writer. I've a few postcards, that's all. "Tony", he'd write, "did you remember to pay the gas bill? Bryan." Never a "dear" or a "love", you see. But he *was* dear, and I did love him.' Tony bent to fondle the dog's yellow head. 'She's called Connie,' he said. 'I couldn't have a dog while Bryan was alive. He couldn't stand them.' He straightened. 'Looks like it's stopped raining. I'd better take her out for a walk, if we're finished, Miss Kingsley.'

India's progress was slow because she stopped every couple of hours at a diner to feed, change and play with Abigail. She had stayed in Montpelier on the first night, where she had bought petrol, maps and warmer clothing for the baby. The next day, she reached Bourchier College, where Marcus had met his first wife, Rosanne. But it was Hester Devereux's story of which India thought as she wheeled the carrycot through the small, pleasant campus, and of the friendship that had grown up between the two women, a friendship whose memory had lasted beyond Rosanne's lifetime, and which had prompted Hester more than twenty years later to try to discover the truth about what had happened to her child.

At the college, a secretary in the bursar's office, charmed by Abigail and coaxed by India, unearthed old files and found out for her what she wanted to know: the address at which Marcus Pharoah had lived during the time he had been at Bourchier. A five-mile drive took India to a small town with a white clapboard church, a general store and a scattering of houses. She stopped at the general store to buy milk for Abigail and to ask directions to Rosanne Pharoah's old home at Aspen Creek.

Another drive, a few more miles north. India turned off the main highway along a narrow, tree-lined road that led up into the hills. After a short distance, she found the house. She parked, climbed out of the car, and with Abigail tucked on her shoulder, walked up the front path. The house ahead of her was small, low and white-painted, set among aspens. All around her, leaves like thousands of pale green pennies quivered in the breeze.

A middle-aged woman came out of the front door and asked her if she needed help. Abigail began to cry, and the woman, who introduced herself as Mrs Greenlaw, invited India indoors. While Mrs Greenlaw was heating up a jug of water for Abigail's bottle, India looked round. You could have fitted the entire building into Fairlight House three times over, but she saw how the late-afternoon sunshine, filtered between the branches of the trees, poured through the picture windows at the back of the house, making liquid patterns on the polished wooden floor. When India knelt down with Abigail on the floorboards, she bobbed her head and reached out a hand, transfixed by the shifting light. Outside, a rectangle of wooden decking, strewn with leaves, looked down over a creek.

While India fed Abigail, Mrs Greenlaw drew up a small table and put a cup of coffee beside her. India asked her about the history of the house. It had been built in the early twenties, Mrs Greenlaw said, as the summer residence of a businessman from Boston, who had liked to fish and shoot in the hills. The house had changed hands frequently in the thirties and had then lain empty for several years. It was an out-of-the-way spot, Mrs Greenlaw acknowledged. She was a painter, and the moment she had set eyes on it she had known it was where she wanted to live for the rest of her life. She could have looked out of that big window for ever. She must have painted the view a hundred times.

India asked her about Rosanne Pharoah. Mrs Greenlaw frowned, pursed her mouth and shook her head. 'You should try the pastor,' she suggested. 'He's been here quite a while. He may be able to help you.'

Staying overnight at an inn in Bourchier, India thought about the house. She tried to imagine Marcus living there, sitting by the picture window perhaps, reading a book. Perhaps they had put a table on the terrace, he and Rosanne, and had breakfast there on fine summer days. Perhaps

Rosanne had paddled in the creek while Marcus had watched her from the rocks above. Perhaps they had planned their future together, a lifetime in that house of flickering light and shivering leaves. Perhaps the destruction of that future had sent Marcus off in a different direction to the one he had originally intended.

The next day, she drove back to the white Congregationalist church she had seen the previous day. The pastor's house was beside it. India knocked on the door.

Half an hour later, leaving the building, she had discovered several things. That Rosanne Pharoah was buried in the churchyard in this quiet town, and that she had been only twenty years old when she had died, a year before the pastor himself had come to live there. The pastor had known nothing of a child, but he had been able to tell India something interesting: that the midwife who had looked after Marcus's wife during her pregnancy and delivery had moved away, returning to her home town in Medway, northern Maine, shortly after Rosanne had died.

The midwife's name had been Kitty Michaud. You wonder, the pastor had said, thoughtfully stroking his beard, whether she had felt responsible — whether, even, there had been some question of negligence. Such a tragedy, after all, for a man to lose his wife and child.

A Saturday: Riley, Ellen and Annie had gone to the Natural History Museum in the morning, where they had gawped at the dinosaurs and Ellen had attempted to explain to Annie about evolution. They had a late lunch in a restaurant in Brompton Road, then called in at a park on the way home so that Annie had the chance to run around.

Back at the house, Riley made tea and parked Ellen in the front room with the Saturday papers. He thought she worked too hard. Annie was upstairs, playing with her dolls' house. Riley carried the tray of tea things into the sitting room.

The doorbell rang as Ellen was reading out some comment Harold Macmillan had made about the testing of nuclear weapons. As he went out to the hall, Riley said over his shoulder, 'There'll be a lot of our people keeping a close eye on what the Russians are up to.'

Then he opened the door. Seeing her, recognizing her, he was for a moment unable to speak.

'Hello, John,' said Pearl.

Riley made more tea, not because any of them wanted it, but because it gave him a few moments to control his shock and anger. And at not quite five o'clock in the afternoon, it was too early for a drink.

'I want to talk to you, John,' she said. 'And I'd like to see Annie. May I come in?'

He had let her in. After all, it was her house as well. By then, Ellen had come out of the sitting room into the hallway. He did not think he would ever forget the expression on her face.

He introduced them. 'Pearl, this is Ellen Kingsley. Ellen, this is Pearl, my wife.' There was a bitter taste in his mouth.

Now, Pearl and Ellen were talking, Pearl with that air of lavishness that always touched her conversation, Ellen polite and composed, though Riley heard the strain in her voice. Pearl was wearing a green and white spotted summer frock with a short green jacket, black gloves and a close-fitting black hat. She looked, Riley thought, well.

Annie sat at the kitchen table, crayoning. Sometimes she looked up at Pearl. Once, catching her eye, Pearl tapped her knee and Annie came and sat on her lap for a few minutes, then slid off, left the room and went upstairs.

Riley could tell that Ellen was finding it hard to make conversation − all those questions that couldn't be voiced − so after he had put the mugs on the table and found a packet of biscuits, he said, 'Where are you living now, Pearl?'

'Cornwall,' she said. 'It's the tiniest little village, so dear, just a funny old pub and a row of dilapidated cottages. I work in a shop in St Ives. You should see me in winter, cycling through the gales.'

Ellen said, 'What sort of shop is it, Mrs Riley?' Her voice had a hollow timbre.

'We sell pottery, mostly. Beautiful pots, the most gorgeous earthy colours. I have some in my house.' Pearl laughed. 'Hardly any furniture but some wonderful pots.'

Riley said bluntly, 'Why have you come back?'

'I told you. Because I wanted to talk to you.'

He felt at that moment a rage so intense he had to look away, as if his gaze might burn.

'How long are you back for?' The question crisp, efficient.

'I haven't decided yet.' She puckered up her mouth in the way that he remembered. 'I promise I won't be too much of a nuisance.'

Was he meant to say, *you won't be a nuisance at all, Pearl?* There were things he must say to her: that she should not assume she could just walk back into their lives, and nor should she assume that she could stay here, in this house. But he had to wait. There was Annie, not knowing what the hell was going on, and there was Ellen, trying hard not to look as if she minded.

'Have you spoken to your parents?' he said.

Pearl looked down, frowning. 'Not yet.'

'You should do.'

'I know, John.' She peeled off her gloves and wrapped her hands round the teacup.

'They've been desperately worried about you. Do you realize what they've been through?'

'It's just that – Mum will cry and I just can't cope with it.' Her words were whispered.

'I'll do it, then.' Though he felt a grating despair in saying so. Because, he thought bleakly, no matter how hard you tried not to let it happen, she sucked you into her chaotic, clamorous life. You did things for her because you felt obliged to tidy up behind her.

Ellen stood up. 'I mustn't keep you,' she said. 'You two will have so much to talk about.'

Riley saw her to the front door. 'Ellen,' he said softly.

'I have to go.'

'This makes no difference to us.'

'Doesn't it?' When she looked at him, her eyes were blank and bewildered. 'I'm sorry. I just need some time to think, Riley.'

She left the house. Pearl had gone upstairs. Riley stood, his hands fisted, breathing hard. Just as the different parts of his life had fallen miraculously into place, Pearl, with her talent for bad timing and disorder, had returned. With her, she would have brought a trail of drama and damage, because she always did.

His anger cooled. No, he thought. Not this time.

He dialled Basil and Vera's number. To Riley's relief, Basil answered the phone. There was a silence after Riley told him about Pearl, and then Basil asked, a catch in his voice, when they could come and see her. Riley told them to come round as soon as they liked.

'Thank you, John, I appreciate it. I'll tell Vera.'

Pearl came back into the sitting room. 'Annie doesn't remember me,' she said.

'It's been a long time. Three years.'

She was standing in front of him, wringing her hands

together. With an effort, he said, 'I expect she does remember you, underneath somewhere, deep in her memory.'

'I tried not to expect anything. But you can't help it, can you?'

'How are you, Pearl?'

'Better, much better.' She was looking round the room, frowning, as if she saw something wrong with it. 'I had to find a way I could live. I know that what I did was unforgivable, and I don't blame you for hating me. But you or Dad would have come after me if I'd told you where I was, and it wouldn't have worked.'

He glanced at the clock. Almost six – what the hell.

'Would you like a drink?'

'No, thanks, I don't any more.' Pearl took a packet of Player's from her handbag and tipped out a cigarette. 'Haven't managed to give up these, though.'

Riley poured himself a whisky. 'Pearl, we have to talk.'

'I know. I want a divorce, John.' She lit her cigarette and looked at him steadily. 'That's one of the reasons I came back here. I'm sorry to be so . . . so blunt.'

'It's OK.' It took a moment for him to absorb what she had said, and then he was left numb, battered, and intensely relieved.

He said, 'Why couldn't you just have written? Why the dramatic reappearance?'

'It would have been cowardly. I knew I should talk to you face to face. And I wanted to make you understand.'

'Understand what?' Fury laced his voice. 'Have you any idea what it's been like? None of us knew whether you were alive or dead. And Annie? What do you think it's been like for her? How could you do that to her? How could you leave her thinking that you just didn't love her enough?'

'Did she?' Her eyes wild, she pressed her fingers against her mouth.

With an effort, he managed to pull himself back. He let out a breath. 'I told her you loved her. I've told her that every single day.'

She whispered, 'Thank you.'

There was a silence. Pearl wiped the tears from her face with her hand; Riley pulled out a chair for her.

'Sit down. Tell me how you are.'

'I'm all right.' She smiled at him, a darting, hopeful smile. 'I'm better on my own, I've discovered. If I'm feeling angry or miserable, I don't annoy anyone else, I just go for a walk by the sea.' She was kneading the cuff of her jacket between finger and thumb. 'There's a nice doctor in St Ives, he's got me some new pills and they don't make me feel as awful as the other ones, and if I feel myself falling ill again I take some. I know that I have to. I know that horrible psychiatrist was right, that I'll always have to, and that I'll never be really well.' She let go of the crumpled cuff and looked up at him, her face blotched with tears. 'I've always been afraid that Annie would turn out like me. I couldn't face it, staying here, looking at her, always wondering, afraid my beautiful girl would end up like me. I love her so much. People talk about broken hearts, don't they, and you think that's just a saying until it happens to you. I was afraid that if I stayed here, I'd poison her somehow, that I'd *make* her like me. I had to go. I've thought of her every day since, every hour of every day.'

Fleetingly, he put a hand on her shoulder. 'Annie organizes me,' he said gently. 'Tells me off if I've forgotten to iron a shirt. A year or two and she'll be checking me out before I go to work, making sure my collar's straight. She's a happy little girl.'

'And sensible, then, like you, John.'

'I suppose she is.'

'We used to have such fun, didn't we, when we were younger? Do you remember?' Her expression saddened. 'And then it all went wrong. It was my fault, of course.'

He shook his head. 'Mine too.'

'Will you let me see Annie?' Her eyes, haunted and afraid, stared at him.

'I don't know, Pearl,' he said honestly.

She didn't scream or cry, as he had been afraid she might. 'I'd like Annie to come and stay in Cornwall with me,' she said steadily. 'She'd love it there, I know she would. It's only a little house, but I could make her up a camp bed in the bedroom.' When he didn't say anything, she said, 'I've changed, John. I'm not the same as I was before. I try so hard. You wouldn't believe how I live now. I've found that I need to lead a very dull life. It's rather a chastening discovery because I'd always thought I needed the opposite. I saw myself as someone who needed adventure and excitement. But they're not good for me, that's what I've realized. I keep an eye on myself. Three meals a day, just like you always said, and eight hours' sleep at night. I go to work and I come home and I read a book or do some sewing. If I'm having a bad time I go for a long walk over the cliffs. It's so beautiful and it's always different, so I never get bored with it.'

'Have you met anyone else?'

'One or two.' She gave her head a shake. 'Not stayers, I don't think. There's a schoolteacher who lives in Zennor, we go for walks together.' She pressed her teeth into her lower lip, then said, 'If you tell me to, I'll leave now and I won't make a fuss. If that's what you want, John. But I always tried to be a good mother to Annie. And I was, wasn't I?'

'Pearl.' Wearily, he ran a hand through his hair. 'I need to think about this.' He glanced at his watch. 'I'd better make tea. Your parents should be here within the hour.'

As he peeled potatoes and chopped carrots, he thought about what Pearl had asked of him. Annie was Pearl's daughter too. Whatever bitterness he felt he must put aside. Annie needed her mother. Yet at the same time, Annie's safety and happiness were paramount. Pearl had told him that she had changed, but he remembered too clearly her unpredictability and wildness.

Vera and Basil arrived, tears were shed and embraces

exchanged. While they were in the other room, talking to Pearl, Riley dialled Ellen's number, but there was no answer.

The serving of supper provided a welcome vestige of normality. After the meal was over, Vera and Basil tactfully took Annie into the sitting room to play a boardgame while Riley spoke to Pearl.

'Look, how about this,' he said. 'You see Annie when your parents are around as well to begin with. I'm sure they'd be delighted to take her down to Cornwall. And if that works out and Annie's happy with it, then maybe, in the future, she can visit you on her own.'

'Thank you, John. I'll make it up to her, I promise, if it takes me the rest of my life.' She kissed his cheek. 'I told my parents I'd go back home with them. I thought you'd prefer that.'

'Pearl, you'll speak to a solicitor about a divorce, won't you?' He had to get this straight.

'I promise. That girl—'

'Do you mean Ellen?'

'Yes, your lovely redhead.'

'I mean to marry her, Pearl.'

'I'm pleased for you, John.' Then her gaze wandered round the room. 'There must have been happy times here,' she said, 'but I can't remember them. That's rather sad, isn't it?'

The phone rang. *Ellen*, he thought. Riley picked up the receiver.

But it wasn't Ellen, it was Janey Kelly. Riley listened to

her, then gave her clear instructions and put the phone down.

Then he went into the sitting room, where Vera, Basil and Annie were playing Ludo.

'Basil, Vera, could you hold the fort for a couple of hours?'

Janey was sitting where Riley had told her to, on a bench on Well Street Common. Dusk was encroaching on the grass and trees of the common. Janey was wearing a mackintosh with the hood up, yet he could see from several yards away that she was shivering. She must have heard his footsteps because she flinched and quickly turned towards him, poised to run. He saw that her face was a mass of bruises and that one of her eyes had closed.

'Janey,' he said. He sat down on the bench beside her. 'Who did this to you?'

'Bloody Lee, who else?' She was breathing shallowly. 'Think he's broken something, Riley.'

'What happened?'

'One of the other girls saw me talking to you. The silly bitch told him.'

'I'll take you to the hospital,' he said.

She scowled. 'I don't like hospitals.'

'They'll make you better.' He spoke much as he would have spoken to Annie, had she hurt herself. 'They'll fix you up and you'll be as beautiful as ever.'

Half of her face managed a mocking grin. 'See, I always

knew you fancied me.' Then she blinked, looking straight ahead of her into the grass and bushes. 'I want to go home, Riley,' she whispered.

'Where's home?'

'Cork. You ever been there?'

He shook his head.

'You don't want to bother. Bloody dump of a place. I got myself into trouble, had to to come over here and sort myself out.' She gave a sour little laugh. 'I thought I was going to be a film star.'

'There's still time.'

'No.' Slowly, she shook her head. 'No, I don't think so.'

She rose and, stooping, her arms wrapped round her chest, limped beside him out of the common. As they neared his car, she said, 'I want to tell you something, Riley.'

'Leave it till you're at the hospital.'

'No, I might change my mind.' She put out a hand to the Wolseley to steady herself, then fixed him with her good eye and said, 'Bernie's got a lock-up in Brixton. It's near the station, under the railway arches. It looks like it's derelict because the door was all burned up in the war, but it isn't. You should go and have a look at it. Bernie keeps everything there.'

His heart speeded up. 'Who told you this?'

'A friend of mine.' She showed her teeth in an expression that was somewhere between a smile and a snarl. 'Pillow talk. You know. You men like to show off to girls, don't you, show us you're the big man.'

Riley helped Janey into the car, then drove her to the London Hospital. While the casualty doctor saw her, he phoned Scotland Yard. The duty officer answered his call and promised to send a WPC to the London.

Sergeant Davies had the weekend off so Riley phoned his home. Davies's wife answered the call. Riley could hear a baby howling in the background.

'Can I speak to Rob, Glenys?'

'He's just having his supper. Hold on a minute, I'll go and get him.'

Riley heard footsteps and muted conversation. Then Davies picked up the phone. Riley told him about Janey and the lock-up in Brixton.

'I'm going to have a look there now. Can you get over there, Davies?'

'I'm on my way.' Davies was chewing something. 'Wait for me, sir. Don't start without me.'

Riley put the receiver down and went back to casualty. They would be keeping Janey in overnight, a nurse told him. While he waited for the WPC to arrive, he went to the phone box and dialled Ellen's number again. Still no reply. She had gone out, perhaps.

Or perhaps she wasn't answering. Perhaps she didn't want to speak to him. What on earth had she thought, when Pearl had turned up like that? Pearl's reappearance must have spelled out to Ellen the complications involved in marriage to him. She would be taking on a daughter as well as a husband — and then there was Pearl, too. He would never completely be able to cut Pearl out of his life because Annie would always tie them together. Might Ellen, realizing that, be having second thoughts?

The WPC arrived. Night had fallen by the time Riley left the hospital. The drive down Whitechapel Road and across Tower Bridge, then through Walworth and Camberwell to Brixton, took him half an hour. The light was going and the streets flew past, marked by the oscillation of the pools of light from the street lamps and the London skyline of terraced houses, gas storage tanks and factory buildings, black against a dirty orange sky.

He parked by the railway station, took a torch out of the glove box and a jemmy from the boot of the car, and walked down Brixton Station Road. A train dragged itself over the railway arches, smoke pluming from its funnel. Some of the arches were infilled with wooden doors, others were open black tunnels. The doors were of varying sizes and Riley saw, as he walked, that only one of them was scorched.

A gleam of headlamps at the top of the road made him sink back into the shadows, but the vehicle, some distance away, seemed to change its mind and reverse back towards the railway station. Riley shone the torch on to the burned door. An incendiary bomb, he guessed; the little that was left of the paint had blistered and much of the surface of the door had turned to charcoal, seamed and criss-crossed like the hide of a crocodile.

Riley applied himself to jemmying off the padlock. The

street was quiet and only a solitary cyclist glided past, hardly bothering to look at him. Eventually the padlock gave, Riley aimed a kick at the scorched wood, and the door opened.

He stepped inside. Shining the torch round, he saw the high brick arch above and heard the rumble of a train, magnified and echoing in the interior space. The circle of torchlight lowered, gliding over boxes and filing cabinets. All the cabinets were padlocked, like the door. As he prised open a padlock he heard a sound behind him and turned.

'Davies, is that you?'

No answer. The padlock snapped, chinking against the metal filing cabinet as it fell to the ground. Riley opened a drawer. Inside it was a row of manilla files. He took one out, and with the torch jammed under his arm, flipped through the pages of figures. Even bent accountants need to keep the books, he thought.

A footstep. Riley switched off the torch, put the file inside his jacket, and stepped behind the cabinet. As his eyes accustomed to the lack of light, he saw a bulky figure silhouetted in the doorway.

'Hello, copper!' Lee Carter's voice boomed beneath the high ceiling of the railway arch. 'Knew the stupid little cow wouldn't be able to keep her mouth shut. Should have finished her off, shouldn't I?'

Riley began to move backwards, one hand holding the torch, the other running over the shapes of the furniture to guide him. He tried to recall the layout of the archway, glimpsed when he had earlier illuminated it. How far did the tunnel go back beneath the railway line? Might there be an exit on the other side of the bridge? And where was Davies?

Carter called out, 'Got you like a rat in a trap, copper. Used to catch rats when I was a boy. It'll be more fun with you.'

Lee Carter's torch found him. Against the curved brick wall of the arch Riley saw his own shadow, huge and black. There was a crack of gunfire, echoing against the walls. Riley began to run between the boxes and cabinets, making for the cover of the darkness at the back of the tunnel.

Carter fired again and a white-hot pain stung Riley's shoulder. He ran on, but it was like running through treacle. He could hear his lungs straining, fighting for air. Stumbling against a cardboard box, he sank to his knees.

The echoing space magnified the sound of his breathing. The light seemed suddenly to expand, filling the tunnel, and he saw Lee Carter, only a few yards away.

Riley closed his eyes.

From Bourchier, it was a drive of almost a hundred miles to Medway in northern Maine. India took her time, resting before setting off again. As she headed north, the settlements became smaller and more widely spaced apart and she stopped at every garage she came across to top up the tank with petrol. The roads narrowed and the forests thickened, the coming change of season flagged by the yellowing of the leaves, and the skies became whiter, more prone to clouds. Now and then she saw a clearing where logs lay tumbled on the razed forest floor like a giant's spent matchsticks. Men worked in the clearings, loading up trucks, and the quiet of the Maine landscape was blotted out by the whine of the sawmill.

She had rarely been so completely on her own before. During her childhood, there had been Sebastian; even when separated from him at various institutions − school, orphanage − she had always been among other people. Then there had been the flat and Rachel, and after Rachel had died, her London friends, and eventually Marcus. She had never really been alone in Vermont, Marcus had made sure of that. Now, apart from Abigail, her days were solitary.

Always with her was the fear that she might become lost. Here, if you mistook your way or if your car broke down, you might walk for miles until you found a house. The logging tracks and the firs that grew to either side of them went on for miles; when she parked at the roadside to feed Abigail she closed her eyes for a few minutes but still saw the endless columns of trees.

A branch moved, a bird rose cawing into the air. You might drive the length and breadth of Britain and see no wild animal larger than a deer, but in these old forests in the heartland of America there were moose and bears. Were there wolves, too? She couldn't remember. Checking the map, India found her gaze drawn sideways to the dense, dark tunnels between the trees. Her hand rested on her baby's chest, feeling the rise and fall of Abigail's breath.

Take a step into those paths, she thought, walk a few paces into the wood, and you'd never find your way out. What was she doing, travelling with her child into the cold north of a foreign land to follow an old, forgotten trail?

The town of Medway was poised at the place where the East and West Penobscot Rivers met. India booked into a motel and asked the receptionist if she knew where Kitty Michaud lived. The receptionist, chewing gum as she leafed through a novel, peered out of the window to where the Austin-Healey was parked, and said, 'That yours? Cute.' Then she directed India to where a road ran alongside the river. 'There's a rusty old Ford out the front of the Michaud place. You can't miss it.'

As India drove out of town, the buildings thinned out and stretches of green dwarfed the few houses. She caught sight of the Ford, a hefty, pre-war vehicle, after a short distance. Parked at the foot of a path, it seemed to have become a part of the landscape, scoured and discoloured to a rusty brown by the Maine weather.

India drew up alongside it and looked at the house. The omnipresent fir trees stood like sentinels to either side of the small wooden single-storey building. A woman was sitting on the porch.

India lifted Abigail out of the carrycot and started up the front path. The woman on the porch stood up. She was short and plump, and she was wearing a cotton skirt and hand-knitted jersey. Her hair, a peppering of brown and grey, was tied back at the nape of her neck. Deep lines were channelled into her broad, weatherbeaten face, and her small, dark, hooded eyes were wary.

India said, 'I'm sorry to trouble you, but I'm looking for Miss Michaud.'

'I'm Kitty Michaud. Who are you?'

'My name's India Pharoah.'

'Pharoah.' Miss Michaud's hand went to her throat.

India began to explain. Miss Michaud interrupted her, saying sharply, 'You know him, don't you? Marcus Pharoah.'

India felt a prickle of excitement. 'He's my husband,' she said.

The dark eyes darted back to the road. 'Is he here?'

'No, Miss Michaud, I travelled on my own.'

'Why have you come here?'

'I was hoping to talk to you about the baby. About Rosanne's baby.'

Kitty Michaud's body seemed to sag and she put out a hand to the porch rail. Then, straightening, she stood aside and held open the door.

'I thought everyone had forgotten him,' she said. 'I thought no one remembered him but myself.'

Tacked to the wall of the parlour were samples of colourful beadwork; on the back of the sofa and rocking chair lay pieces of quilting. 'Winters here are long,' said Miss Michaud, when India admired them. 'I like to keep myself busy.' She motioned India to sit down. 'You look a little like her,' she said.

'Rosanne?'

'The same colouring. And she was very slight, like you. How old is your baby?'

'Abigail's nearly five months old.'

'And she's well?'

'Very well, thank you, Miss Michaud.'

The older woman went to the dresser, opened a drawer and took out a book. She turned a page, then offered it to India. 'That's him. That's my Jimmy.'

India found herself looking down at a black and white photograph of a baby. It was a moment before she could say, 'This is Marcus's and Rosanne's child?'

'Yes.'

Abigail began to whimper. India adjusted her position, propping the baby against her stomach so that she could sit on her knee and look out of the window. 'Marcus told me the child was stillborn,' she said.

'Well, that was a lie. But you didn't believe him or you wouldn't be here.'

'Rosanne died, though, didn't she?'

'Yes.' Kitty Michaud closed the album and put it back on the sideboard. 'He blamed me,' she said quietly. 'He said I'd killed her. The baby was breech and she was such a little thing.'

'What happened?'

Haltingly, Miss Michaud told her story. It had been January, and there had been a snowstorm when Marcus Pharoah had come for the midwife. It had taken them more than an hour to travel the few miles to Aspen Creek. At first, Miss Michaud had been confident that all would be well. She had delivered half a dozen breech babies before, all of them fine and healthy. By the time she had realized things were going badly and had sent Mr Pharoah off to fetch the doctor, the blizzard had worsened and he had been unable to get through to Bourchier, where the doctor lived.

'Even if he had got through it would have been too late,' said Miss Michaud sadly. 'I had to drag that little soul out of his mother or he would have died inside her. That poor girl died of a haemorrhage. There was nothing I could do for her, nothing at all.'

'And Marcus?' whispered India.

'He told me I should have saved the mother rather than the child. I tried to explain to him that I'd had no choice, that he'd have lost the pair of them, but he wouldn't listen to me. I tried to persuade him to hold his child, thinking it might give him some comfort, but he wouldn't. He said it disgusted him. That's what he called his own son. It. He wouldn't even give him a name. It was me who called him Jimmy.' Miss Michaud paused. 'That was the longest night of my life. I couldn't leave that house, you see, because of the snow and because of the baby. And you wonder, when something so dreadful happens, whether there was something else you could have done. I kept going over it in my mind, thinking should I have done this, should I have done that. I was very young, about the same age as you, I'd guess, and I'd never had much confidence in myself.' Miss

Michaud gave a raw laugh. 'My daddy always told me I'd never be up to much and I guess some of that rubs off.'

Her eyes slid back to Abigail, who was playing with the beads round India's neck. 'I got Jimmy to take a little milk,' she said, 'and I held him in my arms all night to keep him warm. I must have fallen asleep around dawn, I was so tired, and when I woke up, Mr Pharoah came to speak to me. He asked me to look after the baby while he made the funeral arrangements and I said yes, I would. The snow thawed after a couple of days and they buried that poor girl. I thought that afterwards he might come round. They say a funeral can draw a line, let you get on with the rest of your life, don't they? Though I can't say I've found it to be true. Anyway, it made no difference. He said he thought the baby looked odd, that there was something wrong with it. Jimmy was very fair, it's true, almost ghostly fair. But he had the most beautiful blue eyes.'

In the silence, India heard a car run along the road and the shriek of the gulls at the river. She said gently, 'So you went on caring for the baby?'

'It was no hardship. He was the dearest little thing. Then Mr Pharoah went away. He told me he needed time to think. He spent his time drinking, I believe. He was in a bad way when he came back a couple of weeks later. He looked like he'd aged five years. Anyway, he made me an offer. He said that he'd pay me to keep Jimmy if I agreed to move away from the area.'

'And did you?'

'Yes. He never spelt it out exactly, but he made it plain that he'd make sure I didn't work again if I didn't agree. But I'd looked after Jimmy since he was born, and I'd come to love him by then. I'd always loved babies, that was why I trained as a midwife, and it would have broken my heart to have given him up to someone else. So I came back here. I was born and brought up in Medway. I told everyone I'd adopted Jimmy, said he was a foundling. I knew that some of my neighbours thought he was my child, born out of wedlock, and I could see them looking down on me. I didn't care, though.'

'And my husband? Did he visit you at all?'

'Just the once.' Miss Michaud smoothed out the patchwork on the back of the chair. 'Jimmy was ill by then. I'll never forget the way Mr Pharoah looked at him. It was as if he should never have been born. He couldn't have stayed more than half an hour. He told me that he'd go on wiring me money each month and he said that if anything happened I was to write to his lawyer in Boston. He left me an address. That was the last I saw of him.'

'What was wrong with Jimmy?'

'I never knew.' Kitty Michaud shook her head slowly. Minutes passed before she began to speak again. 'I kept hoping it was some childhood ailment that would pass, but it never did. He was fine to begin with, but from about three months old he seemed to go downhill. He became such a restless baby. He couldn't sit and smile like your little girl, and his skin was bad, so dry. He used to get sores, even though I did my best with calamine and zinc and castor oil. And he had a musty smell, such a strange thing. The worst thing was he didn't come on the way a child should. He just seemed to stop learning and slip backwards.'

'I'm so sorry,' said India. She found that she was holding Abigail more tightly. 'Couldn't the doctor do anything?'

'It didn't seem so. I took him to see a paediatrician in Augusta and he prescribed some medicine, but it didn't do him any good. I could comfort him when he was upset, but no one else could. We'd sit in the garden under the trees, and it would soothe him to watch the leaves move. But then he started having fits. In the end, he had such a bad fit he never came round again. He was just two years old when he died.' Miss Michaud glanced out of the window. 'I should fix us some coffee,' she said.

'Let me.' India stood up. 'I'm good at making coffee. Perhaps you'd take Abigail for me?'

India put Abigail on Kitty Michaud's lap. As she gently stroked the baby's head, Miss Michaud said, 'I pitied him. I pitied him for losing his wife and for not being able to love that child at all. He was the dearest little thing, my Jimmy. So dear.'

Ellen thought how pretty Pearl Riley had been, how elegant, well-dressed and vivacious. She thought that although Annie hadn't seemed to know Pearl, Pearl was still Annie's mother. And though Riley might not love Pearl any more, he might nevertheless feel bound to her. Pearl was his wife and the mother of his child. These were ties that could not easily be brushed aside.

A couple of times that evening the phone rang, but Ellen didn't answer it. It seemed to her that Pearl's return might have changed everything. Her engagement to Alec had foundered on the rocky shores of Alec's sense of obligation to his mother. Riley was an honourable man. Could she even risk the possibility that he might feel a sense of obligation to Pearl? A part of her, remembering the grief she had endured after her broken engagement, wanted to run. Stop it now, cut it off before she got in deeper.

Before she went to bed, she drank a glass of whisky and took a couple of aspirins and, to her surprise, slept soundly for nine hours. After she had breakfasted, she read through some journal articles. But it was hard to concentrate on a complex discussion of Fourier analysis when a part of her was thinking: Pearl will only hurt him again, because people who are capable of tearing another person apart are not to be trusted. Hard to concentrate, too, while she was waiting for the phone to ring.

Why didn't he ring? The clock ticked on and she gave up all pretence of trying to read the journal. If Riley felt he had to give Pearl a second chance, even though he no longer loved her, then he was sorely mistaken. She, Ellen, must point that out to him. And as for worrying about getting in too deep, she was already in over her head — drowning, almost.

She phoned Riley's house: no answer. She tried again at intervals over the next couple of hours, but still there was nothing. At midday, she went out to buy a Sunday paper. Returning to the flat, she was sure she would hear the phone ringing as she walked up the stairs. That was what always happened, wasn't it? You waited in all morning for a call, then the minute you went out it rang, you rushed to answer it and it stopped ringing just as you picked up the receiver.

But the phone remained silent. Once again, she dialled the number of the Tufnell Park house. Could the Rileys have gone out for the day? Might they have gone to visit Pearl's parents? Yes, that must be it.

Ellen peeled potatoes and chopped runner beans. While she was waiting for them to boil, she scanned through the newspaper. A paragraph at the bottom of the front page caught her eye. *Scotland Yard Detective Shot*. Her heart made a painful squeeze and she read the paragraph through, quickly the first time, then more carefully. The detective wasn't named, but he was listed as critically ill in St Thomas's Hospital. The incident was described as a gangland shooting, which had taken place in Brixton.

The potatoes were boiling over; Ellen turned down the gas. She put a lamb chop on to cook, then dialled Riley's number again. But part of her knew as it rang that no one would answer. *Scotland Yard Detective Shot* . . . *critically ill* . . . *gangland shooting*. A great many detectives must work at Scotland Yard, she told herself; she had no reason to believe the injured detective was Riley.

Yet she couldn't eat the lunch she had cooked, and after she had scraped it into the bin, she searched through the phone directory for the number of St Thomas's Hospital. A lot of holding on and being put through ensued, during which her mouth went dry and she plaited the flex of the phone round her fingers. Then a series of inventive lies was required, and at last a staff nurse on the men's surgical ward was saying, 'Mr Riley's sister, you said? The surgeon had to operate to remove the bullet. Yes, his progress is satisfactory. Yes, visiting hours are between two and three. Only one family member at a time, Miss Riley, he mustn't be tired.'

He had woken in the night and wiggled his toes to make sure his legs were still working. It had been dark, and beside the adjacent bed a doctor and a nurse had been murmuring to each other. He had been aware of a deep, pleasurable relief in finding himself still alive. Then a doctor in a white coat shone a torch in his eyes, which reminded him of Lee Carter, in the tunnel. The doctor said, 'Where are you, Mr Riley?' and Riley thought, in what sense? In a hospital, obviously, but perhaps the question was referring to his life. He was at a crossroads, he thought of saying.

'Hospital,' he said eventually. He spied a nurse in uniform. 'St Thomas's.' Then he closed his eyes and drifted off again.

The next time he woke it was daytime. There was a clattering of trolleys and a school dinner smell. A nurse checked his pulse and temperature then pounded his pillows into shape. There was something he needed to tell her, some message he wanted to give, but he couldn't remember what it was.

If he wasn't eating or washing or having his dressing changed, he was sleeping. Sleep kept the pain away. Surfacing, he was aware of Basil, sitting beside the bed, explaining that Annie wasn't allowed to visit, but that Vera was looking after her and that she was fine.

He must have dozed again, because he was woken by a nurse scolding someone. 'Those are for the *patient*, officer.'

Davies was sitting beside the bed, munching. 'You can spare a grape, can't you, sir?' he said, aggrieved.

Riley hauled himself into a more upright position and stifled a groan.

'You should have waited for me, sir,' said Davies. 'I was on my way.'

'Did you arrest Lee Carter?'

'Yes, sir. He's been charged with attempted murder and possession of an illegal firearm.'

'And Perlman and Rossiter?'

'They're being interviewed as we speak. And we've already rounded up some of the others. Perlman's accountant, Gerry Marks, has been telling us some interesting things about that fellow we found in the Great Dover Street warehouse.' Davies glanced at the staff nurse, who was glaring at him. 'I'd better go, sir, or I'll be told off again.'

Davies left the ward. Though Riley tried to stay awake, sleep was irresistible. He dreamed of bones, glimpsed like pieces of broken white china beneath dead leaves. There was still something he needed to say; he struggled, and something cool and soft stroked his palm.

He opened his eyes and saw Ellen. She said, 'Hello, Riley.' Leaning forward, she touched his lips with hers. 'I only just found out. I'm afraid I haven't brought you anything.'

She sat down beside the bed. She was the only thing worth looking at in the dreary hospital ward. The clock over the door showed that there was only five minutes of visiting hour left.

He said, 'I love you, Ellen. I expect I'll forget I said it and say it all over again tomorrow. I think I'll just say it every day and then we'll know we're all right, won't we? But I love you so much, and when I've got things straight with Pearl I want you to marry me. You haven't changed your mind about that, have you?'

'No.' There were tears in her eyes, yet she was smiling. She stroked his face with the back of her fingers. 'No, I haven't changed my mind. There's one thing, though.'

'What's that?'

'Maybe, because we're to be married, I should call you John. Riley – it's starting to seem a bit formal, a bit academic. Would you like that?'

'Yes,' he said.

She smiled at him and linked her fingers through his. He was very tired, and when he tried to speak, she said softly, 'Hush, John. It can wait. Rest now.'

*　*　*

India stayed on in Medway, at the motel. She liked the thin light and the flat, brackish scent of the water. She liked the boats moored on the banks, with their peeling paint and phut-phutting engines, and she taught herself to like the quiet of the place, the evenings in her room with Abigail, the long walks by the river. She was testing herself by passing a winter in this remote town. She was teaching herself to tolerate boredom and loneliness, making herself into the sort of woman Abigail's mother needed to be. She kept a close eye on her daughter but Abby remained healthy, learning new things every day.

She made friends with the motel receptionist, who was called Karen. Karen mentioned that they were short-staffed in the diner, so at lunchtimes, while Karen kept an eye on Abigail in reception, India helped out, serving meatloaf and shepherd's pie to hungry loggers and truckers and the occasional hiker.

She wrote letters to Sebastian and Ellen in England. She wrote to Marcus, telling him where she was living, and recounting her conversation with Kitty Michaud.

A week later, he arrived in Medway. He wanted her to come home, he told her. He wanted her to come back with him.

'I can't,' she said. 'I'm sorry.'

They were sitting in her bedroom. Outside a full moon cast a silver light on the parked cars.

He said, 'I know you don't love me, but I can live with that. If it's because of the child,' he glanced at Abigail, asleep in the carrycot, 'I felt the same way when Rowena was a baby. Surely, now that you know what happened, you can understand that?'

'You were afraid to love her because you were frightened she might fall ill as well.'

'I believe it to be inherited, you see. The ultimate irony, I think, is that such diseases have always been my interest, my passion. To begin with I was fascinated by the patterns they made, their symmetry and predictability, and what they tell us about inheritance. And then, after what happened to the child, I became consumed with the possibility of finding a cure.' Again, his gaze drifted to the sleeping baby. 'I could tell there was something wrong with it. I could see it wasn't right.'

'He was your son, Marcus.'

'To think that Rosanne and I could have produced such a child . . .' He pushed his fingertips against the lines on his forehead. 'I couldn't be sure. I kept hoping I was mistaken, but the infant's condition became more apparent as time went on. And if the disease is hereditary, as I believe it to be, then I may be a carrier. I've had to live with the knowledge that I could transmit this, this curse to the next generation. I never wanted a child with Alison but she wouldn't have married me otherwise. Thank God, Rowena was healthy.' He sighed. 'I knew it was improbable that a different marriage would result in another abnormal child. If the pattern of inheritance is as I believe, then Rosanne and I must have both been carriers. It was always unlikely that Alison would carry the same faulty gene as well. Or you, India. But there remained the possibility.'

'So you hid it. You pretended it had never happened.'

'I buried my wife, left the child with Miss Michaud, and went home to England. All I wanted to do was to put it behind me, to start again. Only a few people knew what had happened. I threw myself into my work. I met Alison, and a year later Rowena was born. And then there was the war, of course, and Gildersleve. You forget. I made myself forget.'

'Did you?' she said. 'Did you really?'

A shadow of a smile. 'It's a part of me, inside me, written in my blood, ineradicable, unchangeable.' His eyes sought hers. 'Do you blame me for abandoning the child?'

'No, Marcus, I blame myself for marrying you.' She was sitting on the edge of the bed; she did not allow herself to turn aside from his gaze. 'I shouldn't have, I see that now.'

'I can change,' he said.

'But not enough for me. We would destroy each other, you see that, surely?'

He left that night. The way he talked, she reflected after he had gone, as if they weren't all faulty, didn't all pick up imperfections along the way.

India stayed on in Medway as the first snows fell. The motel was quieter in the winter and she helped out with the cooking and cleaning as well as in the restaurant. Abigail learned to sit and to crawl. India received a letter from

Sebastian. The girl he had been dating for months — Jenny — he was in love with her and they were thinking of getting married.

During the coldest months, the daylight limited itself to a few murky hours. The water in the Penobscot thickened, slopping against the shores. India bound Abigail to her in a papoose as she walked to the shops or headed along the river to visit Miss Michaud. Her boots sank into the snow and slabs of snow settled on the ranks of fir trees, tumbling now and then to the ground below, sending up white dust. Snowflakes rushed across the window of her room in the motel and clung to the glass.

In the New Year, she received a letter from Marcus. He was returning to England, he wrote. His position at Midhurst College had not worked out as he had hoped. He had made arrangements to pay a sum each month into an account in a bank in Montpelier, Vermont. If she did not want the money herself, he would like her to keep it towards Abigail's college fees.

Spring came. In the thaw, the river swelled and the wind fractured its surface into crescents. Abigail learned to walk round the furniture in the motel reception room, hands resting on the sofa as she sidestepped like a ballerina. One day, India was fetching a room key for a trucker who had driven in from Canada when she looked up and saw Abigail launch herself off from a table. Six steps, unsupported: India and the trucker applauded.

She wrote to Linc. She had thought of him every day

throughout that winter and spring, of the hard warmth of his body and the exploring softness of his mouth. She had thought of him standing on the stoop outside his house as the snow covered the mountains, and she had thought of him walking into the coffeehouse in the afternoons. Did he still look for her? Did he still think of her?

He wrote back to her. He had been to Medway once before, he said. A nice little town; he had liked the look of it.

The sky became bluer and the air warmed. The jukebox in the café played 'All I Have to Do Is Dream', and India looked out of the window, searching for a tall, brown-haired man with an easy smile.

Working in the diner one morning, she found herself considering a number of things. How soon she would be able to afford to go back to England to visit Sebastian. Whether it was time to move out of the motel and find a place to rent, and if so, whether she would stay on in Medway another winter or move south.

As she wiped and laid a table, she noticed a green truck draw up in the parking lot outside. A customer called out to her for more coffee; India went to fetch the pot but her gaze kept going back to the truck. She poured out the coffee and heard the door of the diner swing open.

And there he was. Denim jeans, red plaid shirt, standing in the doorway.

She put the coffee pot back on the hotplate and crossed the room to him.

'Would you like a table, sir?'

'That's why I'm here, ma'am.'

'Do you know what you want yet?' She was standing in front of him. He rested a hand on her hip.

'Yes, ma'am. Yes, I sure do. And you?'

'Yes.' She stood on tiptoe to kiss him. 'Hello, Linc,' she said.

Chapter Fourteen

Ellen was only just in time for the London train. The guard, perhaps noticing her bump, held open a door for her and waited until she had climbed inside the carriage before raising the flag and blowing his whistle. The train was busy and she murmured apologies as she made her way along the corridor, her briefcase held in front of her like a shield. All the second-class seats were taken; she was glad that John had insisted she buy a first-class ticket.

The corridor shifted and jolted as the train gathered speed. Reaching the first-class carriage, she peered through the windows of the compartments. In one, only a single seat was taken. She was about to open the door when, with a shock, she recognized that the man sitting in the window seat was Marcus Pharoah.

She could have walked away, and was tempted to, but then she opened the door and went inside.

'Good afternoon, Dr Pharoah,' she said.

He had been looking out of the window. Turning to her, he frowned. 'Miss Kingsley.'

'Are these seats free?'

'Yes, all of them.'

She sat down opposite him. She wondered whether they might travel to London in silence, nothing said, but then he spoke.

'Presumably you're not Miss Kingsley any more.'

'I'm Mrs Riley. Though I keep my maiden name at work.'

'Did you get on the train at Cambridge?'

'Yes, I was attending a conference there. And you, Dr Pharoah?'

'I was visiting my ex-wife and daughter.'

A heaviness seemed to settle over him; she thought how greatly he had changed. Though he looked older, and his hair was now almost entirely grey, it was not that which struck her, but the loss of vitality and resolution.

He said, 'And the happy event? When is it to be?'

'In two months' time. January.'

'A new decade. A child of the sixties.'

The train had reached the open countryside south of Cambridge. If she had been able to look further over the fields through the darkness and the rain, she would have been able to see as far as Gildersleve.

He must have had the same thought, because he said, 'They were good days. I miss them.'

She asked curiously, 'When were you happiest?'

'In the war, I think.'

'When you were living in the cottage with Dr Kaminski and Dr Redmond?'

'Yes.' His gaze moved back from the window to her. 'Jan told me he'd spoken to you.'

'Yes.'

'You have such a curious nature. A valuable quality in a scientist, I acknowledge.'

'I think I found out what I wanted to know.'

His smile was disbelieving, and she found herself saying, 'I think that you and Dr Redmond grew apart after the end of the war because you'd found out that he was a homosexual. I expect the division between you deepened after Dr Redmond realized that because Gildersleve was running out of money you were planning to sell the woodland. I think that he threatened to expose you, and either to make public the fact that you'd passed Dr Kaminski's work off as your own, or that you'd been a member of the Communist Party when you were young. That was what he meant when I overheard him tell you that he could destroy you.'

In the silence that lay between them there was only the clatter of the wheels on the rails and the scream of the slipstream as the train raced through a tunnel.

Dr Pharoah said, 'Both those things may be true, but the reason I sent Gosse to the cottage that evening was to find the letters I'd written to Redmond about my first wife.'

Her heart tripped; she felt the baby startle and put a hand on her belly.

'You sent Gosse to the cottage?'

'Yes.' He smiled, sadly. 'We fear most what lies inside us, don't we? And *that* was what I most feared, that he would tell Alison – and Rowena – about my son. *That* was what I thought he had meant. Afterwards, I wondered whether I'd been correct. But by then it was too late.'

'So Dr Redmond knew about the child?'

'He was one of the few people who did. I met him shortly after I returned to England, after the death of my wife. I had to talk to someone and I talked to him. He was a good listener. I'm afraid I sometimes drank too much and bored him with what had happened to me in America. No, that's not right. You couldn't *bore* him. He either listened or he walked away.' A smile flickered. 'Sometimes some bigwig would come to the hall, someone I was trying to extract money from, and Redmond would walk away while he was talking. It used to make me laugh at first, but then, as time went on, it began to annoy me. Why he couldn't *dissemble*, like other people.' Pharoah shrugged. 'I suppose I had to get it out of my system. Most people will listen to you once or twice and then you'll see them becoming impatient. Bryan never became impatient. I think,' here, Pharoah brushed a hand down the sleeve of his coat to wipe away some beads of rain, 'I think his peculiar nature allowed him to listen. He felt no need to be listened *to*. You have to give most people their turn, don't you? But not Bryan. He wasn't a talker. You know that.'

The rain had sharpened, shooting horizontally across the window. 'My mistake was that I wrote to him,' Pharoah said. 'I poured out my heart to him in those letters. About Rosanne, about the child, about the fact that I believed the illness to be hereditary, and about the pattern I ascribed to it. Everything was there. I knew he would have kept the letters because he never threw anything away.'

'And that was what you were afraid of?'

'Yes.' His dark eyes burned. 'I was afraid for my daughter. I did not want her to be burdened with *that*.'

She wondered whether it had been only for Rowena that he had been afraid. Or whether he had taken such pride in his invulnerability, in his good health, intelligence and looks, he had found it impossible to countenance public knowledge of his imperfection.

She said, 'So you sent Gosse to the cottage to find the letters. What happened? Was there a fight? Did he lose his temper and push Dr Redmond downstairs?'

'What an imagination you have. No, nothing so sordid.' Pharoah made a short, quick sigh. 'Gosse was searching the bedroom when Redmond came home. If he hadn't taken the wretched dog with him everything would have been all right. Gosse would have hidden upstairs until Redmond went out to the garden or to Peddar's Wood, and then he would have returned to Gildersleve with the letters. But the dog got out of the room somehow. It must have startled Redmond. He was always afraid of dogs. Perhaps he thought the creature was going for him. In his rush to get out of its way he tripped on the carpet and fell downstairs.' He met her gaze. 'It was a damnable thing to happen,' he said quietly. 'But it was an accident.'

'Then why not tell the police?'

'Don't be ridiculous, Miss Kingsley. It would have all come out – the reason I'd sent Gosse there, the letters, our quarrel. It would have been splashed across the newspapers and the inevitable questions would have been asked. And what good would it have done? None whatsoever. It would have ruined my reputation and Gildersleve's and it wouldn't have helped poor Redmond at all.'

Someone put their head round the door; Pharoah flung them a fierce glance and they retreated, shutting the door behind them. She said, 'Did Dr Redmond die instantly?'

Pharoah became motionless. Minutes seemed to pass before he said, 'No. He was still alive when Gosse left the house.'

His profile seemed to have been carved out of stone, immovable and severe. 'Did you go to him?' she said.

He shook his head. 'No.'

She whispered, 'But he was your friend!' And for the first time, a look of shame crossed his face, and he turned away, towards the window once more.

The train drew into a station. Passengers climbed off and on; this time, three men in trilbies and overcoats joined them in the carriage.

She thought they would not speak again but as they reached the outskirts of London, Pharoah leaned towards her and said, his voice low, 'If you think that I deserve to be punished for what I did, then let me assure you, I have been. My daughter, Rowena, is to marry her cousin. I went to Barton today to try to put a stop to this poisonous alliance, but it's too late. She is expecting Rufus's child.'

Ellen saw that his eyes glittered. She remembered Sunday lunch at the Pharoahs' house, all those years ago: Pharoah's dark, beautiful daughter and her saturnine cousin, huddled together in the dining room. And how Rufus had taken Rowena's plaits in his hands and pulled her towards him, and how she had let out a peal of laughter.

'I'm sorry,' she said. 'A child . . .'

'I'm sure you can work it out. If the disease is recessive, assuming I inherited the faulty gene from my parents, then it's possible that my brother Devlin has done so as well. And if so, it's also possible that we've passed it on to both Rowena and Rufus. Which would mean there's a one in four chance that Rowena's child will inherit the disease.'

There was in his eyes such an expression of horror that Ellen found herself pitying him.

He said, 'I went there today to try to tell Rowena about my son. But I couldn't. This is what I shall have to endure, Miss Kingsley, this is my punishment. This wretched and hasty wedding and a year of waiting to see whether my grandchild is healthy. And that would be the best outcome. The worst – I can hardly bear to think of it.'

He turned away. The lights of the approaching city made orange smears on the rainswept window. Ellen thought of her own child, hers and Riley's, longed-for, already beloved. She felt it move in her womb and she muttered a silent prayer for its health and survival.

He spoke to her only once again, as the train drew into King's Cross. They were rising, doing up buttons and tying scarves.

'Do you see her at all?' he said.

'India? No.' She picked up her briefcase. 'We write, though.'

'Is she happy?'

'Yes, very.'

'Please tell her — please tell her that I miss her.'

He left the carriage. Ellen waited for a few moments before also leaving, not wanting to cross his path again. But as she made her way through the crowds pouring along the platform, she was haunted by them, by Pharoah and Dr Redmond and Rowena Pharoah and her unborn child, by the cold-hearted mathematics of genetics and the way that misfortune and greed and lovelessness could write itself into future generations. And when she went through the barrier and saw Riley waiting for her, Annie at his side, she found herself rushing towards them, throwing her arms round him and burying her face in his shoulder.

'What's this?' he said, concerned. 'What's wrong?'

'Nothing,' she said. His features were blurred by her

tears; but in that moment, among her family again, her meeting with Marcus Pharoah slipped into the past and she was able to say, 'Nothing at all, love. I missed you, that's all.'

And together they walked out of the station.

JUDITH LENNOX

Catching the Tide

1933
Tessa and Frederica Nicolson enjoy one last summer at the beautiful Villa Millefiore, overlooking Florence.

Four years later, Italy is a distant memory and Tessa is revelling in the excitement of modelling in London. Unconventional and impulsive, she believes love is just a game, until a passionate affair with married author Milo Rycroft leads to tragic consequences. In the wake of disaster, Tessa flees to Florence. Following her sister to Italy, Freddie is soon swept up in adventure, danger and romance, and makes a chance encounter that will change her life.

With the outbreak of World War Two, Tessa and Freddie must fight for their own survival and happiness, unsure if they will ever see each other again . . .

Acclaim for Judith Lennox's novels:

'The beautifully written story is a compelling and emotional read' *Woman's Way*

'A compelling novel . . . a beautiful tale' *Sunday Express*

978 0 7553 4489 5

headline
review

JUDITH LENNOX

Before the Storm

A wild autumn day in 1909: Richard Finborough catches sight of twenty-year-old Isabel Zeale at the harbour at Lynmouth and is captivated by her beauty. Scarred by her past, Isabel has no intention of letting anyone get close. But Richard pursues her, and his persistence and ardour win her heart.

The couple marry and have three children, Philip, Theo and Sara. A fourth is added when Ruby, the daughter of Richard's old friend, comes to stay with them after her father mysteriously disappears. The Finboroughs' lives seem enviably perfect.

Then, in the 1930s, the reappearance of an old acquaintance turns Isabel's world upside down, while Ruby uncovers a series of dark truths about her father that lead her to a terrible conclusion. As conflicts simmer in Europe, it seems that love, war and secrets are set to tear the family apart . . .

Judith Lennox's novels have been highly acclaimed:

'A beautifully turned, compassionate novel. Judith Lennox's writing is so keenly honest it could sever heartstrings' *Daily Mail*

'Great, old-fashioned storytelling in the best sense' *Daily Express*

978 0 7553 3134 5

headline
review

You can buy any of these other **Headline Review** titles
from your bookshop
or *direct from the publisher.*

FREE P&P AND UK DELIVERY
(Overseas and Ireland £3.50 per book)

Catching the Tide	Judith Lennox	£6.99
The Heart of the Night	Judith Lennox	£7.99
Before the Storm	Judith Lennox	£8.99
A Step in the Dark	Judith Lennox	£8.99
The Thread	Victoria Hislop	£7.99
Better Together	Sheila O'Flanagan	£7.99
The Lonely Desert	Sarah Challis	£7.99
A Walk in the Park	Jill Mansell	£7.99
The Secret She Kept	Amelia Carr	£7.99
The Last Summer	Judith Kinghorn	£6.99

TO ORDER SIMPLY CALL THIS NUMBER

01235 400 414

or visit our website: www.headline.co.uk

Prices and availability subject to change without notice.

the wives and eunuchs that she was with child, and, as she had hoped, they turned her out. When she first entered the prison enclosure, Idris es Saier, the head gaoler, shackled her with a light chain and attached her to his harem, but she was permitted to tend her former master. Neufeld was allowed to sit outside now during the day and, for the first time, permitted to talk with the other prisoners, many of whom were old soldiers from the Egyptian army and eager for news of the outside world.

One morning he was lying in the shade amid the filth and flies of the prison enclosure when two camelmen rode in. They had orders from the Khalifa to bring Neufeld to him, they could not say why. It was generally known that there was to be a large parade that day, and it was assumed by most of the prisoners that Neufeld was to be executed. Some of his fellow prisoners tried to be encouraging: one told him to be brave, as 'when they tried to burst your head with the ombeÿas'. Neufeld was hoisted on to one of the kneeling camels and taken off to the parade ground just outside the town.

The swinging strides of the camel rubbed his shackles into his now festering legs. Some of the ulcers broke open and the blood and pus ran down the camel's side. Neufeld was in agony, and by the time they reached the Khalifa on the parade ground he was near fainting. The Khalifa noticed his condition and ordered the chains to be removed that night and lighter ones put on him. In the meantime, Neufeld looked out on a plain covered with cavalry, camelmen and foot soldiers. It had apparently been the Khalifa's intention to display his entire army to him, but seeing that in his present condition he was unable to pay attention, he turned to one of his emirs and said, 'Tell Abdallah (Neufeld) that he has seen only a quarter of the army, and let him be brought for the parade tomorrow.'

His fellow prisoners were astonished to see him return alive that evening; they were even more surprised to hear Idris es Saier ordered to remove his chains and put on a lighter set. The gaolers tried to carry out the Khalifa's orders, but the rings around his ankles were now so buried in the swollen flesh that they could not be brought near enough to the anvil's face to be struck. Therefore, he was brought to the parade ground the next morning in the same wretched condition as the day before. The Khalifa was furious when he saw this and sent for the gaoler to demand why his orders had not been obeyed. Idris es Saier replied that he had no lighter chains and that Neufeld's legs were too swollen. The Khalifa refused to take this as an excuse and ordered that the irons be removed that evening. And so they were, but it was a terrible ordeal for Neufeld.

During the parade Neufeld saw Slatin and tried to get near enough to speak to him, but he found it impossible. He did not know that Slatin dared not disobey his orders not to talk with him. One of the emirs asked Neufeld for his impression of the great Dervish army. Neufeld answered shortly, 'You have numbers, but not training.'

The proud Khalifa heard the remark. He was not pleased. Neufeld was sent back to prison – for four years.

14

Neufeld: Life in Chains

In 1887 the prison in Omdurman consisted of a large zariba of thorn trees and branches about six feet high located near the banks of the Nile. Inside was the one common cell – the 'Umm Hagar', House of Stone – where the prisoners were locked up at night. About thirty gaolers kept order with the aid of their curbashes. There were no sanitary arrangements whatsoever; not even a ditch for a latrine; the Umm Hagar and the prison yard swarmed with scorpions and vermin. Prisoners were fed by friends or relations; if they had neither, they starved.

Of all the people appointed by the Mahdi to posts of importance in his government, only two managed to retain their positions until the end of the Mahdiya. One was the head of the arsenal and the other was Idris es Saier, the chief gaoler. A shrewd man was Idris, and he acquired considerable fame in his profession. In fact, his name became synonymous with prisons. Not only the prison in Omdurman, but all the prisons in the Sudan were called Beit es Saier – House of Saier – or simply the saier, and all the head gaolers were also called saier, as though it were a title. He was a tall, well-built Black who had once enjoyed a different kind of fame as a thief. He liked to tell stories of his exploits, always ending them by pointing out how, thanks to his conversion to Mahdism, he had risen in the world and was now the trusted guardian of all thieves – as well as murderers, traitors, unbelievers and run-away slaves. It was true that Idris es Saier no longer stole now that he was a Mahdist. He had no need to. He had learned to be a clever extortionist, milking his prisoners of their money with simple but effective guile. Almost daily he harangued his charges, telling them how he had once been a robber, but now was an honest man; how grateful he was to the Mahdi for his conversion; and how all the prisoners should also be grateful to the Mahdi and the Khalifa for leading them into the true faith. He then vowed that because he had given all his money to the poor, he now had no money to feed his wives and children. 'I am going to see my starving children now,' he would say near the end of his speech, 'and then I will pray to Allah, asking him to release you if you repent and turn the Khalifa's heart to you.'

To win favour, some of the prisoners gave Idris various sums of oney according to their means. Sometimes he would apply a little pressure. He would tell them mournfully that someone must have done something wrong as he had been ordered to put more chains on the principal prisoners, i.e. those with money. This was the signal for the prisoners to collect enough money to make a donation to the gaoler's wives and children; then the 'Khalifa' would learn of their kindness and generosity and the chains would be struck off.

The hundred dollars Wad Nejumi had returned to Neufeld had been given to Hasseena to hold for him, but Idris es Saier took the money from her 'for safe keeping'. Gradually, under one pretext or another, Neufeld was forced to give it all to Idris.

Idris was an extremely superstitious man, and although the Mahdi had forbidden fortune-telling and the writing of talismans, much of his money went to fortune-tellers. He had also about twenty-five or thirty boards of hard wood, twenty inches square, which he used as tablets. Every day he had someone write suras (chapters) from the Koran on the tablets with ink made from soot, gum arabic, water and some perfume. As soon as it was written he would wash his hands and then very carefully wash off the ink, collecting every drop in a cup. If a drop spilled, the writing would have to be done over again. When he had the sacred words in solution, so to speak, he would then drink it, and his soul felt fortified.

Daily life in the prison when Neufeld first entered began with the opening of the door to the Umm Hagar at sunrise. The prisoners were allowed to shuffle down to the bank of the Nile to wash and to relieve themselves. Then all were assembled for the first prayer of the day. This was followed by the reading or recitation of the Mahdi's ratib (book of sayings), which took about three-quarters of an hour. Each prisoner had to purchase or copy out these sayings of the Mahdi and then memorize them. Although copies had been printed on the old Egyptian government press, it was considered more meritorious to write out a copy by hand. It was usually carried in a small leather case suspended from a cord around the neck, and it was generally considered as a talisman.

At noon, the second prayer was said, and between noon and sunset the third prayer, followed by another recitation of the ratib. The fourth prayer was said at sunset and then everyone was driven into the Umm Hagar. The good Muslim prisoner should have said his evening prayer in the Umm Hagar, but the nightmare inside made this impossible. Filthiness prevailed. Excrement was thrown about the crowded room; parasites made sleep an impossibility. As the night slowly wore on, the heat grew more and more oppressive and the stench from the sweating bodies became overpowering; men clawed and bit and kicked each other with their fetters; anyone who fell to the floor was trampled, and was seldom able to rise again. Sometimes more than 250 men were jammed into the small room. When the pandemonium became too great, the guards would come and lash at those nearest the door with their curbashes, and more men would be trampled. Neufeld fought and kicked and bit with the others to save his life. When the door was opened in the morning, there would frequently be trampled corpses on the floor, sometimes as many as five or six. This went on for night after night, week after week, month after month, for years.

The prisoners worked for a while at making bricks for a wall around the prison to replace the thorn zariba, and digging a well for infiltration water. To lighten the load of chains and bars on their legs, the prisoners attached a cord to them; by lifting up on the cord, they were able to walk, or at least shuffle about. Until the wall and well were completed, Neufeld described life in the prison as 'I might say endurable'. The prisoners were allowed to go down to the river to wash and drink, and this gave them an opportunity to exchange news and gossip with the townspeople. It also afforded a number of prisoners an opportunity to escape. These were usually Blacks. As most of the slaves in town wore chains, the Black prisoners were able to pass for ordinary slaves in spite of their chains. Besides, any blacksmith would remove the chains free for the sake of the valuable iron. This means of escape was not practical for Neufeld, he knew, for he would be quickly recaptured if he remained in Omdurman, but he was not without hope of escaping in some manner. Most of the gaolers kept large establishments with many wives and concubines and the prisoners were often put to work making additions to their houses or doing household tasks. The household tasks were the least distasteful chores and they frequently offered an opportunity to escape. In such large households it was rare that there was not at least one wife or concubine who felt herself neglected or unjustly treated. If a prisoner could win the affections of one of the gaoler's women, he was often able, through her help, to make his escape. The usual procedure was for the woman to report a goat or sheep missing just at sunset. She would take her prisoner-lover with her to find the missing beast, and they would simply not return.

Each month, Idris es Saier had to report on the prisoners and give an account of their 'education'. When a prisoner was missing, he would be reported as having completely repented and reformed and was therefore recommended for mercy. If the Khalifa approved, the prisoner was officially free and the gaoler escaped the charge of having allowed a prisoner to escape; he was only minus a wife or a concubine.

Neufeld had once studied physiology and medicine at the universities of Königsberg and Leipzig. In Upper Egypt he had had a reputation as a doctor and, as he did not charge for his services, his practice had been large. His reputation accompanied him to Omdurman, where he was frequently called upon to administer to the gaolers or their wives. In the course of his 'professional' visits to the harems, he made dozens of proposals of marriage, but he never succeeded in arranging an escape.

One day there entered the prison yard a man he knew: Ahmed Nur ed Din of the Kababish. Neufeld had worked with him when he was in the caravan trade and when he was with the British army. Before he could speak to him, Ahmed made a sign for him to be silent and walked off in another direction. That evening, when they were being driven into the Umm Hagar, Ahmed whispered, 'I have come for you. Be careful. Keep your eyes open. Try to obtain permission to sleep outside the Umm Hagar.'

It was two weeks before they had another opportunity to exchange a few words. Ahmed spent them ingratiating himself with the prisoners who associated with Neufeld so that he was gradually introduced into the circle of prisoners with whom he talked. Ahmed Nur ed Din had an interesting story: he was engaged in a bitter feud with Gabou, the guide who had betrayed Neufeld and the Kababish caravan, and he reasoned that if he could bring Neufeld out of the Sudan his enemy would soon be swinging from the gallows. He had therefore made his way to Omdurman for the express purpose of rescuing Neufeld. At first he had waited in the hope that Neufeld would be released from prison. Finding that this was unlikely, he had arranged a quarrel with a friend in the market-place in order to get himself put into prison.

Ahmed Nur ed Din had friends outside the prison and he had arranged with them to procure camels and provisions for the flight. He had also arranged that when he gave the signal through the boy who brought him his food, his friends were to make a hole in the prison wall through which they would escape. Instructions were also sent out to obtain pistols and ammunition. Finally, all was nearly ready, but only seventeen cartridges could be found. Ahmed decided to wait a few days more in the hope that additional ammunition could be procured. Just at this time, however, he became feverish and Neufeld soon saw that he had all the symptoms of typhus. Ahmed urged Neufeld to make his escape without him, but he refused to consider it. Neufeld and Hasseena nursed the sick Kababish, but he weakened every day and died one night in the hell of the Umm Hagar. Two days later, Neufeld himself fell sick.

Hasseena nursed him carefully and enlisted the help of two boys to carry him from shade to shade as the sun travelled across the sky. Often, in moving him, they tripped on his neck chain and they all fell to the ground. Idris es Saier, who was not deliberately cruel, had the chain removed. Hasseena had her own cure for typhus: vegetable marrow soaked in salt water; the water was drunk and, when the patient was able, the marrow was eaten. This was followed by cramming the mouth with butter. The next operation was to rub the whole body briskly and cover it with oil or butter. Neufeld had nothing to say about his treatment. He was helpless. The vegetable marrow acted as a purgative, the butter felt like boiling oil in his throat and, by the time he had arrived at the final stage of the cure, when he was wrapped in old camel-cloths and sweated, he was too weak to protest. After thirteen days he recovered, in spite of the treatment, but he was terribly weak and thin. By the time he was strong enough to get about, the men Ahmed Nur ed Din had organized for his escape had lost heart and gone away. He was often to regret that he had not steeled himself to leave the dying Kababish and fled while he had the chance.

During his convalescence, the Khalifa sent religious teachers to convert him. One was an old kadi who had served under Slatin. He urged that it would be more politic if he would pretend to be converted and submit, as had Slatin, who now lived in his own house with his own slaves, horses and cultivated land outside the city. Neufeld refused. The kadi pointed to Neufeld's chains, then weighing about forty pounds, and said the Khalifa would surely torture him with them until he submitted. Neufeld knew better than the kadi what those chains meant, but he would not accept nor pretend to accept Islam. The reasons he gave for his refusal, curiously, were not religious ones. He once said that he refused to turn Mahdist because he did not want to be found dead in a jibba, killed by an English bullet. Yet, at the time of his capture and for years after there was little or no fighting between the British and the Dervishes except around Suakin. At another time he said he refused to become converted because the Khalifa would make him proclaim his conversion publicly and then would behead him to prevent him from slipping back into Christianity. Yet, he knew that neither the Mahdi nor the Khalifa had ever executed a single European captive and he had no reason to believe he would be an exception. A stubborn Christian was Charles Neufeld.

For the prisoners in the saier, the most trying time of all was during the great famine of 1888–9. As no food was provided by the prison authorities, many whose friends and relatives could not even provide for themselves starved to death. At the height of the famine, dozens died each day, yet the prison population did not grow smaller, for it was increased daily by those arrested in the market-place trying to steal food. These wretches were dragged to the anvil where they watched while the chains were struck off the corpses of men who had starved to death and then fastened on to themselves.

A portion of all the food brought to the prison by relatives and friends was regularly taken by the guards. Once inside, those bringing food had to fight with the starving prisoners, many almost living skeletons, who ran to the end of their chains or struggled to run in their fetters to grab a mouthful of food. Neufeld was fortunate in having his faithful servant Hasseena, as well as friends such as Father Ohrwalder and Sister Catarine Chincharini who managed to get food to him. Slatin, too, secretly contributed to his support. Hasseena, after being knocked down and robbed several times by starving prisoners, hit upon an ingenious device. She obtained a gazelle skin and made it into a bag which she filled with food and hid between her legs under her dress. She carried a few scraps of food with her, but waited until she reached her master before dropping the bag beside him. Thanks to such charitable and ingenious friends, Neufeld survived the famine.

Of all the tasks given the prisoners, the hardest was unloading Nile boats. Shortly after the death of Ahmed Nur ed Din, when Neufeld was recovering from his own bout of typhus, one of the young gaolers, who had been pestering him unsuccessfully for money, ordered him to go to work unloading boats. Neufeld refused and sat down on the ground. When the gaoler seized him and began dragging him towards the gate of the prison, Neufeld, struggling, managed to kick loose, scramble to his feet and knock him down. The young gaoler jumped up and made off to tell his story to Idris es Saier, who, when he heard it ordered Neufeld to obey. He still refused, complaining to Idris that the young gaoler had tried to extort money from him. Idris answered by hitting him on the head with a large flat stick he had with him, breaking the stick in the process. He then ordered that Neufeld be given 500 lashes with the curbash. Neufeld was so stunned by the blow on his head that he was only half conscious when his flogging began. After sixty or seventy lashes, he lost consciousness altogether. Idris, fearing that he was dead or about to die, stopped the flogging. As Neufeld was considered one of the more important prisoners, the Khalifa would not have been pleased to learn that his gaoler had killed him. Neufeld was carried into the shade and Idris turned on the young gaoler, abusing him for starting the affair; he knew that Neufeld had been telling the truth when he said the gaoler was trying to get money from him. Idris was not adverse to bribes, but he insisted they be paid to him, not his underlings.

Often the gaolers were bribed to allow prisoners to sleep outside the Umm Hagar. Neufeld paid Idris himself for this privilege and further bribed one of the guards to allow him to sleep in a small mud hut in the prison enclosure. One evening when an unusually large number of prisoners had bribed gaolers to allow them to sleep outside, Idris made his appearance and, seeing so many men outside the Umm Hagar, demanded to know the reason. The guards, pretending that they had had difficulty in getting the prisoners into the Umm Hagar, began laying about them with their curbashes and driving the prisoners into the cell. The young guard with whom Neufeld had had trouble, not knowing that the privilege had been purchased from Idris, took this opportunity to single him out with his lash and drive him towards the Umm Hagar, about fifty yards away. Idris saw it and the young gaoler paid dearly. He was dismissed from his post, given 200 lashes, and put in prison himself. Neufeld had the satisfaction of seeing the beating and watching the former guard work at unloading the Nile boats. He thought this the only piece of real justice he ever saw during his entire stay in the Sudan.

Flogging was common in the prison, but there were certain rules that were always followed. One thousand lashes was the maximum number ever awarded and the prisoner was always allowed to keep his clothes on. Five hundred lashes was a common punishment and it was always given in the same way; the first two hundred were given on the buttocks, the next two hundred on the shoulders, and the final hundred on the breast. One thousand was usually ordered to extort a confession, and these were always given on the buttocks. Clothes offered some protection, of course, but after the first seventy or eighty blows they were in shreds and soaked with blood.

Neufeld received his worst beating one night when Idris es Saier again came into the prison enclosure to find an unusual number sleeping outside the Umm Hagar. Although Neufeld had bribed Idris well, the latter was so furious at the money being paid to his guards instead of to himself and his 'starving children' that he ordered all the prisoners without exception to be given 150 lashes. Most set up such a clamour, begging for forgiveness and swearing repentance, that they escaped with twenty or thirty lashes at the most, but Neufeld refused to beg for mercy. As the lash cut into him, he clenched his teeth and bit his lips, resolved that not a sound of pain would escape him. 'Will you not cry out?' demanded the gaolers who were beating him. 'Are your head and heart still like black iron?'

Years later, writing about the flogging, he remembered most keenly the humiliation of it:

> There was I, a European, a Prussian, a man who had fought with the British troops . . . now in the clutches of the tyrant and his myrmidons, whom we had hoped to rescue Gordon from; a white and a Christian – and the only professing Christian – chained and helpless, being flogged by a black, as much a captive as I was, and yet my superior and master. It is impossible for anyone not having undergone a similar experience to appreciate the mental agonies I endured.

In May 1887 Hasseena had escaped the Khalifa's harem by maintaining that she was pregnant, which she was not; in November 1888 she was indeed pregnant, and this presented a difficult situation for both Hasseena and for Neufeld. Hasseena could be stoned to death if it could be proved that she had had sexual relations with anyone other than her master. If Neufeld claimed the child, Idris es Saier would be in trouble for allowing Neufeld so much freedom; and for a prisoner to get Idris es Saier in trouble was to get into serious trouble himself. The matter was complicated by the fact that Idris wanted Hasseena for himself. As for Hasseena, she had no idea who the father of her unborn child might be. She had turned to prostitution and thievery to obtain food for herself and Neufeld during the famine; she had not changed her ways since.

Neufeld consulted his friends among the other prisoners and was advised to claim paternity, even if it did mean trouble for Idris. The Khalifa, they thought, might then release him, for a wife and child represented hostages as it was obviously impossible to escape with them. Neufeld followed their advice and claimed the child, and Idris was indeed unhappy: he was deprived of a chance to obtain Hasseena for himself and he was in danger of suffering the Khalifa's wrath. Fearing the Khalifa's displeasure, Idris worked out a unique solution to his problem: he empanelled a jury of women to decide whether Neufeld could indeed be the father of the child about to be born. The jury examined the matter at length and, either because of Idris es Saier's bribe or to protect their own future activities, came to a most remarkable conclusion: Hasseena was indeed with child by Neufeld but the conception had not taken place in the prison, but nineteen months earlier! Some of the women even maintained that it was possible for gestation to take years.

The child was born in January 1889 and was named Makkieh, meaning 'shackles'. When the Khalifa heard the verdict of the women jury and of the name of the child, he was much amused. He sent Neufeld his congratulations and offered him his freedom if he would promise to make gunpowder for him. Neufeld replied that he did not understand the manufacture of gunpowder, and so remained in prison.

Every prison has its prison aristocracy, and the Khalifa's prison in Omdurman was no exception. Here it was often composed of sheikhs and emirs who had formerly occupied important positions in the Mahdist government, and Neufeld had an opportunity to meet and talk with many of them. Of them all, the man who impressed him most was that remarkable and able man, Ibrahim Wad Adlan, sometime chief of the Beit el Mal. Before the Mahdiya, he had been one of the principal merchants in Kordofan, and rich. He had travelled to Cairo and other parts of Egypt a number of times; he could read and write Arabic, and possessed a brilliant mind. When he succeeded Ahmed Wad Suliman as head of the Beit el Mal in 1889 he completely reorganized the treasury and introduced an intelligible system of accounting, employing experienced Egyptian clerks and accountants. He was a friend of both Slatin and Neufeld, and Neufeld said of him: 'He was a man himself, acted as one, and despised heartily those who, in his opinion, were carrying their obedience to the confines of servility.' Neufeld, like Slatin, confided to Adlan his longing to escape, and Adlan offered to do all in his power to help. But first it was necessary for both of them to be out of prison.

Adlan did not believe he himself would be kept long in prison; affairs at the Beit el Mal were going badly without him and the worse they became, the higher were his hopes of returning to the Khalifa's good graces. Getting Neufeld out was more difficult. Adlan urged him to pretend to be converted, saying that otherwise he would never be allowed out of prison. The old argument was persuasive coming from the one man Neufeld was able to respect, and he finally agreed, sending word through Idris es Saier of his conversion. When the matter was reported to the chief kadi however, he said, 'What! Abdallah Noful a Muslim? No, his heart is the old black one. He is not with us. He is deceiving. He is still headstrong. He is a deceiver. Tell him so from me.'

Neufeld failed to win his release by his unconvincing conversion, but Adlan, as he had predicted, was shortly released and reinstated in his old position as head of the Beit el Mal. Adlan now did his best to obtain Neufeld's release from prison. It was about this time that the Khalifa was searching for someone to design the Mahdi's tomb, and Adlan suggested that Neufeld be supplied with drawing materials and told to submit a design. He accordingly drew up a rough sketch of a proposed tomb based upon tombs of Egyptian rulers he had seen in Egypt. He was then told to make a clay model of the tomb, which he did. A great number of people came to see the model until one day a fanatic kicked it to pieces, saying that the Mahdi's tomb should not be designed by a dog of an unbeliever. Nevertheless, the finished tomb was almost a copy of Neufeld's design except for its distinctive conical roof. Now Adlan sent word to Neufeld to draw up a design for the interior of the tomb. The object of all these efforts was, of course, the hope that if the design was approved, Neufeld would be released from prison to take charge of the work. Adlan recommended Neufeld's designs for the tomb's interior to the Khalifa, adding that it would cost nothing as there was sufficient paint in the Beit el Mal.

It was some time before the Khalifa finally approved the project, but one day Neufeld was led out of the prison and taken to the Mahdi's tomb to inspect it. Adlan met him there and confidently assured him that this would be his last day in chains. And so it might have been if just at this time a European had not escaped from Omdurman. A half-witted Bohemian minstrel who had wandered by accident into the Sudan and had been captured, now as casually wandered out of Omdurman. He never reached safety, for he was murdered not far from the town. Nevertheless, his escape so infuriated the Khalifa that Neufeld, all hope of freedom now dashed, was not only kept in prison, but an extra bar of iron was added to his fetters.

Not long after this Neufeld was astonished and dismayed to see Adlan brought back into the prison and heavily weighted with chains. Neufeld was anxious to speak with him, but everyone was strictly forbidden to go near him and he was put into a small hut some distance from the others in the prison yard. Nothing was possible during the day, but that night Neufeld shuffled towards the hut. When he was a few yards away, he lay on the ground and wriggled close, keeping his chains spread as taut as possible to prevent their rattling. In a whisper he asked, 'What has happened?'

Adlan was startled but whispered back, 'Go away! Go away! Do not speak to me. A big dog has me by the leg this time. Go away, or he will get your leg.'

Neufeld was insistent and asked again what had happened, but Adlan ignored the question and simply begged him to go away. Neufeld reluctantly wriggled back and regained his own hut without being detected, but he knew no more than before. The next day, Adlan's slave boy passed Neufeld and said, 'Do not speak to my master. If you do, you will hear the ombeÿa.'

When asked what he was doing, the boy replied, 'Burning papers. Do not speak to my master.'

A few days later, Adlan was taken out of his hut and led to the anvil to have his chains struck off. All knew what this meant: his execution. Neufeld and the other prisoners were not allowed to go near him, but Adlan called out to them, 'This is my day! Have no fear, any of you. I am a man. I shall say and do nothing a man need be ashamed of. Farewell!'

While still more chains were being fitted to Neufeld's ankles, he heard the sounds of the ombeÿa announcing the death of Ibrahim Wad Adlan. He had run foul of Yakub.

With the execution of Adlan, Neufeld fell into a state of abject despair. All hope was gone. He had, when supplied with drawing material to sketch the Mahdi's tomb, succeeded in writing letters to his agent and friends in Egypt – not, curiously enough, to his wife. He had even found means of getting the letters into the hands of men who would take them to Egypt. Nothing came of his efforts; no answer had come back.

One day an Egyptian doctor, Hassan Zecki, who had married Frank Lupton's widow and was now in charge of the medical stores at the Beit el Mal, came to the prison and talked with Neufeld about the manufacture of saltpetre. Neufeld had seen crystals made in a laboratory while at the university, but he had no experience in bulk production. Nevertheless, Hassan Zecki was interested and said that his assistant was trying to extract saltpetre in and around Khartoum.

Three days later Neufeld was summoned by Yakub to explain the making of saltpetre. On the way from the prison to Yakub's house, Neufeld considered what attitude he should adopt. He knew that if he confessed he did not know anything about bulk manufacture of the chemical, he would not be believed and would probably be flogged; if he pretended to know, he would probably be let out of prison for a while. He therefore assured Yakub that he could make saltpetre, but that he would require the construction of three large tanks about six feet long and four feet wide in which arable soil could be mixed with water and the solution drawn off and allowed to evaporate.

The following morning, Neufeld was taken to the anvil; his iron bars were struck off and his heavy ankle chain was replaced by a piece of light awning chain taken from one of Gordon's old steamers. It was a tremendous relief to have the dead weight of fifteen to twenty pounds removed from his feet. He was then led to the river where Yakub and some emirs, with about thirty workmen were waiting for him beside a Nile boat. A two-hour sail downriver brought them to Halfaya. After nearly four years in prison, this sail on the Nile was a delight Neufeld never forgot. They were met at Halfaya by a Fellata called El Fiki Amin. 'Fellata' is the name used in the Sudan for the West Africans who for centuries have passed through the Sudan on their way to and from Mecca. The trip usually took years, the pilgrims being poor and the journey long and hard. Like a very sluggish stream, the Fellata moved, and still move, across the Sudan, creating an enduring aspect of Sudanese life without its individuals ever becoming part of it. As the Mahdi had forbidden pilgrimages to Mecca, the stream was broken during the Mahdiya, but it is doubtful if even then it was completely dammed.

The Fellata held the secret of making saltpetre and had a virtual monopoly on its production, but most was made in Darfur and had to be transported hundreds of miles by camel to reach Omdurman. Here, however, El Fiki Amin was engaged in producing by very primitive methods small quantities of very good saltpetre, and he did not look kindly on the intervention of a potential competitor.

Yakub ordered Neufeld to search for deposits of earth that might be rich in potassium nitrate. He looked around. Coming upon a dark, damp patch of earth he took some and mixed it with water, pouring off the solution and boiling it in a small coffee pot. He added more solution as the water boiled away, and after two hours he obtained a small deposit of a thin syrupy consistency; this he poured on to a porous brick. When the moisture was absorbed, crystals remained; these burned away when placed on hot charcoal. He then dried some of the earth, rubbed it fine and allowed it to fall in a thin stream on to the fire. The hissing noise it made, combined with an occasional coloured spark, convinced those present that a new deposit had been found. One of the emirs was sent back to Omdurman to tell the good news to the Khalifa.

After he had gone, the Fellata told Yakub that burning the crystals did not prove the substance was saltpetre. Yakub, not knowing whom to believe, ordered Neufeld to make more and send it to Hassan Zecki. This he did, and Hassan Zecki sent back a secret message to Neufeld saying that the crystals were not very good, but that he knew Neufeld would be sent back to prison if he said so; therefore, he would give his approval of the crystals if Neufeld would try to produce them in the form of needles instead of grains. Hassan Zecki then made a favourable report to the Khalifa and asked that Neufeld be sent some large pans. Shortly after this, Neufeld received several copper kettles and an officer's camp bath-tub, probably taken from Khartoum or from the baggage of one of Hicks Pasha's officers.

Neufeld now began to make saltpetre, but the Fellata so resented the competition that it was decided Neufeld should look elsewhere. Neufeld, with an eye to escape, suggested that he search for new deposits further north, but Yakub would not permit it. About this time, Hasseena's child died and the Khalifa thought it would be safer if Neufeld stayed closer to Omdurman. So after about two weeks in Halfaya Neufeld was removed to Khartoum. There he was put in the old Catholic mission, occupying one of the priests' rooms. The mission was in ruins: windows, doors, and all metal and wood had been removed; only the garden, with its fruit trees and vegetables was still maintained. In the chapel, cocks crowed, and hens laid their eggs where the altar had been.

For six months Neufeld worked with fifty slaves constructing large tanks to produce saltpetre in bulk, while at the same time carrying on limited production of four or five pounds a day in the copper kettles and bath-tub. The results of their work were sent over to the arsenal in Omdurman and turned over to Joseph Pertekachi, the Khalifa's maker of gunpowder. As the quality of Neufeld's saltpetre was not good enough to make gunpowder, Pertekachi mixed the gunpowder made from it half and half with good powder from old government stocks when he tested it. As good powder came in from Darfur, Pertekachi simply stored away Neufeld's saltpetre and the deception went unnoticed.

Father Ohrwalder came to visit Neufeld several times while he was at Khartoum. They talked about the past and commiserated with each other, but they never discussed plans for escape, although escape was uppermost in the minds of both men. Father Ohrwalder never tried to explain why he did not try to work a concerted escape plan with Neufeld or other prisoners, but many years later Neufeld wrote:

> That we did not openly discuss such plans now appears to me strange – and yet it is not strange. Where all led for years a life of falsehood, in which deception of self had a no less part than that of others, suspicious of everyone around us, trusting no one, what wonder that deceit became a second nature, and that truth, honour and morality – that is to say, morality as preached in Europe – should have retired to vanishing point!

Although the European prisoners did what little they could to help each other, they trusted no one. In January 1888 a spy-messenger sent to the Sudan by the Anglo-Egyptian army in Egypt with letters for Slatin and Lupton reported back that they had refused to accept the letters in the presence of each other 'owing to mutual mistrust'. Slatin never mentioned this incident.

Among the letters Neufeld had managed to smuggle out was one to an old friend, Mankarious Rizk, the Greek station-master at Aswan. Mankarious had tried to help. He had found a reliable Ababdeh Nubian who was willing to go to Omdurman and give Neufeld 100 dollars and to try to arrange an escape. He arrived in Omdurman while Neufeld was still in prison, so he turned over the money to a Greek to keep. Concluding that it was impossible for Neufeld to escape from prison, he returned to Aswan. The news of Neufeld's position put an end, for a time, to his friends' efforts to free him.

When Neufeld heard of Father Ohrwalder's escape, he cursed him, for he thought he had gone off with some guides with whom he himself had plotted. When Mankarious learned of Father Ohrwalder's escape, he tried again to get in touch with Neufeld. It took him some months to find someone willing to make the trip, but at last he found an old but wiry Arab named Ahmed Abou Hawanein who agreed to go.

With two camels, some money and goods with which to trade, Ahmed set off to make his way up the Nile. In the summer of 1894 he reached Omdurman and found Neufeld in the garden of the mission house in Khartoum. He brought no letters and Neufeld was at first suspicious, but after questioning him thoroughly he became convinced that the man had indeed been sent by his friend and he was soon talking enthusiastically of escape. Unfortunately, Ahmed Abou Hawanein did not think the camels he had were good enough for a rapid flight; he suggested that he return to Aswan to buy two good trotting camels and the two revolvers which Neufeld thought necessary.

Not long after Ahmed Abou Hawanein had left, Neufeld was asked to visit a sick man in the house of a friend of his and he received permission to go. The 'patient' turned out to be a perfectly healthy Arab named Abdallah who gave him a piece of paper on which Neufeld could make out only faint marks. Abdallah told him the writing would emerge when heat was applied to the paper. As cauterization was a common remedy, Neufeld called for some hot coals to be brought to him. With the aid of the coals the writing stood out and Neufeld read that Abdallah had been sent by the War Office in Cairo. In the course of several meetings, an elaborate escape plan was worked out. It was to be put into effect as soon as Abdallah returned to Berber and collected the camels and rifle he had left there. He left and Neufeld never saw him again in the Sudan.

Abdallah's story was a curious one. In Cairo he had been given as his primary mission the task of bringing out Neufeld, being promised £300 if he succeeded; he was also promised £100 if he brought out any of the other captives. This last clause was Neufeld's undoing. Seeing the difficulties of trying to carry off a man who was in chains and closely guarded, Abdallah decided to forget the £300 and to assure himself of the smaller but safer sum by taking one of the other captives. He therefore contacted Father Rossignoli and arranged an escape plan for him. He and Father Rossignoli went as far as Berber on donkeys. When they reached Berber, Father Rossignoli threw himself on the ground and refused to go any further; he demanded that he be taken back to Omdurman. Abdallah was startled and frightened: to return to Omdurman now would be suicide. Father Rossignoli then started wandering about the town; he even told several people that he was being taken by Abdallah to Cairo against his will.

Abdallah knew that he would never collect his £100 if he left Father Rossignoli in Berber. He had procured a camel, and in desperation and exasperation he broke off a branch of a tree and flogged the priest until he climbed upon it. He then mounted in front of him and forced him to escape. Once back in Egypt, he decided he would never again run such a risk. But he had created false hope and left Charles Neufeld bitterly disappointed again.

After Pertekachi blew himself up, there were closer examinations of the saltpetre Neufeld supplied and he was given several warnings about the quality. Fortunately, it was about this time that he obtained a new job working in the mint. Neufeld suggested that they try to make coins with a punch press. He and his companions experimented until they had spoiled several sheets of copper, a number of dies and finally the press itself.

Although still wearing light chains and still closely guarded, Neufeld's life was considerably more bearable than it had been in the prison. However, he had domestic troubles. Hasseena's morals had never been of the best, but she had been loyal to him and undoubtedly had saved his life when he had first been thrown into prison. He owed her much. But now she had become a nuisance and a danger to him. During the famine, she had risked the punishment of a caught thief to provide him with food; now she continued to steal for herself, taking advantage of her position as the wife of a European to steal from the other Europeans, knowing they would not report her. Neufeld's friends strongly urged him to get rid of her before he became involved as an accomplice. He at last decided reluctantly to do it, but as she had been given to him by the Khalifa, he felt that he must have his permission to divorce her.

When Hasseena came to see him, he quarrelled with her openly so that it could be seen they no longer got along well together. Then he asked through his superior if the Khalifa would consent to a divorce. The Khalifa agreed, but said that he would select another wife for him. When Neufeld learned that the woman the Khalifa had in mind was a half-breed French subject, he was horrified. An Islamic marriage was, in his eyes, simply a liaison, but marriage to another European was bigamy. He appealed to his European friends to find him a Muslim wife, and quickly. Casting about for an eligible woman, they found Umm es Shole, an Abyssinian who had been raised in the household of a Greek family in Khartoum and had married one of the sons. On the fall of Khartoum, her husband had been killed and she became the property of the Beit el Mal, eventually being turned over to an emir as one of his concubines. As she refused to lie with the emir, he retaliated by torturing her children to death. Abdel Kader, the Mahdi's uncle, heard of her case and gave her a document declaring her to be a free woman.

When the Khalifa gave his order for all women and girls to marry, Umm es Shole married an old and ailing Jew, whom she nursed until he died two years later.

The Khalifa gave his consent to the marriage, but Umm es Shole objected; she did not want to marry again. Only when told that Neufeld was ill (which he was just then) and would surely die unless cared for did she give her consent. Neufeld was married by proxy and only after the wedding did Umm es Shole see her new husband. She at once set about nursing him and establishing her small household.

The new marriage seemed to be satisfactorily arranged, but the divorce from Hasseena proved somewhat more difficult. Normally, divorce (for a man, but not for a woman) is a simple and private matter in Islam: a man need only say three times, 'I divorce you.' Neufeld followed the prescribed rules, but Hasseena promptly countered by declaring that she was pregnant. The Islamic divorce rules as practised in the Sudan required a husband to keep his pregnant wife until the child was born, and if the child was a son the divorce was null and void. Neufeld decided to send her off anyway, but she returned about eleven months later with a baby boy. Neufeld then kept her for two years more.

Originally, Hasseena had figured in Neufeld's escape plans, and he had intended to take her with him when he fled. Now she was replaced in these plans by Umm es Shole. Abdallah had not returned, but there was still the plan he had worked out with Ahmed Abou Hawanein.

On 28 February 1895 Neufeld was seized without warning, loaded with chains and placed under a double guard at the house of the Governor of Khartoum. Four weeks later he was returned to the saier in Omdurman. As he passed through the prison gate, he saw another prisoner being brought in: it was Ahmed Abou Hawanein.

15

Neufeld: Hell's End

Knowing that all hopes for escape were now crushed, and being once more in the hated saier, Neufeld was in a state of absolute despair close to insanity. For days he shuffled about the prison yard, dragging his chains and irons, refusing to speak to anyone, his eyes on the ground. It is difficult indeed to live without hope, and he would have been a most unrealistic optimist to have seen any reason to support hope in his present position.

Neufeld's sudden return to heavy chains and the saier was the direct result of the escape of Slatin. Ahmed Abou Hawanein was in prison for the same reason. When he returned to Omdurman, he was at once seized and accused of having helped Slatin to escape and of returning to help Neufeld. He was flogged to make him confess, but he refused. Another flogging was ordered, but some of his own people interceded on his behalf and he was finally released. He at once returned to Aswan, where he showed his torn back and festering wounds. This cooled all enthusiasm among the Arabs for further attempts to assist Europeans in Omdurman.

One day Neufeld was near the prison anvil when he heard a man crying. Looking up, he saw a man being shackled and recognized him as Ibrahim Pasha Fauzi, an Egyptian officer whom Gordon had found as a subaltern when he first came to the Sudan, but whom he had continually promoted until he became Governor of Khartoum and Commandant of Troops. Neufeld was shocked to see such a man crying. It was disgraceful. A man of his standing should not act like a child, and Neufeld told him so. Suddenly a change came over Neufeld. Confronted with the wreck of a man that Fauzi was, he felt a responsibility thrust upon him. His own despair lifted and he became the protector of the former governor: as a disappointed child finds comfort and distraction in lavishing affection on a doll, so Neufeld now saw Fauzi: someone who needed him, someone to be comforted.

As Neufeld was in prison only to prevent his escape from Omdurman and not because of any misdeed, Idris es Saier had been instructed to treat him well, and Umm es Shole and her child were allowed to come and visit him at any time. But he was never to be permitted to sleep in the open and was forced to spend all his nights in the Umm Hagar. On the evening of Fauzi's first day in prison, he was placed in the corner furthest from the door with his back against the wall. At first he had enough room to stretch out his legs on the foul floor. When the second batch of prisoners was driven in about an hour and a half later, there was only room for the prisoners to squat. Fauzi, heavily chained and unable to get to his feet, remained with his legs outstretched while four other prisoners sat on him. Neufeld was driven in with the third batch of prisoners, and when all were inside, there was only room to stand. Fauzi, still on the floor, begged those around him not to stand on him.

Neufeld heard him and, fearing that he would be trampled to death, he began to fight his way towards him, lashing about in all directions at friend and foe alike. As the men could see little in the dark and could not tell exactly who had hit them, they struck back indiscriminately at those around them. The Umm Hagar was soon a mass of brawling humanity. Neufeld continued to fight his way towards Fauzi, calling on friends to help him. The guards, hearing the uproar, threw open the doors and laid about with their whips and sticks.

In the confusion Neufeld and a few of his friends managed to fight their way through the swaying, sweating, yelling mass to Fauzi. They pushed men off him and made a human barricade around him. Fauzi himself, who could not tell whether an attempt was being made to save or murder him, fainted.

About midnight, the doors of the Umm Hagar were again thrown open and the guards tried to push in twenty men, each wearing a shebba. There was no room for them, but the guards were determined. They set fire to handfuls of straw and grass and threw them into the cell, at the same time laying about them with their curbashes. Fauzi, still dazed and seeing the fire falling on the heads of the men, thought he was surely in hell. The men bound with shebbas were somehow driven into the Umm Hagar, the doors were pushed shut, and so they were left until sunrise.

Among those in the Umm Hagar that night were Zeki Belal, the brave guide who had helped Slatin to escape. Zeki had been forced to confess that he had helped a man with 'cat's eyes' to leave Omdurman, but swore he did not know who the man was.

During the first few weeks after Neufeld was back in prison, Umm es Shole had little difficulty in begging small quantities of grain and borrowing an occasional dollar to keep him supplied with food. After a time, however, people grew afraid of assisting him and he began to feel the agony of starvation. Then, in September 1895, an Abyssinian woman came to the prison to see him under the pretence that she wanted medical treatment. She slipped him a small packet of letters and whispered that it had been given to her by a man outside the prison who said that he also had money for him and asked to whom he should pay it.

It was three days before he found an opportunity of being alone and opening the packet. In it was a letter from his sister written four years earlier, a letter from Father Ohrwalder and a note from Major Wingate: all told him not to lose hope for attempts were being made to assist him. At irregular intervals over a three-month period, he was visited by the Abyssinian woman and through her he obtained money, plotted for escape and himself managed to write letters for the man to carry back to Egypt. The man was Onoor Issa, and one of the letters he carried out was to Father Ohrwalder. In it Neufeld gave news of mutual friends in the Sudan, asked about his business in Aswan and begged Father Ohrwalder to send him instructions and materials for making coins that would look like silver.

Neufeld's desire to make coins was based on his belief that if he could do work of this sort he would be transferred from the prison to work at the Beit el Mal. However, he was fortunate enough to make this transfer without knowing how to make coins. Awad el Mardi, the head of the Beit el Mal, became interested in trying to extract gold and silver out of certain stones found in the neighbourhood of Omdurman. Neufeld was detailed to assist in this enterprise. His iron bars and heavy chains were replaced by a single pair of ankle rings connected with a light chain, and he was transferred to the government workshops in Khartoum. Here he enjoyed the easiest life he had experienced since his captivity. Awad el Mardi told him: 'I am your friend. Do not be afraid. If you cannot find gold and silver, tell me of anything else you can do, and I will see that work is given to you so that you may not be sent back to the saier.' He was housed in one of the best buildings still standing in the town, sharing the lower floor with an Egyptian who had formerly been the telegraph clerk in Berber. A number of Beit el Mal slaves were put there to guard him, but they were told that his chains were only to prevent his being carried off by the Egyptians. Thus, in effect, his guardians became his servants.

In April 1896 rumours reached Omdurman that British and

Egyptian troops were advancing. Then came news that Dongola had been taken. At first Neufeld could not understand what was meant when he heard that the British were crossing the desert in 'iron devils'; then he understood that a railroad was being built, but this seemed almost equally improbable. It was about this time that Onoor Issa sent him a message that he had been detained in Berber by the emir there, but that he hoped to get away soon and arrange his escape. Neufeld's hopes soared.

With the advance of the Anglo-Egyptian troops into the Sudan, the Khalifa became concerned about his supplies of ammunition. An inspection of the stores and arsenals revealed that large quantities of powder had caked with moisture. The Khalifa threatened to cut off a hand and a foot of the arsenal chief if he did not make the powder into a good explosive. Neufeld was ordered to help, and he set to work with some carpenters to produce a wooden model of a powder machine. He knew that materials for a full-sized machine were not available and he built into the design some serious defects that would make the machine break down if it were ever built, but it looked real enough. When it was shown to the Khalifa, he was so delighted with it that he ordered all Neufeld's chains to be removed.

For ten years Neufeld had been in chains, and for most of the time he also had the additional weight of irons. He had learned to shuffle about, his step limited to the ten or twelve inches of chain and the irons making each step an effort by their weight. When at last he stood freed of chains and irons, he could not contain himself. All that day he ran and jumped about, stretching his legs for the sheer joy of it; intoxicated with his new-found lightness. The next morning, his legs were swollen from his hips to his ankles and his muscles ached so excruciatingly that he was unable to walk. He was still laid up when, thirteen days later, the Khalifa changed his mind and put him once again in chains.

The Khalifa also ordered Neufeld to make a cartridge machine for him. He set to work and designed a model, but Berber had been taken by the time it was ready to show to the Khalifa, who only looked at it and said sourly, 'I want cartridges, not models!' He ordered that Neufeld be removed from his house, kept at work all day in the arsenal and that he spend his nights locked up with other prisoners in the arsenal prison with the convict labourers. The Khalifa's half-brother Yakub was, of course, consulted about the machines Neufeld made. He did not understand them any better than the Khalifa, but he is reported to have said that 'there must be something in the head of the man who invented them, and he was better employed in the arsenal than idling his time in the saier'. Yakub gave orders that Neufeld was to be given whatever materials he needed for his work.

Neufeld now began gleefully to destroy everything he could lay his hands on. He demanded the paddle axle of one of the steamers and cut it into discs, then he turned his attention to destroying as much brass and copper as he could obtain.

In August 1897 Onoor Issa returned to Omdurman and sent a message to Neufeld through Umm es Shole. Neufeld was able to get a letter written and passed to Onoor Issa with instructions for him to give it to the first officer he saw. In it, he gave such information as he knew concerning the forts around Omdurman and asked that Onoor Issa be given a list of medicines, as 'practising medicine facilitates my communication with the outer world'. Onoor Issa took the letter but he was not able to leave Omdurman until the end of December and it was six months before he returned with money and a noncommittal letter from the commandant at Suakin. Meanwhile, towards the end of November, the arsenal was removed from Khartoum to Omdurman and Neufeld was returned to the prison.

The Anglo-Egyptian army under its Sirdar, General Horatio Herbert Kitchener was steadily making its way up the Nile, and the Khalifa and his followers grew more and more apprehensive. Their greatest fear seems to have been of the Sirdar's gunboats, which might appear at any time to bombard Omdurman. It was suggested to the Khalifa that mines placed in the river would stop the gunboats. One mine was made and tested. It worked so successfully that the Khalifa ordered more. When they were completed and being placed in the river they unaccountably exploded, blowing up the *Ismailia*, one of Gordon's old steamers, and killing more than thirty men.

As General Kitchener's army drew closer and closer to Omdurman, the prison boiled with rumours. There were many who had reason to dread the coming of the English, and there were those such as Neufeld who, for years, had dreamed of a British advance, so that almost any rumour dropped on fertile ground and flourished. The prisoners were afraid that they might all be killed by the Dervishes before the army arrived, or that they might be thought Mahdists and shot by the British when they marched in. Many decided that it would be a wise precaution to establish their sympathy with the British cause and they came to Neufeld to give him information or otherwise to prove their loyalty. Neufeld sent out a number of messages to the advancing army through Onoor Issa, giving what he hoped would be useful military information. Idris es Saier turned particularly kind to Neufeld and nervously asked what he should do in case the English won the coming battle; treat him well, Neufeld advised him, and he would speak 'good words' for him.

There was an old prophecy that the final great battle with the infidels would take place in the plains of Kerreri. Accordingly, the Khalifa moved his mighty army, numbering about 80,000 men and including every male inhabitant of Omdurman, to the plains north of Khartoum.

On 1 September 1898 the cry flew through the prison that the gunboats were coming up the river. Next, the prisoners heard a distant booming of guns that grew nearer and nearer. A boy stationed on the roof of a gaoler's house came tumbling down with the news that the gunboats were in sight and had passed Halfaya. A few moments later, the prisoners were covered with a shower of dust and stones as a shell hit the top of the prison wall and ricocheted off without exploding. Everyone ran to the shelter of the north wall and squatted there, thinking this the safest place. More shells went screeching overhead.

Charles Neufeld went mad. He stumbled out into the open prison yard, shouting, laughing, crying, trying to dance in his shackles, kissing his hands to each shell that raced overhead. The Baggara prisoners tried to kill him. Idris es Saier saved him and locked up all the prisoners except Neufeld, Fauzi and the other government sympathizers in the Umm Hagar.

Suddenly, the shelling stopped and the guns fell silent. In the prison yard they waited tensely and expectantly for the next phase of the battle. Nothing happened. Some said that two of the gunboats had been sunk and that the remainder had fled down the river. Neufeld and Fauzi sat in a daze in the prison yard; mad joy gave way to despair. Neufeld broke down and cried.

That night he could hear the Baggara in the Umm Hagar shouting what they would do to that 'son of a dog, Abdallah Nofel', promising themselves that they would drink his blood the moment his brothers reached Omdurman. All night long he could hear the pat-pat-pat of running feet outside the prison walls. No one knew what it meant. It was only later they learned that it was the sound of men running back to Omdurman from the plains of Kerreri.

The next morning at sunrise, the boom of cannon was heard

again in the prison. Later they heard the sound of musketry as well, and among themselves, in complete ignorance, they tried to guess the probable course of the fight. To calm his nerves, Neufeld began to illuminate a ratib with red and black designs. About noon he left this work to attend to the wounds of two young men who had been attached to the prison but had gone off to fight. One had a bullet over the left temple and the other a bullet in his left arm. Neufeld cut out the bullets with a penknife and dabbed the wounds with a bit of carbolic acid. When he questioned them about the battle, they told him that Yakub had been killed and that the Khalifa Abdullahi was retreating.

In the afternoon, the prisoners heard the braying ombeÿas and the beating drums that called the faithful to gather, but did not know what they meant. Idris es Saier came to Neufeld and asked him what he should do. Neufeld told him to shut the gates of the prison and use his rifles on any Baggara that might try to get in; he could then wait and see who would ask for the keys, the Khalifa or Kitchener. Idris took this advice and then linked all the prisoners into gangs connected with chains. This work had just been completed when Idris came to Neufeld in great excitement and told him that the place was filled with his 'English brothers' and that a big, tall man was asking for him.

The chain connecting him to the other prisoners was cut off, and he was led by Idris to the gate of the prison. Neufeld was so filled with emotion that he could only make out a blurred group of officers standing before him. Then he heard the first words of a European language he had heard in seven years: 'Are you Neufeld? Are you well?'

A tall figure approached him and shook his hand. It was the Sirdar, General Kitchener. Neufeld stammered something, shook hands with someone, and felt a friendly slap on the shoulder. The Sirdar looked at his three sets of heavy leg irons and said, 'Can these be taken off now? I am going on.'

A British officer stayed with him and tried to find Idris or one of his gaolers to remove Neufeld's chains, but all had fled. So instead the officer gave him his horse and helped him to mount side-saddle, chains and all, and walked beside him as he led the way to the officers' mess of the headquarters staff in the desert just north of town. It was not imposing. It was dark by the time they arrived, and tired, hungry and thirsty officers and men worked on orders and dispatches by the light of guttering candles. They celebrated their victory that night with a supper of biscuits, water and some of

Neufeld's prison bread. Ernest Bennett of the *Westminster Gazette* saw Neufeld and thought 'he looked very little the worse for his stay in Omdurman'. Shortly after arriving at the mess, Neufeld heard someone calling, 'Where's Neufeld?' The inquirer was Bennet Burleigh, correspondent for the *Daily Telegraph*. Finding Neufeld still in chains, he rushed off to get farriers. With strong language and strong blows, the chain was cut, but the iron anklets remained until the next day when they were removed on board the gunboat *Sheik* with the aid of a vice and a cold chisel.

When Neufeld boarded the steamer that was to take him down the Nile to civilization, he was a man secure in his honour. Throughout his twelve years of captivity, he had maintained his manhood and his faith; he felt proud, too, that he had been able to be of some help to the conquering army by the information he had smuggled out to the Sirdar. The nightmare was over now. He stood on the deck of the steamer, a free man looking forward eagerly to resuming the broken path of his life. He did not yet know of his reputation in the civilized world. He was soon to learn.

Part 3

The Sudan Reconquered

16

Kitchener and the War the Railroad Won

At the end of the last century, the old, poverty-stricken, rotten Ottoman Empire was a ramshackle affair, propped up and preyed upon by a number of European powers. The vibrations caused by the fall of the Sudan reached back to Constantinople and caused the tottering structure to lean even more precariously towards the brink. It still pretended to rule Egypt, but the real pharaoh was the cool, efficient Evelyn Baring. It also pretended to rule, directly or through Egypt, a considerable stretch of the African coastline running all the way along the Red Sea, around Cape Guardafui and the horn of Somalia, down to where the Sultan of Zanzibar vaguely claimed, without effectively controlling, his stretch of African coastline. With the fall of the Sudan, there was a good deal of what Baring called 'Egyptian debris' left over which European powers began to sweep up into their own hands.

British forces occupied Berbera and Zeila, establishing what became British Somaliland. The French seized the area just north of Zeila and began to construct French Somaliland. The Italians, after asking the British if they would mind, grabbed the land around Massawa and formed Eritrea; then Cape Guardafui itself and the south-running coastline to below the equator to create Italian Somaliland. The British garrisoned Suakin, but did not claim it.

Abyssinia, too, came in for her share of Egyptian debris. In 1884, by treaty with Britain, chunks of Sudanese land were given to Abyssinia in exchange for allowing the Egyptian garrisons along the Abyssinian border to withdraw to Massawa. The British also helped the Egyptian garrisons to withdraw from Harar, and Abyssinia occupied – or rather reoccupied – this territory.

In Darfur, the country was so torn and bloodied by revolt, and so reduced by famine and migration, that the Khalifa no longer bothered to keep an army there. In the south, Emin Pasha, the last of Gordon's provincial governors, remained until 1888 when Henry M. Stanley, after near incredible hardships, reached him and carried him, reluctantly, out of the country to the eastern sea-coast. Events in Equatoria have an even vaguer, more unreal quality about them than events in the rest of the Sudan. The Khalifa started to conquer it, recalled his forces for other purposes, and then apparently forgot about it. Emin did not control the entire province and it is doubtful if he actually was capable of governing any of it. When he left, Equatoria drifted into anarchy.

In Egypt, after Wolseley's forces withdrew from the Sudan, steps had to be taken to prevent the Dervishes from coming down the valley of the Nile into Egypt proper. A line was drawn, which remains almost the same to this day, between the Sudan and Egypt, at Wadi Halfa. The border was guarded by British, Egyptian and Sudanese soldiers – all led by British officers – collectively known as the Frontier Field Force. From such information as this force could gather from refugees, deserters, merchants, spies and patrols was pieced together nearly all that was known to the outside world of events in the Sudan. The weekly intelligence reports make interesting reading, not only because of their stories of camel and cavalry patrols and interrogations of people coming out of the Sudan, but because the writers included a human element missing from most modern military reports. Doubtless the officers were bored by the routine. Colonel Josceline Wodehouse wrote on 4 October 1891: 'I understand that the statements of the refugees and others are required in full, more or less. Their information is usually so inaccurate and improbable that it seems hardly worth noting.' When Zubair Pasha's son deserted to the Dervishes, General Grenfell noted that he was a 'lazy, drunken man, who had quarrelled with his father'.

In the eastern Sudan there was some action. In February 1891 Colonel Holled Smith set out from Suakin with a force of 2,000 men and defeated the forces of Osman Digna near the town of Tokar, which he occupied. This was the first attempt to reoccupy any of the Sudan. In England there was considerable agitation to reoccupy more of it. Politicians pointed out that it was dangerous for Egypt to have such a barbarous neighbour, but after the battle of Toski in 1889 no further attempt was made by the Dervishes to invade Egypt and it was quite obvious that no real threat to Egypt existed.

In 1895 there was a change in government in England, bringing into power a Conservative and Unionist administration that was strongly opposed to the Egyptian policy of Gladstone. Governments in democracies generally tend to reflect popular opinion, and popular opinion favoured the reconquest of the Sudan. Queen

Victoria favoured it too, writing that these 'wild Arabs . . . would not stand against regular good Troops at all'. Since the fall of Khartoum and the death of Gordon there had been a strong feeling in England that Gordon ought to be avenged; Britain felt guilty about the loss of the Sudan, although it was believed, certainly in official circles, that she was in no way responsible for it. Writing ten years after the event, Lord Cromer (Evelyn Baring) said: 'Indeed, one of the principal arguments in favour of recapturing Khartoum was that the British public had evidently made up its mind that, sooner or later, Khartoum had to be recaptured.' The escapes of Father Ohrwalder and Slatin, and the accounts of their experiences given to the English-speaking world by Wingate, tended to increase the feeling that something ought to be done; the victories at Toski and Tokar convinced most that it could be, for they had proved that well-disciplined troops, even Egyptian troops, could defeat the much-dreaded Dervishes.

Of course, men always go to war for the sake of high ideals, and suitably noble ones were easily found and eloquently expressed by young Winston Churchill in *The River War*:

> What enterprise that an enlightened community may attempt is more noble and more profitable than the reclamation from barbarism of fertile regions and large populations? To give peace to warring tribes, to administer justice where all was violence, to strike the chains off the slave, to draw the richness from the soil, to plant the earliest seeds of commerce and learning, to increase in whole peoples their capacities for pleasure and diminish their chances of pain – what more beautiful ideal or more valuable reward can inspire human effort? The act is virtuous, the exercise invigorating, and the result often extremely profitable.

Beyond the ideals and the mere desire to reconquer the Sudan, probably the most potent argument for transforming desire into action was the possession of the weapon to do so: the new, British-trained Egyptian army. Of course, somewhat different reasons were given for taking the first belligerent steps. On 1 March 1896 an Italian army was defeated by the Abyssinians at Adowa. The British supposed that the Dervishes were in league with the Abyssinians – a curious supposition as, far from being allied with the Abyssinians, the Dervishes had been fighting them. It was thought that the Dervishes, encouraged by the success of the Abyssinians, might attack the Italians at Kassala, endangering European prestige, then regarded as a valuable, if intangible, asset. Actually the Italian disaster at Adowa tended more to solidify British desire to reconquer the Sudan than to create any real alarm. Neverthe-less, it was decided that a British demonstration on the Egyptian–Sudanese border might deter the Mahdists from initiating any aggressive plans they might have, and on the night of 12 March 1896 the Sirdar of the Egyptian army received orders from Evelyn Baring to advance south of Wadi Halfa towards Dongola. Three weeks later, Baring wired Kitchener: 'There is at present no question of a general reconquest of the Sudan. Pray bear this carefully in mind.' But the first step, once taken, could not be withdrawn and the next steps followed each other with a stately cadence: the war of reconquest had begun.

The order to advance into the Sudan meant many things to many people, but to the almost unknown forty-six-year-old Sirdar with the improbable name of Horatio Herbert Kitchener it was a ticket to fame and honour. Born in Ireland, the eldest son of a Lieutenant-Colonel, he did not attend school until he entered the Royal Military Academy at Woolwich. In many ways he was like the man he was now to avenge: both Gordon and Kitchener were sons of army officers, both served in the Royal Engineers, both were extremely religious, both spent time in Palestine studying the archaeological remains of early Christianity, both taught themselves to speak Arabic, and both had served as provincial governors in the Sudan before becoming eventually governors-general. In other ways, however, the two men were quite different. Where Gordon had been exotic and quixotic, Kitchener was methodical and careful. Gordon was flamboyant and colourful; Kitchener was cold and dull.

As a young man, Kitchener was not considered promising. His instructors and fellow students at Woolwich characterized him as 'in no way remarkable', 'quite an ordinary youth' and 'rather slow in learning'. He was considered somewhat below the average standard of a Royal Engineer officer when he passed out of Wool-wich in December 1870. Shortly after this he went over to France to offer his services to the French army in their brief struggle with Prussia. This seems to have been a quixotic act contrary to his general character, until it is remembered – as it generally is not – that his father took him there. He caught a chill going up in a balloon with a French officer and fell ill. His father took him home.

His next attempt to see action came twelve years later and ended almost as badly. He was making maps in Cyprus when Arabi's rebellion broke out in Egypt. He asked to be transferred there, but the request was refused. He then took sick leave and went to Alexandria, arriving just in time to be evacuated by the British ships. He witnessed the naval bombardment, but was refused permission to accompany the party that went in to spike the guns of the shore batteries. He did have his first chance to do some intelligence work: with another officer, he went ashore in disguise and made some sketches at Zigazag. When he returned to Cyprus, however, he found himself in trouble for leaving the island without permission and over-extending his leave.

Late in the year 1882 Sir Evelyn Wood was trying to persuade British officers to join the Egyptian army and create it anew in their own image. Posts in the Egyptian army were not considered to be stepping stones for advancement in the regular establishment, but each officer was immediately given an Egyptian rank two steps above the rank he held in the British army and the pay was good. Sir Evelyn Wood found Lieutenant Kitchener and twenty-four other young officers who could not afford to live in good regiments in England. They were good men and service in the Egyptian army gave them an opportunity to prove it: twelve of them became generals.

The young officers, together with a set of excellent drill sergeants, set about the task of remaking the Egyptian army. Kitchener, then thirty-three years old, was given the post of second-in-command of the cavalry and the rank of bimbashi, or major. One of his fellow officers wrote in his diary: 'We all hated the sight of him, for two reasons – (1) because he was a "Sapper", and (2) because he designed a light blue uniform for his cavalry much finer than anything we had!' In general, his associates in Cairo thought him gauche, shy and unclubbable.

Kitchener did not spend much time on cavalry duties. He was soon given a two-month assignment surveying in the Sinai desert, from which he was recalled on the news of the disaster of the Hicks Pasha expedition. Then he was sent to the Sudan border to report on road conditions. From April to June 1884, he was in Aswan organizing a small force of Ababdeh irregulars. On board a Nile steamer near here he wrote to his friend Walter Besant in England on 3 May:

> I am now having an exciting time in Upper Egypt. I have got 1,000 Bedawin under my command and expect 1,000 more, all mounted on dromedaries. I hope to advance soon on Abu Hamed. I am just going back to Cairo to explain matters to the authorities. Excuse scrawl, as this d—d boat is very unsteady.

In June he moved to Korosko and then to Dongola, gathering

information, bribing tribes to be loyal and, from Dongola, sending messengers to Gordon in Khartoum. He was now working for Colonel Sir Charles Wilson, head of intelligence for the Egyptian army, and for the first time he was beginning to make something of a name for himself.

In his dealings with the Sudanese Arabs, Kitchener appears to have been somewhat naïve, giving them more credit for good intentions than they deserved, although he was close enough to the Mahdist movement to form a higher opinion of Dervish character than was generally held by those in Europe. To his friend Besant he wrote: 'Unless an English expedition comes, I do not think we shall be able to hold this frontier, as the rebels mean coming on, and are much more disciplined and fanatical than people give them credit for.'

In September 1884 Lord Wolseley arrived in Egypt to take charge of the relief expedition. In a letter to his wife Wolseley announced his intention of taking '1,000 or 1,500 men on camels into Khartoum, *capture* Gordon, and bring him back with me'. Lord Wolseley appears to have understood Gordon's character better than Kitchener and his immediate superiors, who were then offering £10,000 to the Kababish if they could rescue Gordon. When Lord Wolseley took command, Kitchener came under him and was appointed to the Intelligence Department with the additional duties of Deputy Assistant Adjutant-General and Quartermaster-General at Dongola.

As the relief expedition advanced slowly up the Nile, Kitchener was again engaged in intelligence work, principally in trying to maintain contact with Gordon. He worked hard, but Gordon was contemptuous of his efforts. In his journal (24 September 1884) Gordon wrote:

It is the most extraordinary thing, quite incomprehensible, that with only one exception . . . not one single messenger has entered this place on the proper initiative of outsiders. It has been invariably *my* messengers, who were sent out by me, from Khartoum, who did bring me any news. . . . Either these officers outside do not care to spend a sou in spies to give me information, or else they think it is a matter of supreme indifference whether I know what is going on or not. . . . There is a lot of 'I hope you are well', etc.; men like Kitchener . . . might be expected to have more brains than that. . . . I never saw such a feeble lot in my life! One has only to compare the telegrams &c, we send down, with the *rubbish* sent in by *our own messengers*. . . . Kitchener's note to Stewart on the same paper – it perfectly exasperates one. Kitchener asks

Stewart 'what he can do for him' – nothing of what has gone on with respect to the Sudan . . .

Meanwhile, Kitchener, who was doing his best to get messages to Gordon, complained that he heard little news from him. Although he did not please Gordon, he pleased his superiors in the field and in Cairo. But with the fall of Khartoum and the death of Gordon, the relief expedition was deemed superfluous and was abandoned. Kitchener went on leave to England for two months, studied Ottoman law in London and then was appointed to a commission in Zanzibar. When at Suez on his way home, he received a telegram appointing him 'Governor-General of the Eastern Sudan and the Red Sea Littoral'. The title was bigger than the territory. Osman Digna's Dervishes held all this land except for the squalid town of Suakin.

On his arrival at Suakin, Kitchener embarked upon a policy of making friends with the local tribes, regardless of their conduct in the past, and he had written over the gate to the town: 'Peace to those who enter and who leave this place.' In January 1888 he felt that he had become strong enough to attempt an attack on Osman Digna, then encamped at Handub, only fifteen miles from Suakin. Kitchener's force consisted of only about 450 men, most of whom were 'friendlies'. Permission to make the attack was given to Kitchener only if he did not use regular troops, but he took along some Blacks from the 10th Sudanese Battalion. It was the first time he had ever actually planned and directed a battle.

He set out from Suakin just before dawn on 17 January, and after a three-hour march he halted and directed his infantry and the friendlies to advance and attack the camp. He made a strange error for an engineer officer: he thought the enemy camp was near by when it was actually three miles from his halting place. After waiting for some time without receiving any news, he advanced himself with his cavalry at a fast trot. The Blacks and friendly tribesmen had apparently taken the Dervishes by surprise when they charged into the village, but Osman Digna quickly gathered his force together and attacked the attackers from the rear. Kitchener's friendlies bolted, leaving the regulars of the 10th Sudanese to extricate themselves as best they could. As usual, the Blacks fought bravely and were holding off an attack from two sides when Kitchener arrived on the scene.

Kitchener dismounted his men and poured several volleys into the Dervishes. With difficulty, he managed to disengage the Blacks and make an orderly retreat, but the Dervishes continued a murderous fire and Kitchener was wounded so severely in the lower jaw that his second-in-command had to take charge of the retreat to Suakin.

For this effort, Kitchener was rewarded by being made a brevet colonel. After leave in England to recover from his wound, he went back to Cairo. He commanded the cavalry at the battle of Toski and then spent a year as head of the Egyptian constabulary before becoming adjutant-general in the summer of 1891. In April of the following year, Sir Francis Grenfell resigned the Sirdarship of the Egyptian army. Kitchener was not the most popular choice to succeed him, but he had the most powerful supporter: Sir Evelyn Baring. As the man most responsible for the finances of the Egyptian government, Baring favoured a sirdar who knew how to save money as well as spend it. Kitchener was his man, for, as Lord Salisbury once said, he was the only soldier he ever knew who understood and practiced economy. Baring had his way and Kitchener was appointed Sirdar of the Egyptian army.

The army Kitchener commanded consisted of 18,000 men organized into fourteen battalions of infantry (eight of Egyptian fellahin and six of Sudanese Blacks), four squadrons of cavalry and three batteries of artillery; there was a small cadre of supply and transport troops, but no engineers – they would be too expensive. Nothing was wasted or thrown away until it fell apart. Old leather and badly worn uniforms were reworked in army workshops; cheaper cloth was used for clothing; men were put in the reserve two years ahead of their time. The parsimonious Kitchener was not popular with his officers, but Baring liked him.

The Egyptian army under Kitchener was a far different organization than it had been in the days before Arabi's rebellion. In spite of their ragged appearance, the soldiers were drilled and trained by honest and conscientious British officers and non-commissioned officers. They were also paid regularly and were not maltreated. Egyptian officers were expected to learn their trade and soldier in the British manner, although none held rank higher than kaimakam, or lieutenant-colonel. Unlike the Egyptian units, the Sudanese battalions were composed entirely of volunteers, many of whom were former bazingers or deserters from the Dervish army. They were Blacks from the forest and swamps of the southern Sudan – Shilluks, Dinkas and Gallas mostly. Each battalion contained 759 men divided into six companies, each with four British officers.

While training his battalions and husbanding his resources, Kitchener was also gathering all the information possible about the

Sudan. He was fortunate in having as the head of his intelligence department a most remarkable officer: Colonel Francis Reginald Wingate. He was born on 25 June 1861, the seventh son of a Scottish merchant who died a year later. He was educated at St James Collegiate School and at the Royal Military Academy at Woolwich and was gazetted as a second lieutenant in the Royal Artillery in July 1880. After service in India, where he learned Hindustani and was bitten by a panther, and in Aden, where he studied Arabic and Freemasonry, he was appointed to the new Egyptian army in 1883 and posted to the 4th Infantry Battalion. His first major assignment was to set up a hospital during the cholera epidemic. Three months later he had won the Order of Osmanieh (4th class) and was himself taken ill and invalided back to England.

Three months later he was back in Cairo as aide-de-camp for the Sirdar, General Sir Evelyn Wood. Word had just been received of the defeat of Hicks Pasha and the twenty-three-year-old Wingate found himself in an interesting and exciting position at headquarters, where he could see and be seen during the rapid development of events in the Sudan: the defeat of General Baker and the fighting around Suakin, Gordon cut off in Khartoum, the disaster to Colonel Stewart and his party, the organization of the relief expedition under Lord Wolseley, the tragic news of the fall of Khartoum, and the retreat of the desert column of the relief expedition. For his staff work, Wingate was given the Queen's Medal, the Khedive's Star, and the Order of Mejidieh (4th class). It had been an interesting and exciting two years, but when Sir Evelyn Wood resigned his Sirdarship and it became evident that the Sudan was not to be reconquered, Wingate also resigned from the Egyptian army and returned to the 'Regular Establishment', still as A.D.C. to General Wood but in England.

He was in England for less than a year, but it was time enough to pass the examination for his captaincy and to become engaged to Miss Kitty Rundle. Not having enough money to marry and live in England, he returned to the Egyptian army and was assigned as Assistant Military Secretary to the new Sirdar, Sir Francis Grenfell. One of his colleagues was Leslie Rundle, his fox-hunting future brother-in-law, who amused himself by teaching English to the natives with some success. Sir Francis, while on a tour of inspection, was once surprised to find himself greeted on entering a village by cries of 'Tally-ho!' and on leaving with 'Gone away!'

In 1887 Wingate was doing recruiting and some intelligence work; two years later he was devoting himself exclusively to

intelligence. His work involved collecting not only military information on the strength and disposition of the Khalifa's forces but also
political and economic information on conditions in the Sudan. In
addition to this, but related to it, was the task of attempting to effect
the escape of the European prisoners of the Khalifa. Wingate
finally collected so much information about the Sudan that he
decided to write a book about it, and *Mahdiism and the Egyptian
Sudan* was published in October 1891. The original manuscript
contained a good deal of political comment regarding the British
government's relations with Egypt and the Sudan, but on Baring's
advice most of this was eliminated. However, he could not resist
saying: 'That a new and better Soudan will be raised over the ashes
of Gordon, and all those brave officers and men who have perished
in the loyal performance of their duty, is the present hope of every
well-wisher for the prosperity of Egypt.'

Two months after the publication of this book, Father Ohrwalder
and the two nuns made their dramatic escape with the help of
Wingate. An account of Father Ohrwalder's life in captivity and his
flight from Omdurman was published by Wingate shortly after.
The book created something of a sensation and undoubtedly
stimulated interest in the reconquest of the Sudan. In 1892, when
Kitchener became Sirdar, Wingate's network of spies and in-
formers was given an official status with the creation of a formal
Intelligence Department, with Wingate as its chief. In 1894 he
helped Father Rossignoli to escape. Then, in 1895, he was primarily
responsible for the escape of Rudolf Slatin. This was rightly considered a great coup, and Wingate was rewarded with the Iron
Crown of Austria, bestowed on him by the Emperor Franz Josef,
while Queen Victoria made him a Companion of the Bath, a rare
honour for a thirty-four-year-old major of artillery. The news of
Slatin's escape and Wingate's translation of Slatin's account of his
experiences, published under the romantic title of *Fire and Sword
in the Sudan*, maintained British interest in the Sudan and height-
ened a desire to subdue the Khalifa and reconquer the country.
Thus Wingate became not only the chief source for gathering news
about the Sudan, but also the chief propagandist for its reconquest.

The Sirdar found Wingate a very useful staff officer. Although it
has never been admitted, there is a suspicion that Wingate's spies
were not all in the Sudan; some, perhaps, were in the household
and government of Abbas Hilmi II, the new twenty-year-old
Khedive of Egypt, who succeeded his father, Tewfik, in 1892. A
private document came into the Sirdar's hands just before the first

inspection by the Khedive of the Egyptian army; in it, the Khedive expressed his intention of discrediting the British officers who were running his army. The document seemed so incredible that at first it was believed to be a forgery, but the young Khedive's conduct followed the plan.

As the Khedive and his retinue, with Kitchener and his staff, proceeded from north to south up the Nile in the khedival yacht inspecting the troops, the Khedive's comments on the efforts of the British officers became more and more acid. At the final review at Wadi Halfa he was particularly cutting. Every British-led battalion was censured and every Egyptian-led battalion was praised. Finally the Khedive turned to his Sirdar and said, 'To tell you the truth, Kitchener Pasha, I consider it disgraceful for Egypt to be served by such an army'.

Kitchener testily replied: 'As Your Highness is evidently displeased with the efforts of myself and the British officers in training your army, nothing remains for me but to place my own resignation and that of all the British officers in your hands.'

The Khedive, realizing that he had gone too far, tried to be conciliatory, but Kitchener was adamant. Wingate drew up a report on the Khedive's inspection tour that was quickly dispatched to Baring, who passed it on to London. Baring supported Kitchener and the British government supported Baring. The result was that the Khedive was forced to issue an official statement to the effect that he was completely satisfied with the work of Kitchener and the British officers and the British government expressed its support of the Sirdar by creating him K.C.M.G.

If it was not clear before, there could be no doubt after this incident that Britain ruled Egypt and Baring was her viceroy; Baring controlled the Egyptian army and Kitchener was his commander-in-chief. Although the Khedive was 'brought to his bearings', he never forgave Kitchener nor Britain, and when World War I began he defected (according to British views) by maintaining his allegiance to the Sultan of Turkey, whose khedive he was supposed to be. There was never the enthusiasm in Egypt for the reconquest of the Sudan that prevailed in England. Although the war against the Khalifa was fought primarily with Egyptian and Sudanese troops of the Egyptian army, *en principe* for Egypt, it was Britain's war, not Egypt's.

It was only the morning after Kitchener had received his marching orders that anyone thought to tell the Egyptian government what their army was going to do; Baring quickly convened the Egyptian cabinet for it to give its approval and vote a decree. The following day the reserves were called up and the next day, after a review by the Khedive of the troops of the Cairo garrison, Kitchener informed the Khedive that the first troops would move south that night. He did not bother to tell him that already, that very day, troops of the Egyptian army had started their march south from Wadi Halfa across that invisible line between Mahdism and the rest of the world. The 11th and 12th Sudanese battalions seized Akasha, about forty miles south of Wadi Halfa, without a fight on 22 March 1896. This first advance into the Sudan was led by an exceptionally capable officer named Hector Archibald Mac-Donald, who shortly rose to command a brigade of Sudanese.

MacDonald was the youngest of five sons of a Scottish crofter. At eighteen he enlisted as a common soldier in the Gordon Highlanders and served nearly ten years in the ranks, rising to the rank of colour-sergeant. He so distinguished himself by repeated acts of bravery and exceptional leadership during the Afghan wars that Lord Roberts gave him a commission. After active service in Natal, where he again displayed his exceptional courage at the battle of Majuba, he came to Egypt to accept an appointment in Valentine Baker Pasha's constabulary in 1883. He was aptly called 'Fighting Mac' for he always seemed to be on hand when there was fighting to be done.

In the next few weeks following MacDonald's advance, Akasha was made into a strong camp while the bulk of the Egyptian army was carried by Nile steamer and railroad to the frontier. Some cavalry skirmishes took place south of Wadi Halfa in May, but it was June before the next major advance was made. By this time Kitchener had assembled about 9,000 men within striking distance of Firket, the closest Dervish stronghold, only ten miles from Akasha. The army was composed of an infantry division of five Egyptian and five Sudanese battalions, seven squadrons of Egyptian cavalry, a camel corps of eight companies, three batteries of artillery and one battery of four Maxim guns. On 7 June this force attacked and captured Firket. Although the bulk of the fighting was done by the Sudanese under Major MacDonald, the Egyptian troops behaved very well; the British officers who had trained them had done their job well. Two days after the battle of Firket, Mac-Donald's brigade occupied Suarda, about twenty-five miles further south, and this became the most advanced post of the conquering army.

Supply was the biggest problem. Most of the river transport on the lower Nile was handled by the enterprising firm of Thomas Cook and Son, but above the first cataract land transport was needed. There had once been a railroad running south from Wadi Halfa to Firket. The road-bed was now in ruins and the sleepers gone, but most of the rails were still around – some had been used by the Dervishes at Firket to construct a gallows. This railroad was now repaired and extended as far as Kosheh, a little village of mud huts ten miles south of Firket. It was used to bring up supplies, reinforcements and even gunboats in sections to be assembled on the banks of the Nile and floated above the second cataract.

The next Dervish position was at Kerma, at the third cataract, 127 miles by river and eighty-six miles by land from Kosheh. The force at the Sirdar's disposal at this time consisted of an additional two battalions of Egyptian troops, a battalion of British troops (the North Staffordshire Regiment) and a flotilla of five gunboats and three armed steamers, a total of 15,000 men. Nearly the entire Egyptian army – thirteen out of the sixteen battalions – was at the front. The advance on Kerma began on 23 August, again led by MacDonald's brigade consisting of the 11th, 12th and 13th Sudanese battalions. The army reached Kerma on 19 September and found that the Dervishes had moved over to the opposite side of the Nile. The action was primarily between the gunboats and the entrenched Dervishes. After a two-hour duel at long range, the Dervishes retreated. The army marched on, and Dongola, thirty miles further on, was taken without difficulty, ending the 'Campaign of 1896'. As such matters are reckoned in war, the cost had been small: forty-three men were killed and 139 wounded in action, while another 130 men had died of cholera and other diseases.

A year passed before there was any further action. The delay was caused by the difficult question of supply. As Winston Churchill said in his colourful prose: 'Victory is the beautiful, bright-coloured flower. Transport is the stem without which it could never have blossomed.' Although the Nile had been the main road for supplies during the Campaign of 1896, the repair of the railroad to Kosheh had been an invaluable asset. To build and run the railroad, a railroad battalion was formed: a motley crew of Egyptians, Blacks and captured Dervishes, many of whom had never before seen a railroad track or a train. There were only eight locomotives and these were so decrepit that at times only three of them were operational. Nevertheless, a handful of young engineer officers managed to keep the railroad running. The Sirdar now considered extending it across the desert to Abu Hamed. After seeking the advice of experienced British railway engineers and of other military men who had built and operated railroads – all of whom agreed that it was impossible – the Sirdar decided to build it. He turned over the entire project to a young Royal Engineers officer of French Canadian ancestry named Lieutenant Edouard Girouard.

Fifteen new engines and 200 cars were purchased in England, 1,500 additional men were recruited for the railway battalion, and workshops were constructed at Wadi Halfa. Eventually, forty engines of ten different makes and of various ages were put into service. The task of extending the railroad into the desert was a formidable one. Added to the difficulties was the fact that nearly every man had to be trained for his job: almost every engineer, switchman and clerk had to be taught his trade; even men who could not read and write were made at least semi-literate in classes under palm trees.

The desert into which the railroad moved was believed to be waterless. Two successful wells were eventually sunk, but in the main the water for the engines and for the men had to be carried out to them on the trains, in addition to food and supplies. The further away they moved from Wadi Halfa, the more difficult it was to supply the graders and track layers. It also became more dangerous, so that in addition to the men working on the railroad itself, soldiers had to be provided to guard the workers and the laid track. Yet, off into the desert the line of track moved, headed for Abu Hamed – which had not yet been captured.

Abu Hamed is 210 miles in a straight line from Wadi Halfa. The railroad had been pushed out 130 miles when it paused to wait for the capture of Abu Hamed. To secure this important position, a flying column was organized under the command of Major-General Archibald Hunter, a brave, experienced, and very popular officer – it was Hunter, not Kitchener, who was the most respected man in the Egyptian army. The flying column consisted of MacDonald's brigade, now composed of the 9th, 10th and 11th Sudanese battalions, plus a troop of cavalry and a battery of field artillery – about 3,600 men. Starting from a little village near Merawi on 29 June, the column had to cross 146 miles of desert. The troops suffered from the heat and from struggling through the soft, deep sand. Three men died on the march. When they reached Abu Hamed early on the morning of 7 July they were nearly exhausted, but Hunter pushed them forward to the attack, for he had heard that Dervish reinforcements were on their way. Although the place was stoutly defended, MacDonald's Sudanese battalions carried the town. Two British officers and twenty-one men were killed and sixty-one were wounded, but now the railroad could continue.

Kitchener had intended to bring his army up to Abu Hamed and carefully build up his supplies for the next big jump to Berber, but an unexpected development caused him to move faster than he had planned. Towards the end of August, a group of forty Ababdeh tribesmen loyal to the government were sent out to reconnoitre in the direction of Berber. They went on, meeting no resistance, until they actually entered Berber; finding that the Dervishes had retreated, they occupied the town and sent word of its capture back to Abu Hamed. Two days later, when the Sirdar heard of it, he had to decide whether to recall the audacious tribesmen and be safe, or move in troops to occupy Berber. He decided to be daring and send his troops ahead; Hunter was dispatched with the 9th Sudanese in four gunboats to Berber, which he occupied on 10 September.

The occupation of Berber had the desired effect on the tribes in the Red Sea littoral and soon the route between Suakin and Berber was opened again by a camel corps patrol and a group of war correspondents, who boasted that they were the first Europeans to use the route in thirteen years.

In October a flotilla of gunboats steamed up the Nile and spent two days destroying the forts at El Metemma. By the end of the year, the army had reached the junction of the Atbara river with the Nile and built a strong camp there. Spies reported that the great Dervish army at Omdurman was about to advance, so Kitchener requested and obtained a brigade of British troops. The brigade consisted of one battalion each of the Cameron Highlanders, the Royal Warwickshire Regiment, the Lincoln Regiment and the Seaforth Highlanders, all under the command of General William Gatacre. The essential railroad pushed further and further south, past Berber and El Metemma to the camp on the Atbara.

In March 1898 a Dervish force of about 16,000 men under the command of Mahmud Wad Ahmed and Osman Digna tried to go around the east end of the Atbara camp and attack Berber. Kitchener countered this by moving the bulk of his army, 14,000 men, up the Atbara to intercept them. For a week both sides sat in their zaribas, seven miles apart, each waiting for the other to attack. Finally, the Sirdar decided to make the first aggressive move. On the morning of 8 April, Highlanders, Egyptians and the Sudanese battalions marched through the sand and heat to the skirl of bagpipes towards the zariba of the Dervishes 'in all the majesty of war', as Churchill said, 'an avalanche of men, stern, unflinching, utterly irresistible'. The Dervish army was defeated, Mahmud Wad Ahmed was captured and the wily Osman Digna fled. On the Anglo-Egyptian side, eighty-two were killed, mostly Blacks from the brave Sudanese battalions; the Dervishes lost about 3,000 men.

Thanks to the railroad, Kitchener had now transported his army to less than 200 miles from the Khalifa's capital. All knew that the next battle would be the biggest one, and decisive. Kitchener put his troops in summer camp and prepared for the struggle ahead. More men and equipment were ordered: another brigade of British infantry, a battery of heavy howitzers, a battery of Maxim machine guns, three new screw steamers and the 21st Lancers. By the middle of August 1898, Kitchener had assembled a force of 17,600 Egyptian and Sudanese troops and 8,200 British troops; counting the weapons on the steamers, there were eighty cannon and forty-four Maxims; there was a flotilla of ten steamers, and on land 3,524 camels, 2,469 horses, 892 mules and 229 donkeys. With this force the Sirdar began his march on Omdurman, where an estimated 50,000 Dervishes were waiting to destroy him.

On 1 September 1898 Kitchener's army was within a few miles of Omdurman. Early that morning the 21st Lancers were sent out to find the enemy, even if they had to go to the gates of Omdurman itself. In command of one of the troops was a young subaltern named Lieutenant Winston Churchill (or Winston Spencer-Churchill as he then called himself). As the squadrons rounded the shoulder of the Kerreri Hills, he saw in the distance a pointed dome rising above the horizon: the tomb of the Mahdi in Omdurman.

17

The Battle of Omdurman

All through the summer of 1898 when Kitchener was bringing up his army, weapons and supplies, the Khalifa was gathering in the tribesmen for his last great effort. Proclamations were sent in all directions summoning the faithful to the jihad, and 50,000 fighting men answered his call. He built seventeen forts to command the river approaches and tried to devise mines and string chains across the river to stop the gunboats. He possessed sixty-three guns, but most of these were in the forts along the river and only five were taken with him on 31 August when he led his army out of Omdurman, north towards the Kerreri Hills to meet the invaders.

The Khalifa arranged his army in battle formation on the plains of Kerreri. In the centre were 12,000 Black riflemen (the jihadia) and 13,000 spearmen with a strong detachment of mulazemin thrown out in front. The Khalifa himself was in the centre of the line with 2,000 of his bodyguard. Behind him was the rearguard of 13,000 spearmen under the command of Yakub. The right wing was commanded by the Khalifa Sherif and was composed of 2,000 Donagla tribesmen plus 1,700 Hadendowa under the command of the wily Osman Digna on the extreme right nearest Omdurman. Khalifa Ali Wad Helu was on the left with 5,000 warriors extending into the desert.

What they lacked in discipline, they made up in fighting experience and in fanatic loyalty to the Mahdist cause. Unfortunately for the Khalifa, he did not have modern weapons. He had fewer rifles than his enemy and those he had were old with faulty ammunition; his cannon were also obsolete and his powder was not the best. But most unfortunate of all was the lack of good generals. The great Abu Anga, brave Wad Nejumi and the stout Zeki Tamal were all dead. The Khalifa himself had little experience in commanding armies, nor had the other khalifas; most of the rifles were under the command of the Khalifa's son Osman, who had no experience at all.

When the 21st Lancers joined the Egyptian cavalry on a ridge they looked down with astonishment on this mighty army, its huge banners flying, drums beating and spears flashing. It must have been a striking spectacle. Those who saw it were the last ever to see such a sight, for never since has such a huge barbaric army been displayed in all its wild splendour. Most impressive of all to young Lieutenant Winston Churchill was the deep murmur of the tens of thousands of voices that came rolling up towards them.

Except for a bit of cavalry skirmishing, the first major action was the fight between the gunboats and the Khalifa's forts along the river. It was an uneven contest. The mud forts with their outdated cannon were no match for the well-armed steamers: the shells from the gunboats blew the mud walls to pieces and the Maxim guns mounted on the decks swept the trenches. The steamers then made their way upstream and bombarded the city itself, killing a number of women and children.

The howitzers were landed and they, too, began to shell the city. In all, 410 high explosive shells were thrown into the mud walls of Omdurman. The dome of the Mahdi's tomb was their aiming point, and they made several direct hits on it. Although the Anglo-Egyptian force did not know it, none of this shelling of Omdurman had the slightest effect on the battle, for, excepting a small percentage of deserters, every man able to hold a spear was with the Khalifa Abdullahi on the plains of Kerreri.

The Sirdar's army expected the Dervishes to attack at once and stood ready to meet it. On 1 September Lieutenant Churchill had lunch with Colonel Wingate and asked him if there was really going to be a battle. 'Certainly, rather,' he replied.

'When? Tomorrow?'

'No. Here, now, in an hour or two,' said Wingate.

But he was wrong. By mid-afternoon it was apparent that there would be no fight that day. As there was some fear of a night attack, the Anglo-Egyptian army did not make a regular camp but slept on the ground in battle positions.

The following morning, 2 September 1898, bugles sounded throughout the camp by the river at four-thirty. There was not the slightest doubt in anyone's mind that this was the day of the great battle. The Anglo-Egyptian forces were arranged in a half-circle with their backs to the river around the little village of Egaiga. The gunboats protected their flanks and the Egyptian cavalry and camel corps occupied the high ground in the Kerreri Hills to the north-west. Shortly after dawn, the invaders saw before them the host of the Khalifa, stretched out for five miles on the open plain. To turn his superiority of numbers to advantage and minimize his defects in equipment, the Khalifa ought to have attacked by night. This was urged on him, but he rejected the suggestion. Perhaps he feared that his warriors would not be brave enough unless under his watching eyes. So it was bright morning as his men charged across an open plain into the mouths of modern rifles, machine guns and artillery.

Six thousand Dervishes poured over the ridge of Surgham and bore down on the left flank of the Anglo-Egyptian army. Then Osman with 8,000 men attacked the centre. Ernest Bennet, an Oxford don who was serving as war correspondent for the *Westminster Gazette*, described this first Dervish charge: 'In the clear morning air the pageant was truly magnificent, a splendid panorama of some forty thousand [*sic*] barbarians moving forward all undismayed to do battle with the largest army which Great Britain had placed in the field for forty years.' The Anglo-Egyptian artillery opened fire at 2,800 yards; the rifles of the infantry at 1,200 yards. The Dervishes were shot down by the score. And when a Dervish was hit by a British bullet he fell, for the British troops were using dumdums: hollowed out, soft-nosed bullets that spread when they hit, creating horrible wounds; called 'man-stoppers', these cruel missiles have since been outlawed by international agreement.

Some of the Maxims ran out of water to cool their barrels; they were filled from the canteens of the Cameron Highlanders. Few Dervishes came as close as 500 yards from the front rank of the Anglo-Egyptian infantry, and none came within striking distance. A number found cover in a small depression, but the artillery searched them out and hounded them with shrapnel. This first attack, begun at 6.45 in the morning, was finished by 8.00 a.m. G. W. Steevens, one of the sixteen war correspondents who were there, said, 'It was not a battle, but an execution.' Even after the enemy had retreated, the excited soldiers kept firing at the scattered writhing wounded stretched out before them. Kitchener rode across the front of the 2nd Egyptian Brigade calling 'Cease fire! Cease fire! Cease fire!' and he was heard to exclaim, 'Oh, what a dreadful waste of ammunition!'

Meanwhile, Colonel Broadwood with the Egyptian cavalry and the Camel Corps in the Kerreri Hills received an order to retreat behind the main lines. But Broadwood knew that his force was in a position to divert the Dervish cavalry, which was now coming towards him. He decided to disobey the order to retreat and instead to lure the enemy cavalry away from the main battle. He therefore moved north, drawing the Dervish horsemen after him.

His camel corps, however, found the rocky ground difficult and the Dervish cavalry was gaining on him. He was fortunate enough to reach the river and come under the protection of the guns of a steamer just in time. Thus protected, his camel corps was able to get back to the main lines, while he rode on with the cavalry and drew the Dervish horsemen another three miles north.

On the other end of the Anglo-Egyptian lines, the 21st Lancers were riding south, around the edge of Jebel Surgham, between the ridge and the river. They found the east end of the ridge unoccupied, but they could see groups of Dervishes making their way towards Omdurman. In a khor, or dry watercourse, directly in front of them was a Dervish force of about 700 men. The 21st Lancers prepared to attack, but before they could, and unknown to them, the defenders of the khor, who stood between the lancers and Omdurman, were reinforced by nearly 2,000 Dervishes detached from the main body by the Khalifa as soon as he learned of the advance of the cavalry. The reinforcements had moved up unseen by another khor.

Colonel R. H. Martin, in command of the lancers, had explicit orders only to reconnoitre and harass the enemy, but he could not resist the temptation, seemingly so strong in cavalry officers, to charge. He ordered his bugler to sound 'Right wheel into line!' and the regiment, 320 officers and troopers, trotted off towards an enemy of unknown strength. The ground in front of them appeared smooth, but they came unexpectedly upon a small khor filled with Dervishes who sprang up to attack the attackers. Each trooper crouched over his lance and dug his heels into his horse in an effort to gain enough momentum to carry him through the dense mob before him. In the brief hand-to-hand fighting that followed, the smart line of lancers was broken by the Dervishes, who pressed the muzzles of their rifles against the flanks of the horses or swung their heavy swords at the cavalrymen. They did not panic under the impact of the charge as undisciplined savages were supposed to do. These men were familiar with this type of warfare and their conduct in the fight was superb.

Lieutenant R. F. Molyneux fell from his horse in the khor amid the Dervishes. Unhurt, he leaped to his feet, pistol in hand. While he fired at one man, his right hand was slashed by another. He jumped out of the khor and ran in the direction taken by his regiment, pursued by four or five of the enemy. Seeing a trooper riding across his path, he called to him for help. With a cheerful, 'All right, sir!' the trooper wheeled and charged Molyneux's pursuers, waving his sword. He was wounded in his chest by a Dervish spear, but his action allowed the young lieutenant to escape. The trooper himself fought his way clear.

Lieutenant Churchill's troop was riding on the right wing of the charging lancers and hit only the edge of the massed Dervishes. Churchill saw two jibba-clad men standing before him in front of the khor. He rode between them. They shot at the future prime minister, but missed him; the trooper immediately behind him was killed. Then his horse dropped into the sandy khor and he found the enemy all around him, though not as thick as on his left, where some troopers were stopped in their tracks, unable to force their way through the densely packed Dervishes. Churchill rode straight through and up the opposite bank of the khor, his horse again trotting on the hard, crisp desert soil. In the excitement, he had no sense of danger or disaster but trotted about, shooting at stray Arabs, until he realized that he was alone and ought to be with his troop. He spurred his horse into a gallop and soon found his men reforming and facing about. A Dervish jumped up among them, and there was some confusion as several troopers jabbed at him with their lances. Churchill shot him.

Finding that he had fired the entire clip from his Mauser pistol, he reloaded and while he did so he asked one of his sergeants if he had enjoyed himself. The man replied honestly: 'Well, I don't exactly say I enjoyed it, sir, but I think I'll get more used to it next time.'

Most of the lancers managed to fight their way through and passed on about 200 yards beyond the khor before pausing to reform and turn back to face the enemy again. This was a separate battle, a private war. Without Maxims or artillery, it was primarily lance and sword against spear and sword. But the romance of the cavalry charge no longer seemed so alluring. In the two minutes it had taken the regiment to pass through the Dervishes in the khor five officers and sixty-five men had been killed or wounded, and out of 320 horses, 119 were dead or wounded. The 21st Lancers had lost a quarter of its strength in less than ten minutes time. The pocket watch of Lieutenant R. Grenfell, who was killed in the charge, was pierced by a Dervish spear; it had stopped at 8.40 a.m.

Colonel Martin, who had bravely and stupidly ridden through the Dervish-filled khor without drawing sword or pistol, finally came to his senses, and instead of charging back into the khor, sounded the order to gather his men together and led them around to the flank of the enemy where he could enfilade them with carbine fire. The Dervishes were routed and, twenty minutes after starting their reckless charge, the remains of the 21st Lancers were taking breakfast in the khor. Near by were about thirty or forty dead Dervishes and the hacked and mutilated bodies of more than twenty lancers. Three Victoria Crosses were awarded for bravery in this action, including one for the trooper who saved the life of Lieutenant Molyneux; Colonel Martin was commended for 'excellent services performed' in Kitchener's official report of the battle. Not for the first time, a blunder by British cavalry was made an example of military glory.

The charge of the 21st Lancers was a minor action; the main event was still taking place behind them on the Kerreri plains. Kitchener, apparently thinking the battle won and anxious to occupy Omdurman before the Dervishes could fall back upon it, ordered his infantry to re-form in marching order and swing south. The brigades of British and Egyptian infantry began their cumbersome movements. Although G. Gorringe, a young lieutenant at the time (he later became a lieutenant-general), said afterwards that Kitchener knew what he was doing, it seems highly unlikely that he was aware of the fact that he was marching his army across the front of the main body of the Dervish army, leaving a strong, undefeated enemy on his flank. The two British brigades, which had been on the left of the arc around Egaiga, were the furthest south and they moved to occupy the east end of the Jebel Surgham ridge. The Egyptian brigades started to follow, but MacDonald's brigade of the 9th, 10th and 11th Sudanese battalions and the 2nd Egyptians, in all about 3,000 men, found Dervishes firing at them from the front (west) and they turned to meet them.

It soon became apparent to the experienced MacDonald that he was being attacked in great force, as indeed he was: this was the Dervish main force under Yakub, nearly 20,000 men. MacDonald's brigade was at this time about a mile from the nearest brigade on his left. He received an order to retreat, but he is reported to have said, 'I'll no do it. I'll see them damned first. We maun just fight.' And fight he did.

Although the Dervishes pressed home their attack with great bravery, they were cut down by superior fire-power, steadily and capably directed. The attack of Yakub's warriors was supposed to have been co-ordinated with those of the troops under the Khalifa's son Osman coming from the Kerreri Hills. Unfortunately for the Khalifa and his cause, MacDonald's men were able to blunt the charge of Yakub's men before those of Osman came on the scene.

MacDonald coolly and skilfully swung his troops by half-battalions in an arc to meet the attack on his flank, his Blacks executing each movement with parade-ground precision. Bennet Burleigh, who saw MacDonald's performance from a distance, said: 'Had the brilliant, the splendid deed of arms wrought by MacDonald been done under the eyes of the sovereign, or in some other armies, he would have been created a general on the spot.' But it was performed under the eyes of Kitchener. Had the attack on Mac-Donald been well co-ordinated, it appears most likely that he would have been overwhelmed by superior numbers and the Dervishes would then have been able to fall on the flank of the Anglo-Egyptian army while they were in motion. Even so, had Mac-Donald's Sudanese battalions not stood firm and the ammunition not held out, or had MacDonald not handled his battalions so skilfully, the results might have been tragic indeed for Great Britain. How close the Anglo-Egyptian army came to disaster can be judged by the fact that when the battle was over and the ammunition counted in MacDonald's battalions it was found to average only two rounds per man.

While MacDonald's brigade fought, Kitchener flew about the field shouting orders in an effort to bring his troops about to face the new menace. He worked neither through his staff nor through the chain of command, but even gave orders to battalion commanders, tossing brigades and battalions about the field. The army swung round clumsily and the other brigades moved ponderously up to MacDonald's support. But MacDonald had handled the situation without the aid of the rest of the army. He had saved the day. His accomplishment was later used as an example of the proper handling of troops in battles of this sort at the Staff College.

The bravery of the Dervishes astonished the British. War correspondent G. W. Steevens wrote:

> Our men were perfect, but the Dervishes were superb – beyond perfection. It was their largest, best and bravest army that ever fought against us for Mahdism, and it died worthily of the huge empire Mahdism won and kept so long. Their riflemen, mangled by every kind of death and torment that man can devise, clung round the black flag and the green, emptying their poor, rotten, home-made cartridges dauntlessly. Their spearmen charged death at every minute hopelessly. . . . A dusky line got up and stormed forward: it bent, broke up, fell apart, and disappeared. Before the smoke had cleared, another line was bending and storming forward in the same track.

The bravery of the Dervishes was indeed magnificent – and useless.

When Kitchener had all his troops in line facing west again, they drove the remnants of the great Dervish army into the desert. By noon the battle was over. So was the campaign. The Khalifa had fled. Yakub was dead. So were 10,800 other Dervishes. On the Anglo-Egyptian side, only forty-eight men were killed (of whom nearly half were 21st Lancers) and 382 wounded. Kitchener's generalship had not been very good, but it had not needed to be. The Khalifa had proved a worse general and victory had gone to the best drilled battalions with the best weapons; cool efficiency had triumphed over hot religious fanaticism.

The battle now definitely won, Kitchener, guided by Slatin, proceeded with his army to Omdurman. With a Sudanese battalion and four guns, he approached the town, entering it through the main gate, and followed the straight road that ran to the Khalifa's house and the Mahdi's tomb. Steevens, one of the first newspaper correspondents to enter the town described its appearance in unflattering terms:

Omdurman was just a planless confusion of blind walls and gaping holes, shiftless stupidity, concentrated filth and beastliness. . . . Oppression, stagnation, degradation were stamped deep on every yard of miserable Omdurman. . . . Everything was wretched. And foul. They dropped their dung where they listed; they drew their water from beside green sewers; they had filled the streets and khors with dead donkeys; they left their brothers to rot and puff up hideously in the sun. The stench of the place was in your nostrils, in your throat, in your stomach.

Of the area around the Khalifa's house Steevens wrote:

Tiny round straw tukls, mats propped up a foot from the earth with crooked sticks, dome-topped mud kennels that a man could just crowd into. . . . On every side, of every type, they jumbled and jostled and crushed; and they sweated and stank with people.

There were still a few small pockets of resistance in the town and the gunboats continued to lob shells into the centre of town until one nearly killed Kitchener. Herbert Howard, a former officer who had served in Matabeleland and was here acting as correspondent for *The Times* and the *New York Herald*, had charged with the 21st Lancers that morning and had been actively covering the fighting all day. Now he had entered Omdurman with the Sirdar. 'This is the best day of my life,' he said to a companion. Then he went into the courtyard of the Khalifa's house to take a photograph and there, ten minutes later, he was killed by one of the last shells thrown into Omdurman. Today, a plaque marks the spot where he fell.

When the battle began, many of the inhabitants of the town had sought sanctuary in and around the Mahdi's tomb. More than a hundred were killed there by the high explosive shells from the gunboats and howitzers. When Kitchener arrived on the scene, he found the area of the tomb covered with blood and corpses. After posting guards over the main buildings, he made his way to the prison, where he released Neufeld and other political prisoners. That night most of the Anglo-Egyptian army slept within the walls of the captured capital.

Rudolf Slatin, who had accompanied the Anglo-Egyptian army as Wingate's assistant, was disappointed that the Khalifa had escaped. Now he rode with the Egyptian cavalry and the camel corps to pursue him. They went about thirty miles south, and the gunboats steamed on a further sixty miles, but the Khalifa, with a few thousand faithful followers, made good his escape, going first south and then west into Kordofan, to his own country which he had left so many years ago to become the leading follower of the Mahdi.

Two days after the battle of Omdurman, Kitchener ordered a memorial service to be held for Gordon at the ruins of his former palace in Khartoum. Representative detachments of officers and men from the British and Egyptian battalions were ferried across the river and amid the weeds and broken walls the band played the Dead March from *Saul* and Gordon's favourite hymn, 'Abide with me'; the Union Jack and the Crescent and Star were again hoisted over the walls; the troops gave three cheers for the Queen. Kitchener was much affected by the ceremony he had created. He burst into tears, and had to ask another officer to dismiss the parade.

On 5 September Kitchener wrote to Queen Victoria, reporting on how he had carefully loaded the wounded on barges to be taken down the Nile and describing the memorial service for Gordon. The Queen was much moved by his letter. Of Gordon she wrote in her journal: 'Surely, he is avenged!'

Most of the British soldiers probably knew about Gordon, and the task of avenging him was doubtless a suitable enough explanation as to why they had come to this remote land to shoot Sudanese with their dumdum bullets and machine guns, but few were aware of the larger political issues involved. Possibly more than one Tommy did not know the difference between the Khedive and the Khalifa. Two days after the battle of Omdurman some prisoners were brought in and it was rumoured that the Khalifa had been captured. As the soldiers in camp ran out to see, one British soldier was heard to call out, "urry up, Bill, come along. They've cotched the bloody Khee-dive!'

Kitchener now had other work before him, which shifted his attention from Dervishes to Frenchmen. A month before the battle of Omdurman he had received sealed orders which he was instructed to open after the capture of Khartoum. The day after the battle he opened them and found himself ordered to take personal command of an expedition south in order to end French pretentions on the upper Nile.

Just as many Britons dreamed of British territory extending from the Cape to Cairo, so many Frenchmen dreamed of French colonies stretching east and west across Africa from coast to coast. These two ambitions were bound to clash and the result was what has gone down in history as the Fashoda Incident. In an effort to grab the southern Sudan for herself, France had, two years earlier, dispatched an expedition under the command of Major Jean Baptiste Marchand to central Africa. After enduring terrible hardships and overcoming fearful obstacles, Marchand reached the Bahr el Ghazal and on 10 July 1898 raised the tricolour at Fashoda, a village on the White Nile sixty miles north of the junction of the White Nile and the Sobat river. The expedition had beaten off one Dervish attack and was awaiting another when Kitchener, accompanied by Wingate and Slatin, arrived on the scene with a battalion of Sudanese infantry and a battery of artillery.

Sir Geoffrey Archer has said: 'I suppose that in the history of the "Scramble for Africa" no episode was so serious or so menacing.' Fortunately, both Marchand and Kitchener, representatives of the bold imperialist policies of their respective governments, realized the seriousness of the situation. Marchand claimed the entire Bahr el Ghazal and said he would have to fight if Kitchener tried to make him lower his flag. Kitchener, who had donned the uniform of an Egyptian general, complete with tarboush, said he was ordered to raise the Egyptian flag and to protest against the raising of the French flag. After a friendly talk over lunch on a gunboat, they agreed that there was nothing to prevent both flags from being raised and referring the entire matter to Paris and London. Kitchener landed his Sudanese battalion, raised the Egyptian flag and steamed away, leaving the two garrisons to stare uneasily at each other and to try to keep out of each other's way until the affair could be decided by the politicians in Europe.

Kitchener's duties in the Sudan were now ended for the time being and he returned to England to receive the honours and hero's welcome that awaited him. W. T. Stead wrote in his *Review of Reviews* that 'not Wellington returning from the Battle of Waterloo could have been accorded more triumphal honours'. He was given the freedom of a number of cities, Cambridge gave him an honorary LL.D., parliament voted him £30,000, and he was elevated to the peerage, becoming Lord Kitchener of Khartoum. There were, however, some dissenters and fault-finders among those who spoke of Kitchener's glory, for, as Baring once said, the Sirdar had 'not the faculty of making friends'. Some criticism of his conduct after the battle was expressed even before he arrived back in England. There was, for example, the question of the Mahdi's skull.

Four days after the capture of Omdurman Kitchener decided that if Mahdism was to be erased the Mahdi's tomb should be destroyed, and the task was given to Gordon's nephew, Major W. S. Gordon of the Royal Engineers. Assisting Major Gordon were Sergeant J. P. Maynard of the Royal Marines and six Dervish prisoners. It was rather naïvely believed that the Dervish prisoners would spread the word and confirm the desecration of the tomb. It would appear, however, that they wisely kept silent about their part in such an affair. The walls of the tomb were about six feet thick and it was found difficult to destroy them. Only after trying three times to dynamite it was the tomb sufficiently demolished. The remains of the Mahdi were dug up and his bones were thrown in the river. His skull was saved, however, and James Watson, one of Kitchener's A.D.C.s, presented it to his chief, who did not quite know what to do with it. It was suggested that he should mount it in silver and make an inkstand out of it, but Kitchener thought perhaps he would send it to the College of Surgeons in London.

When news of this affair reached England there was a considerable reaction. The desecration of the Mahdi's tomb was condemned by the press, by the army and by members of parliament. The Queen thought it savoured too much of the Middle Ages. Baring advised Kitchener to get rid of the skull as decently as he could, and he had it buried somewhere near Wadi Halfa on his way home.

There was also criticism of Kitchener's handling of the Dervish wounded. Ernest Bennet said: 'It is certain that in many cases wounded Dervishes, unarmed and helpless, were butchered from sheer wantonness and lust of bloodshed. The whole formed a hideous picture, not easy to forget.' On the other hand, Captain

Adolf von Tiedemann of the Prussian General Staff, who accompanied the expedition as an observer, defended the practice: 'As regards the killing of the wounded on the battlefield, that was a necessary measure which was as regrettable as it was indispensable.' The justification was that even the badly wounded Dervishes continued to fight the 'Turk' as long as they had any strength left in their arms.

Still another criticism was that even days after the battle, Kitchener found it impossible to care for the vast number of wounded Sudanese, estimated at 16,000. Some lay on the battlefield in the sun until they died; many dragged themselves to the Nile to relieve their thirst and died along the river banks; thousands made their way to Omdurman. Kitchener's medical department was not equipped to cope with such numbers. Hassan Zecki, the Egyptian medical officer who had married Frank Lupton's widow, set up a makeshift hospital in the centre of town and the army surgeons did what they could, but unknown hundreds must have died of untreated wounds.

Kitchener's critics were in the minority, however, for he had achieved that for which all generals strive: victory. Lord Salisbury, speaking in the House of Lords on 8 June 1899, said admiringly that his victory had been achieved 'with absolute accuracy, like the answer to a scientific calculation'. In a sense, this was true. In spite of the dramatic battle of Omdurman with its romantic charge of the 21st Lancers and the exotic setting of the entire campaign, victory had really been made possible by Lieutenant Girouard's prosaic railroad, which pushed into the desert and brought the soldiers with their arms, ammunition, food and all the cumbersome material of European warfare into the heart of the Sudan. Evelyn Baring, Kitchener's chief, summed up the Sirdar and his war quite succinctly:

I have no wish to disparage the strategical and tactical ability which was displayed in the conduct of the campaign. It is, however, a fact that no occasion arose for the display of any great skill in these branches of military science. When once the British and Egyptian troops were brought face to face with the enemy, there could – unless the conditions under which they fought were altogether extraordinary – be little doubt of the result. The speedy and successful issue of the campaign depended, in fact, almost entirely upon the methods adopted for overcoming the very exceptional difficulties connected with the supply and transport of the troops. The main quality required to meet these difficulties was a good head for business. By one of those fortunate accidents which have been frequent in the history of Anglo-Saxon enterprise, a man was found equal to the occasion. Lord Kitchener of Khartoum won his well-deserved peerage because he was an excellent man of business; he looked carefully after every important detail, and enforced economy.

Kitchener boasted that he had conquered a million square miles and two million inhabitants at a cost of £2 6s. 6d. per square mile and £1 3s. 3d. per head. In spite of all criticism, he was very pleased with himself. The reconquest of the Sudan was acclaimed, at least in Britain, as an achievement of British arms, but although all of the senior officers and, in the final stages, about one-third of the force engaged were British, the bulk of the soldiers were Egyptians. Yet, there were more men killed in the six Sudanese battalions than in all of the rest of the force combined. By chance or design, it was the brave, dependable Blacks who bore the brunt of the fighting.

Although the Khalifa Abdullahi and the slippery Osman Digna had escaped and there were still great numbers of tribesmen loyal to the Dervish cause scattered throughout the vast Sudan, Mahdist rule was ended. It had lasted for more than thirteen years and the great human upheaval of the Mahdiya has left its mark to this day.

18

Epilogue

The Sudan had been reconquered. The question remained: What was to be done with it? There was also the question of who would, or had a right to, do anything with it. In short, who was to rule the Sudan? The British felt that it was they who had conquered the Sudan. They were obviously the masters of the political situation, but they had, after all, only conquered in the name of Egypt; Kitchener, the conquerer, although British, had commanded the victorious troops as Sirdar of the Egyptian army. And it was Egypt that paid two-thirds of the cost of the reconquest.

Legally, Egypt seemed to have the most right to the Sudan. It had belonged to her before the Mahdi's rebellion and it had been reconquered in her name. Yet it seemed intolerable to British minds that so much money and effort should have been spent and British blood spilt simply to return the land to Egyptian misrule. Turkey, too, had her claims, but these could easily be ignored, as could any thoughts of allowing the Sudanese to rule themselves, which was not even considered. For Britain to convert the Sudan into a colony would have been to flout world opinion and insult Egypt. After all, the French had been told to get out of Fashoda on the grounds that it was Egyptian territory. Nevertheless, Britain now demanded control boldly and baldly on the basis of 'right of conquest'.

Yet Britain managed to usurp Egypt's rights without seeming to do so. This trick was achieved by that very clever man, Evelyn Baring. It was Baring who conceived the idea of creating what he himself once described as a 'hybrid form of government, hitherto unknown to international jurisprudence'. It was called a condominium. H. C. Jackson, who spent twenty-four years in the Sudan Civil Service, called the condominium, 'A curious experiment in administration which only the British could have devised, and which none but they would have had the slightest hope of being able to carry through.' It is probably true.

Baring's scheme took the form of an agreement between Britain and Egypt whereby the two countries would jointly rule the Sudan – at least there was the appearance of joint rule: both the Egyptian and British flags would fly in the Sudan, the Governor-General would be appointed by khedival decree on the recommendation of the British government and the country would be called the Anglo-Egyptian Sudan. The laws of the land were to be simply the proclamations of the Governor-General. Nothing was ever said concerning the nationality of the Sudan's ruler, but as long as there were Governors-General they were British. There was to be no interference from other European powers: no foreign consuls could reside in the Sudan without the consent of the British government.

The geographical boundaries of the country were kept as vague as its political status. The northern frontier was fixed at the 22nd parallel, but the southern and western frontiers were left undefined. The actual boundaries of the country were not completely fixed until 1926. Baring was once asked what would happen to Europeans who were married or buried in the Sudan. He blandly replied that 'any European who considered it essential that his marriage or burial should be attested by a Consular representative of his country, would do well to remain in the territory lying north of the 22nd parallel of latitude'.

The Convention that created the condominium was signed on 19 January 1899. When the faint murmured objections of the Egyptians died away and the European powers recovered from their shock of amazement, this strange political creature of Britain was accepted by the world and the British set out with their usual perseverance and efficiency to tame and control it. The first Governor-General was Lord Kitchener of Khartoum.

It was doubtless Baring's intention to rule the Sudan through his own hand-picked man, for Kitchener, as Governor-General, was to be ruled by Baring. The entire campaign for the reconquest of the Sudan had been classed as a 'Foreign Office war' and Kitchener's immediate superior had been Baring throughout. It was only necessary that this chain of command be continued. But now that Kitchener was a peer and a hero, he was no longer content to be Baring's agent. He wanted to rule the Sudan without Baring's guidance or control. He appeared to feel that it was *his* country. He had conquered it; now he would rule it. And Kitchener's rule was a stern one.

The capital of the Sudan was again to be Khartoum, and Lord Kitchener wanted it to be a suitable one. First of all, the palace was to be rebuilt. While still in England, before his return, he wrote to

Wingate instructing him to 'loot like blazes. I want any quantity of marble stairs, marble pavings, iron railings, looking-glasses and fittings; doors, windows, furniture of all sorts.' Five thousand men were set to work rebuilding the town: new streets were laid out, 7,000 trees were planted and government buildings were built. He called on Britain for money to build a school and more than £100,000 was subscribed by the British people to build Gordon College (now the University of Khartoum).

Kitchener never consulted Baring; he refused to take his advice; and he even refused to account for any of the money he spent. He ruled the Sudan as though it was a regiment and he resented any criticism, however mild, from Baring. At first, Baring was reluctant to criticize his own man to his superior, Lord Salisbury, but he was obviously disturbed. In January 1899 he wrote that Kitchener's methods were 'a little more masterful and peremptory than is usual in dealing with civil affairs'. When Baring warned Kitchener that land speculators were sending money to the Sudan for Greeks to make purchases, and that Kitchener should take care as they had no legal means for acquiring titles to the land, Kitchener simply snapped back that he could not expel every Greek who bought and sold anything. In April, Baring confessed to Salisbury: 'He is, I fear, terribly bureaucratic.'

Although Kitchener had broken the back of the Mahdiya, the Khalifa and some of his leading emirs, including Osman Digna, and several thousand faithful ansar were still free. Expeditions were sent out from time to time to apprehend them; one was led by Kitchener personally. When famine once again broke out in the Sudan, Kitchener told Baring that this suited his policy admirably as it would deprive the Khalifa and his followers of local support.

In November 1899 spies reported that the Khalifa was making for the Nile about 180 miles south of Khartoum. Wingate was dispatched with a column consisting of 250 camel corps soldiers, the 9th and 13th Sudanese battalions, some light artillery and about 1,000 irregulars. The column left Omdurman on 19 November. Four days later it surprised a large Dervish raiding party and killed 400. Scouts brought in word that the Khalifa himself was camped only a few miles away at a place called Umm Diwaykarat, near present-day Kosti. Wingate made a forced march by night and dawn found him in position on high ground overlooking the Khalifa's camp.

Wingate's force consisted of 3,700 well-armed men; the Khalifa had about 5,000 badly-armed Dervishes. As soon as it was light, the Dervishes attacked. Wingate's men cut them down with rifle and machine-gun fire and then advanced for the kill. It was over in half an hour. The Khalifa Abdullahi along with Khalifa Ali Wad Helu and most of their principal emirs were found dead, the Khalifa lying on his sheepskin rug facing Mecca. Only the wily Osman Digna, that expert in escaping from lost battles, managed to escape again, the last of the great Dervish generals.

It was more than a year later before Osman Digna was finally betrayed. He was found, not with an army but alone with a servant in a cave near Tokar. A British captain, together with the Suakin commandant of police, Mohammed Bey Ahmed, led a small force of Sudanese policemen to surprise him. Although the entrance to the cave was surrounded, he nearly escaped again. He was waiting for his servant to prepare his breakfast when the police appeared. As soon as he saw them, he jumped up and ran back into the cave and out another entrance. He was soon spotted, however, and the police set out after him as he scrambled up a steep hillside. One of the policemen paused to call out to him to stop: 'Your time for running away has now passed!'

'I do not run away,' Osman Digna shouted back, 'but now, as ever, and in accordance with my master's commands, I turn my face away from the unbelievers.'

He was caught nevertheless. He refused to give his name and as none of his captors had ever seen Osman Digna before, they were at first not sure that they had actually captured him. Then Mohammed Bey remembered past battles from which the wily old warrior had escaped but not unscathed. They looked over their captive and found the known scars of old battles: the sword wound in the middle of his head, the bullet wound on his left wrist and the mark of a bayonet on his back. There was no doubt. This was Osman Digna, and they carried him back to Suakin in triumph.

When he was brought to Cairo, Wilfrid Scawen Blunt quoted a newspaper account and recorded his indignation in his diary:

Osman Digna has been captured at last and brought in chains to Cairo. 'A large crowd pressed forward eager to see the dark, long face, brilliant eyes, large mouth, and long grey beard, of a frightened and dignified old man who sat with chains round his sore ankles and swollen, bare feet.' I quote 'Our own correspondent.' This is how the British Empire makes its 'Roman holiday'!

Osman Digna was about sixty-four years old when he was cap-tired on 19 January 1900, but he lived on for another twenty-six years. He was transferred about to several prisons, but as the years went by his prison life became easier and easier. Towards the end, he had a pleasant house at Wadi Halfa and lived the life of a religious recluse, more like an honoured pensioner than a prisoner: the government supplied him with food and a military guard that served more to keep the curious from bothering him than to prevent his escape. In 1924 he was given his complete freedom and made the pilgrimage to Mecca. He died in 1926.

One month after the battle of Umm Diwaykarat and the death of the Khalifa, Kitchener left the Sudan to become second-in-command of the army fighting the Boers in South Africa. Although a hero to countless English schoolboys, he was never popular with his associates. He added to his honours, and his prestige became enormous, but he never mellowed. He organized the British forces to fight the guerrillas in South Africa and then spent seven years as commander-in-chief in India. He was made a field-marshal in 1909, and when World War I began he became Secretary of State for War. This cold, harsh man died in the cold, harsh waters of the North Sea when H.M.S. *Hampshire* struck a mine on the evening of 6 June 1916. He had been on his way to visit the Tsar and the Russian front.

Kitchener was succeeded as Governor-General of the Sudan by Sir Reginald Wingate, the man who had organized and operated so effectively the Military Intelligence Department of the Egyptian army. Wingate ruled wisely and well for seventeen years. They were difficult years, for in spite of the defeat of the Dervish forces and the death of the Khalifa, the Sudan was far from subdued. Wingate faced his first crisis only one month after Kitchener left: a crisis caused not by the Mahdists but by the stern discipline of Kitchener. The 14th Sudanese battalion, led by its Egyptian officers, mutinied in Omdurman.

Wingate was in Cairo when the mutiny occurred, but he hurriedly returned to the Sudan. Refusing the offer of British troops, he listened to the complaints of the Egyptian officers, who were merely dissatisfied with Kitchener's economies, particularly in regard to their field allowances, and made an investigation into the reason why the brave and faithful Blacks had turned on their British masters. It had been rumoured in the officers' messes that the Sudanese battalions would be sent to fight in South Africa. The disgruntled Egyptian officers had made good use of the rumour, telling their ignorant soldiers they were to be sent out of the Sudan to be slaughtered by the Boers. Wingate won back the soldiers by promising them an amnesty and the seven officer ringleaders were drummed out of the service and returned to Cairo under escort.

There were no more mutinies, but there were continual revolts, most of which were of a messianic nature. In 1900 there was trouble among the ansar who expected the coming of the Prophet Jesus. The leaders of this movement were tried by a religious council and sent into exile as heretics. In 1903 a new mahdi sprang up in eastern Kordofan. He was captured and hanged. In 1904 a Prophet Jesus appeared at Sinja on the Blue Nile. Four years later a former Dervish emir raised a fair-sized revolt that had to be crushed by a military expedition. In 1912 there was still another Prophet Jesus in Kordofan who had to be put down. There were also numerous revolts created from other than religious motives. In 1913 there were no less than nine expeditions sent out to stop intertribal wars, halt the arms traffic and uphold the authority of the government. There were a number of military operations over the years in the Nuba Hills to bring the refractory Nuba tribes under the control of the government. The fighting went on intermittently for years. In the first thirty years of the condominium more than 170 military expeditions were sent out.

But perhaps the most serious disturbance to the condominium was created in 1924 by the Egyptians, who wanted complete control again. Zagloul Pasha, one-time Egyptian Prime Minister, declared in a speech that 'The Sudan belongs to Egypt, and we must have it. We will dispose of it as any landlord disposes of his own property.' The Egyptians formed secret societies and created a barrage of anti-British propaganda. Sir Lee Stack, then Governor-General of the Sudan, was shot and killed in the streets of Cairo. The British retaliated by throwing all Egyptian officials out of the country and Egyptian battalions in Khartoum were surrounded by British troops and unceremoniously shipped north. The British remained masters of the Sudan.

After the fall of Omdurman, Darfur became an autonomous state under Sultan Ali Dinar, a descendant of the ancient ruling family. He had an army of slaves whom he equipped with rifles and, although supposedly subordinate to the condominium, he refused to allow officials of the Sudanese government to enter his realm. It was not until 1916, in the middle of World War I, that Darfur was reconquered by a force of between two and three thousand men supported by three aeroplanes. One of the pilots, John Slessor (who was wounded in the leg by an old Remington), later became Marshal of the Royal Air Force.

Darfur remained turbulent, and there was an uprising in

southern Darfur in 1921, when a religious fanatic assured his followers that bullets from government rifles would turn to water when directed against them.

There has never been any common ground for understanding between the Arab of the north and the Black of the south, and hatred has grown through the years. In August of 1955, there was an army revolt in the southern Sudan. The Blacks killed their Arab officers and the revolt spread to the police, game wardens and tribesmen. Northern Sudanese officials were killed or fled and soon all of Equatoria and the Bahr el Ghazal were in revolt and only Malakal remained in government hands in the Upper Nile province. Being without proper leaders, the revolt failed, but to this day there are sporadic uprisings and much discontent among the restless Blacks.

Wingate's greatest service to the Sudan was not in suppressing revolts but in building up a sound government administration. All the senior officials were British; the minor officials were Egyptians who, after about fifteen years, were gradually replaced by Sudanese. Thanks to Wingate, the Sudanese Civil Service (later renamed the Sudan Political Service) developed a reputation for being the best in the British Empire. There was no nonsense about competitive examinations. University graduates were examined by a board in London, and sometimes Wingate himself sat with the examiners. Character was what they were looking for, but as character is difficult to detect in untried young men, the board generally settled for athletes. It used to be said that the Sudan was a country of Blacks and Browns administered by Blues. Considering the climate in the Sudan, its diseases, and its lack of civilized comforts, this was probably not a bad method. In any case, many of the young men thrived, few were dishonest, and most worked hard to make the Sudan civilized.

An interesting aspect of the condominium was that slavery was not abolished. One of the great moral reasons the British had given themselves for interfering in the Sudan had been the need to abolish the slave trade, but when the Sudan was finally conquered they decided that Sudanese life had been disrupted enough by the Mahdiya without attempting to abolish a custom so deeply rooted. Besides, emancipation of the slaves would have been dangerous. The government therefore embarked on a plan of gradual abolition, which began by giving freedom to all children of Arab fathers and slave mothers. Slavery was not completely abolished in the Sudan until 1940.

Wingate's chief assistant in ruling the Sudan was the man he had helped rescue and who became his close friend: Rudolf Slatin. When Wingate was appointed Governor-General, Slatin was made Inspector-General, a title created specially for him. After his escape, he had gone home to Vienna to see his family, then to England, where he was welcomed as a hero and had an interview with Queen Victoria. On 19 August 1895 the Queen wrote in her journal:

> Slatin Pasha, who had escaped from his long captivity with the Mahdi, three months ago, and Major Wingate, who had been instrumental in his escape, arrived. After dinner I decorated Major Wingate with the C.B. Had a great deal of conversation with him and Slatin Pasha, which was most interesting. The latter is a charming, modest little man, whom no one could think had gone through such vissicitudes, for he looks so well; but there are lines in his face which betoken mental suffering. . . . What has been a great sorrow to him, is that his mother died before hearing of his escape.

When Slatin's account of his captivity, translated and edited by Wingate, was published in 1896, it was dedicated to the Queen, 'who has ever shown deep solicitude for and gracious sympathy with the European prisoners in the Sudan'. Wilfred Scawen Blunt, the ardent arabist and anti-imperialist, read the account and wrote in his diary:

> Slatin is a mean wretch to have published it, and the Mahdi made a mistake in not cutting his head off at once when he surrendered, and sending him straight to paradise. His professions of loyalty to the Khedive and to our gracious Queen are fulsome, and those of disloyalty to the people whose religion he adopted to save his miserable life, disgusting.

After Blunt met Slatin he described him as 'a commonplace little German, quite unworthy of ever having served the Mahdi'.

Blunt's feelings were the exception. For most, Slatin was a hero and a wonder. Baring called him 'a gallant and very capable officer'. Wingate asked if some medal could not be given to him, even though he was not a British subject. Lord Wolseley approved, and in October Slatin was decorated with the Civil C.B. The Khedive had made him a Pasha and other honours followed through the years: He was knighted in 1898 (K.C.M.G.); in 1906, he was made a Baron of the Austrian Empire; and in 1907, he became an honorary Major-General in the British army. From plain Rudolf Slatin he had added to his name the titles of three countries;

he became Major-General Baron Rudolf von Slatin Pasha, K.C.M.G., C.B. He received so many medals, in fact, that according to Sir Geoffrey Archer, Governor-General of the Sudan in 1925–6, King Edward VII is alleged to have said, 'The next time you come here, Slatin, I shall have to pin the decoration on your back-side.'

Slatin, with his intimate knowledge of the language, customs and people of the Sudan, was an invaluable aide to Wingate, but he did not always understand the outlook of the young English athletes from Oxford and Cambridge who came to the Sudan to assist them. He took them in tow and tried to tell them about the country and to teach them their duties in it, but he had little knowledge of sports and once introduced a young man who had won his post in the Sudan Civil Service by his ability to pull an oar as the man who had rowed the fastest in the Oxford boat.

After a short training period in Khartoum, the young men of the civil service were sent out to rule in the remote provinces. Among the pieces of advice given them by Slatin was that they should always try cases and judge disputes with a stick between their teeth. If they did not, he warned, the Sudanese would tell by watching their lips if they were believed.

In the spring of 1914, Slatin returned to Austria on leave. On 21 July of that year, at the age of fifty-seven, he married Alice von Ramberg, a baroness. She was forty-one. Two months later, World War I broke out and Slatin found himself torn between his loyalty to Austria and his loyalty to Britain. When he received his C.B. from Queen Victoria, she had written in her journal that he was a man who was 'ready at any time to shed his blood in my service'. But he was not prepared to fight his own countrymen and he resigned his post. Although offered a military post in the Austrian army, he could not bring himself to fight against the British either. He joined the Austrian Red Cross and was responsible for aid to prisoners of war: a fit post for one who had himself been a prisoner for so long.

The outbreak of war between Britain and Germany found Slatin in possession of a set of cipher books. Wingate received a letter from him through the British Consul in Zürich in which he swore that he had sealed the books and locked them in his safe at home. It did not matter. Slatin did not know it but the ciphers were obsolete as far as the Foreign Office was concerned and had simply been allowed for use in the Sudan. Still, it was a decent gesture.

On 12 November 1916 Alice von Slatin gave birth to a baby girl,

Anne Marie. In June 1918 Wingate's youngest son was killed in action and Slatin wrote a letter of condolence. In the same year, Slatin received one of his last honours when he was elected Honorary Chief Scout, and to this day there is a scout group in a Vienna suburb that bears his name. The war, with its conflict of loyalties, the unaccustomed cold climate of Europe and age combined to erode his vigour and put an end to his career, and he did not return to his post in the Sudan. In 1921 his wife died and he was left a sixty-four-year-old widower with a five-year-old child to raise on a meagre pension.

In the winter of 1927 Slatin returned to the Sudan as a guest of the Sudanese government. There is a story, perhaps apocryphal, that he made a visit to the Khalifa's house as an ordinary tourist. The official guide pointed to the spot where, he said, Slatin used to stand when he was a mulazem at the gate. The visitor spoke up to correct the guide. There was a brief argument which the visitor ended with, 'But I am Slatin.' It was the sort of theatrical gesture Slatin loved. Perhaps it really happened, for his name appears in the visitors' book for 24 November 1927.

Throughout his life, Slatin remained a close personal friend of Wingate, and to Wingate's children he was always 'Uncle Rowdy'; after the war it was Wingate who was instrumental in having his medals restored to him. Almost every summer Slatin went to England with his daughter. Once he was staying with Sir James Currie, a former Director of Education in the Sudan, when a party of Sudanese came to visit. That evening, when the Sudanese slipped outside to say their evening prayers, Slatin quietly went out and prayed with them.

Slatin Pasha died near Vienna on 4 October 1932 at the age of seventy-five and was buried in the cemetery at Ober St Veit, where he was born and where there is still a street named after him: Slatingasse. There was once a street in Omdurman named Shari Salatin, but this has now been changed to Shari Wad al Nejumi.

In 1917 Wingate became British High Commissioner to Egypt. He did not last long. He quarrelled with Lord Curzon and, although not yet fifty-eight years old, he was retired in 1918 on a pension of only £1,300 per annum. He had always been an active Freemason – he had been Grand Master of Egypt and the Sudan – and he now became Grand Warden of England. He lived on to a ripe old age, outliving his wife and all his old friends, and died in London in 1953 at the age of ninety-one.

Even Wingate did not outlive one of the subalterns who had

taken part in the charge of the 21st Lancers at Omdurman and who wrote, if not the best, at least the most dramatic account of the campaign for the reconquest of the Sudan. When the war was over, Lieutenant Winston Churchill paused in Cairo on his way home to collect material for his book, *The River War*. He later returned with a draft, which he showed to Baring, asking for his comments. Baring, now Lord Cromer, slashed up the manuscript of the young officer ruthlessly, but he sent him an encouraging letter, saying: 'One of the very few things which still interest me in life is to see young men get on.' This young man did.

Evelyn Baring, who became Baron Cromer in 1892, a viscount five years later and the Earl of Cromer in 1901, retired in 1907 to devote himself to classical studies and to writing about the Egypt he had known and whose affairs he had directed. In 1916 he presided over the Dardanelles Commission; he died following one of its meetings on 29 January 1917.

Besides Slatin, one other provincial governor escaped from the Sudan – although 'escape' is perhaps not the right word. Edouard Schnitzer, better known by his alias of Emin, was governor of Equatoria, southernmost province of the Sudan. He was never actually in the hands of the Dervishes, but the Khalifa could have had Emin and his province any time he wished. Equatoria was isolated on three sides by savage tribes and unknown country and in the north by the Dervishes. Emin managed to get several letters out to Europe and when it became known that one of 'Gordon's lieutenants' was still alive there was a great cry for something to be done to rescue him.

The man selected to go to the relief of Emin Pasha in his remote province was Henry Morton Stanley, the man who had found Livingstone, who had discovered the course of the Congo river and who had founded the Congo Free State. An expedition was launched via the Congo and eventually, after near incredible hardships that resulted in the loss of 512 men out of 702, Stanley reached Emin. But Emin was not unhappy in his lost province. True, he had had difficulties in controlling his soldiers, but he was really more interested in flora and fauna than in political administration, and Equatoria was a marvellous place in which to study botany and zoology. He was not sure he wanted to leave. Nevertheless, Stanley carried him out.

On 4 December 1889 they reached Bagamoyo, on the shore of the Indian Ocean in Tanganyika. That night the German officers stationed there gave them a banquet. Emin perhaps had too much to drink; he wandered out on a balcony, fell off and cracked open his skull. When he recovered, he turned his back on civilization and went back into the interior of Africa. A few months later, Arab slavers slit his throat.

The colourful and tragic career of Valentine Baker Pasha ended in Egypt when he died of angina pectoris on 17 November 1887, two and a half years after his disastrous defeat at El Teb.

After the reconquest, Father Ohrwalder, like Slatin, returned to the Sudan. H. C. Jackson, one of the athletic young men from Oxford who made his career in the Sudan during the condominium, described meeting Father Ohrwalder in Omdurman. He was 'tall, sad and placid' with lines of suffering etched on his face. He was still handsome with a fine beard, now turning white. While Slatin delighted in describing his experiences as a captive of the Mahdi and Khalifa, Father Ohrwalder was reluctant to speak of this part of his life. When he met him, Jackson assumed that his air of sadness was the result of his sufferings during the Mahdiya. It was not. Father Ohrwalder was forbidden to say mass because of some unknown sin he had committed some time during his years under the Khalifa. He died in the Sudan in 1912.

Sister Elisabetta Venturini, one of the nuns who escaped with Father Ohrwalder, also returned to the Sudan after the reconquest. She served in missions at Khartoum, Omdurman and Atbara before, advanced in age, she died in Khartoum in 1937. Of Sister Chincharini, the other nun who escaped with Ohrwalder, nothing is known. Sister Grigolini, who married the Greek, bore her husband two sons and remained for many years in the Sudan, assisting the Roman Catholic missionaries in re-establishing themselves. She eventually returned to Italy and died in Verona in 1931.

After his escape in 1894, Father Paolo Rossignoli remained for several years in Egypt until called to Rome where he was made a canon. He died in 1919 at the age of sixty-seven.

Father Bonomi, who had been Father Ohrwalder's superior at the Dilling mission station and who escaped from El Obeid shortly after his capture, became a chaplain in the Italian navy in 1888. He was later in Eritrea as chaplain of an Italian military hospital in Asmara, where he died in 1927.

Of all the prisoners of the Khalifa, the stubbornest, stoutest and one of the bravest was Charles Neufeld, yet the reception he received from the civilized world he had longed for and dreamed of was disgraceful. He had thought that perhaps he would be honoured in some way for the information he had been able to send out to the advancing Anglo-Egyptian army. He had certainly risked his neck to do so. Instead of honours, he found his reputation ruined by slander. What little was known of his life in the Sudan was interpreted in the worst possible manner in Egypt and in Europe. At first he was reported dead, then it was said that he was alive but that as he had taken a Negro wife he did not want to leave the Sudan. Worst of all was the charge that he had made gunpowder for the Khalifa. No one reported his staunchness or his sufferings, his defiance of the Khalifa or his faithfulness to his religion. Both the Austrian and the Anglo-Egyptian governments tried to help Slatin; government and Church worked to secure Father Ohrwalder's escape; but no such powerful allies made any vigorous attempt to assist Neufeld.

When his friend Mankarious wrote to the German Consul in Alexandria about his business affairs, he was told in a letter dated 12 March 1889, that

> Mr Neufeld is no longer a German subject nor *protégé*, because during his stay in Egypt Mr Neufeld has never claimed the protection of Germany, where he was born. Thus he has lost his nationality. This is according to what we learn from the parties interested in Germany. Upon this, this Consulate can in no way look into the affairs of Mr Neufeld nor protect his rights.

Neufeld's English wife was apparently able to do nothing. In September 1888 it was reported to her that he had attempted to escape, but had been recaptured and executed. On 10 March 1890 the Intelligence Department of the Egyptian army informed her that her husband was alive, but mixed a considerable amount of wormwood with the sweet news:

> Mohammed Effendi Rafai, late Sub-lieutenant, 4th Battalion, 5th Regiment, who left Khartoum three months ago, states he knew Neufeld very well, and saw him at Omdurman only a few days before he left. Neufeld had been under surveillance until about five months prior to this, but was now free. His release was owing to one of the Emirs representing to Abdullah Khalifa the great service Neufeld had been in enabling arms and ammunition to be taken from the Kabbabish at the time Neufeld was captured. He now was employed as one of the Khalifa's mulazimeen, and received a small salary; the Khalifa gave him two wives, and treats him well. Neufeld has very little to complain of except want of funds, which renders living difficult, good food being very dear. He is frequently staying with Ibrahim Bey Fauzi, who has opened a small coffee shop. It is untrue that the

Khalifa ever threatened Neufeld's life; he was only threatened with imprisonment unless he turned Mussulman. Does not think it possible that Neufeld can receive any letters, etc., from outside. Neufeld does not occupy himself in business in any way. Has never heard Neufeld express any wish to go away, but does not think he would be able to do so even if he wished it, as everyone knows him.

Neufeld returned to find a story circulating that he had actually been fighting with the Dervishes and had galloped from the battle-field to the prison just in time to be found in chains by Kitchener. In Egypt he found his business ruined. Claims had been filed against him by people he had never heard of, and some of these had even been paid from his assets. At the German consulate he was informed that his citizenship had lapsed because he had been away from his homeland for too long. When he had first been captured, an English newspaper had raised a fund by subscription to try to rescue him; he was now asked to repay the money subscribed. The War Office demanded repayment for £20 that had been given him just before he left for the Sudan. When offered money by a magazine to write his experiences, he was at first told that as he was technically a prisoner of war he was not at liberty to enter into agreements of this sort.

Neufeld was hurt most by the false stories about him that appeared in print. One such story, that appeared in a number of London and provincial newspapers read:

Twice had every preparation been made. The relays of camels to take the exile across the desert were ready. Nothing remained but for Neufeld to pluck up courage and quit Omdurman. Each time he backed out at the last moment. At length he confessed the truth, namely, that he did not care to come away. He had married a black wife. His friends in Germany were dead or had forgotten him. He would stay where he was.

This article was also reproduced in German newspapers and Neufeld found himself socially ostracized by both Englishmen and Germans.

Ernest Bennett wrote a hastily written book, *The Downfall of the Dervishes*, in which he spoke of Neufeld:

The prisoners were released from their fetters on the night of the battle. . . . I saw Charles Neufeld, and he looked very little the worse for his stay at Omdurman. A great deal of English sympathy has been wasted on this person. The harrowing stories we have read in the papers of the poor captive languishing in hopeless captivity are sheer nonsense. On two separate occasions Neufeld had the chance of escape, for a clever and courageous Arab named Oman had been dispatched by the Intelligence Department to rescue the captive. Neufeld, however, refused to leave Omdurman unless he was accompanied by a black woman with whom he lived. This was obviously out of the question. So Father Rossignoli was rescued instead, and brought safely to Assouan.

On his way down the Nile to Cairo, Neufeld learned that Hasseena was in Berber. He stopped off there to look for her, and finally found her living in a brothel. He brought her out and made arrangements for her to lead a respectable life again, but shortly after arriving in Cairo, he received a telegram telling him that she had returned to her old way of life. In the international colony in Cairo, however, it was said that he had brought her back with him and that his English wife, after her years of anxiety, was confronted with her husband's 'black wife'. What Neufeld did about Umm es Shole is not known. He did not bring her to Cairo with him, but he had married her. True, it was an Islamic, not a Christian, marriage, but their relationship was more than platonic: Neufeld had a daughter by Umm es Shole called Bakhita.

In a Cairo hotel one day a newspaper friend was showing Neufeld some newspaper articles about him when the Cairo correspondent for Reuters came up and said, 'Hello, how is that book of Neufeld's getting on?'

Neufeld's friend asked if he knew Neufeld. 'Know him!' exclaimed the Reuters man, 'No. Nor do I want to know him, considering the number of English soldiers he has sent to eternity with his gunpowder. I would not even look at the fellow's face.'

'This is Neufeld,' said his friend.

The man from Reuters fled.

Fortunately, Neufeld had some friends left and there were some who did not believe all the stories told against him. Duke Johann Albrecht, the Regent of Mecklenburg, sent him money through the German consulate, but when Neufeld called for it the money was refused him because of the claims against him. It was five months before he was able to obtain it.

Hard pressed for money, he went to see a German friend of his, Hewlett Moxley of the Imperial Ottoman Bank. When he had stated his case, Moxley turned over the papers Neufeld had given him and made some passing remarks to the effect that Neufeld's 'guarantees were not of the highest order' and that his 'credentials were not of a very satisfactory nature'. Neufeld's heart sank, but Moxley was a friend indeed. He gave Neufeld £150 for his immediate needs and opened a credit for a further £250. It was the first helping hand he had seen in Cairo.

The strain of returning to freedom and civilization, the anxiety caused by his reception and the worry caused by his financial plight, proved too much for him. The Khalifa could not break this strong stubborn man, but his fellow Europeans did. Neufeld fell ill. When he heard that Sir George Newnes, the British magazine publisher wanted to see him, he had to climb from his sick bed to talk with him. He had been told that Sir George was an 'ogre', but instead he found in him a sympathetic friend. Sir George encouraged him to write his book and collect every scrap of evidence he could to substantiate his story. Neufeld was much heartened by this interview. Later, Newnes introduced him to Chapman and Hall, who published his book in 1899, and Newnes himself ran the story in *The Wide World*, a weekly.

Very little is known of the subsequent history of this remarkable man. He established a tourist agency at Aswan, but when World War I broke out, he was repatriated to Germany. In 1916 he was the Arabic interpreter for a German military mission that sought to enter Abyssinia and the Sudan by travelling through the Hejaz. It got as far as Yenbo, but shortly after was turned back by hostile Arabs who captured part of their baggage. Colonel Baron Othmar von Stotzinger, head of the unsuccessful mission, spoke highly of Neufeld's fluency in Arabic and mentioned his eighteen-year-old Kurdish wife. Back in Damascus, Neufeld wrote a long report which outlined a method for dealing with the Arab revolt and recommending the establishment of a German intelligence unit in the Middle East. He died in Germany in 1918, just before the end of the war.

When Slatin returned to the Sudan, he made it a point to find Zenuba, the wife of Frank Lupton. She was happily married to Hassan Zecki, by whom she bore three other children in addition to her two daughters, Fatma and Victoria, by Lupton. Slatin later tried to send the eldest girl, whom he called 'Fanny', to Europe to be educated, but both mother and daughter were against this. Fanny later married a Sudanese. A few years after the re-conquest, Frank Lupton's brother Malcolm visited the Sudan, met Zenuba, and arranged to have his brother's grave transferred to the Christian cemetery in Khartoum. Zenuba's descendants by both Frank Lupton and Hassan Zecki are alive in the Sudan today.

To end this account of those whose lives became entangled in Sudanese history by the revolt of Mohammed Ahmed, it remains to say a few words concerning two officers who were primarily responsible for the success of the reconquest of the Sudan: Hector Archibald MacDonald, who led the gallant Sudanese battalions and saved the battle of Omdurman for Kitchener, and Edouard Girouard, who built the railroad. For his services in the Sudan MacDonald was made C.B., a brevet colonel and an extra A.D.C. to Queen Victoria. Some Scots thought the honours given MacDonald were too skimpy and a Scottish newspaper, the *North Star*, pointedly asked Britain if she wanted no more Highland recruits. It was also noted that being appointed A.D.C. to the Queen was a fine honour but brought in no extra pay and would even cost the Scottish hero money for a fancy uniform. MacDonald continued his fighting career in India and South Africa, rising to the rank of Major-General; he was created K.C.B. in 1900. He was in command of the troops in Ceylon when there was 'an opprobrious accusation against him' (according to the *Dictionary of National Biography*), and he went to London to defend himself at the War Office. The authorities there ordered a court of inquiry to be held in Ceylon. He started back to Ceylon, but on 25 March 1903 this exceptionally brave and capable officer shot himself in the Regina Hotel in Paris.

Edouard Girouard was only twenty-nine when he became director of the Sudan railways and built Kitchener's lifeline into the Nubian desert. (The railroad was later extended and the first train reached Khartoum on 10 January 1900.) After the Sudan was won, Girouard was appointed President of the Egyptian Railway and Telegraph Administration. This appointment was brief, for he was soon called to South Africa to control the vital railroads needed to defeat the Boers. In 1907 he went to Nigeria and a year later succeeded Frederick Lugard as Governor of Northern Nigeria; there he built the country's first railroad. He resigned in 1912, but returned to government service three years later as director-general of munitions supply. He died in London in 1932.

Kipling had predicted that 'In due time the demand will go up "the Sudan for the Sudanese"', and so it did. The condominium came to an end when the Sudan became independent on 1 January 1956. Sudanese political figures, like other African leaders, delight in throwing verbal spears into the corpse of colonialism; but if one country can ever successfully rule another, the British can be said to have ruled the Sudan well. The Sudan owes much to British rule: it gave her diverse peoples a measure of peace and freedom from famine, enabling the population to increase and to enjoy a prosperity they could not have hoped to achieve under the Egyptians or by themselves. Young, British-educated Sudanese today are not yet wise enough in the ways of the world nor of history to appreciate the foundations on which they were given to build.

When the British left the Sudan to the Sudanese, there was an attempt to form a democratic government, but as in all other African countries, the attempt failed. First there was an election to determine whether the Sudan should be independent or join Egypt. One of the strongest of the political parties was the Umma Party, headed by Sayyid Abdel Rahman el Mahdi, posthumous son of the Mahdi. It favoured independence and this view prevailed. There were the usual political difficulties of a people struggling with democratic methods and institutions for the first time; then the military took over the government in 1958. The military dictatorship of General Ibrahim Abboud provided the country with reasonably stable government until 1964.

One of the sights of Khartoum when the British ruled the Sudan was a large bronze statue of Gordon mounted on a camel that stood near the palace. It has had a curious history. There are two identical statues, the creation of Onslow Ford. One, the original, stands today where it has always stood: at Brompton Barracks, Chatham, Kent. Its double once stood near Trafalgar Square where the statue of Nurse Edith Cavell now stands. Kitchener thought it should be in Khartoum and it was sent there in the early days of the condominium. After independence, the Sudanese, long since bored by England's Christian martyr hero, packed up the statue and shipped it back to England. In 1959 it was presented to the Gordon Boys School at West End, Surrey, near Woking. In Khartoum the statue looked from the palace out over the desert; now it stands in the corner of a green playing field.

Khartoum still has the trees Kitchener planted, and they have now grown tall and beautiful. Today the city contains the offices of the government, the bulk of the European population of the Sudan, and the homes of the wealthier Sudanese, including the residence of Imam El Hadi el Mahdi, grandson of Mohammed Ahmed and religious leader of the ansar, still some three million strong.

Khartoum now has a small but modern airport, built by the British. The first aeroplane to land there, on 21 January 1914, was piloted by Marc Pourpre, a French aviator. As he climbed out of his cockpit, an excited Sudanese woman ran up to him, demanding to know if he was a man or an angel. When M. Pourpre assured her that he was a man, and, in answer to her next question, admitted that he was also a Christian, she was amazed. This was the only fine thing she had ever known a Christian to do, she exclaimed. A few months later, Slatin, to celebrate the nineteenth anniversary of his escape, flew over Omdurman in the second aeroplane ever to visit Khartoum.

A bridge connects Khartoum with the African city of Omdurman, which is not much different now from the days when the Khalifa made it his capital. The streets are narrow and twisting, the houses of mud. The Khalifa's house still stands, now a museum of the Mahdiya, but there is a football stadium on the site of the Beit el Mal. For fifty years the Mahdi's tomb remained in ruins. In 1924 a visitor to the Sudan, Major A. Radclyffe Dugmore, described it:

> The ruined remains of the Mahdi's tomb may still be seen on the eastern side of the town, and this is gradually falling apart in its walled enclosure, which is always kept locked. The native Mohammedan still has a certain respect for it, for on entering the place he always removes his footwear.

The tomb was finally rebuilt in its original shape by the Mahdi's son in 1947. The ansar have chosen to forget Kitchener's act of desecration and it is commonly believed that the Mahdi's remains are still in the grave.

In the early days of the condominium Mahdism was outlawed and it was forbidden to read the sayings or recite the prayers of the Mahdi, but over the years the attitude of the government softened. After the battle of Umm Diwaykarat Wingate had telegraphed his wife: 'Hurrah Mahdism finished.' But Mahdism did not die, it only grew respectable. The man primarily responsible for keeping it alive and for making it respectable was Abdel Rahman el Mahdi. The other nine sons and ten daughters of the Mahdi died at an early age, but Abdel Rahman lived to be seventy-five years old and did not die until 1959. He was knighted by the British and created a pasha by the Egyptians. He made himself one of the richest men in the Sudan, and Abba Island, birthplace of Mahdism, became one of his country estates. On a visit to London, Abdel Rahman called at No. 10 Downing Street while a cabinet meeting was in progress. A cabinet meeting is rarely interrupted, but a private secretary thought Sir Winston should be advised. The Prime Minister, told the private secretary that the Mahdi would have to wait, but added, 'Unless you think he will go off and make another revolt.'

The Nuba Hills, where Father Ohrwalder and his colleagues began their work, has remained one of the more backward areas of the Sudan, although Dilling now boasts a government institute of education. Today a gravel road connects Dilling and El Obeid, but the surface is usually corrugated and it takes a heavy toll of the trucks that use it.

The Fashoda Incident ended in the removal of Captain Marchand's gallant little force. For a time there was talk of war in London and Paris, but as Wingate said in a letter to his wife, 'For England and France to quarrel over a mud fort in a swamp was futile.' Britain, having the most might on the scene, carried the day, but in deference to French sensibilities Fashoda had its name changed to Kadok, and by this name it is still known. Although not shown on any map, there exists a small village about eight miles from Kadok that is called Fashoda. The chief of the Shilluks lives there.

It is doubtless foolhardy to predict the future of such an unpredictable country as the Sudan, but Mahdism has proved durable as both a religious and a political concept. At the time of writing (1967) the Mahdi's Umma party has become the main political force, and today a grandson of the Mahdi rules over the land of his grandfather.

Glossary of Arabic and Sudanese Words

angareb – A low bed consisting of a wooden frame laced with leather thongs.

ardeb – A unit of capacity in many Islamic countries. The amount varies from place to place, however. In the Sudan at this time about $5\frac{1}{2}$ bushels.

ashraf – The name given to the relatives of the Mahdi.

asida – Sorghum (durra) mixed with water and made into a paste over which is poured a strong sauce of spices and peppers. A staple dish in the Sudan, eaten with meat or milk.

Baggara – Cattle-owning Arab tribes living mostly in southern Darfur and southern Kordofan.

bazingers – Armed slaves, usually Blacks from the southern Sudan who were trained to use fire-arms and fight as soldiers. They were the main strength of the slave hunters.

beia – The Mahdi's oath of allegiance.

Beit el Mal – Storehouse and treasury. In the Mahdist government this housed slaves, animals, furniture and anything else of value. There were several of these, located in all the principal towns.

Blacks – Hamiticized Negroes from the southern Sudan. Nilotes.

curbash – A whip, usually made of rhinoceros hide.

Dongolawi (pl. *Donagla*) – A native of Dongola and its vicinity.

durra – A kind of millet (*sorghum vulgare*). It was, and still is, the staple food crop of the Sudan.

emir – A chieftain.

farda – Cotton or woollen shawl.

Fellata – West African pilgrims working their way across the Sudan to Mecca.

gellabas or *jellaba* – Itinerant merchants, traders, usually in slaves. Many kept armed slaves as retainers. Most came from the Nile valley and among the Arabs of the western Sudan the name was synonymous with a Nile valley native.

imam – A Muslim priest or anyone who is considered an authority on theology or Islamic law.

jebel – A hill or mountain.

jibba – A patched, shirt-like garment worn by the Dervishes.

jihad or *jehad* – In Islam, a religious war against unbelievers.

kadi – In the Sudan during the Mahdiya the word meant simply 'judge'.

khor – A dry watercourse.

Mahdiya – The period when the Sudan was ruled by the Mahdi and the Khalifa, 1885–98.

Mudiria – A district, ruled by a mudir. Also, the building or buildings which constituted the headquarters for the district's governor; government house of the district.

muezzin – In Islam, the man who calls the faithful to prayer.

mulazem (pl. *mulazemin*) – A combination servant, bodyguard and courtier serving the Khalifa or the Mahdi.

muslimaniya – Former Christians who have renounced Christianity for Islam.

Nubia – Egyptian Kosh; biblical Cush; Arabic Bilad el Barabra. This is the desert and steppe-land between Khartoum and Aswan, an area of about 22,000 miles. It forms a broad hyphen between Egypt and the Sudan.

ombeya – A horn made from an elephant's tusk.

ratib – A small book of sayings of the Mahdi, which largely replaced the Koran itself during the Mahdiya.

rekuba – A light hut consisting of poles supporting a roof of matting and palm leaves.

shebba (*shayba*) – A forked stick which was fastened to the neck of slaves to prevent their escape.

sirdar – Commander-in-chief. Here, the head of the Egyptian army.

Turkiya – The period of Egyptian rule in the Sudan, 1821–85.

ulema – General term for religious leaders.

Umm Hagar – Literally, 'stone house'. This was the name given the house inside the prison zariba at Omdurman that acted as a common cell in which the prisoners were locked up at night.

zariba – Thorn bushes placed for protection around a temporary camp.

Manuscript Sources

Diary of Abbas Bey in the Library of the University of Khartoum.

The War Office Library contains:

FFF 1–106	Dairy of the Frontier Field Force
FFF 107–127 and 166–249	Staff Diary and Intelligence Report of the Frontier Field Force
GMRES (1890) and GMRES (1891)	General Military Report on the Egyptian Sudan. Intelligence Division, War Office, London.

The British Museum possesses a number of letters from Gordon, Slatin, Emin Pasha and Gladstone:

Add. MS 33222
Add. MSS 34474–34479
Add. MS 40665
Add. MS 41340, ff. 6–60b
Add. MS 42181, f. 73
Add. MSS 44147, f. 11, and 44629, ff. 71, 73 and 192
Add. MSS 44768, ff. 15–91 *passim* and 44769, ff. 15–85 *passim*.

The School of Oriental Studies of the University of Durham holds the papers of Sir Reginald Wingate and of Slatin Pasha.

Selected Bibliography

NEWSPAPERS

Fortnightly
Nineteenth Century
Pall Mall Gazette
Punch
Sudan Notes and Records
The Graphic
The Times
Westminster Gazette

BOOKS

ALFORD, H. S. L. and SWORD, W. DENNISTOUN. *The Egyptian Soudan – Its Loss and Recovery.* London, Macmillan, 1898.

ARCHER, SIR GEOFFREY. *Personal and Historical Memoirs of an East African Administrator.* Published for the author by Oliver & Boyd, Edinburgh and London, 1963.

ARCHER, THOMAS. *The War in Egypt and the Sudan.* London, Blackie, 1887.

ARKELL, A. J. *A History of the Sudan to A.D. 1821.* London, Athlone Press, 1955.

ARNOLD, SIR THOMAS and GUILLAUME ALFRED, eds. *The Legacy of Islam.* Oxford University Press, 1931.

ARTHUR, SIR GEORGE, ed. *The Letters of Lord and Lady Wolseley.* New York, Doubleday, Page, 1922.

— *Life of Lord Kitchener.* 3 vols. London, Macmillan, 1920.

ATTERIDGE, A. HILLARD. *Towards Khartoum.* London, A. D. Innes, 1897.

BARBOUR, K. M. *The Republic of the Sudan.* London, Athlone Press, 1961.

BENNETT, E. N. *The Downfall of the Dervishes.* London, Methuen, 1899.

BLUNT, WILFRID SCAWEN. *My Diaries.* Part One (1888–1900). New York, Knopf, 1922.

— *Secret History of the English Occupation of Egypt.* New York, Knopf, 1922.

— *Gordon at Khartoum.* New York, Stephen Swift, 1911.

BRACKENBURY, HENRY. *The River Column.* Edinburgh and London, Blackwood, 1885.

BURLEIGH, BENNET. *Khartoum Campaign 1898; Re-Conquest of the Sudan.* London, Chapman and Hall, 1899.

CALVILE, H. E. *History of the Sudan Campaign.* (Official publication, compiled in the Intelligence Division of the War Office.) 2 vols. H.M. Stationery Office, n.d. (1889 or 1890).

CASATI, GAETANO. *Ten Years in Equatoria.* 2 vols. trans. by J. Randolph Clay and I. Walter Landor. London, Frederick Warne, 1891.

CHURCHILL, WINSTON S. *My Early Life.* London, Cassell, 1930; Fontana Books, 1959.

— *The River War.* London, Eyre & Spottiswoode, 1899; Landsborough Publications, 1960.

COATES, THOMAS F. G. *Hector MacDonald.* London, S. W. Partridge & Co., 1900.

COLBORNE, J. *With Hicks Pasha in the Soudan.* London, Smith, Elder, 1884.

COLLINS, ROBERT O. *The Southern Sudan, 1883–1898.* Yale University Press, 1962.

CRABITÈS, PIERRE. *Gordon, the Sudan and Slavery.* London, George Routledge, 1933.

— *Americans in the Egyptian Army.* London, George Routledge, 1938.

CROMER, EARL OF. *Modern Egypt.* 2 vols. New York, Macmillan Co., 1908.

DARLEY, HENRY. *Slaves and Ivory.* London, Witherby, 1926.

DAVIES, REGINALD. *The Camel's Back.* London, Murray, 1957

Directory of the Republic of the Sudan 1960. London, The Diplomatic Press and Publishing Co., 1960.

DUGMORE, A. RADCLYFFE. *The Vast Sudan.* London, Arrowsmith, 1924.

FARWELL, BYRON. *Burton.* London, Longmans, 1963.

— *The Man Who Presumed.* New York, Henry Holt, 1957

GORDON, C. G. *The Journals of Major-Gen. C. G. Gordon, C.B. at Khartoum.* London, Kegan Paul, 1885.

GRAY, RICHARD. *A History of the Southern Sudan 1838–1889.* Oxford University Press, 1961.

GROGAN, E. S. and SHARP, A. H. *From the Cape to Cairo.* London, Hurst & Blackett, 1900.

GUNTHER, JOHN. *Inside Africa.* New York, Harper, 1953.

HANSON, LAWRENCE and HANSON, ELIZABETH. *Chinese Gordon – The Story of a Hero.* New York, Funk & Wagnalls, 1954.

HENDERSON, K. D. D. *The Making of the Modern Sudan.* London, Faber, 1953.

HILL, RICHARD. *Egypt in the Sudan 1820–1881.* Oxford University Press, 1959.

— *Slatin Pasha.* Oxford University Press, 1965.

— *A Bibliography of the Anglo-Egyptian Sudan from the Earliest Times to 1937.* Oxford, London, 1939.

HITTI, PHILIP K. *History of the Arabs from the Earliest Times to the Present.* London, Macmillan, 1964.

HOLT, P. M. *A Modern History of the Sudan.* New York, Grove Press, 1961.
— *The Mahdist State in the Sudan 1881–1898.* Oxford University Press, 1958.
HYSLOP, JOHN. *Sudan Story.* London, The Naldrett Press, 1952.
ISHAQ, IBN. *The Life of Muhammad,* edited by Michael Edwards. London, The Folio Society, 1964.
JACKSON, H. C. *Behind the Modern Sudan.* London, Macmillan, 1955.
— *The Fighting Sudanese.* London, Macmillan, 1954.
JAMES, F. L. *The Wild Tribes of the Soudan.* New York, Dodd, Mead, 1883.
The Koran, translated by George Sale. London, Frederick Warne, n.d.
KUMM, H. KARL W. *The Sudan.* London, Marshall Bros, n.d.
LONGFORD, ELIZABETH. *Victoria R.I.* London, Weidenfeld & Nicolson, 1964.
MACMICHAEL, SIR HAROLD. *The Anglo-Egyptian Sudan.* London, Faber, 1934.
— *The Tribes of Northern and Central Kordofan.*
MAGNUS, PHILIP. *Kitchener; Portrait of an Imperialist.* London, Murray, 1958.
— *Gladstone.* London, Murray, 1954.
MANDOUR EL-MAHDI. *Short History of the Sudan.* Oxford University Press, 1965.
MANN, ANTHONY. *Where God Laughed.* London, Museum Press, 1954.
MAXWELL, J. LOWRY. *Half a Century of Grace.* London, Sudan United Mission, n.d.
MEEK, C. K. *A Sudanese Kingdom.* London, Kegan Paul, 1931.
MIDDLETON, DOROTHY. *Baker of the Nile.* London, Falcon Press, 1949.
MILNER, ALFRED. *England in Egypt.* London, Edward Arnold, 1892.
MOOREHEAD, ALAN. *The White Nile.* London, Hamish Hamilton, 1960.
NEUFELD, CHARLES. *A Prisoner of the Khaleefa.* New York, Putnam, 1899.
OHRWALDER, FATHER JOSEPH. *Ten Years' Captivity in the Mahdi's Camp 1882–1892,* trans. by F. R. Wingate. London, Sampson Low, 1893.
PETHERICK, JOHN. *Egypt, The Soudan and Central Africa.* Edinburgh and London, Blackwood, 1861.
POPE-HENNESSY, JAMES. *Monckton Milnes; The Flight of Youth.* London, Constable, 1951.
POWER, FRANK. *Letters From Khartoum Written During the Siege.* London, Sampson Low, 1885.
ROBINSON, RONALD and GALLAGHER, JOHN, with DENNY, ALICE. *Africa and the Victorians; The Official Mind of Imperialism.* London, Macmillan, 1961.
ROYLE, CHARLES. *The Egyptian Campaigns 1882–1885,* new and rev. edn, continued to December 1899. London, Hurst and Blackett, 1900.
RUSSELL, HENRY. *The Ruin of the Soudan.* London, Sampson Low, 1892.

SAID, BESHIR MOHAMMED. *The Sudan, Crossroads of Africa*. London, The Bodley Head, 1965.

SCHWEINFURTH, G., RATZEL, F., FELKIN, R. W. and HARTLAUB, G. eds. *Emin Pasha in Central Africa*, trans. by Mrs R. W. Felkin. New York, Dodd, Mead & Co., 1889.

SELIGMAN, C. G. *Races of Africa*. Oxford University Press, 1957.

SHIBEIKA, MEKKI. *British Policy in the Sudan 1882–1902*. Oxford University Press, 1952.

SLATIN, RUDOLF C. *Fire and Sword in the Sudan*, trans. by F. R. Wingate. London, Edward Arnold, 1896.

STEEVENS, G. W. *With Kitchener to Khartoum*. New York, Dodd, Mead & Co., 1899.

STRACHEY, LYTTON. *Eminent Victorians*. London, Chatto and Windus, 1918.

Sudan Almanac. Government Printing Press, Khartoum, 1963.

SYMONS, JULIAN. *England's Pride*. London, Hamish Hamilton, 1965.

TAYLOR, DON. *The British in Africa*. London, Robert Hale, 1962.

THEOBALD, A. B. *The Mahdiya; A History of the Sudan, 1881–1899*. London, Longmans, 1951.

— *Ali Dinar, Last Sultan of Darfur 1898–1916*. London, Longmans, 1965.

TOYNBEE, ARNOLD, *Between Niger and Nile*. Oxford University Press, 1965.

TRIMINGHAM, J. S. *Islam in the Sudan*. London, Frank Cass, 1965.

WHYTE, FREDERIC. *The Life of W. T. Stead*. 2 vols. New York, Houghton Mifflin, n.d.

WILSON, SIR CHARLES W. *From Korti to Khartum*. Edinburgh and London, Blackwood, 1886.

WINGATE, F. R. *Mahdiism and the Egyptian Sudan*. London, Macmillan, 1891.

WINGATE, SIR RONALD. *Wingate of the Sudan*. London, Murray, 1955.

WOOD, SIR EVELYN. *From Midshipman to Field Marshal*. 2 vols. London, Methuen, 1906.

— *Winnowed Memories*. London, Cassell, 1914.

WRIGHT, H. C. S. *Soudan '96*. London, Horace Cox, 1897.

WYLDE, A. B. *'83 to '87 In the Sudan*. 2 vols. London, Remington, 1888.

ZETLAND, THE MARQUESS OF. *Lord Cromer*. London, Hodder & Stoughton, 1932.

Index

Index